Raves for Adam Fawer's
IMPROBABLE

"A remarkable novel that combines a gritty, expert plot with serious ideas and speculations. A skillful, fascinating debut."

Caleb Carr, author of *The Alienist* and *Angel of Darkness*

"I was hooked from the first sentence . . . *Improbable* is an ingenious melding of thought-provoking mathematical theories and thriller mayhem, reminiscent of Michael Crichton and Robert Ludlum. A truly great read."

Ben Mezrich, author of *Bringing Down the House*

"[*Improbable*] creates a complex, frightening world, takes the reader into it and through it, and doesn't let the reader out until the last word of the last page, if then . . . Fawer's story unfolds relentlessly, always moving forward even as the plot twists and turns . . . One of the most complex, fresh, and enjoyable novels of its type to come along in a while."

Richmond Times-Dispatch

"Exciting action scenes and an interesting character study elevate *Improbable*. Fawer keeps the tension high . . . And he delivers a slam-bang ending that is truly nail-biting."

Ft. Lauderdale Sun-Sentinel

"The success of *The Rule of Four* and *The Da Vinci Code* has shown that plenty of readers enjoy their science, as long as there's a compelling plot encircling it, which there is here."

Publishers Weekly

"There's a very strong probability that you'll read this book . . . [A] very promising debut."

Philadelphia Inquirer

ADAM FAWER

IMPROBABLE

HarperTorch
An Imprint of HarperCollins*Publishers*

This is a work of fiction. Names, characters, places, and incidents are products of the author's imagination or are used fictitiously and are not to be construed as real. Any resemblance to actual events, locales, organizations, or persons, living or dead, is entirely coincidental.

Excerpt from *Big Deal* by Anthony Holden reprinted by permission of Time Warner Book Group U.K.

HARPERTORCH
An Imprint of HarperCollins*Publishers*
10 East 53rd Street
New York, New York 10022-5299

ISBN-13: 978-0-06-073678-1
ISBN-10: 0-06-073678-X

First HarperTorch paperback printing: February 2006
First William Morrow hardcover printing: February 2005

Printed in the United States of America

Visit HarperTorch on the World Wide Web at www.harpercollins.com

10 9 8 7 6 5 4 3 2 1

For my dad, Philip R. Fawer
I still think of him every day

Okay, let's talk about probability. First up, everybody's favorite topic: the lottery.

The odds of winning Powerball are approximately 120 million to 1. Since its inception in 1997, over 50 people have "defied the odds" and won the jackpot, making them some of the luckiest, and wealthiest, people on the planet. I hate those people. But I digress.

Now let's talk about another low-probability event: civilization getting wiped out by a giant asteroid colliding with the earth. Astrophysicists have calculated that the chance of this happening in any given year is approximately 1 million to 1.

Since our simian ancestors have roamed the planet for over 7 million years, the probability that an asteroid would have wiped us all out by now is roughly 700 percent. In other words, we should all be dead—not once, not twice, but *seven times over.*

However, as most of you already know, since the recorded history of mankind, humanity has never been annihilated.

So what's my point? Well, it's not that we're all going to be killed by an asteroid. Instead I want you to understand something about low-probability events, and that is this:

Shit happens.

—Excerpt from a statistics lecture by David T. Caine

MEDICAL FACT

When the brain's nerve cells become overactive, they fire off uncontrolled, seemingly random signals. These signals may cause abnormal sensations, bizarre movements, or even psychic aberrations. Such occurrences are commonly known as seizures.

Two percent of adults will have at least one seizure before they die. Of those that do, most will never have another. However, some will endure repeated seizures throughout their lives. This malady has been known by many names throughout history—lunatism, unspeakable misery, daemonic suffering, and even the scourge of Christ. Today we call it epilepsy.

Sometimes doctors are able to trace the cause of an epileptic's seizures—usually to either microscopic cerebral scars, brain tumors, or genetics. However, 75 percent of all epileptics—over 1.9 million in the United States alone—are told that their condition is idiopathic.

"Idiopathic" comes from Greek, where *idio* means "peculiar, separate, or distinct" and *path* means "feeling or suffering." Literally, "idiopathic" can be defined as "peculiar suffering," although the modern definition is "of, relating to, or designating a disease having no known cause."

In other words, despite the dramatic advances medical science has made during the last few centuries, doctors still have no idea why most epileptic seizures occur.

None at all.

IMPROBABLE

PART I

VICTIMS OF CIRCUMSTANCE

A gambler, be he one who bets on horses or sports events,
on casino games or raindrops running down windowpanes,
is someone who wagers unfavorable odds.
A poker player, if he knows what he is doing,
is someone who wagers favorable odds.
The one is a romantic, the other a realist.

—Anthony Holden, poker player

It is almost always gambling that enables one to form
a fairly clear idea of a manifestation of chance;
it is gambling that gave birth to the calculus of probability . . .
it is, therefore, gambling that one must strive to understand,
but one should understand it in a philosophic sense,
free from all vulgar ideas.

—Louis Bachelier, mathematician

"It's twenty to you, Caine. In or out?"

David Caine could hear the words, but he couldn't respond; his nose wouldn't let him. The smell was unlike anything he had experienced before—a perverse stew of rancid meat and rotten eggs floating in a vat of urine. He had read on the Internet that some people killed themselves because the smell got so bad. At first he didn't believe it, but now . . . now it didn't seem so crazy.

Even though he knew that the smell was a by-product of a few confused nerve cells, it didn't matter. According to his brain, the smell was real. More real than the cloud of cigarette smoke hovering over the table. More real than the greasy scent of McDonald's that still hung in the air from Walter's midnight snack. More real than the smell of sweat mixed with despair that permeated the entire room.

The smell was so bad that his eyes had begun to water, but as bad as it was, Caine didn't hate it as much as what it represented. The smell meant that another one was coming, and judging by the intensity of the vomit-inducing, brain-crying *stench,* it was going to be a doozy. Worse still, it was coming on fast, and of all the times it could happen, he couldn't afford to have it happen now.

Caine squeezed his eyes shut for a moment in a vain attempt to hold off fate. Then he opened them and stared at the crumpled red-and-yellow box of fries sitting in front of Walter. It pulsed before his eyes like a cardboard heart. Caine turned away, suddenly afraid he might puke.

"David, are you okay?"

Caine felt a warm hand on his shoulder. It was Sister Mary Straight, an ex-nun with oversize dentures that were older than he was. She was the only woman at the table—hell, she was the only woman in the whole club except for the two emaciated Romanian waitresses Nikolaev kept around to make sure no one ever had a reason to get up. But Sister Mary was the only female player. Despite that everyone called her "Sister," she was more like a surrogate mother to the men who lived down in the cellar or, as the Russians liked to call it, the *podvaal.*

Technically, no one truly lived in the *podvaal,* but Caine was willing to bet that if he asked any of the twenty-odd men crowded around the tables where they felt most alive, they'd say it was here, in the cramped, windowless basement fifteen feet below the East Village. All the regulars were like Caine. Gamblers. Addicts. Sure, some had fancy offices on Wall Street or important-sounding jobs in midtown and business cards with raised silver lettering, but they all knew none of that mattered. All that mattered were the cards you were dealt and whether you were in.

Every night they returned to the cramped basement beneath Chernobyl, the Russian supper club on Avenue D. Although the bar was dirty, the games Vitaly Nikolaev ran were clean. When Caine first laid eyes on Vitaly, with his pasty white complexion and thin, girlish arms, Caine would have guessed he was a CPA rather than a Russian mobster.

But all his doubts disappeared the night when Vitaly Nikolaev beat the living shit out of Melvin Schuster, a harmless old man who picked the wrong club to cheat. Before Caine knew what was happening, Nikolaev had transformed the paunchy grandfather's face into a red, pulpy mess. No one ever cheated at the *podvaal* after that.

And yet this was the place Caine chose to call home. The minuscule studio he had on the Upper West Side was just where he slept, showered, and occasionally shaved. Every now and then, he would get a girl to come up, but that hadn't happened in a long while. Not surprising, considering the only woman Caine had any interaction with was Sister Mary.

"David, are you all right?" Sister's question brought Caine back to the world of the living. He blinked his eyes and gave Sister a quick nod, which was enough to make his nausea return.

"Yeah, I'm cool, Sister. Thanks."

"You sure? Because you look a little green."

"Just trying to *earn* some green," Caine said with a half-hearted grin.

"Are we through coffee-housing, or you two wanna get a room?" Walter sneered through yellowing teeth. He leaned in close enough for Caine to smell the onions on his breath. "Twenty. To. You. In. Or. Out?"

Caine looked down at his hand and then again at the up cards, stretching his long, sinewy arms over his head of unruly black hair. He pushed the nausea back down his throat and forced himself to ignore the smell as he decided what to do.

"Stop running the odds and bet," Walter said, picking at a hangnail.

Caine was known for doing the complex math in his head necessary to calculate the odds of nearly anything. The only variable that Caine couldn't quantify was the probability that his opponents were bluffing, but he tried nonetheless. Caine felt like Walter was purposely trying to rush him, so he gave the old man a bored look and continued analyzing the board.

The game was Texas Hold 'Em and the rules were simple. Each player was dealt two cards, which was followed by "the flop" when three cards were turned over for everyone to see. Then the dealer would flip over a fourth card, known as "the turn," and then the fifth and final card, known as "the river." There was a round of betting after each flip, and then the players revealed. Whoever had the best five-card poker hand—out of the five shared cards in the middle and the two cards in his hand—won.

The beauty of the game was that at any given moment an intelligent player could look at the board and know the best possible hand that could be made. When Caine looked at the flop, he didn't see three cards, he saw hundreds of probabilities. The probability that he cared most about was whether he had a shot of winning. With his current hand, Caine judged that probability to be high. He was holding a pair of bullets—an ace of hearts and an ace of diamonds. The flop consisted of an ace of clubs and a couple of spades—the jack and the six. Caine's trip aces was the "nuts"—the highest hand possible on the board—but there were still a lot of outs.

He began calculating the odds of every possible scenario. For the few precious seconds that Caine ran the numbers, the neurons that kept insisting that the air was filled with the smell of burning flesh were mercifully silent.

Anyone holding two spades had a total of four spades—two in his hand, two on the board. That person would need another spade on the board to complete his flush. Caine did the math, his mind twisting and turning the numbers with the ease of a child singing her ABCs.

There were a total of thirteen spades in a deck, so if someone was holding two spades, at most there could only be nine spades left (in this case the "outs"). Assuming someone had the two spades, the probability that one of the next two cards would be a spade was 36 percent. High, but then again the odds that someone had been dealt two spades in the first place were only 6 percent per player.

Caine turned the mental key in the lock to get the final answer, the odds of getting dealt two spades *and* having another appear on the board. He sighed as the number appeared in his head, spinning around like a glorious neon sign—only 2.1 percent. He could live with that.

He repeated the exercise, this time calculating the likelihood of someone having only one spade in their hand and then completing the flush—barely 2.0 percent per player. The odds of someone hitting the flush with clubs instead of spades was even tinier—0.3 percent per player. Nothing to be concerned about.

The straight was more worrisome. With an ace and a jack showing and not another face card or a ten in sight, that meant there were twelve outs that would make a straight possible (any one of the four kings, queens, or tens). Still, there was only a 3.6 percent chance that someone was already holding the two other cards necessary to make the straight. Theoretically, the straight flush was also still alive, but this was so unlikely he didn't even bother to calculate the odds.

Since Caine already had trip aces, what he really needed was another ace, a jack, or a six. If he got the ace, he'd have quads. A jack or a six would give him the nuts full house, either aces over jacks or aces over sixes. With seven outs (one ace, three jacks, and three sixes) the odds of getting any one of the necessary cards was—Caine blinked, his blood pumping—28 percent. Not bad.

He looked at Walter, trying to read the geezer's watery eyes, but there was nothing except for a dull weariness Caine recognized from his own reflection in the mirror. That and a nervous yearning, an intense desire to play, play, play. And then it hit him again, another wave of the foul stench. A hot stream of bile bubbled into his mouth, but he swallowed it back down.

Caine knew he should hit the john, but he couldn't. Not in the middle of a hand when he had the nuts. No fucking way. Even if he was bleeding out his eyes, there was no way he would walk until the cards were raked. Caine reached down and blindly tossed four chips into the pot.

"Raise twenty."

"Call." Sister Straight was in—Caine hoped she had

paired up on the jack and wasn't chasing the straight as she was known to do.

"Call." Shit, Stone was in, too. As always, he sat still as a statue. He almost never moved, but that wasn't how he got his nickname; he earned his alias because he was a fucking rock. Stone always played by the rules, never stayed in on a whim or a hunch, and always ran the odds. No way would he be in unless he was in line for the straight or the flush.

Caine cursed himself for not betting higher before the flop to get out all the straight seekers. They wouldn't have stayed in if he had hit it harder out of the gate. But the smell was clouding his brain, making him play like crap. He tried to tell himself that no, he had just bet light to sucker them in because he was greedy, but that wasn't true. It was the smell. The smell, the smell, *the smell.* If he closed his eyes, he could picture the piles of rotting meat covered with wriggling white maggots.

Walter fingered his chips, flipping them over his knuckles with a tired ease. For a second Caine thought Walter was going to raise, but instead he just called. Yeah, they're all just waiting for the turn, holding their own until they had a better idea of what was coming.

The next card was a joyous sight. To Caine it was prettier than a *Playboy* centerfold and more beautiful than the Grand Canyon at sunset—an ace of spades. With a pair of bullets now on the board and another pair in his hand, he had quads.

The only hand that could beat him was a straight flush, but hitting it was unlikely. The next card would have to be a king, a queen, or the ten of spades, plus someone would need to have the other two royal spades necessary to complete it. No way.

Still . . . Caine did a quick calculation in his head, his lids drooped to hide his darting eyes—the odds of being dealt any of the necessary three spade combinations (king-queen, king-ten, or queen-ten) was 442 to 1. The probability of getting dealt one of those pairs *and* hitting the third card was 19,448 to 1. Yeah, there was no way.

The pot was his; now it was just a question of how big he could make it before the hand ended. If he bet too hard, he might scare off all the fish. But if he decided to be a possum and slow-play, then he might waste his killer hand. He had to bet a Goldilocks—not too big, not too small . . . just right.

"Twenty." Walter threw in four red chips and leaned back, as if preparing for a long wait.

Caine looked down at his chips and slowly picked out a pair of greens. "Make it an even fifty."

"Out." Sister Straight said in disgust, throwing down her cards with one hand while fingering the silver cross around her neck with the other.

"Me, too," Stone said. He didn't move, as his cards were already facedown in front of him. Both were probably looking for a straight and figured that someone else had hit either a boat or a flush on the turn.

"That just leaves you and me," Walter said, absently munching on a cold french fry. "Let's say we make it interesting. Raise another fifty." His voice was as oily as his skin. His chips clinked into the middle of the pot.

Caine tried to block out the smell and focus. What was Walter doing? He could be completely full of shit, but Caine didn't think so—not with a pair of bullets on the board. Plus, there was something about the man's arrogant smirk that made Caine think he had something. Then Caine knew—Walter had either a pair of jacks or a pair of sixes in his hand. He had a full house, probably jacks over aces—the only problem for Walter was that his boat wouldn't beat Caine's four of a kind.

If Caine hadn't felt so nauseous, he would have smiled. When he was vomiting in the stall after the hand was over, at least he would be comforted with a nice pile of chips. He concentrated on making his voice sound normal, even though each word that exited his mouth tasted like curdled milk.

"Fifty more." Caine threw in a hundred-dollar chip. The matte black circle caught Nikolaev's eye, and he sauntered over to watch the action. Walter tossed in a black of his own and stole two greens for change. Then the dealer flipped over the river—a king of spades—and Caine's stomach did a little flip of its own.

With an ace, king, and jack of spades showing, the straight flush was officially alive and kicking. He looked back at his hand and then at the board, trying to ignore the stench. He took a long swig of his Coke to chase it away, but it was no use. *Think, think, think. Don't focus on the smell, focus on the cards, the numbers.*

That was the way. The numbers would help him. They would be his guide. He recited them in his mind, putting all his energy into the litany of probability. He had four of a kind. Quads. What did that mean?

The smell, the awful smell, it was everywhere.

No, focus. Focus on the numbers.

There are almost 134 million possible hands that can be made from seven cards. Of those 134 million hands, only 224,848 result in a four of a kind. Hence there is only a 0.168 percent chance of getting quads—595 to 1.

What about the straight flush?

There are only 38,916 seven-card combinations that result in a five-card straight flush. Only a 0.029 percent chance. One in 3,438 hands.

But what about getting them both at the same time? How many combinations was that? His head was spinning. He couldn't think. How many combinations? Not a lot. Small. Tiny. Insignificant. The math was beyond him in his current state. All he knew was that it was some small subset of 38,916 hands that would also include quads. Probably something like 5,000 hands. Five thousand seven-card combinations out of 134 million possibilities—26,757 to 1.

There was no way. No fucking way . . . but possible. Christ, the smell was killing him. He closed his eyes, hoping that when he opened them, everything would be back to normal. But when he raised his lids, the world looked like a reflection in a funhouse mirror. Walter's haggard face stretched from floor to ceiling. The dark circles beneath his eyes were the size of Frisbees. His mouth could swallow a twenty-inch television set.

"Child, are you *sure* you're all right?"

The voice was a million miles away. Caine turned his head, and the whole room jerked so suddenly that he almost fell over.

"Whoa, big fella." It was Stone—he had reached out and grabbed hold of Caine's arm. At first Caine didn't understand why, but then he realized he was sitting at a forty-five-degree angle to the left. He grabbed the felt table with both hands and righted himself.

"I'm okay," Caine gasped, "just a dizzy spell. Sorry." His voice sounded like it was coming from a long tunnel.

"I think you should lie down for a spell, dear."

"First he's got to finish the fucking hand," Walter said, then turned to Caine. "Unless you want to fold."

"Don't be such a cocksucker, Walter. Can't you see he's sick?"

"*Cocksucker?* You pray to Jesus with that mouth, Sister? I mean—"

"Walter, be quiet!" Sister Straight said the last with such authority that Walter snapped his mouth shut. Then she leaned in front of Caine. "Do you want to lie down on the couch for a bit?" Out of the corner of his eye, Caine could see Vitaly Nikolaev hovering over the Sister's shoulder. He didn't look worried—he looked pissed.

"No, no, I'm good," Caine said, willing all of the strength he had into his voice. "Let me just finish up the hand." Before Sister Straight could respond, Caine pushed one black chip into the pot. "One hundred," he said. Now that the last card had been dealt, the game was pot-limit—the size of the raise was limited only by the size of the pot.

Walter stared at Caine, trying to size him up. If Caine had any tells, he was sure that his acute illness had hidden them.

All Walter would see from his inspection was that Caine looked like walking death.

After a second, Walter muttered over his shoulder. "Vitaly, gimme a count." Nikolaev walked over to the table and expertly stacked all the chips in the pot. Five blacks, eight greens, and fifteen reds—a total of $775.

"I see your hundred and raise you the pot," Walter said as he pulled ten hundred-dollar bills from the money clip resting by his elbow. "That's $875 to you."

Walter wanted Caine to think that he had hit the straight flush, but there was no way. Not with those odds. Walter was just trying to buy the pot—but Caine wasn't going to let him. He looked down at his paltry stack of chips and then at the slip of paper beneath. It was a credit line for fifteen grand, to reward Caine for always paying his debts promptly. When Nikolaev had given it to him, Caine swore to himself that he would never use it unless he had an absolute sure thing. If four bullets didn't qualify, he didn't know what did.

He nodded at Nikolaev, but he needn't have bothered. Nikolaev had already signaled his mountainous bodyguard, who immediately placed a stack of fifteen purple chips in front of Caine. If he called the $875, it would be over in five seconds. If he lost, he would be in the hole to Nikolaev for a grand—not desirable, but he could scrape it up in a few weeks. Caine tried to fool himself into thinking that he was considering this option, but he knew it was a lie. He couldn't fucking call. Not with quads. Not after Walter had tried to steal the pot from him. Calling was no longer an option. He had to raise.

Caine slowly pushed four purple chips toward the pot, taking back five blacks for change. "That's $3,500. Raise the pot back to you."

There was a quiet gasp from Sister Mary. Even Stone was impressed—Caine could tell by the tiny crease that appeared in the man's brow. All the air sucked out of the room. Even the god-awful smell subsided for a moment as Caine met Walter's watery eyes.

"$2,625 to you, Walter. In. Or. Out?"

Walter just smirked. "You're really gonna kick yourself tomorrow." He nodded at Nikolaev, and ten purple chips were placed in front of him. Walter pushed them all forward, along with five blacks, which he tossed into the pot one at a time.

"Pot-raise back to you," Walter said. "You callin'?"

Caine felt his heart sink. There were no more raises left. This was it. He had to put in $7,875 to call. If he lost, he'd be in the hole eleven grand to Nikolaev—which was about $10,600 more than he had in his bank account. That was a serious debt to a very serious man. At least Caine could put to rest the question of whether or not he still had a gambling problem. His Gamblers Anonymous sponsor would be so proud.

But none of that mattered. If he folded his four bullets on the chance of taking the pot—now bubbling over with $15,750—he'd kill himself.

"I'm in," he said with a halfhearted sigh, his stomach tying itself in a double knot. He slid eight purples into the pot and then said, "Show 'em."

Caine could feel the whole table lean forward in anticipation to see whether Walter really had the queen-ten of spades to make the straight flush or if he was full of shit. Walter turned his cards over one at a time. When Caine saw that the first was a queen of spades, he knew Walter had it. But still, he watched transfixed as the old man flipped over the black ten. Royal straight flush. It was the nuts—the only possible hand that could have beaten Caine's quads. He had lost everything. It didn't seem real. The odds were so low as to be next to impossible.

Caine tried to say something but couldn't. He succeeded in moving his mouth a little, but before a sound could escape his throat, the smell washed over him, swallowing him up like a tidal wave. He could feel it seeping into his skin, pulsing through his veins, pushing in through his nose, his mouth, and his eyes. It was worse than ever before. It was the smell of death.

The world went black as Caine tumbled to the floor. In the split second before he slipped into unconsciousness, Caine discovered an emotion he was surprised to find—relief.

CHAPTER two

At exactly 2:15 A.M., Nava Vaner stopped at the corner of Twentieth and Seventh to light a cigarette. It was her only vice, and as with everything else in her life, she had complete control over it. She allowed herself one cigarette a day, unless she was doing surveillance, in which case all bets were off. However, today she was not on assignment, so this would be her first and last.

She tilted her head back and took a long drag, watching the red ember glow against the dirty night sky. Exhaling, she pretended to check if any cars were coming before stepping onto the crosswalk. However, it wasn't traffic that she was looking for—it was a tail.

Even though it was well past midnight, the sidewalk was smattered with club kids, street people, and other Saturday-night adventurers. Instinct told her she was being followed, but by whom, she wasn't sure. Abruptly she turned around and thrust herself into the throng of pedestrians, trying to identify her pursuer.

A scraggly, homeless black man stumbled out of her path, bumping into a trio of goths who roughly shoved him aside. Alarms instantly went off in Nava's head, but it took a second to determine why. There was nothing about the man's appearance to suggest he was anything other than what he appeared to be, but Nava knew different.

It was his scent that gave him away, or rather the lack thereof. Despite his tattered clothes and dirt-smudged face, he did not smell like someone living on the streets. As Nava continued walking, she removed a compact from her black leather knapsack and studied the man reflected in the tiny circular mirror. Now that Nava knew what he was, his disguise became more obvious. His enormous stained poncho and hunched walk masked his large, muscular frame.

She would have to go where he couldn't follow to suss out his partner. When Nava spotted her new destination, she quickened her pace until she meshed into the crowd waiting outside Twi-Fly. She took one last drag on her cigarette and stubbed it out beneath her heel with a pang of regret that her daily nicotine fix had been cut short.

As Nava was a striking woman with a lean athletic figure, long brown hair, and an olive complexion, she had no problem cutting through the crowd and sidling up to the bleached-blond bouncer. She flashed him a smile and pressed a hundred-dollar bill into his palm. Without a word he unhooked the velvet rope in front of the door and ushered her inside.

She walked down a dark, mirrored hallway that opened up into a room the size of an airplane hangar. The driving techno beat and pulsing lights immediately assaulted her senses. She knew that this would make it harder to ID her second tail, but it would also make Nava harder to follow.

Standing with her back to a wall of strobe lights, Nava kept her eyes focused on the door. She stood there for almost ten minutes before the redhead with the alabaster skin strolled through. Although the woman had positioned herself in the center of a gaggle of party girls, it was obvious from her wardrobe and makeup that she wasn't really with them. Sure enough, when the girls hit the dance floor, the redhead stayed behind, doing her best to lean casually against the bar as she scanned the room.

Nava waited another five minutes to see if anyone else suspicious entered after the redhead, but no one did. She knew there could be more operatives, but her gut told her that it was just this one and the homeless man. As Nava watched the woman, she considered her next move.

Nava didn't think they would try to kill her. If they wanted her dead, then it would have made more sense to use a sniper, rather than track her. Unless they were trying to make it look like an accident. Nava had killed others that way—waited until the last possible moment before delivering a quick shove toward a speeding bus or truck. But that was unlikely. They were probably just trying to spot a dead drop or a handoff. Either that or see who she interacted with.

Nava decided it was time—if they were indeed assassins, she wanted to operate on her schedule, not theirs. Tensing her muscles, Nava walked purposefully toward the bar. Once she was sure the redhead had spotted her, Nava hurried toward the exit. As she emerged into the cold night air, she crossed the street toward the large black man.

Although he was physically superior to the redhead, Nava wanted the element of surprise on her side; while the man would underestimate Nava, the woman would be prepared for an altercation. Nava passed five meters in front of him and continued walking along Seventh Avenue, looking for a place with some cover.

She needed to take the man when his partner was out of sight. The Twenty-third Street subway station was the obvious choice. She walked faster, hoping that only the man would try to keep up and the woman would hang back a little. Nava hurried toward the stairs leading beneath the city and took them two at a time.

Once she reached the sublevel, she rounded the corner and pressed herself against the wall. She reached into her knapsack to remove the sap, which contained a half-pound molded lead weight and a spring-steel shank surrounded by heavy leather casing. Simple but effective. She bent her elbow and pulled her arm back slightly so that she could build up some momentum when she struck.

Seconds later she heard the man's shoes clop down the steps. Keeping her eyes on the floor, she watched his long shadow approach. Nava didn't wait for him to turn the corner before she attacked. She spun out from her hiding spot and grabbed his throat with her left hand as she smashed the sap across his skull with her right. He grunted in pain and brought up his arm to shield his head. Nava grabbed his wrist and gave it a vicious twist, stopping just short of snapping it.

Still holding his wrist in one hand, she dropped her sap, removed his gun from the shoulder holster hidden beneath his poncho, snapped off the safety, and rammed the muzzle against his neck, forcing him to back up against the wall.

"Who are you working for?"

The man's eyes darted down to the gun and then back to Nava, as if he couldn't understand how this had happened.

"Your partner will be here in thirty seconds. I can't deal with both of you, so unless you start talking, I'll kill you and get the information from her." Nava didn't blink. "I'll give you ten seconds. Nine. Eight. Sev—"

"Jesus Christ," he grunted. "I'm Agency like you, just doing routine surveillance! My wallet's in my front pocket, see for yourself!"

The second he blurted out his identity, Nava knew he was telling the truth, but she still had to make sure. She pressed the muzzle of her gun deeper into his neck while she searched for his wallet. Like most agents, he had two. The one in his left pocket had a regular driver's license, while the one in his right contained a CIA badge—Agent Leon Wright. Nava exhaled and took a step back.

Wright slumped against the wall and gingerly rubbed his sprained wrist. Just then Nava heard his partner's shoes echo off the walls as she raced down the stairs. Nava gave Wright a nod, and he called out.

"I've been made, Sarah. You can relax now."

Nava stepped around the corner and held up her hands, loosely holding Wright's gun by her thumb so his partner wouldn't be alarmed. The redhead's face registered surprise, disappointment, and anger before masking itself in bland acceptance. When Sarah spotted Wright, she let out a low whistle. A purple welt the size of a pinball had already risen out of the side of his head.

"I'm willing to forget this ever happened if you let me resume my late-night stroll in peace," Nava said.

Sarah was about to protest, but Wright cut her off.

"Deal," he said, managing to restrain the grimace that was trying to contort the edges of his mouth. Nava flicked the safety back on Wright's gun and tossed it to Sarah along with his badge.

"Have a good night, then," Nava said.

Without looking back, she walked up the stairs, her hands shaking. She had almost killed him. Christ. She was slipping. There was a time when she would have been able to determine the intention of a fellow spy just from the way he walked, but lately she felt tired, frazzled. Nava spun around, suddenly wondering if the whole thing had been a trick. But there was no one. She was alone.

Nava knew that just because her movements were being tracked, that didn't mean the U.S. government suspected her of treason. If they had, then the two agents wouldn't have let her walk away so easily. She was being paranoid. It was just what Wright had said—routine surveillance, which was conducted on all agents from time to time to make sure everyone stayed kosher.

Still, Nava circled the block three more times just to be certain. She then opened the door of the dirty walk-up with the keys her contact had wordlessly slipped into her pocket the night before. Once inside, she climbed to the second-story landing, stopped, and withdrew her gun—a Glock 9-millimeter. She exhaled slowly, already feeling more relaxed with the heavy weapon in her hand. She trained the pistol on the front door and waited for five full minutes to make sure no one else was following her.

No one was.

Satisfied, she climbed the remaining three flights to the vacant apartment, slid the key in the lock, and turned the knob. She pushed the door open with one hand while sweeping her gun across the room with the other. The small Korean man sitting in the room's only chair barely moved. His smooth, broad face was expressionless. Nava took a step into the room and quickly looked around to make sure they were alone.

"Why so jumpy tonight?" His English was very good, but there was still a slight accent, his words too close together.

"Not jumpy. Just careful."

He nodded, then motioned to a laptop; its screen painted the dark kitchen with a greenish glow. She held up her index finger and then unpacked a small device from her knapsack, a cylinder about five inches long with a two-inch diameter. She pressed a tiny black button on its base, and three steel prongs sprang from the tip. She gently placed the apparatus on the floor, aiming the prongs at the ceiling. After a few seconds, the machine emitted a low-pitched hum; the indicator light flashed red.

"Another careful precaution?" the *Spetsnaz* agent asked.

"It prevents any directional microphones from picking up our conversation," Nava said, noticing for the first time the tiny earpiece he wore. She knew that her signal jammer wouldn't disrupt his transmitter, but it wasn't the Koreans from whom she was trying to avoid detection. She ran her hand across the smooth lines of the laptop. "Is this secure?"

"The cellular modem has a 128-digit encryption-code key. Once I verify the data, I will transfer the money to your account. Then you can call Switzerland yourself."

Nava unclipped her belt buckle, extracted the tiny circular laser disk, and slid it into the side of the computer. After she input the fifteen-character password, the screen went black for a split second before coming back to life.

Seeing this, the man she knew as Yi Tae-Woo stood and walked over to the computer. His movements were so fluid he seemed to float across the floor. Judging from his grace, she knew he was an expert at hand-to-hand combat. But then again, all *Spetsnaz* agents were—especially those in Unit 695, the elite group of operatives assigned to build clandestine cells around the globe for North Korea's counterespionage division—the Research Department for External Intelligence, the RDEI.

Nava remembered when the men from the Democratic People's Republic of Korea first appeared at the camp where she'd trained as a girl. It had been 1984, and Kim Jong-Il had decided to send his best fighters to Pavlovsk to learn from the Soviet special-forces soldiers known as the *Voiska Spetsialnogo Naznacheniya,* or *Spetsnaz* for short. Their training included all forms of armed and unarmed combat, terrorism, and sabotage.

The North Koreans so admired their Soviet teachers they adopted the *Spetsnaz* moniker for their own troops. However, the DPRK retained its own slogan: "One against one hundred." And they meant it. Nava wondered again if she had made a mistake in dealing with them. Although they weren't any deadlier than the Israeli Mossad or British MI6 agents she normally sold information to, she didn't trust the North Koreans. No matter—it would all be over soon. This would be the last time she dealt with them.

She watched Yi Tae-Woo at the computer. He scrolled through the information, intermittently slowing down to read specific pages and then speeding up to bypass entire sections. Nava left him to his work, waiting patiently until he was confident she had delivered what was promised. After five minutes he stepped back.

"Everything seems to be in order. The money has been transferred. You can use the laptop to check for yourself."

Nava smiled. "You'll understand if I decide to pass on your offer."

"Of course," Yi Tae-Woo said, nonplussed.

Nava had no intention of using a computer owned by the RDEI to verify the transfer. Not only could the RDEI falsely feed her information, but if they recorded her keystrokes, they would know her passkey and could bleed her account dry. Although Nava would have been surprised if the North Korean's foreign-intelligence arm had cheated her, embezzlement in the world of espionage was certainly not unheard of. After all, spies had budgets, too.

She snapped open her cell phone, which had its own

128-digit encryption-code key, and made the call. After she gave the foreign banker her passkey, he confirmed that three-quarters of a million dollars had just hit her account. She gave the banker another passkey, signaling him to execute the wiring instructions she had provided him the day before. Nava waited a few seconds for his response and then hung up the phone. By the time she turned around to face Yi Tae-Woo, her money (less a 1.5 percent carrying fee) was safe in the Cayman Islands.

"Everything is as it should be?" he asked.

"Yes. Thank you," Nava said. She packed up the signal jammer and replaced it in her knapsack. Yi Tae-Woo was standing between her and the door. He was about to move aside and let Nava pass when she heard his earpiece begin to buzz loudly. Tae-Woo took a step back and removed his gun in one smooth motion, aiming it directly at Nava's chest.

"There is a problem," he said plainly.

"What is it?" Nava asked. She forced herself to remain calm.

"One of the files is unreadable. There must be a problem with the disk," Yi Tae-Woo said. He motioned to the computer with a slight nod of his chin. "Check it."

Nava turned around and ejected the disk. Holding it between her thumb and index finger, she angled the disk to catch the light. Sure enough, she saw a tiny scratch the size of an eyelash. It must have been damaged when she was fending off Wright.

"The disk is scratched," Nava said.

"You must return the money," he said.

Nava felt her blood go cold. "I can't," she said without turning around. "I gave strict instructions not to move the money for at least twenty-four hours after arrival." When she had told her banker this precaution the day before, Nava had thought she was being clever. Now she thought otherwise.

"Then we have a very serious problem."

Nava knew she had only one chance. Whipping around, she grabbed his forearm and forced it to the ceiling before he was able to squeeze off a shot. With her other hand, she sliced the disk across his cheek, instantly drawing blood. The shock of the sudden laceration gave Nava the edge; she slammed the heel of her hand into his face, shattering his nose. Dropping his gun, he staggered backward.

Nava reached into her jacket for her Glock when the door burst open and three men dressed in black rushed in, guns drawn. She instantly put her hands behind her head and fell to her knees, knowing there was no way out. One of the men kicked her in the stomach. She rolled to the floor in pain; the man held her there, his boot resting on the base of her skull, an Uzi submachine gun aimed at her back. The men spoke hurriedly in Korean for nearly a minute, and then they tied her to a chair.

Yi Tae-Woo bent over so that they were eye to eye.

"What do you want?" Nava asked.

"We want you to return the money," Yi Tae-Woo said, his voice nasal due to his broken nose. "Now."

"I told you—I can't."

He stood up and pointed his SIG Sauer at her head.

"Tae-Woo, wait. Within twenty-four hours, I can get you the data. I just need to go back to the field office and download it."

Yi Tae-Woo had a brief conversation in Korean with whoever was on the other end of his earpiece. Then he returned his attention to Nava.

"In twenty-four hours, you will give us the rest of the information *and* return the money."

"That's unfa—" Nava decided not to finish the rest of her sentence due to the solemn look in Yi Tae-Woo's eyes. She started over. "Thank you for being so reasonable."

"You are welcome." Yi Tae-Woo nodded to his men, who quickly untied her and helped her up. "Remember—twenty-four hours."

"I'll remember," Nava said, resisting the urge to rub her wrists.

Without another word she was out the door and down the

stairs. She didn't unclench her jaw until she had put eight blocks behind her, at which point she surprised herself by stopping to vomit on a pile of dark green garbage bags. When she was through, she wiped her mouth on her sleeve, leaving a tiny yellow stain.

As she continued walking, Nava found herself unconsciously lighting another cigarette. She was about to stab it out when she changed her mind, deciding that she would allow herself as many as she wanted today.

She wasn't sure there were going to be many more tomorrows.

As Dr. Tversky reviewed the data from his latest experiments, he thought about Julia. Lately she flitted across the lab, all smiles and giggles, worlds away from the timid demeanor she had displayed during her first two years there. Pretty soon people would start to suspect something—that is, if they hadn't already.

That didn't bother him much; after all, professors had been screwing their grad students since the dawn of time. The administration didn't care, as long as you were quiet about it. Hell, they even expected it; it was one of a professor's unspoken fringe benefits.

Of course, that's not what he told Julia. She was a bit naïve in the ways of the world, and he sensed that the secrecy of the affair added to her excitement, so he did what he could to fuel her fantasy. In truth the sex wasn't that good. She was eager but clumsy—all teeth and fingernails when she was servicing him, and when he was on top, she just lay there like a sack of potatoes with a goofy grin on her face. And the way she insisted on calling him "Petey" when they were alone together. Just the thought of the juvenile moniker made him cringe.

After the first month, he had decided to break it off, but then he realized that her severe case of puppy love presented a unique opportunity. At first she had been hesitant to participate in the human trial, but when he explained how important it was to him, she quickly acquiesced. Thus far the results had been nothing short of extraordinary. The information he was able to extract from Julia during her fugue states was incredible. Tversky suspected that he could push her even further, but he was worried about the side effects of the treatments.

Although for the most part she seemed fine, her newfound love of rhyming was quite disturbing. Disorganized speech patterns like hers were an early sign of schizophrenia. He knew that altering her brain chemistry would probably disrupt her mental stability, but he was surprised that it had happened so quickly. Still, it was worth it, whatever the risks to Julia.

After all, if he were successful in bringing the experiments to their projected conclusion, then it wouldn't be Julia's safety that he had to worry about—but his own.

Dr. James Forsythe had always known that he wasn't brilliant.

However, the short, bald-headed, bearded man also knew that brilliance wasn't a necessary attribute to become a great scientist. Of course, having a keen intellect helped—to a point. But anything beyond that point was typically detrimental. Classical scientists were introverts, lacking the people skills necessary to excel in the real world, and Forsythe was glad not to count himself among them.

Whenever he overheard one of his researchers declare that Forsythe wasn't a real "man of science," he would smile. Forsythe knew that it was meant as an insult, but he took it as a compliment. After all, the so-called "genius" scientists were merely the Science and Technology Research lab's worker bees, while Forsythe was its director.

Despite that the STR was a government lab, most civilians didn't know of its existence, which was probably for the best. Although the lab itself was about twenty years old, its true history dated back to 1952 when President Truman signed the National Security Council Intelligence Directive that gave birth to the National Security Agency.

By the early eighties, the NSA was eavesdropping on

more than 250 million conversations a day from over 130 countries. Though their mission was to analyze only those communiqués related to national security and ignore the rest, like a boy who picks up the phone only to hear his older brother talking about sex, when the NSA heard something interesting, they couldn't help but listen.

With so much information at their fingertips, the NSA struggled with what to do with it—specifically the scientific data. That is, until the Director of Cryptography dreamed up a solution. His vision was to create a research lab dedicated to decrypting, analyzing, and interpreting data gathered from scientists all over the globe, so that no country would ever become more advanced than the United States.

When the plan was pitched to Ronald Reagan's White House as another means of keeping tabs on the world's communist regimes, the administration welcomed the idea with open arms. And so, on October 13, 1983, the Science and Technology Research lab was born.

Initially the STR spied only on foreign scientists. But as the Cold War ended and the Internet led to more international cooperation, the STR soon found itself inadvertently spying on domestic scientists as well. However, by that time the U.S. government was benefiting by the STR's research too much to care.

The STR's "research" process was simple. Their analysts read through thousands of pages of research culled from mainframes from around the world and flagged any interesting new technology for their in-house scientists to investigate. They then replicated key experiments and verified the viability of any newly developed technology.

Once the new technology was validated, the STR lab passed the information along to the appropriate government agency. If, however, the technology was developed by a foreign country and commercial in nature, the STR leaked it to two or three American-based multinational corporations that were currently "in favor" with the administration. It didn't take long for the STR to become the most powerful clearinghouse of new technology on the planet.

Once Forsythe assumed the role of director in 1997, he was amazed to discover how much money and political capital the previous STR director had left on the table. The STR controlled the dissemination of stolen technology to no fewer than six government agencies (the CIA, DoD, FBI, FDA, NASA, and NIH) as well as a handful of the most innovative Silicon Valley powerhouses. The only entity that stood between Forsythe and his "clients" was the STR Oversight Board, which consisted of three senators who fully appreciated the power their position afforded them.

Forsythe knew that the real power was in being the sole decision maker. However, in order to be that man, Forsythe needed to have control. It was then that Forsythe enlisted an unlikely ally in his quest for power, a greasy young NSA hacker named Steven Grimes. It took Grimes less than two weeks to discover information that would compel the board, led by Geoffrey Daniels, the senior senator from Utah, to be more amenable to Forsythe's recommendations.

Although Grimes's endless desire to watch others was disturbing, his voyeuristic and prying nature proved very useful. Forsythe still didn't know how Grimes had come up with the photos of Daniels with that young boy, and quite frankly he didn't want to know. All that mattered was that after Senator Daniels saw those pictures, he had been more than happy to follow Forsythe's "suggestions."

John Simonson, the most junior senator on the board, also became much friendlier once Grimes discovered Simonson's illegal tax shelter in the Cayman Islands. After that, no request Forsythe made to the board was rejected again. True, the vote was typically two to one, but a majority was all Forsythe needed, which was a very good thing, as Grimes had never been able to find anything on the third board member, an ultrareligious right-wing senator from Louisiana.

For nearly six years, Forsythe had controlled the STR

board and made no secret of that fact, culling money and favors from CEOs and government officials alike. Life had been very good. But now all that was coming to an end, thanks to the untimely demise of Senator Daniels, who had gone into cardiac arrest in his sleep and woke up dead.

When Forsythe saw reports of Daniels's death on the news, he silently cursed. He knew that Daniels's replacement would be John "Mac" MacDougal, a liberal senator from Vermont. Two years earlier MacDougal had made a failed bid for the board position and had hungered after it ever since. Forsythe was certain that MacDougal was already maneuvering to fill the spot.

Forsythe, anticipating that MacDougal might one day achieve his goal, had taken the preemptive measure of having Grimes try to find some dirt on him. Unfortunately, the only information the hacker unearthed was that MacDougal had a cousin in the pharmaceutical industry who had his eye on government work.

By the time Forsythe arrived at the lab that morning, there was already a message from MacDougal's office requesting a meeting. It was then that Forsythe knew for sure—by the end of the month, he would be replaced. He had always known that his position wouldn't last forever, but he thought he had at least until the next Senate elections.

Fortunately, he wasn't entirely unprepared. During the previous few months, he had lined up $12 million in funding for the development of his own research lab. Venture capitalists rarely gave out blank checks the way they did to Forsythe, but then again, rarely did they have a chance to finance a man with literally thousands of workable ideas at his fingertips.

The only problem was that Forsythe had always assumed he would have at least a full year to find the perfect idea, rather than less than a month. But he could still pull it off. He would spend the next two weeks reviewing abstracts of all the research projects on the planet until he found one that was worth stealing. Once he identified the project, he would bury the STR files to make sure the government wouldn't pose any future competition.

As luck would have it, one of the abstracts that he'd read a few days before seemed promising. It described illicit experiments being conducted by a biostatistician that the STR had been watching for quite some time. The good doctor had been injecting a human subject with an intriguing compound that had a very interesting effect on the man's brain waves. Although Forsythe didn't know the human guinea pig's name (as he was referred to only as "the Alpha Subject"), he did know the professor.

Coincidentally, the professor already had a meeting request pending. He was probably looking for a grant. It was perfect. Forsythe buzzed his secretary.

"I need you to make an appointment for me as soon as possible. You should already have the contact info. . . . Tomorrow is fine. . . . The name is Tversky."

Caine nervously sniffed the air. It was cool and sterile, with the faint hint of alcohol. After he ran his hands over the starched sheets, he knew he was in the hospital. He slowly opened his eyes, still afraid the world would be long and distorted, but everything was in proportion, just a bit blurry without his contacts. He brought his arm up to rub his gummy lids and noticed the IV needle stuck in the back of his hand. He had a weird sense of déjà vu, as if he had woken up in this bed a few other times and had the same series of thoughts.

He wondered how long he'd been here.

"About eight hours, little brother. You've been in and out, talking in your sleep. Welcome back."

Startled, Caine snapped his head to the left. Jasper held up his hand in a brief wave. Caine caught his breath, thinking, *That's what I'd look like if I went crazy.*

Jasper looked terrible. His skin was pasty, and his bones seemed to pull at the flesh of his lanky frame. Even so, there was a glint in Jasper's sunken green eyes that reminded David Caine of the fierce intellect trapped within his brother's tortured mind.

"I didn't know that you—" Caine fumbled for words. "I mean, wow, you're here. That's great, man."

"It's okay, you can say it," Jasper said, shifting his weight from one foot to the other. "You didn't know they'd let me out of the loony bin."

Caine looked sheepish, then nodded. His brother always could read his mind.

"Yeah," Jasper said, his voice both tired and amused. "The good folks at Mercy gave me a clean bill of health in January. I've been out for over a month now."

"Christ, man, why didn't you call?"

Jasper shrugged. "I don't know. Just wanted to sort things out first. Thanks for visiting, by the way."

Caine winced. "Jasper, I—"

Jasper held up his hand like a stop sign. "Don't." He turned away from his brother and stared out the window for a while before breaking the silence. "I'm sorry. I understand. I probably wouldn't want to visit me in that place either."

"Still, I should have come."

"Well," Jasper said with a sly smirk, "there's always next time."

Neither of the two brothers spoke for a moment, and then, simultaneously—as identical twins are likely to do—they burst out laughing. It felt good to laugh. It seemed like a long time since Caine had really laughed, longer still since he'd laughed with his big brother. Even though his brother had beaten Caine out of the womb by only ten minutes, Jasper would never let him forget who was little and who was big.

"How did you know I was here?"

"Some intern called my cell after they checked you in. When I got here, the nurse told me you had a seizure."

Caine nodded.

"She also mentioned that you've been having seizures for about a year now. Evidently she thought I knew. Care to share-*pair-fair-dare?"*

Caine looked at Jasper in fear, but his brother merely cackled like he'd just made the funniest joke in the world. Whatever they'd done to him in the mental institution, it hadn't been enough. Caine now recognized the other thing the glint in Jasper's eye reminded him of—his brother's condition.

"Did the nurse say anything else?" Caine asked, trying to ignore Jasper's odd behavior.

"Not much, except that it was a fairly severe episode. According to your Russian buddies, you were unconscious for about twenty minutes before the ambulance came to pick you up."

"Shit," Caine said, suddenly wondering what Nikolaev's reaction had been when Caine went down. "They had to call 911?"

"Yup," Jasper answered. "By the way—what were you doing at a Russian dinner club on Avenue D at two in the morning?"

Caine shrugged noncommittally. "They have good vodka."

"Yeah, I bet—or, should I say, *you* bet." Jasper raised his eyebrow.

"I guess that wouldn't be entirely inaccurate."

"How much are you in for?"

"Nothing, I'm fine," Caine said, a bit too quickly.

"If that was the case, I doubt Vitaly Nikolaev would have called here three times asking about your condition."

Caine's shoulders sagged. "No shit?"

"No shit, little bro. Unless he wanted to send over some get-well vodka, I'm guessing he's looking after his investment. So I ask again: How much?"

Caine closed his eyes and tried to remember that last hand. As it came back to him through his cloudy mind, he groaned. "Eleven," he said without opening his eyes.

"Eleven hundred? That's not so bad. I think I've got a CD I could cash in—"

"No."

"David, come on, I can help."

"Yeah, but I don't owe eleven hundred."

"How much, then?" Caine just stared at the haggard face of his twin. "Fuck," Jasper finally said as he realized the true amount. *"Eleven grand?"*

"Yeah."

"Christ, David. How could you lose that much?"

"I shouldn't have lost, it was a sure thing."

"Not sure enough."

"Look, Jasper, I've got enough problems without you coming in here and judging me. I fucked up. I admit it, okay? Last time I checked, you've fucked up once or twice yourself."

Jasper sighed and sat down in one of the neon orange hospital chairs. "What did you have?" Jasper asked, obviously trying to smooth over Caine's outburst.

"Quads."

"Little ones?"

"No. Bullets."

Jasper let out a low whistle. "You lost on four aces? Shit," Jasper said with true respect. "What happened?"

"The other guy hit the straight flush on the river."

"Wow," Jasper said, shaking his head. "How long do you have to pay it back?"

"Knowing Vitaly, he's going to want the first installment by tomorrow. But since I'm a friend, he'll probably let me slide until the end of the week before he has one of his thugs put me in the hospital on a more permanent basis."

"The nurse tells me you're getting enough hospital time on your own."

"Yeah. Basically if Nikolaev doesn't kill me, then probably my seizures will."

"Christ, man," Jasper said, real emotion in his voice. "Last time we spoke, you were in perfect health and hadn't made a bet in . . . what, a year? What the hell happened?"

Caine didn't know what to say. The reality of his situation began closing in around him. This whole last year had been one giant train wreck. Jesus, had it been a year since that first seizure? It couldn't have been that long, could it? Then he realized it had been more like a year and a half since he'd last stood in front of a class as an adjunct professor. His stomach dropped. Funny. He thought it would take longer than that to totally fuck up his life.

Guess he was wrong.

Unlike most of the instructors in the statistics department, Caine loved to teach. After leading his first class, he discovered that he had a unique gift to convey his passion for statistics in a way that both intrigued and excited his students.

Although it wasn't quite the same high as he felt after winning a huge pot, there was something about opening up his students' minds to the world of probability that gave him a thrill. Ironically, it was losing all his money in the underground poker rooms throughout the city that had first brought him to the classroom. He had no other choice; he needed money, and as a fourth-year statistics Ph.D. student at Columbia University, running a section of Introduction to Probability Theory was the only job he could get.

Since he was all out of both credit and cash, he couldn't play any poker until after he got his first paycheck. But once he was paid, Caine had realized he didn't feel like gambling anymore. That night, instead of dreaming about cards, he dreamed about the next day's lecture.

That's when everything started to turn around. Sure, he still awoke the following morning with the hunger and yearning that only a true gambler could understand, but he forced himself to swallow those feelings and channel them into academics. Teaching had finally given him what scores of Gamblers Anonymous meetings had failed to provide: control.

The next couple months were almost peaceful as he learned that he could indeed master his addiction. For a while, Caine actually believed that things were finally going his way—right up until it all fell apart. He could still remember the exact moment when his life began to unravel. It was in the same place where things had finally started to gel for him—the classroom. He had been leaning against the blackboard, a piece of chalk in one hand and a Styrofoam cup of coffee in the other. That's when he'd launched into his impromptu history lesson.

"So . . . anyone know where probability theory came from?"

Silence.

"Okay, I'll make it multiple choice. Probability theory

came into being through a series of letters exchanged between two French mathematicians who were discussing (a) physics, (b) philosophy, or (c) dice."

No response. "If someone doesn't raise their hand in the next five seconds, this stuff *will* be on the exam." Twenty hands shot into the air. "That's better. Jerri, what's your guess?"

"Physics?"

"Nope. The correct answer is (c) dice.

"The man who laid down the principles of probability was born in 1623, and his name was Blaise Pascal. Like a lot of privileged children at the time, Pascal was schooled at home by his father, along with several tutors. However, because Pascal's father didn't want his son to be overworked, he decided that Blaise should concentrate on languages and ignore mathematics.

"Being an ordinary kid, the fact that mathematics were off limits only served to fuel Pascal's curiosity, so he decided to study geometry in his free time." A few students rolled their eyes, and Caine added, "Look, this was before Xbox and PS2; there wasn't a lot a kid could do to have fun." A few laughs.

"Once his father learned about Blaise's natural gift for numbers, he encouraged him with the gift of Euclid's *Elements*—again, remember, there was no such thing as TV back then, so people read things called *books*." He got a couple chuckles on that one. "Anyway, after Blaise's father saw him burn through Euclid, he hired the best math tutors, which proved to be a wise move, since Blaise Pascal became one of the most important mathematicians of the seventeenth century.

"In fact, he affected the life of everyone in this room with one of his inventions. Anyone know what it was?"

"The abacus?" a sorority girl guessed.

"I think you're confusing the French with the ancient Chinese," Caine said. "Although you were on the right track. He invented the first arithmetic machine, which later evolved into the modern-day calculator. Throughout the rest of

Pascal's life, he studied mathematics and physics, although a few years before he died, he gave up his obsession with numbers, ironically because he quantitatively proved that his time would be better spent focusing on religion and philosophy."

"How did he do that?" a bearded student in the back row asked.

"Good question, I'll get to that in a bit. Now, where was I? Oh, right." Caine took a sip of his coffee and continued. "Before Pascal abandoned mathematics, he was posed several questions in 1654 by a French nobleman known as the Chevalier de Méré. Intrigued by the mathematical issues the questions raised, Pascal began a correspondence with an old friend of his father's—a retired government councilor named Pierre de Fermat.

"As it so happens, de Méré was a compulsive gambler, and his question was about a popular dice game, in which the shooter would roll four dice. If he did so *without* rolling a six, then he would win even money, but if he *did* roll a six, then the house would win. De Méré wanted to know whether or not the odds were in the house's favor.

"Now, if you only take away one thing from this class, I hope it's this." Caine went to the board and wrote in ten-inch-high letters:

The odds are ALWAYS in the house's favor.

He got a few appreciative laughs. "Now, can anyone tell me why this is? Jim."

Caine's favorite student perked up. "Because if the odds *weren't* in the house's favor, then the house would lose money more often than it won, so eventually there would be no more house."

"Exactly," Caine said. "In my opinion, even before the creation of probability theory, de Méré should have been able to figure that one out, but of course if French noblemen had been smart, they probably wouldn't have all gotten their heads chopped off.

"In any case, Pascal and Fermat mathematically demonstrated—surprise, surprise—that the odds *were* in fact in the house's favor. They showed that if a shooter played a hundred games, he would likely *not* roll a six and win 48 times but he *would* roll a six and lose 52 times. Thus, the odds of the game were in the house's favor, 52–48. And that is how probability theory was born—because a French nobleman wanted to know if betting that he wouldn't roll a six on four dice was a smart move."

A few heads nodded, which Caine had learned was code for *hmmm, interesting*. An African-American student in the back raised his hand. "Michael?" Caine asked.

"How did Pascal prove that he should spend his life on religion?"

"Oh, right, almost forgot about that," Caine said. "He used a theory that would later be named 'expected value.' Essentially what you do is sum the products of several events' probabilities by what you would receive if each event occurred."

Caine was greeted by glassy stares. "Um, all right, let's take a real-world example—the lottery. How much is this week's Powerball jackpot? Anyone know?"

"Ten million bucks," offered a jock in the back row.

"Okay, for the moment let's pretend we live in a fantasy land where there are no taxes. Now, I happen to know that the odds of winning that jackpot is roughly 120 *million* to 1, since that's how many possible numeric combinations there are. The way I would calculate what I *expected* to win if I paid one dollar for a lottery ticket is this: Multiply the probability of winning by the amount I would win and then add that to the probability of losing multiplied by zero, since you don't win anything if you lose."

Expected Value (lottery ticket)

=prob(winning) * jackpot +
prob(losing) * ($0)

$$=(1 / 120{,}000{,}000) * (\$10{,}000{,}000) + (119{,}999{,}999 / 120{,}000{,}000) * (\$0)$$

$$=(0.00000083\%) * (\$10{,}000{,}000) + (99.99999917\%) * (\$0)$$

$$=\$0.083 + \$0.000$$

$$=\$0.083$$

"This means that if you played Powerball this week, you would *expect* to win only 8.3 cents. However, since the ticket *costs* one dollar and the *value* is 8.3 cents, according to probability theory, it doesn't make any sense to play, because the cost is higher than the expected value.

"Thus, even though you might think it's worth it to pay a dollar for a chance to win $10 million, you would be wrong, because in truth it's not even worth a dime." Caine took another sip of his coffee while his last statement sank in. After he felt confident that everyone understood his explanation, he posed a question: "When *would* it make sense to play? Madison."

The perky blonde sat up straight in her seat. "Um, only when the jackpot was over $120 million."

"Right. Why?"

"Because if the jackpot was, say, $125 million and the odds of winning were 1 in 120 million, then the expected value of each ticket would be—" Madison paused as she punched some numbers in on her calculator—"$1.04, which is more than the cost of one dollar."

"Exactly," Caine said. "From an expected-value standpoint, it only makes sense to play when the *value* is greater than the *cost*. Hence in this case you should play only when you can win more than $120 million."

"But what about Pascal's decision to devote his life to religion?" Michael asked again.

"Pascal used expected value to prove that he should dedicate himself to religion. Like all good mathematicians, he boiled the question down to an equation."

Which is greater?
(a) Expected value (hedonistic life)
or
(b) Expected value (religious life)
Where . . .
(a) = Prob(no afterlife) * (joy from hedonism) +
Prob(afterlife) * (eternal damnation)
and
(b) = Prob(no afterlife) * (joy from religion) +
Prob(afterlife) * (eternal happiness)

"Pascal's logic was simple: If (a) was greater than (b), then he should be hedonistic, but if (a) was less than (b), then he should be religious."

"But how did he solve the problem without knowing the values of the variables?" Michael asked.

"He made a bunch of assumptions, namely, that the value of eternal happiness was positive infinity and that the value of eternal damnation was negative infinity."

eternal happiness = + ∞
eternal damnation = – ∞

"Whenever you input infinity into an equation, it cancels everything else out because it's such a big number, so you can say that (a) hedonistic life has an expected value of negative infinity while (b) religious life has an expected value of positive infinity."

(a) hedonism = – ∞ and (b) religious = + ∞
so . . .
(a) < (b), thus . . .
exp. value (hedonism) < exp. value (religious life)

"Get it? Even if the probability of an afterlife is incredibly small, the joy Pascal expected to gain from a religious life would still be greater than the joy he expected by living a hedonistic life and risking eternal damnation.

"Once Pascal realized that, the answer to whether he should devote the remainder of his days to religion was obvious."

"So does that mean *you* live a religious life?" Michael asked, to the amusement of the class.

"Actually," Caine said with a smile, "I don't."

"How come?"

"Two reasons: First, I believe that the joy of a sufficiently hedonistic life is positive infinity while the joy of a religious life is negative infinity." Several students clapped appreciatively. Caine held up his hand. "And second, I live a hedonistic life for the same reason I play the lottery—sometimes you just gotta say 'to hell with statistics' and go with what feels right."

Everyone laughed, and a few students even whistled. Caine was about to let everyone leave when he looked down at the piece of chalk in his palm. That's when he noticed that it had started to grow.

It extended from his hand like a giant wooden staff. He reached out his fingers to touch the tip, and they, too, seemed to grow, stretching out like four giant pieces of taffy. For a moment he couldn't move. But then, as the chalk seemed to bend back toward him, he threw it on the floor, where it shattered, the pieces squirming like a pile of earthworms.

Gasping for breath, he looked up at the blackboard to center himself, but it only made things worse. The board towered over him, his equations fluttering like ribbons. Desperate, he turned to face his students, hoping the sight of animate objects would bring him down. He couldn't have been more wrong. Three of the undergrads had their hands in the air, and their arms rose up out of their bodies like massive palm trees, gently swaying in the breeze.

That was when the smell hit him. Putrid and rank, it filled his brain with images of rotting flesh and decayed meat. His mind struggled to grasp what was happening, but it was too late. He suddenly felt like someone had punched him in the chest, as all the air was sucked out of his lungs. He barely made it to the wastebasket before he vomited and passed out, smacking his head against a desk on the way to the floor.

Fortunately, one of his students was interning at Mount Sinai's neurological ward, so Caine was spared the humiliation of waking up with a wallet stuffed into his mouth like he had when he passed out on the N train two months later. Of course, at the time he didn't know he should be grateful. All he knew was that his new life seemed to have died before his eyes.

It took almost three weeks before he was able to muster up enough courage to return to the classroom, but when he did, it was a disaster. As he looked out at the sea of expectant faces, all his mind could see were monstrous hands waving back and forth like wayward props from a bad Tim Burton movie. When he opened his mouth to speak, no sound emerged. Caine took a deep breath, and his nostrils flared as he remembered the awful stench.

"Are you all right, Professor?"

Caine heard the words from one of the students in the front row, but he was unable to respond. Instead he ran up the steps to the back of the class and staggered through the heavy steel double doors. Once outside, he could feel his heart slow. He cautiously sucked in the cool air, relieved to discover that the smell was gone.

He tried to teach once more after that, but it was no use. This time his panic attack began the second he walked into the room. When he reached the lectern, he could barely breathe. Sweat poured off his brow, stinging his eyes. In a horrifying repeat of his first seizure, he stumbled over to the wastebasket and vomited up the breakfast burrito he'd eaten an hour before.

As he stared at the disgusting orange mix of partially digested eggs and salsa, he knew that it was over. He would never teach again. He pushed himself to his feet, wiped his mouth, and left the classroom, secure in the knowledge that he wasn't coming back.

At first he tried to convince himself it was a good thing—without having to teach three times a week, he could concentrate on finishing his Ph.D. dissertation, *The Influence of Statistically Significant Outliers in Logistic Regression Analysis.*

And, for almost a month, it seemed he was right. He channeled all his nervous energy and the dull yearning that he awoke with each morning *(Come on, man, don't you want to play some POKER?)* into his doctoral thesis. He spent his days holed up in Columbia's voluminous stacks hunched over his laptop, diligently graphing distribution curves for various natural phenomena until he passed out each night from exhaustion.

And then it happened again, this time even worse than before. One afternoon as he stared at his laptop, he was suddenly overcome with the stench. The smell seemed to emanate from the computer itself—the screen stretched wide before his eyes like a giant, toothless maw.

Caine tried to back away, but he froze. Then everything went black. He woke up on the cold cement floor. He rolled over and spit out a mouthful of hot, salty blood, along with a piece of broken enamel from one of his front teeth. His computer lay on the floor by his feet. It looked like it had been run over by an eighteen-wheeler—the screen was cracked, the keyboard smashed beyond recognition.

His mind groggy, he tightened his fist at the sight of his $2,500 Sony Vaio, whose only use now was as either a paperweight or a piece of modern art. It wasn't until the shard of plastic pierced his skin that he realized a piece of the keyboard was embedded into his hand. He pulled back his fingers to reveal the F key stabbing into his palm.

It seemed to be mocking him. F. Finished—as in *You are now finished, buddy boy. Might as well pack it in. You blacked out, trashed your computer—which you don't even remember, by the way—and now you're lying on the floor spitting out pieces of your front teeth. Let's call a spade a spade—you're over.* F *is for "finito," and that means you.*

What, you thought you could get away scot-free? You got the crazy gene, my friend. Your twin brother has it, and guess what? You've got it, too. Welcome to the party.

Caine threw the key against the wall, where it left a tiny red mark before falling to the floor. It was then that he finally admitted to himself that his little "problem" wasn't going to go away on its own. The next morning he made an appointment with one of the neurologists at the Columbia Neurological Institute. Three days, a CAT scan, a PET scan, and two MRIs later, a moon-faced doctor from India came into his room to deliver the bad news.

Caine had TLE—temporal lobe epilepsy. His doctor informed him that olfactory and visual hallucinations were typical before a seizure, as was hearing voices or having a flash of déjà vu. The smells, sights, sounds, and feelings were all grouped into the same classification, called a pre-seizure "aura." Caine supposed knowing that auras were common for TLE patients should have made him feel better, but it had the opposite effect.

The next year passed like a bad dream, as he bounced in and out of the hospital, the seizures growing worse every time.

"David, I had no idea," Jasper said, when Caine finally finished his story. "I'm sorry."

Caine shrugged. "Even if you had known, there was nothing you could have done."

"I know, but still, I wish you had told me." Jasper twitched his shoulders. "Do they know what's causing your seizures?"

"My doctor said it's 'idiopathic,' which means they have no idea."

"And they can't treat it?"

Caine shook his head. "During the last year, I tried six different AEDs—antiepileptic drugs—but all they did was make me puke my guts out."

"Christ," Jasper said. "I thought epilepsy was treatable."

"The drugs and other procedures work for about sixty percent of people with epilepsy. I happen to be in the lucky forty percent."

Before Jasper had a chance to respond, there was a knock on the door. "May I come in?" Dr. Kumar asked perfunctorily, breezing into Caine's room without waiting for a response.

"Sure," Caine said, even though the man was already inside. Dr. Kumar picked up Caine's chart and began paging through it, nodding vigorously, as if he were having an intense conversation with himself. Finally he put it aside, shone his penlight in both of Caine's eyes, and then took a step back.

"How are you feeling?"

"Tired, but okay."

"How long did you experience the aura before you had the seizure?"

"Just a few minutes."

"Hmmm. And this is the shortest aura since the VNS procedure?"

"Yes." Caine unconsciously rubbed the scar where the doctors had sliced him open. Three months before, Dr. Kumar had implanted a battery-operated device below a nerve in his neck. The technique, known as vagus nerve stimulation, worked on only 25 percent of the patients who received it. Despite this, out of desperation Caine had tried the procedure. Unfortunately, he wasn't among its successes.

Dr. Kumar sighed. "I don't know what to tell you, David. There aren't any more procedures available, and you were unresponsive to all the pharmaceuticals on the market. Quite frankly, you're out of options." Dr. Kumar paused. "Unless you've changed your mind about my study."

Dr. Kumar had first asked Caine to participate in his experimental drug trial almost nine months before. Initially Caine had said yes. He even suffered through all the blood tests and paperwork, but at the last second, when Dr. Kumar listed the possible side effects, Caine had backed out.

But that was before the VNS procedure, when there was still hope. Now, as Dr. Kumar had so delicately put it, Caine was out of options. If the seizures continued, he would wind up a vegetable within a few years. And in the meantime he lived in fear, never knowing when he would suddenly pass out, flopping on the floor like a fish out of water.

"Is there still room in your study?"

"As of yesterday it was full, but one of my patients dropped out this morning, so—"

"Why did the patient drop out?" Caine interrupted.

"What? Oh, she complained that the drug was giving her terrible nightmares. Personally I think it was psychosomatic."

The doctor paused suddenly and took a long breath. "In any case, I currently have one open spot. But you must decide immediately."

"Okay." Caine nodded with resignation.

"You remember the possible side effects?"

"How could I forget?"

"Oh, yes—you have a history of schizophrenia in your family, correct?"

Jasper raised his hand. Dr. Kumar turned to him, as if noticing Caine's brother for the first time.

"Ah, you must be the twin. David told me that you had a recent break."

Jasper looked at Caine, who nodded as if to say, *Just answer the questions, and I'll explain later.* Jasper turned back to the doctor. "Yes."

"How long since your release?"

"Five weeks."

"What medications have you used?"

"Currently I take Zyprexa, although I've also been on Seroquel and a dash of Risperdal."

"Interesting. And your symptoms are currently under control?"

"The voices have stopped telling me the government is after my brain, if that's what you mean-*kean-lean-seen,*" Jasper said with a pained grin.

Caine watched Dr. Kumar eye Jasper and tried to put himself in the doctor's shoes, to see what he saw. Jasper's appearance had been ravaged by his schizophrenia; he was no longer handsome and looked like someone any sane person would cross the street to avoid. After a moment Dr. Kumar turned back to Caine.

"So what would you like to do?" Dr. Kumar asked.

"What choice do I have?" Caine sighed. "I'll do it."

"Good," Dr. Kumar said, almost smiling. "I'll have my research assistant take care of the paperwork. You will be released from the hospital tomorrow, but you must return every three days for a blood test. I would like you to record the time and duration of all your auras and seizures. And if you experience any schizophrenic symptoms such as delusions, disorganized speech, or hallucinations not related to a partial seizure, then—"

"Whoa." Jasper stood up, holding out his hands to stop Dr. Kumar's monotonous litany. "Why would he experience schizophrenic symptoms?"

Dr. Kumar turned to Caine's twin as if he were a petulant child, but when he saw the fierce look in Jasper's eyes, he decided to answer the question.

"The antiepileptic drug I am testing has a side effect of increasing the brain's production of dopamine. As I'm sure you are well aware, high levels of dopamine have been linked to schizophrenia. Because the AED encourages dopamine release, it is *possible* that David could have a schizophrenic break."

When Dr. Kumar saw Caine and Jasper exchange a nervous look, he barreled on. "I'm not saying that it will happen. I'm just saying that there is a slight risk."

"How slight?" Jasper asked.

"Less than two percent," Dr. Kumar said quickly.

"And if that starts to happen, I stop taking the drug, right?" Caine asked.

Dr. Kumar shook his head. "Oh, no, that could be very dangerous. Even if the AED appears not to be working, it could still be having an effect. If you were to suddenly stop taking the medication, then it is likely you would have some extremely severe seizures."

"So if I start to go crazy, I should do what, exactly?"

"It is very difficult to self-diagnose a mental illness, so I suggest that you meet with my research assistant once a week for a psych evaluation."

Caine slumped back in his bed. He could see by Jasper's expression that his brother, of all people, was feeling sorry for him. Jesus Christ. Caine closed his eyes, trying to block out the world. Dr. Kumar's words still rang in his head—*schizophrenic break.* Caine couldn't believe that he was voluntarily putting himself at such risk. But the seizures . . . if they continued unabated, he would end up worse than Jasper. There was no other choice.

"Okay," Caine said, feeling simultaneously relieved and terrified.

"Good." Dr. Kumar started to walk toward the door, when he stopped and turned around. "That reminds me, you'll have to sign a waiver allowing me to commit you to a mental institution if necessary." Before Caine could respond, the physician was gone.

"Nice guy," Jasper said dryly.

"Oh, yeah. He's a fucking prince."

A beat of silence. Then: "So you're really going to go through with it?" Jasper asked.

"I have to."

"Aren't you afraid of ending up like your big brother? Crazy and foaming at the mouth like a rabid dog-*bog-hog-log?*"

Caine caught his breath. "Jasper, are you sure you're all right? Isn't rhyming symptomatic of—"

"It's nothing," Jasper said, cutting Caine off. The edges of Jasper's mouth curled into a smile. "Rhyming just makes me feel good, that's all. I like the sound." He clicked his tongue against the roof of his mouth a couple times, as if punctuating his sentence. "So back to you. Are you sure about this?"

"I don't have any other choice. I can't keep living like this. And if the seizures continue like they have, well . . ." Caine let his words trail off.

"You want me to stay? I can crash on your couch for a couple of days if you want."

Caine shook his head. "No, I'll be okay. I want to do this on my own. You understand."

"Yeah," Jasper said, scratching his stubbly chin, "I guess I do."

"Can I ask you a question, though?"

"Sure."

"What's it like? Schizophrenia, I mean," Caine said awkwardly, realizing he had never asked his brother the question before. "What's it feel like?"

Jasper shrugged his shoulders. "It doesn't feel like anything. The delusions seem real. Natural, even obvious. Like it's the most ordinary thing in the world that the government is spying on your thoughts or that your best friend is trying to kill you." He didn't say anything for a beat. "That's why it's so fucking scary."

Jasper swallowed before continuing. "The thing is, whatever is happening—or whatever you *think* is happening—you're still in control. Just try to remember that you're still you. Ride it out. Try to find ways to anchor yourself, places to be safe or people to be safe with. And try to make smart decisions within whatever world you create. Eventually you'll find your way back to reality."

Caine nodded, praying that he wouldn't need to use Jasper's advice.

"So," Caine said, trying to steer the conversation back to some semblance of normalcy, "where are you living these days?"

"Same old apartment in Philly, a few blocks off campus."

"Cool." Neither said anything for a while, each brother lost in his thoughts, worried about things to come. Finally Jasper looked at his watch and stood up. "If you don't want me to stay, I should head out now to catch the next bus back."

Caine was surprised how disappointed he felt that his brother wanted to leave. It must have shown in his face, for Jasper immediately backpedaled.

"Of course, if you want, I can call in sick and stay a couple days."

"No, it's all right. I wouldn't want you to get in trouble at work. I'm sure it's not easy getting a job when—" Caine stopped himself before he finished the sentence, but the implication was obvious.

"What, when you're crazy?" Jasper asked.

"Come on, man," Caine said, feeling exhausted. "You know what I mean."

"Yeah. Sorry, I'm just a bit on edge these days."

"No problem. Me, too." Caine extended his hand to his twin, a near stranger in his life, wondering how things had gotten so screwed up. "Thanks for coming. I really appreciate it, especially considering I haven't been around lately."

Jasper waved off Caine's words. "What's a twin brother for?" He turned and started to leave but stopped in the doorway, one foot in, one foot out. "If you need anything, you've got my cell-*bell-dell-well.*"

"Thanks," Caine said, a little uneasy. "That means a lot." After Jasper had left, Caine was surprised to realize that it did.

Julia knew she was in love.

She knew it by how her heart ached when they were apart and how her hands trembled when they were together. How she could barely breathe when they were making love and how she felt after she came, warm and tingly all over, as if her bones had been replaced with Jell-O. More than that, she always felt incredibly safe. When she was in Petey's arms, nothing could hurt her.

Petey. He loved her pet name for him. She couldn't believe how much he had changed her life. When she'd met him, she was still just a girl, but now she was a woman.

Two years earlier, when she'd started graduate school, Julia had given up on ever finding someone. She knew she was probably too young to swear off romance, but as she had never dated, she wasn't sacrificing much. Not one boy in high school or college had ever showed the slightest bit of interest. She began to think there was something deeply wrong with her. Something everyone could see. And she became so tired of hoping, so tired of the letdowns. So she closed herself off. That is, until she met Petey.

He was the last person in the world she had expected would take her virginity. More than twenty years her senior, her thesis adviser was a furry little man, with wild eyebrows and tufts of gray hair growing out of his ears. She knew that the other girls in the department thought he was dorky, but Julia didn't care. It wasn't how he looked that had made her fall in love with him; it was how he thought. Petey was simply the most brilliant man she'd ever met. And his work was groundbreaking. She felt certain that if—no, not if—*when*—he proved his theories, he would become a household name.

Not only would he win the Nobel, but she was sure the talk shows would fall all over themselves to get the great doctor to explain how the very fabric of all their lives was interconnected, traced out in a giant, shifting tapestry of energy, space, and time. If only the university hadn't given him such a hard time about funding, he would be finished by now.

She cringed as she thought of their last conversation about the topic.

"Do you really think you'll get the grant this time?" Julia asked as she ran a hand through his thick, salt-and-pepper hair.

Petey froze; their perfect moment was ruined.

"I'm sorry," Julia said, instantly regretting her words. "I didn't mean—"

"No, it's all right. I have to face facts. If this last round of testing doesn't show the results that I need, then the small-minded university bureaucrats will have won."

Petey was right—they were all bureaucrats. If they really cared about science, they wouldn't have left the world of research to become glorified administrators. Instead they were all out to get him because they were jealous of his brilliance, throwing up roadblocks whenever he was about to cross the threshold into discovery. But they couldn't stop him. She was certain his recent experiments would prove his theory. Then they would trip all over themselves to give him money, and his ideas would be valued for the genius that they were.

She couldn't wait. Once that happened, he promised that they would be able to go public and they could end the experiments. She sighed, anticipating the relief she would feel, knowing that she would never have to go to that . . . that place again. A chill rippled through her body, terror mixed with a bizarre sense of eagerness. She closed her eyes and could almost see it, but then it was gone.

She found it hard to remember that place when she was awake, but every night it was there in her dreams. Lately she'd been dreaming a lot. In her dreams all the weird things made sense, but as soon as she awoke, they would become muddled. For a few weeks, she dreamed of numbers trapped in giant spheres that glowed white and red, pulsating so brightly they made her eyes throb.

Last night's dream had been about poker, which was strange since she didn't even know the rules. But in her dream she was a master player and could calculate all the odds in the blink of an eye, despite the putrid smell of rotten fish that had flooded her brain.

Petey said the dreams didn't mean anything, but Julia suspected they were because of the experiments. As much as it thrilled her to be a part of Petey's study, she knew that it was wrong, and the day the tests ended would mark a new stage in their relationship. No more meeting in skeevy bars halfway across town or having sex in the lab late at night. She rolled over in bed and stared at the ceiling, stretching out her legs, imagining him lying next to her.

What would it be like, to wake up in his arms? They could make love in the morning, and then she would serve him breakfast in bed. After his morning coffee (milk, no sugar) they would have sex again. She reached down to caress her inner thighs and felt a warmth spread through her.

For the first time in her life, Julia was happy. As she inched her fingers down her naked stomach, her watch began to beep. Without a moment's hesitation, she jumped out of bed and ran into the bathroom, where she kept her pills. There was no label on the clear container; Petey didn't want there to be any way to trace them back to his lab.

"Pill, fill, lil', nil," she said aloud, laughing at her senseless rhyme as she poured out two 50-milligram tablets. She found herself rhyming a lot lately. She wasn't quite sure why, but for whatever reason, she found it hysterically funny. Unfortunately, Petey didn't seem to share her amusement. The first time she had rhymed after one of their lovemaking sessions, she felt his body go stiff—and not in a good way. If it bothered him, she would stop. Nothing mattered as long as he was happy.

She tilted her head back and swallowed the two pills, quickly washing them down with a glass of water. They always left a bitter and chalky aftertaste that stayed with her. But that wasn't as bad as the smell. At first it had scared her, but Petey said that it was just a minor neurological side effect, nothing to worry about. So she put it out of her mind.

After all, Petey would never lie to her.

Things didn't seem any better in the morning light. As Nava slapped her buzzing alarm clock, she realized she couldn't go on like this. She had been selling U.S. secrets to various governments without incident for over six years, but last night had been her wake-up call. Eventually she was going to get either caught or killed—it was just a matter of time.

If she had been willing to sell out her fellow CIA agents or deal in weapons technology, she would have been living on a tropical island by now, but those were two areas she wouldn't touch. Instead Nava sold only information she thought could be used to either save lives or level the playing field. Whether it was locations of Palestinian terrorists to the Israeli Mossad or satellite photos of the Czech Republic to Austria's Counterintelligence Service, it didn't matter. She had no loyalty, no country.

Last night's payday had been her biggest yet, the result of over eight months of work. She now had a total of $1.5 million in her Cayman Islands account. It wasn't enough to live like a queen, but it was enough to escape. She could leave right now. Just grab the documentation from one of her six identities and hop on the next plane to anywhere. Within forty-eight hours, she could make herself disappear.

The thought was tempting, but she knew that it was impractical. Although the CIA wouldn't be happy about having one of their assassins disappear, she doubted they would come after her. Unfortunately, she couldn't say the same about the RDEI's *Spetsnaz*. The North Koreans would never let her go. It might take them years, but eventually they would hunt her down and kill her.

No, running was impossible; she needed to resteal the information about the errant Islamic terrorist cell from the CIA databanks and turn it over to the RDEI. After that she could turn into a ghost. The second she was through with the North Koreans, she would leave New York and start over. She had just made her decision when her BlackBerry wireless communicator began to vibrate.

The messages were always the same—the time and location of that night's dead drop, where she would retrieve the data disk containing her new assignment. Although physically transferring the information about her upcoming missions was old-fashioned, it was still the only way the Agency could be certain that no one else listened in. Only the mechanism had changed.

While twenty years ago, agents received mission briefings produced by dot-matrix printers, today they were given photosensitive DVDs that would become unreadable within twenty minutes of being exposed to the light. The DVD could be read only by specially configured laptops, like the one Nava had in the next room, which was equipped with a tiny camera. Its sole purpose was to scan the retina of whoever was looking at the screen to verify that only the intended recipient could unlock the information.

Nava went to the bathroom and splashed some water on her face before checking the message on her BlackBerry. When she saw it, her heart froze. Instead of a coded time and address, there were just two words on the screen:

Report in.

The only person who could call her in was her director. Did he know? Impossible—she was sure no one had followed her to the apartment the night before. Still, why else would he want to meet with her face-to-face? No, she was being ridiculous. If the director knew she was selling government secrets, he wouldn't ask her to come to the office; there would be an armed escort on her doorstep.

Still, maybe that's what they wanted her to think. If they tried to take her by force, there was a chance she might get away, but once she was in the CIA's New York field office, escape would be impossible. If she was going to flee, she had to do it now—unless it was already too late. If they were already watching her apartment, they would never let her leave the city.

Her mind raced, knowing that she didn't have much time to make a decision. When she'd checked the message, her handheld had automatically sent the Agency her GPS location. If she wasn't in the office within the next half hour, they would know something was wrong. Closing her eyes, Nava took a deep breath, painfully aware that the clock was ticking.

Stay or go. Her two options couldn't have been simpler. The repercussions, however, were anything but. After nearly a minute, Nava opened her eyes, her decision made. Armed with her three weapons of choice—a SIG Sauer 9-millimeter in her shoulder holster, a Glock 9-millimeter semiautomatic strapped to her calf, and a dagger in her boot—along with four fake passports and five clips of ammo, she headed for the door.

Before she left, she looked over her shoulder at her apartment one last time. She doubted she would ever see it again. Once on the street, she hailed a cab. She would have to hurry.

It was so cold Jasper could see his breath, but he didn't mind. The cold felt fantastic, the dull ache in his fingers reminding him what it was like to be alive again. He was back for the attack. He had stopped taking his antipsychotics a few weeks before and the drugs were nearly out of his system. He felt as if someone had stuck a hose in his ear and washed out all the gauze clouding his brain. If the streets weren't crowded with throngs of people, he would have run down the sidewalk just for the sheer thrill of racing past the buildings.

Christ, he felt great. "Great-*late-date-fate!*" he yelled out to no one in particular. Although Jasper received more than a couple bizarre stares, he didn't care. He loved the way rhyming made him feel. The sound echoing in his ears, bouncing around like a perfectly round sphere.

He couldn't wait to get back to Philly. He—

You can't go back yet.

Jasper stopped so suddenly that someone walked into him. Ignoring the physical world, Jasper tilted his head as if he were trying to hear a distant sound. It had been the Voice. The Voice that had been his constant companion for almost an entire year, until the drugs drove it away.

It wasn't until he heard the Voice echo in his brain that he realized how much he had missed it. He loved the Voice so much he wanted to cry. There was a soft buzzing in his ears, letting him know that the Voice had something to say. Jasper squeezed his eyes closed. He could always hear the Voice better with his eyes closed.

You havvvve to stay.

—Why?

Becauzzzzzz you havvvvve to protect your brother.

—What's going to happen to him?

Soon they'll be coming. You havvvve to be here, to help him.
—Who's "they"?
The govvvvernment.
—Why are they after him?
Becauzzzzz he's special. Now, lizzzzen closely . . .

And listen Jasper did, standing still in the middle of the busy midtown sidewalk, people streaming around him as if he were a rock jutting out of a roaring river. When the Voice finished buzzing in his brain, Jasper opened his eyes and smiled. He turned around and began walking as fast as he could, rejuvenated with a new sense of purpose.

He was going to help David. His brother didn't know they were after him. But Jasper did. As long as he did what the Voice instructed, everything would be just fine. Oblivious to the angry stares of the pedestrians whom he jostled out of his way, Jasper began to jog. He would have to hurry.

He still had to buy a gun.

Nava steeled herself as she passed through the gunmetal gray security doors of the Central Intelligence Agency's New York City field office. If they were going to arrest her, it would be here, in the anteroom. As the doors locked shut behind her, she eyed the two armed guards, looking for some clue as to their agenda. But their faces were blank.

Slowly she marched toward the last checkpoint. The frame of the metal detector flashed red as she walked past, but the guards didn't search her. They already knew she was allowed to carry firearms into the building. She placed her hand on the scanner beside the door and waited while the line of white light scrolled beneath her fingers.

There was a click as the electronic lock disengaged and the bulletproof door slid open. Nava walked through, feeling relieved. The first thing she saw was a reception area. Except for the CIA seal emblazoned on the wall, it looked like any corporate setting, complete with a pair of secretaries—one perky, the other bookish. When Nava told them her name, the bookish one escorted her through the maze of cubicles to the director's office.

Director Bryce stood to shake Nava's hand as she entered the small, windowless room. He was a tall, thin man with thick silver hair, sharp brown eyes, and a firm grip. He looked more like a Fortune 500 CEO than an intelligence officer. He wasted no time in getting to the point.

"I'm transferring you."

"What?" Although Nava had been ready to be arrested, she was completely unprepared for this.

"The Science and Technology Research lab at the NSA is short on manpower and has put in a request for a field agent."

Nava didn't understand. The NSA had more than five times the number of agents as the CIA. Besides, such an interdepartmental transfer was completely unheard of. This must be a trap. She had to stall and get more information.

"But, sir, I can't—"

"You can and you will. The transfer is effective immediately. Here is your new identification card," he said, pushing a freshly laminated badge across his desk. "You can turn in your agency ID to security when you leave."

"Sir, why would the NSA need a CIA agent?"

"Evidently they don't care to tell us—else they would have requested our assistance rather than a full-fledged transfer," the director spat. The venom in his voice told her everything she needed to know. The transfer had not been his choice. It wasn't a trap after all, just something he'd been forced into.

"But why me?" she asked, still confused.

"You are the only agent currently not on assignment who has the requisite skill set." When she heard his last three words, everything clicked into place. The only reason the NSA would request the use of a CIA operative such as Nava was if they needed someone interrogated, kidnapped, or killed. The director pulled a piece of paper off his laser printer and handed it to her.

"This is the address of the STR office. You're due to check in by noon, so you better get a move on." He returned his attention to his computer screen, obviously done with her. "Now, if you'll excuse me."

An armed guard was waiting for Nava outside the director's office. He looked down at her sternly.

"I've been asked to escort you out, ma'am."

Nava's mind raced. She had to log in to the network and copy the intel onto another disk. She looked up at the guard, batting her eyelashes.

"Can I just get onto one of the terminals to check my e-mail? It will only take a second."

"I'm afraid not, ma'am. Your security codes are no longer active. I have to ask you to come with me."

Nava shrugged her shoulders as if it were no big deal and let the guard lead her out of the building. She wondered what the RDEI would do when she told them she no longer had access to the information. The second Nava was outside, she lit a cigarette with trembling fingers. Across the street she spied a tall Korean man wearing mirrored sunglasses talking on his cell phone. Shit. They were already following her.

She pretended not to notice and began walking toward the STR lab fifteen blocks away. The man kept pace, barely trying to hide his purpose. She knew that the *Spetsnaz* were more skillful than this. She'd been able to spot him easily only because he wanted her to see him. He was there to remind her that they were watching. As if she could forget.

Putting the man out of her mind, she forced herself to think. Her original plan of burning another data disk at the field office was now impossible. She would have to think of something else to give the RDEI. If she failed to deliver in the next sixteen hours, they would kill her.

Nava's only hope was that she would discover some data at the STR that would be considered an even trade. It was a long shot, but she had to try. If she couldn't find anything, she would have to run.

Nava was still thinking about escape plans as she entered the downtown office building that housed the NSA's Science and Technology Research lab. After she was cleared through security, she rode the elevator to the twenty-first floor. A smiling receptionist was there to greet her.

"Welcome, Agent Vaner," the woman said. "Please follow me. Dr. Forsythe has been expecting you."

When Dr. Tversky kissed Julia gently on the forehead, he felt her body tremble.

"Are you all right, dear?"

"I'm perfect," Julia murmured, her eyes closed. "I'm always perfect when I'm with you, Petey."

Christ. He knew she had a bad case of puppy love, but this was getting ridiculous. He wondered how much longer he would have to keep up this charade. In the back of his mind, he rationalized that if the experiment was a complete failure, at least he could extricate himself from the relationship.

Feigning what he hoped would be perceived as tenderness, Tversky gave her arm a quick squeeze and then stepped back to survey his lover, his subject. She was lying on the table, naked except for a thin cotton sheet that was carefully positioned over her nether regions. Her tiny breasts were exposed, their dark brown nipples erect in the cold, crisp air of the lab.

Six shiny electronic leads were taped directly below her breasts, their wires trailing down her stomach before they disappeared beneath the table, snaking into the electrocardiograph machine. Eight more electrodes were affixed to her scalp, two for each lobe—occipital, central, frontal, and temporal. These wires fed into the electroencephalograph, which measured the electrical impulses given off by her brain. He turned his attention away from Julia and toward the bank of monitors next to her, focusing on the readout that displayed her brain waves.

A student of history as much as of science, Tversky marveled at the chain of events that had brought him here. It could all be traced back to 1875, when a Liverpool physician named Richard Caton first discovered neural electric signals while he was probing the exposed brains of animals. Fifty years after that, Hans Berger, an Austrian psychiatrist, invented the electroencephalograph, which measured both the strength and frequency of human brain waves. Like Tversky, Berger was also a believer in human trials. In 1929 he published the first seventy-three EEG readings all from the same subject—his son, Klaus.

But it was the research that Berger had done with epileptic patients in the 1930s that truly interested Tversky. Berger had discovered that the electrical impulses displayed by epileptics' brain waves during seizures were stronger than those of normal patients. Even more interesting was that their brain waves nearly flatlined immediately after a seizure, as if they had temporarily short-circuited. It was this polarity that Tversky credited as the spark that led him to study the brain waves of those suffering from the illness once referred to as the scourge of Christ.

Tversky had always known that brain waves were the key to what he was looking for. Beta, alpha, theta, delta—therein lay the answer. As he monitored Julia's readout, he found himself momentarily hypnotized by the bouncing electronic ball with its long silvery tail that represented Julia's alpha waves.

The frequency of the wave, measured in Hertz, illustrated the number of times a wave repeated itself each second; the amplitude or height of the wave represented the intensity of the brain's electric impulses. Although there was always activity within each of the four brain-wave categories, at any given time one category was dominant.

Currently Julia's alpha waves were dominant, which was no surprise. Alpha waves were the natural rhythm for relaxed adults. These waves were strongest when a person was having a mild daydream and were often described as a bridge to the subconscious, linked to both memory and insight. The frequency of Julia's alpha waves was 10 Hz, precisely in the middle of the normal range.

Tversky decided to check out her beta waves before bringing her down. Beta waves were dominant only when people had their eyes open or were actively listening, thinking, or otherwise processing information, so he gave Julia a task to literally get her brain working.

"Sweetheart, I want you to begin counting prime numbers until I tell you to stop, starting now."

Julia nodded slightly and then began counting aloud. "Two, three, five, seven, eleven, thirteen . . ."

At first there wasn't a lot of change in her brain-wave activity, probably because she had the first ten prime numbers memorized. However, as Julia counted higher and higher, she had to put her conscious mind to work, and her beta waves spiked, cycling rapidly at around 19 Hz, as expected.

"That's fine, Julia. You can stop now."

Julia ceased counting; the amplitude and frequency of her beta waves immediately began to drop. Once again her alpha waves became dominant. Tversky tapped out two cc's of a yellowish solution into his hypodermic. "I'm going to give you a gentle sedative now. It will sting for a second."

Tversky slid the needle into her arm, and Julia tightened for a moment. After a few seconds, he felt her relax, as if all the muscles in her body had simultaneously exhaled. She started to breathe deeply, and her head lolled over on its side. Tversky snapped his fingers inches from her face. Julia slowly blinked her eyes a few times but then let them close.

"Julia, can you hear me?"

"Hear you," Julia murmured.

She wasn't totally out, but she was close, exactly where he wanted her—lost in la-la land. He glanced over to the monitor and nodded to himself. Now her theta waves were dominant, showing that Julia was somewhere between wakefulness and sleep. It was the theta waves that were most connected with creativity, dreams, and fantasies.

Although it was rare for theta waves to be dominant in conscious adults, it was perfectly normal in children through the age of thirteen. Scientists didn't know if the dominance of children's theta waves was the cause or the result of their vivid imaginations, but they did know that, at least from a biochemical standpoint, the average child was much more creative than most adults.

Tversky's mind continued to wander as he watched Julia's theta waves increase in their intensity. Her eyelids seemed to pulse above the darting pupils beneath. He measured out one more cc and gave Julia another dose. He waited a few minutes for the drug to take full effect.

After a time her theta waves slowed in frequency and amplitude, making room for her delta waves. These waves cycled at a much lower rate than all the others—only 2 Hz—but their intensity was far greater. Julia was now in a deep, dreamless sleep, her unconscious mind finally in control. The delta waves were what he was most interested in, for they tapped in to the ability that Tversky endeavored to understand—pure intuition.

It was then, when Julia's delta waves were at their strongest, that Tversky gave her one more final injection, although this one he inserted into the base of her skull. Unlike the others, it was not a sedative; it was a new serum that Tversky had developed. It had taken him no less than four years of research before he was able to synthesize the base compound that had the desired effect on rhesus monkeys, then another two years of human trials.

The first few poor sods he found at epilepsy clinics around the country, all of them searching for a miracle cure. They were so desperate they would have done anything. Had they fully understood what Tversky was trying to achieve, he suspected they would have been less cooperative. It would have been a lie to say that he felt guilty about their fate. True, he regretted the final outcome, but more for science than for the test subjects.

Once he'd worked the kinks out of the system and felt confident about success, he had proceeded to experiment on Julia. After all, if he was able to achieve his goal, he wanted someone he could control, and what better person than a lovesick grad student? He looked down at his lover and gently caressed her head, careful not to dislodge any of the electrodes as he did so. What a sweet little guinea pig.

Suddenly the EKG began beeping excitedly. Her heart rate had nearly doubled, to 120 beats per minute. Tversky could feel his own heart hammering in his chest, as if trying to match her rhythm. Julia's beta, alpha, and theta waves were cycling at the same intensity as her delta waves. Tversky could barely breathe. If he was right, she should now be able to process information while simultaneously being in touch with her unconscious.

He was so nervous his hands were shaking. He forced himself to take a deep breath; he held it for a moment and then exhaled slowly. A quick glance at the video camera confirmed that everything was being recorded. He had a perverse desire to check his hair in the mirror—after all, if he was right, this was a historic moment, but he chased the thought out of his mind. Worry about the present, not the future. Worry about the now. He nodded to himself, repeating the sentence over and over in his brain.

Worry about the now. Worry about the now.

When he felt confident that his voice wouldn't crack or tremble, he leaned forward, inches from Julia's face, and asked the question that had plagued him for years.

"Julia"—his voice was scratchy—"what do you see?"

Without opening her eyes, Julia turned her head to face him.

"I see . . . infinity."

Caine stared down at the oblong capsule, wondering if the drug would push him over the edge of sanity.

"I can't leave until you take your medication, Mr. Caine," the nurse said.

"I know," Caine said softly.

"Is there a problem?"

"Not yet." The nurse didn't get his joke. Without further thought, Caine put the pill cup to his lips and threw his head back, dropping the capsule down his throat. Then he picked up the Styrofoam cup of water and toasted it toward the nurse. "And here's to hoping things stay that way."

The nurse returned Caine's nervous smile with a confused look. After she checked beneath his tongue to make sure he had swallowed the capsule, she walked out of the room, leaving Caine alone with his fears. It would take twenty minutes for his stomach to digest the disposable plastic shell around the grains of Dr. Kumar's new experimental drug. After that, all bets were off.

Caine wondered what he should do with (potentially) his last moments of sanity. He considered writing a will, but he owned nothing of value. Had he not seen Jasper today, he would have jotted a note to his twin, but he felt that was no longer necessary. In the end he settled on turning on the television and watching the last half of *Jeopardy!*

A pudgy man named Zeke was destroying the other two competitors. He went on a tear during Double Jeopardy, constantly adjusting his thick, black-framed glasses in between turns. But then Zeke got greedy on the Daily Double and lost more than half his winnings, putting him in second place by a few hundred dollars. It would all come down to Final Jeopardy. After a spate of commercials pushing dog food, minivans, and brokerage firms, Alex Trebek returned to give the final answer.

"When Napoleon asked this eighteenth-century astronomer why his book on the solar system failed to mention God, this scientist answered, 'Sire, I have no need of that hypothesis.' " Alex said, carefully enunciating each word before the *Jeopardy!* theme began.

"Who is Simon-Pierre Laplace?" Caine asked the empty room.

He was sure he was right; however, before he was able to confirm his answer, Caine drifted asleep, dreaming of a schizophrenic future.

Forsythe used all kinds of euphemisms to describe what they did at the Science and Technology Research laboratory, but none of them fooled Nava for a second. She could summarize the STR's mission statement in one word—"steal"—and that was a word Nava was very familiar with. She only hoped that whatever it was Forsythe wanted her to steal would be of interest to the RDEI.

Once she was assigned a workstation, Nava began scrolling through the file names of the documents the STR hackers had lifted off Tversky's computer. Next to each document was the size of the file, the date it was created, and the last three dates it was modified, which helped her estimate usage rates. Nava then sorted the files and began skimming the ones that had the highest activity levels.

As she expected, the bulk of the material was well beyond her. She would need to go back to school for nearly a decade and study up on biology, physics, and statistics to make heads or tails of Tversky's journal. Still, it had been worth a try. She always attempted to go directly to the source before depending on others' interpretations; however, in this case, she had no choice.

She pulled up a few of the abstracts written by Forsythe's team of in-house research scientists. As Nava read, her eyes widened. For the first time in the last twelve hours, luck shone down on her. What Tversky claimed to have discovered was nothing short of science fiction. Although his data was not yet conclusive, it appeared that he was extremely close. Nava couldn't believe her good fortune. The black-market value of his raw data was priceless.

Even if the RDEI wasn't interested, Nava thought she could stall them long enough to find another buyer. Personally, she didn't believe in Tversky's project. Nava didn't understand the biochemistry or quantum physics underlying his theories, although she understood enough about the world to know that what he suggested was simply impossible. It had to be. But that didn't mean a foreign government wouldn't believe in it; Nava was certain she could find a buyer somewhere for Tversky's wild ideas.

Once she sold the information, she could get out forever. Nava reached into her knapsack and put on a pair of reading glasses. She made sure to keep her head perfectly still as she paged through the abstracts and original files, so that the fiber-optic camera hidden in the arm of her glasses would get a clear image of the screen. Once she got to the last page, she began scrolling back up through all the data a second time to make sure she hadn't missed anything.

When Nava was finished, she stared at the title of the theory, wondering why in the world Tversky had decided to give his project such a bizarre name. No matter. She put the thought out of her head and looked at her watch. It was one o'clock. She still had fourteen hours to bargain for her life.

On her brisk walk home, she smoked two cigarettes. By the time she arrived at her apartment, she had formulated a plan. She spent the next few hours corresponding with the RDEI, the Mossad, and the MI6 via encrypted e-mail. While she waited for each response, she paced back and forth, cigarette in hand. By five o'clock she had set the meet, and an hour after that she took a cab to the Bronx, then boarded the last car on the D train, headed back toward Manhattan.

In a barely audible voice, the conductor announced they were making all local stops to Coney Island. As the train traveled southwest, it became more and more crowded, the congestion reaching its peak at Forty-second Street. From then on, the number of passengers slowly declined until there were only a few riders left. The only two that remained of the twelve who had gotten on with her in the Bronx were two Koreans—a beefy man reading a newspaper and the man in the mirrored glasses.

As Nava now felt confident the CIA had not followed her onto the train, she closed her paperback book and put it in her knapsack. That had been the signal. Almost immediately the beefy man folded his newspaper beneath his arm and sat down next to her.

"Where's Tae-Woo?" Nava asked.

"Yi Tae-Woo is getting his nose fixed," he said solemnly. "My name is Chang-Sun." Nava knew that "Chang-Sun" was an alias, but she didn't care. She was certain Tae-Woo's name had also been a fabrication. All that mattered was whether Chang-Sun had the power to deal.

"Do you have an answer?" It was unnecessary to trade pleasantries with the man.

"Our scientists at the ministry have analyzed the data and found it quite interesting," Chang-Sun said noncommittally.

"And?"

The man bristled at Nava's abruptness but answered nonetheless.

"Our business will be complete upon delivery of the unedited data files along with the Alpha Subject."

"The Alpha Subject was not part of the offer."

"There is no agreement without him," Chang-Sun said simply, opening his hands on his lap as if to show that there was nothing he could do.

Nava had expected as much. Her two other conversations, the first with the Brits, the second with the Israelis, had gone similarly. Neither government was interested in the raw data without the subject who had generated it. However, each had offered her north of $2 million, far more than the value of the information Nava had previously delivered to the RDEI. She knew she had room to negotiate, as Tversky's files were worth more to the RDEI than having her dead.

"I will need an extra million dollars," Nava said.

"That is out of the question."

"Then we have nothing to discuss. Your bid is too low." Nava stood as if she meant to get off the train; the *Spetsnaz* agent put his hand on her arm. She turned to look him in the face for the first time, enjoying her position above him.

"I was unaware this was an auction."

"Despite my current situation, you didn't expect I would only come to you with such a unique commodity?"

"Who are the other bidders?"

"That's irrelevant."

Chang-Sun nodded to himself. "Offering to sell to Mother Russia, perhaps?" he asked. Although Nava was startled, she held her emotions in check. Still, he knew he had her attention. "I'm sure your old comrades at the SVR would be very interested to know how their wayward spy has embraced capitalism so fully."

Nava concentrated on her breathing. She wondered how

the RDEI had found out her identity when her own country had not. Nava stared down at Chang-Sun as if he were an insect.

"I am unsure of what you are talking about. However, it does not change the price."

"Doesn't it?" Chang-Sun gave her a wide smile, revealing his perfectly capped teeth, clearly a product of Western dentistry. He knew he had her. Anything the RDEI would do—including killing her—would pale in comparison to what would happen if the SVR discovered her existence.

"Five hundred thousand. If you're still not interested, I'm sure the ROK will be."

The *Spetsnaz* agent's neck turned red at the mention of the Republic of Korea. It was a bluff on Nava's part, as she did not have a reliable contact within the South Korean government. Regardless, her words had the desired effect. Chang-Sun gave a quick nod.

"I will have to clear the higher price with my superiors, but we have a deal in principle."

"I will contact you once I have the subject in my care."

"Which will be when?"

"Within the week."

"Two days."

"That's not enough ti—"

Chang-Sun dug his fingers into her arm and yanked her close, his voice low and menacing. "We are no longer operating on your timeline. In two days you will deliver the Alpha Subject to us, along with the rest of the scientist's primary research materials. If you are late, two things will happen. First, I will tell my superiors that you fabricated the scientific documents. Second, I will personally call Pavel Kuznetsov at the SVR and tell him all about your activities during the last ten years. You have already missed two deadlines. Do not miss a third."

Chang-Sun let go just as the train jerked to a stop and the subway doors hissed open. Without waiting for a response, he exited the car, leaving her alone with the man in the mirrored sunglasses. As the subway pulled out of the station, Nava wondered how she was going to snatch Dr. Tversky's Alpha Subject without the NSA figuring out what had happened. As she ran through different scenarios in her head, she didn't see a way she could pull it off without killing someone.

It would be regrettable, but if that's what it took to get out, then she would do it. She had no choice.

Tommy was licking the inside of the oily muzzle when he heard the ring. The phone scared him so badly he almost blew his brains out.

Although he had planned on killing himself, planning wasn't the same thing as deciding. Once he pulled that trigger, he knew there was no do-over, so he wanted to be absolutely, 100 percent sure. The shrill ring had almost robbed him of that decision. Tommy extracted the .45 from his mouth and put it down on the table.

Next time I'll take the phone off the hook.

"Hello?"

"Tommy! Did you see?!"

It was Gina, his ex-girlfriend. She was the last person Tommy had expected to hear from tonight. "See what?"

"The news! The numbers!"

"I don't know what you're talking about, but I'm kinda in the middle of something. Can I maybe call you later—"

"You don't know, do you?" Gina gasped, her voice low and excited.

"No, I told you—"

"Tommy, you won! Your numbers came up. Did you hear me? *You . . . fucking . . . won.*" She said the last three words slowly, sounding out each syllable as if she were talking to someone not quite right in the head. Despite her careful enunciation, it took Tommy a few seconds before he understood what she was saying.

"You mean . . . ?" Tommy let his voice trail off, afraid of finishing the sentence.

"Yes, Tommy."

"Are you sure?"

"Fuck yeah, I'm sure! I was in the kitchen when they announced the numbers. As soon as I heard 'em, I knew. After all those years of listenin' to you go on and on about 'em, how could I not, ya know? But then I ran in and kept switchin' to the other stations until they repeated 'em, and I wrote 'em all down and everything, just to make *super*sure. Jesus fuckin' Christ, Tommy . . . you're a *millionaire!*"

Tommy just stared out the window, not knowing what to say, the truth slowly dawning on him. He was a millionaire. Tommy DaSouza, Millionaire.

"Tommy? You there, Tommy?"

"Um, yeah."

"Hey, Tommy, you want me to come over? We can celebrate, just like old times—'cept this time we'll actually have sumpin' to celebrate, ya know?"

Gina's words caught him off guard. He had missed her so much he literally wanted to die. But after hearing the desperate tone in her voice, he realized that being with Gina right now might make him feel more lonely, rather than less.

"I think . . . um . . . I think I'm gonna take a rain check, okay?"

"Let me just get my shoes on and—" Gina cut herself off when she processed Tommy's words. "Oh. Sure, you want to be alone. I get that."

"Thanks," Tommy said, suddenly feeling ten feet tall. He had never said no to Gina before. Hell, he had never even dreamed it.

"Tommy . . . um, I still love you. You know that, right?"

Funny, that's not what you said three weeks ago when you screamed at me to stop calling, Tommy wanted to say. But instead, all that came out of his mouth was, "I gotta go." He hung up the phone before she had a chance to reply, afraid that if he stayed on too long, they would end up getting back together. Weird, considering a couple of minutes ago he would have given anything to be with her again. But now . . .

He sat back down on the couch and reached past the gun for the television remote. It only took him a couple minutes of channel surfing before he caught one of the newscasters repeating the winning numbers—6-12-19-21-36-40—and the red Powerball of 18. He didn't have to write them down like Gina did, nor did he have to pull out his ticket to see whether it was a match. They were *his* numbers. He'd been playing them every week for the last seven years.

He couldn't exactly pinpoint why 6-12-19-21-36-40+18 were his numbers. It wasn't like any of the digits were his birthday or anything. The numbers had just always been there, flashing in his brain, like giant neon characters on the backs of his eyelids. All of them were bright white, except for the last digit, which glowed red like an ember from a dying campfire. He never knew what they meant until Powerball came to Connecticut.

The first time he saw the numbers on the ten o'clock news—six white and one red, just like the ones in his dream—he knew it couldn't be a coincidence. He was meant to win Powerball. At first he was scared that he'd missed his chance, that the numbers—*his* numbers—had already been picked. But when he got the package in the mail from the Multi-State Lottery Association listing all the winning numbers, he was relieved to discover that his numbers were still virgins.

The next day he rode the train out to Connecticut to play the numbers that had been in his head for as long as he could remember. Although it took him over two hours to get to the 7-Eleven and back, it was worth it. He reasoned that with a jackpot of $86 million, it was like making $43 million an hour. The night they announced the winning numbers, he'd been so positive that his destiny was about to be fulfilled that he bought all the guys at O'Sullivan's a round of drinks. It cost him $109, plus tip, which totally cleaned him out, but it didn't matter. He knew that by the end of the night he was going to be so rich he'd be able to buy the entire bar.

Only the numbers on the news that night weren't his numbers. Out of seven, he got just two right. Tommy had been so certain he was going to win that he thought the TV was wrong. But the next day the newspaper confirmed that the white-haired anchorman hadn't been mistaken. Tommy had lost.

Although his confidence was shaken, it wasn't destroyed. He just had to keep at it, that was all. The next week he got back on the train to play his numbers. But just like the first time, he got only two digits right. After a few months, he'd begun to lose hope. He would have given up had the numbers not burned like fire in his brain every time he slept. And so Tommy kept buying lottery tickets, never once missing a week for fear that it would be the week his numbers finally appeared.

After the first couple years, Tommy stopped expecting to win, but he never stopped buying tickets. And whenever he would get drunk, which was more and more often lately, he'd tell anyone who would listen that he was going to be a millionaire someday. Just wait and see. Unfortunately, "someday" never came.

The days kept marching forward, and things kept getting worse. Well, not worse, exactly, but not really better either, which was pretty much the same thing. It had been ten years since he'd graduated high school, and he was still in the same shitty Brooklyn apartment with the same shitty job. Both the apartment and the job seemed really cool at first, but Tommy learned that what was cool at eighteen is pathetic at twenty-eight.

Worse still, chicks knew it, too. Chicks like Gina. Sure, he was fun for a booty call now and again, but as Gina had painstakingly explained to him, Tommy had no "long-term potential." He had tried to change into the man she wanted him to be, but it was impossible. Twenty-eight-year-olds without a college education whose only work experience was as a cashier at Tower Records just didn't wake up one day with long-term potential.

Except for today. Today I have long-term potential, don't I? Tommy walked over to the coffee table and picked up the gun. Turning it over in his hands, he wondered why he still wanted to put the muzzle in his mouth and pull the trigger.

He no longer needed to kill himself. Now that he'd won the money, everything would be all right . . . wouldn't it? For some reason he wasn't so sure. Deep down he knew that the money didn't change anything; he was the same loser he'd always been. But he also knew something else—that even though he was the same guy who had been ready to blow his brains out a few minutes ago, he didn't have to *stay* that guy. He could transform himself into . . . into what?

Into someone with a purpose, that's what. He sighed longingly, nodding to himself. *At least I can try.* Yeah. Making an effort not to think, Tommy hid the gun in the back of his closet, beneath the pile of black concert T-shirts he'd acquired over the years. He used to wear them all the time, but lately he found himself using them only on laundry day when he was out of clean clothes.

After the closet door was shut, Tommy finished his beer and lay down on the couch. And although he thought a lot about the numbers before he finally fell asleep, for the first time in ten years, they didn't glow in his dreams.

It was night when Caine awoke. Light from the television flickered on the dark walls, casting amorphous shadows that leaped across the room. On the screen a bubbly young woman was ticking off the winning Powerball numbers. He clicked the remote, and the room went black. Caine stared at nothing, waiting for his eyes to adjust.

He had a nagging feeling that he was forgetting something. Was it something he had dreamed? No, that wasn't it. He had slept hard. If there had been any dreams, they'd already been eclipsed by his conscious mind. Then he remembered. He had swallowed the capsule. He grabbed his cell phone off the nightstand to check the time. It was almost two—the drug had been in his system for eleven hours.

He turned his head to the left and then to the right, blinking his eyes as he did. He didn't feel any different. So far, so good. But then again, isn't that what Jasper had said? *It doesn't feel like anything.* Still, Caine thought he would recognize the difference if something had jarred loose in his mind. He would know. He would have to.

His cell phone suddenly started to tremble in his hand. It scared him so badly that Caine nearly dropped it. He looked at the display to see who was calling him.

ID Blocked

He considered not answering for a second and then decided against it. He fumbled the phone open with hands that were still tingling with pins and needles.

"Hello, Caine, it's Vitaly. How are you feeling?"

Caine felt his stomach knot. "Oh, hey. I'm feeling good, thanks. How are you?" Caine asked, not knowing what else to say to the man he owed eleven grand.

"Not so good, Caine. But I'm hoping you can help fix that." Nikolaev paused. Caine wasn't sure he was expected to speak, but after a few moments, he felt compelled to fill the silence.

"So . . . ah, I guess you're calling about the money." No response. Caine's tongue went dry, like a sponge left out in the hot sun. "I've got it, Nikolaev. As soon as I get out of the hospital, I can pay you back."

"Plus interest."

"Right, plus interest. Of course." Caine tried to swallow, but it was impossible. "How much is the interest, by the way?"

"Standard rate. Five percent a week, compounded weekly. So I just want to be clear—you have the money, right? I mean, I love seeing you in the club. I want to make sure I keep seeing you, you know?"

"Yeah, of course I've got the money," Caine lied. "No problem."

"Fantastic," Nikolaev said, his voice low and menacing. "Is it at the bank?"

"Um, yeah." Caine wanted to vomit.

"Good. Since you're laid up, I will send Sergey over. You can give him your bank card, and then I'll just take the money out for you. That way you don't have to worry about coming downtown," Nikolaev said. "You can focus on getting well."

"Oh, thanks," Caine said dumbly, trying to stall. The last thing he wanted was a visit from Sergey Kozlov, Nikolaev's 250-pound bodyguard. "The thing is, Vitaly, that I may have to move some funds around, you know? I've got about two grand in the bank, but the rest is securities. I'll need to cash in a couple of CDs, stuff like that."

"I thought you said you had all the money at the bank." Nikolaev was silent a moment. "Now is not a good time to start lying to me, Caine."

"I do . . . I mean, I'm not. I've got it—it's just not all liquid. But it can be." Silence. "It *will* be, Vitaly. Just as soon as I get out."

"Okay. Here's what I will do. Sergey is waiting in the lobby. I'll send him up to get your bank card. He'll withdraw one thousand tonight and another five hundred each day until you get out of the hospital and cash in those CDs. Good?"

"Sure, Vitaly. That's cool," Caine said, although he thought it would be much cooler if there were actually more than four hundred dollars in his account.

"Good. Sergey should be up in a few minutes."

"Okay, thanks, Vitaly."

"No problem," Nikolaev said magnanimously. "Oh, and Caine, one more thing."

"Yeah?"

"Get well soon." There was a soft click, and the phone went dead.

As Caine closed his phone, he decided it was time to check out of the hospital. Pulling back the starchy sheet, he gingerly lowered himself off the bed, worried that his legs might not hold his weight. The linoleum floor felt cold and smooth against the bottoms of his feet. It was nice to be standing again. Once he was sure he wasn't going to fall over, he hurriedly dressed himself in his street clothes.

He looked at the clock. It had been less than three minutes since he'd hung up. Assuming Nikolaev called Kozlov the second he was off the phone, Caine didn't have much time to make his escape. He didn't doubt that the big Russian would make it past hospital security; the only question was how long it would take him. Caine hoped he wouldn't find out, as he wanted to be gone long before Kozlov paid him a visit.

Caine poked his head outside his room into the dimly lit corridor. Just as he did, he saw Kozlov lumbering down the hall. The huge bodyguard didn't walk so much as he waddled, shifting his massive bulk from one large foot to another. Caine felt his heart drop. It was too late. He would have to give Kozlov his bank card. And when Nikolaev discovered that Caine had lied about his balance, it was all over.

Suddenly intangibles like seizures and schizophrenia seemed a whole lot less scary than the physical world did. Caine looked around the room, desperate to find someplace to hide, but all he saw was the pale form of his roommate, who was breathing so shallowly Caine wondered for a second if the man was still alive. The only thing that proved his status among the living was the soft beep of his EKG monitor.

As Caine stared at the bouncing electric ball, he got an idea.

"Code blue—1012. Code blue—1012."

Nurse Pratt spoke into the microphone with a practiced, calm firmness. Best not to scare the patients by alerting them that someone was dying in Room 1012. She grabbed the crash cart and barreled down the hall. She didn't notice the massive bearded man until she rammed into him.

He spun around with a fierce look on his face, but she didn't have time to chew him out. She steered the cart around his hulking form and kept moving. She was first on the scene. Christ, why did the old ones always have to croak on her shift? This was the third this week. When she entered the room, she hit the lights and ran over to Mr. Morrison, who was so gray he already looked like a corpse.

It was then she saw it—the lead was lying on the floor. Suddenly one of the new baby-faced interns ran into the room, nearly knocking her over.

"How long has he been—"

"False alarm. The lead came unattached."

"What—oh," the intern said as he followed her finger toward the wire, which lay limply on the floor.

She bent down and picked the lead off the floor. Strange—the tape was still sticky. She wondered briefly how it came unattached but discarded the thought almost immediately. After being a nurse for sixteen years, she had learned not to question the weird things that took place in this building.

After all, it was a hospital. Strange stuff happened all the time.

From the dark doorway of Room 1013, Caine tried to make himself invisible as he watched the nurse and intern leave his old room. When Kozlov slipped inside 1012 a few seconds later, Caine darted down the hall and walked briskly toward the red neon exit sign. As he stared at the glowing letters, they suddenly seemed to grow larger, stretching down to the floor. Caine's heart stopped in his throat.

Not now, not fucking now.

Caine squeezed his eyes shut, willing his visual hallucination to pass. As he did so, he felt a wave of dizziness wash over him. He reached out and grabbed a cart by the wall to steady himself. When the world stopped spinning, he opened his eyes and saw that the cart was piled high with discarded scrubs and white doctors' coats. Acting on instinct, he pulled a coat from the stack and slipped it on.

Just then he heard the heavy clop of boots from behind him. It was Kozlov. Caine braced his shoulders for impact as the giant Russian barreled down on him. When he felt Kozlov's meaty hand grab his shoulder, Caine knew there would be no escape. But instead of smashing him up against the wall, Kozlov shoved him roughly aside and then was gone, disappearing around the corner.

Caine stood stunned for a moment, unsure of what had just happened until he realized that his coat must have fooled the giant Russian into thinking Caine was a doctor. Pushing himself onward, Caine quickly slipped through the set of double doors at the end of the corridor. When he found the elevator bank, he reached out to press one of the silver buttons when he began to feel a trembling near his thigh just as his phone began singing.

"Shit!" Caine dug into his pocket to silence the device. But it was too late—the double doors swung open to reveal Kozlov holding a cell phone in his hand. He was smiling.

Caine looked desperately at the elevator doors, willing them to slide open and provide an exit, but they remained closed. Kozlov slowly marched down the hall, enjoying the calm before the storm. Just then the elevator doors opened, revealing an elderly Hispanic man holding a mop in a large bucket on wheels.

"Sorry about this," Caine said as he grabbed the mop out of the confused janitor's hands and sent the bucket rocketing down the hall. His timing couldn't have been better. Kozlov managed to sidestep the rolling projectile, but as he did so, the mop handle collided with his shoulder, turning over the bucket and spilling soapy water across the smooth floor. Kozlov slipped and crashed down.

Caine jumped into the oversize elevator car and madly stabbed at a random button, hoping the elevator would close before Kozlov had a chance to right himself. Just as the doors began to slide shut, Caine caught a glimpse of the giant man's frame. His arm reached forward to halt the elevator, but he was too late. The metal doors snapped shut, and the car began its ascent.

As Caine watched the floor numbers flash, one after another, the ridiculousness of the situation settled on his shoulders. What was he doing? Running around a hospital trying to evade a Russian gangster? How had everything gotten so crazy?

And then it hit him—the pill. He had taken the pill, awoke and then . . . what?

Maybe this was it—maybe he was having a schizophrenic episode, just *imagining* that the Russian mob was after him. But that was impossible. This was real. He had lost the money to Vitaly Nikolaev *before* he had ever taken the capsule. Sure, the last few minutes had been a little crazy, but that didn't mean *he* was crazy, did it?

Then again, maybe this was all a nightmare, triggered by the medication. He pinched his forearm to make sure he wasn't dreaming. It hurt, but did that really prove anything? Maybe he'd just *dreamed* that it hurt. It was an endless loop of logic, or illogic, depending on the point of view. How could a delusional mind identify when it was having a delusion?

What if this was it?

What if he'd just slipped into madness, lost forever?

Jasper's words echoed in his mind, mockingly: *It doesn't feel like anything . . . That's why it's so fucking scary.*

Suddenly the elevator came to a stop with a mild bounce and a *ping* that reminded Caine of a cooking timer. The doors opened, and, without thinking, he stepped out onto the fifteenth floor. There were no hints as to what illnesses were housed here; it looked identical to his own. The doors slid shut behind him.

Caine considered summoning another car, but something told him not to. It was almost as if there were a voice inside his head saying, *Not yet . . . you're not done.* Further evidence that he was going insane? No. He refused to accept that. He told himself that it was just an instinct. He had instincts all the time, and for the most part, they were pretty good—except, of course, for the one that told him to bet eleven G's on a losing hand.

Ignoring his internal dialogue, Caine walked down the naked hall, his footsteps echoing across the hard linoleum floor until he reached the double doors. As he touched their smooth handles, he felt an incredible sense of déjà vu.

Everything was familiar—the slick, cool metal beneath his fingers; the flickering fluorescent light above his head; the antiseptic smell of alcohol and medicine. The power of the sensation overwhelmed him, washing over him like a giant wave that left him feeling . . . what? Prescient? Aware? Psychic?

Suddenly he was filled with a strange confidence, as if he were holding a royal straight flush and knew there was no way he could lose. And so he pushed through the double doors to see what lay on the other side. The cold air rushed by his face as he walked down the dimly lit corridor past the quiet rooms. He sucked it all in, wanting to savor every moment as it played out before him, just as he knew it would.

Caine found that there was something restful about the experience, walking past the sleeping bodies, wondering what dreams and nightmares plagued their unconscious minds.

Blueberry muffins piled to the ceiling . . . rabid dogs foaming at the mouth . . . a heated confrontation with an ex-lover.

Each thought drifted through his mind like vivid memories long since past. He felt oddly comforted and connected . . . but connected to what?

Their minds, the voice (instinct?) whispered to him. He told himself that it was crazy.

Of course it is. But that doesn't make it untrue.

He shook his head, feeling scared. This was it. He was losing it, he was hallucinating. But it was all too real to be a delusion. The feelings, they were true. Then he heard Jasper's words echo in his mind:

The delusions seem real. Natural, even obvious. Like it's the most ordinary thing in the world that the government is spying on your thoughts or that your best friend is trying to kill you.

His skin suddenly felt cold and clammy. He had to focus. He started paying closer attention to his surroundings. Each doorway he passed had a number and a white card, upon which was written the name of the occupant in large block letters. HORAN, NINA. KARAFOTIS, MICHAEL. NAFTOLY, DEBRA. KAUFMAN, SCOTT.

It wasn't until he had passed the fourth room that Caine realized he'd been reading the names as if he were looking for someone. In his head, as he paused outside each door, his brain had been saying, *No, no, no, no.*

He stopped when he read the name next to the fifth door. He could hear a soft whimpering coming from within.

Yes, she's the one.

Without hesitating, Caine stepped inside.

The sheets were slightly rumpled on the large hospital bed, though there didn't seem to be anyone beneath them. As his eyes adjusted to the dark room, he saw the small head of a doll. Then it turned toward him and blinked its giant, wet eyes.

Caine almost screamed, but he was able to bite down on his tongue before the shriek crossed his lips. It was then he realized that this creature was no doll at all. It was a little girl. In the oversize bed, the poor thing seemed so small and alone.

"Are you okay?" Caine asked hesitantly.

The girl didn't speak, but Caine thought he saw her head inch up and down slightly.

"Do you want me to get a nurse?"

She slowly shook her head.

"Do you want me to stay with you for a minute?"

A tiny nod.

"Okay." Caine softly pulled up a chair beside the little girl's bed and sat down. "My name is David, but my friends call me Caine."

"Hi, Caine." The girl's voice sounded so weak, but inside, there was a spark of something—hope, maybe? Or was it something else? Caine wasn't sure. He suddenly felt ashamed of how scared he'd been just a few hours ago. After all, he was an adult. This girl in front of him was only a child. He couldn't imagine being alone in a hospital at her age.

"Your name is Elizabeth, right?"

"Uh-huh," she sniffed.

"That's a real pretty name. You know, if I ever had a little girl, I think I'd name her Elizabeth, too."

"Really?" the girl asked, absently wiping at her nose.

"Really," Caine said with a smile. Then he bent toward her with a conspiratorial wink. "Now, this is the part where you say you like *my* name—even though it's not as pretty as Elizabeth."

Elizabeth giggled. "Your name is pretty, too."

"Really?" Caine asked, imitating her high-pitched voice.

Elizabeth giggled again. "Really," she said, flashing a gap-toothed smile. Then, "You're different from the others."

"What others?"

"The other doctors," she said, as if it were the most obvious thing in the world. "None of the others ever talk to me besides to make me say 'ahhhh' and stuff like that."

"Yeah, doctors can be a tough bunch. But they've got a hard job, working with sick people all day long, so I try to cut them some slack."

"I guess so," she said, with more wistfulness than any girl her age should know. "I just get tired."

"Yeah," Caine said, suddenly feeling very tired himself. "I know."

She peered closer, squinting to make out his face among the shadows. "Are you *really* a doctor, Caine?"

Caine smiled. "Would you like me less if I weren't?"

"No way. I'd like you *more.*"

"Well, in that case," he said, "I'm not a doctor."

"Good, 'cuz I don't like doctors too much."

"Me neither," he said.

Caine said nothing for a while, and Elizabeth opened her mouth in a wide yawn.

"I think that's my cue to leave. It's way past your bedtime." Caine stood up, but before he could step away, Elizabeth shot out her hand and grabbed his arm. He was surprised at the strength of her grip.

"Please don't go yet. Stay a little while longer. Just till I fall asleep, okay?"

"Okay," Caine said, and settled back down. He gently removed Elizabeth's hand and placed it on her lap. "I promise I won't go anywhere until I hear you start to snore."

"I don't snore!"

"We'll see about that," Caine said, tucking in her covers. "Now, close your eyes and start counting sheep."

Elizabeth obeyed. After a few seconds, she turned to him, eyes still closed.

"Will you come and visit me tomorrow night?"

"I think I'll be gone by then, Elizabeth."

"Maybe in my dreams, then?"

"Sure. Maybe in your dreams."

A few minutes later, Elizabeth began breathing heavily, and Caine tiptoed from the room, strangely confident that whatever had brought her to the hospital would somehow work itself out.

Jasper paced around the block, waiting for the Voice to tell him when it was time. He had never fired a gun before, but he wasn't worried. It was just like taking a picture—point and shoot. The only difference was that a Nikon didn't have the recoil of a Lorcin L 9-millimeter.

He had considered taking a couple of test shots in Harlem, where he'd bought the illegal firearm, but he had only two clips of ammo and didn't want to waste any bullets. He didn't know how many he would need, as the Voice was rather vague on the whole subject. It had just told him to buy a gun and get his ass back downtown, so that's what he did. Any practicing would have to be done on-site.

Jasper wondered if he would have to kill anyone. He didn't want to, but he knew that if the Voice instructed him to kill, then he would. The Voice wouldn't steer him wrong. It was simply impossible—the Voice knew everything, all there was to know.

Jasper wasn't sure how he knew this, but he did. The Voice had never told him that it knew everything, but when it spoke to him, a part of his brain could see what it saw. And when that happened, Jasper could see everything. All the people plotting and scheming to hurt David. Some wanted to trade him for money. Others wanted to experiment on him. A few wanted him dead.

That was why Jasper had to get the gun. For protection. For protection against the ones who wanted to hurt David. He would never let them hurt his baby brother. Never—

It's time.

Jasper stopped on the empty sidewalk and cocked his head.

—I got the gun like you told me to.

Are you ready?

—Yes.

Good. Here is what you need to do . . .

As Jasper listened, he closed his eyes so he could see a piece of infinity. And when he did, an idyllic smile stole across his face as he finally understood his true purpose. Then the Voice went quiet. When Jasper opened his eyes, the images he'd seen fled his conscious mind, leaving behind only shadows.

And although he couldn't remember all that he'd seen, he still felt light and airy, as if his insides were filled with pure joy. He tightened his grip on his gun and hurried down the street. He would have to run to make it in time.

Once he was on the other side of Elizabeth's door, Caine felt relieved. Whatever instinct *(Voice?)* had urged him into her room had fallen silent. Suddenly he had no reason to be there, so Caine walked back down the hall toward the elevator. But when he reached the ground floor, he again felt something tugging at him, whispering in his ear.

Don't go out the main exit—he'll be waiting for you. Go through the emergency room.

Afraid to ignore his instincts *(don't you mean the Voice?)*, Caine snaked through the corridors until he found himself in the ER. It bore little resemblance to the television show that was its namesake. There were no handsome doctors shouting things like "CBC!" or "Chem 7!" Instead there were only scores of chairs filled with unhappy people, coughing, sneezing, bleeding, and oozing.

Spotting the exit, Caine began to weave his way through the chairs. He passed a pregnant woman arguing with her husband, and a wave of dizziness made the room ripple, as if he were watching it from behind a crystal waterfall. Caine stopped and gripped the closest chair, squeezing his eyes shut. He tried to ignore the bickering couple standing near the door, but their conversation cut through his consciousness.

"I can't be by myself. You're gone all day on that ridiculous train, and I'm stuck here, hundreds of miles away."

"But, honey—"

"Don't 'but, honey' me. It's not safe. Let's ask him. What do you think?" There was a moment of silence. "Doctor? Doctor?"

Caine opened his eyes, relieved to discover that his dizziness was gone. The pregnant woman was staring at him.

"Huh?" Caine asked, confused.

"Is it safe for a woman who's gone into premature labor three times and lost her first child to stay home all alone while her husband drives a train up and down the East Coast?"

Caine looked at the pregnant woman's husband for help, but he only shrugged.

"I'm not sure," Caine said, grasping for something intelligent to say. "Do you have any family in the area?"

The woman shook her head. "Just a sister in Philadelphia."

"That's funny; my brother lives in Philly. Small world, I guess," Caine said, almost to himself. Suddenly he blurted out, "Why don't you stay with your sister? You know, just until the baby is due."

The husband's face brightened. "Hey, that's a great idea, honey. You can stay with Nora for the next two months. Then, when the baby's born, you can come back home. Everybody wins."

The woman looked down at her pudgy hands, which were holding on to each other as if each was afraid to be alone. Slowly she nodded. "Okay. I'll call her."

The man sighed with relief, gave his wife a gentle peck on the forehead, and held out his hand to Caine. "Thank you so much, Doctor."

"My pleasure," Caine said, relieved himself that the bizarre conversation was over. "Good luck with everything."

"Thanks," the man said, still pumping Caine's hand.

As he helped his wife to the door, she started telling him to call every hour while he was at work. She forced him to repeat her cell-phone number over and over again to prove that he had it memorized so that there would be "no excuses" if she didn't hear from him.

Caine waited a minute before following the couple outside, fearing that he would accidentally end up mediating another argument. Once he felt confident the coast was clear, he walked the final twenty steps toward his freedom. The instant he passed through the exit, the frigid air swirled around him.

Despite hating the cold, Caine savored the way the fresh air burned his ears and cut through the thin white coat as he strolled down the street. He'd made it. He felt as if everything was going to be fine—until a rough pair of hands grabbed him by his collar and slammed him against the building.

Caine's head ricocheted off the concrete, the pain racing down his spine. Before he had a chance to fight, the man wrapped a giant arm around his chest and half carried, half dragged him around the corner to an abandoned lot, where he tossed him to the frozen ground. Then he lifted Caine by his throat and pushed him up against the brick wall.

Although Caine couldn't make out his assailant's face in the dim light, the man's thick accent told him what he needed to know.

"Mr. Caine," Kozlov growled. "I've been looking for you."

CHAPTER eight

The gunshot was deafening. Much louder than he thought it would be. Upon hearing it, his brother's attacker froze, his fist hanging in the air, cocked back like a cartoon boxer's.

"Let him go." There was a slight tremor in Jasper's voice, but he didn't care. The beefy hand that had been closed around his brother's throat released its pressure and slowly raised itself up. David collapsed to his knees, coughing violently.

"You okay?" Jasper asked.

"What the hell are you doing here?" David asked between coughs.

"You wouldn't believe me if I told you. Who's he?" Jasper motioned to the goon who still had his hands above his head.

"This is Sergey," David said hoarsely as he got to his feet, careful to stay out of the big Russian's reach. "Sergey, tell Vitaly that I will get him his money by the end of the week."

"Mr. Nikolaev will not like that," Sergey grunted.

"Yeah, probably not," David said. "Just tell him, okay?"

Sergey shrugged as if to say, *It's your funeral.*

David moved away and stood behind Jasper, who flipped the gun in his hand and smashed the handle against the back of Sergey's head. The big man crashed down like a felled tree.

"We need to get the hell out of here before your friend wakes up," Jasper said, breathing heavily.

For the first time, David really looked at his brother. "How did you know . . . ?"

Although Jasper wanted to tell him, he knew that David wasn't ready. It was important to sound normal with David. If he acted crazy, then David wouldn't trust him. But Jasper wasn't worried—he'd been pretending to be sane most of his life; he knew how to fake it.

"Just lucky, I guess," Jasper lied. "Come on, let's go."

Jasper took his brother by the arm and led him away from the scene. After walking a few blocks, David stopped.

"Wait, where are we going?" he asked.

"Back to your apartment."

"No, we can't," David said, shaking his head. "Nikolaev will be looking for me there."

"No he won't," Jasper said with a cool confidence.

"How can you know that?"

Jasper didn't answer. Instead he grabbed David's arm again and broke into a jog, dragging his brother beside him.

By the time they arrived at Caine's apartment, a patch of early-morning light was already creeping across the floor. Through the window he could see the sun peeking over the horizon. The clock on his wall read 6:28 A.M. It was the only piece of electronic equipment left in the apartment besides his answering machine. Everything else had been stolen. He had to give Nikolaev credit—at least he was thorough.

Polished stone chessmen were scattered across the floor. Caine bent to pick up a black knight. Its snout was now chipped. A pang of sadness and loss welled up in his chest. The chess set was the only thing he owned of any real value, a gift from his father on Caine's sixth birthday. From the moment that his dad had laid out the strange-looking pieces across the black and white squares, Caine had been spellbound.

"Chess is like life, David," his father had said. "Every piece has its own function. Some are weak, others strong. Some are good at the start of the game, and others are more valuable at the end. But you need to use them *all* to win. And, as in life, there's no score. You can be down ten pieces and still win the game. That's the beauty of chess—you can always come back. All you have to do to win is know everything that's happening on the board and figure out what the other guy is going to do before he does it."

"You mean like predicting the future?" Caine asked.

"*Predicting* the future is impossible. But if you know enough about the present, then you can *control* the future."

At the time Caine didn't understand what his father had meant, but that didn't stop him from enjoying the game. Every night after he and Jasper cleared the dishes, his dad would sit down and play a game with each of them before the twins did their homework. Although Jasper never beat their father, Caine did on a regular basis.

Caine picked up a white king and placed him on his square. It had been more than ten years since his father had died. He still missed their games.

"You know," Jasper said, pulling Caine out of his thoughts, "I think Dad liked you better because you played so well."

"Dad didn't like me better," Caine said, even though he knew there was more than a grain of truth in Jasper's words. "Besides, you were a good player when you concentrated. Your problem was that you could never sit still long enough. You always made careless mistakes that left you wide open for attack."

Jasper shrugged. "Concentration is your gig. Not mine," Jasper said. "You got a pillow?"

So much for reminiscing, Caine thought. Understanding that their conversation was now over, he set Jasper up on the couch before settling onto his own bed. He was asleep almost instantly. Slowly his mind drifted down, floating away into the sea of unconscious. And then he was . . .

. . . riding on a train to Philadelphia.

The car swings gently left and right, making him sleepy. The clickety-clack, clickety-clack becomes a constant hum in his brain; the trees outside his windows meld into a brown blur. He looks down, mildly surprised at what he sees. In the palm of his left hand is another much smaller hand. It belongs to Elizabeth. She gives Caine a big smile and squeezes one of his fingers.

Caine looks at his right hand. His fingers are pressed tightly together, held there by a large, soft hand with long, red nails. Caine looks over to ask the woman to ease her grip. When she turns to face him, she seems somehow familiar. He doesn't realize who she is until he sees the curve of her belly. The pregnant woman from the hospital.

"Where are you going?" Caine asks the two of them.

"Same place you're going," they answer in unison.

"Why?" Caine asks, unsure of exactly what he is trying to learn by his question.

"Because," Elizabeth says, "that's the way it works."

"Oh," Caine responds, as if her answer makes perfect sense.

. . .

And, in a corner of his brain now flooded with dopamine, it did.

Dr. Tversky straightened his tie before the doors slid open. Two men dressed in green-and-black camouflage greeted him. He never could understand why, in an urban environment, military personnel dressed in clothing specifically designed to blend in with jungle foliage. In the gray room, their camouflage clothes were anything but, making the bulky men seem hyperreal, like 3-D action figures.

"May I have your ID, sir." The words fell hard and flat. The guard's request was an order.

Dr. Tversky handed over his driver's license and waited while the guard printed up a temporary ID badge and handed it to him. He quickly glanced down at the laminated surface before pinning it to his chest. Large block letters proclaimed TVERSKY, P. above a series of vertical black lines. He wondered when people had started taking for granted that it was perfectly acceptable to be labeled like a bar of soap.

He was surprised to see a picture of himself in the upper-right-hand corner. It must have been taken moments before by one of the many hidden cameras in the STR installation. Tversky stared at the image; he had never seen such a candid photo of himself. He was momentarily taken aback—the man in the picture didn't look well. He appeared angry and more than a little afraid. Tversky wondered if the emotions he saw on his own face would be as obvious to Forsythe.

That wouldn't do for this meeting. Forsythe would sense the fear and exploit it, especially since the likelihood Forsythe would believe him was low. In Tversky's opinion Forsythe had never been much of a thinker. He was more of a glorified administrator than anything else. Yet here Tversky was, asking this man, this lesser man, for his money.

And his help.

Forsythe sat behind his large desk and stared at his old colleague. What Tversky had just described was nothing short of incredible. No, not incredible—*impossible.* But even if his story contained only a shred of truth, Forsythe couldn't ignore it. In fact, it could be exactly what he needed. He decided to push Tversky hard, to see how much the man believed in his own theories.

"Well, you've certainly made an interesting case," Forsythe said noncommittally. "But what do you want from me?"

"I need your support. Obviously I don't have the funds necessary to effectively study this phenomenon. But with your resources . . ."

"You would," Forsythe finished, folding his hands in his lap.

"Yes. I would," Tversky responded through gritted teeth. Forsythe mentally shook his head. He would have thought that such an intelligent man as Tversky would have learned to hold his anger in check at this stage in his career. Especially when talking to a potential funder. Of course, it was Tversky's—and that of the people like him—ineptitude at human interaction that allowed Forsythe to succeed while they failed.

"I would like to help you," Forsythe began, "but what you're describing flies in the face of over seventy years of quantum physics. As you're well aware, the Heisenberg Un—"

"Heisenberg got it wrong," Tversky said.

"Is that so?" Forsythe was used to dealing with the incredible hubris of scientists, but Tversky's bold statement took him aback. Although there were still a few renegades who insisted that Heisenberg's Uncertainty Principle was wrong, almost all the top physicists on the planet agreed with the tenets of quantum mechanics as laid out by Werner Heisenberg.

In Heisenberg's famous 1926 paper, he mathematically demonstrated that it was impossible to observe a phenomenon without affecting its outcome. To prove this, he envisioned a scenario in which a scientist wished to ascertain the precise position and velocity of a subatomic particle.

This could be accomplished only by shining a light wave on the particle. Then, through analyzing the light wave's resulting disruption pattern, scientists could determine the particle's position at the time it was struck by the light wave. However, this experiment had an unwanted effect—because the particle's velocity was unknown until the light and the particle collided, the particle's velocity was therefore changed in an unpredictable way.

Thus Heisenberg showed that it was impossible to predict both a particle's position *and* its velocity simultaneously, proving that there was always a level of *uncertainty* in the physical world. Therefore Heisenberg rejected the notion of absolutes that Newtonian physicists had always championed, claiming that the world was not black or white—but gray. He asserted that, in the real world, subatomic particles did not have exact positions, they only had *probabilistic* positions, meaning that even though an individual particle is *probably* in one place, it is not actually in any one singular position until it is *observed.*

Heisenberg was therefore able to demonstrate that the only information one could gain through observation was not the position of a particle as it truly *existed* in nature but the position of a particle *being observed* in nature. And although many scientists felt uncomfortable with this notion, Heisenberg's theory of a probabilistic universe was completely consistent with previously accepted (albeit unexplainable) physics equations.

Finally, in 1927, physicists came together to agree on what would be known as the "Copenhagen interpretation," which supported Heisenberg's theories and stated that observed phenomena obeyed different physical laws than did nonobserved phenomena. Not only did this raise some very interesting philosophical questions, it also forced scientists to admit that literally anything was possible, since all outcomes exist in a world ruled by probabilities rather than certainties.

For instance, even though a particle may *probably* be in a scientist's lab, it could *possibly* be halfway across the universe. Such was the birth of modern quantum physics, and even though most couldn't claim to understand how it was possible, no one could refute Heisenberg's contention.

Still, the theory was not welcomed by all, especially those scientists who were devout Newtonians and believed in the theory of determinism—that the universe was governed by immutable laws and that nothing was uncertain. The determinists believed that everything was a consequence of some earlier cause that could be predicted perfectly if only humanity could understand the "true" laws and current state of the universe.

As Forsythe mulled this over, he thought of the best way to attack Tversky's assertion.

"To disregard Heisenberg is to embrace determinism," Forsythe said carefully. "Is that what you're saying?"

"Maybe it is. In my point of view, determinism has never been fully disproved."

"What about Charles Darwin?"

Tversky rolled his eyes at Forsythe's mention of the man who was one of the first to dispute determinism. Although Heisenberg's Uncertainty Principle was often regarded as the *final* (albeit most abstract) nail in determinism's coffin, Darwin's theory of evolution was one of the biggest and most easily understandable nails.

When Darwin wrote his revolutionary *Origin of Species,* he presented philosophers and physicists alike with a view of the world that was not mapped out by some divine power but one that had evolved over millions of years through countless *random* mutations. After *Origin*'s publication in 1859, anyone who accepted the hypothesis of evolution over creationism also had to discard any notions of predestination and, therefore, determinism.

"Are you now saying that you deny evolution? Please don't tell me you're a creationist."

Tversky ground his teeth for a second before answering; Forsythe smiled. The only thing he loved more than an intellectual debate was getting under the skin of one of his ivory-tower brethren. He knew that labeling Tversky as a creationist was ludicrous, but that's what made it so much fun. It was clearly too much for Tversky, however, as he switched into diatribe/lecture mode.

"Obviously I believe in evolution. However, Darwin's postulate that evolution and natural selection result from random mutations is completely *un*proven. Just because modern science has not been able to determine what causes mutations does not mean that they are random. Randomness is merely the appearance of a phenomenon that is currently incomprehensible.

"There are over 3.2 billion nucleotide bases within the human genome. Who's to say that there aren't chemical structures within those genomes that *purposefully* reprogram the physical characteristics of a person's offspring when faced with certain environmental adversities—like darkening the skin in tropical climates or raising the cheekbones in areas of high winds?"

Forsythe held out his hands. "All right, you've made your point. I take it back—I don't think you're a creationist. But still, determinism? What about Maxwell?"

James Clerk Maxwell, a philosophical great-great-grandfather to Heisenberg, was one of the most brilliant physicists of the nineteenth century, best known for his study of electromagnetic waves as well as thermodynamics, or the movement of heat. His greatest achievement was the discovery of the law of entropy, which stated that heat always flowed from a body of higher temperature to a body of lower temperature until the temperatures of the two bodies became equal.

He showed that when an ice cube was dropped into a glass of warm water, it wasn't the "coldness" of the ice that seeped into the water but the relative heat of the water that was absorbed into the ice. The water would heat up the cube until it melted and the entire liquid reached a thermal equilibrium. Like Heisenberg, however, Maxwell wasn't a huge believer in absolute laws, and although he spent the first part of his career trying to discover them, he spent the latter part trying to tear them down.

His chief success in that arena was when he proved that the Second Law of Thermodynamics wasn't a law at all. The famous Second Law stated that in any system, energy tended to flow from being concentrated in one area to becoming dispersed and spread out. Essentially the Second Law was used to explain everything from why rocks didn't roll up mountains to why a dead battery didn't suddenly reenergize. The reason being that both those events would require energy to become spontaneously concentrated, the polar opposite of what the Second Law stated—that energy always spread out; a system always flows toward the state of greatest disorder. Hence the Second Law gained the nickname "Time's Arrow," since it seemed to literally direct the flow of time.

However, Maxwell was able to prove that the Second Law was not, in fact, absolute. He did so by imagining a test tube that was injected with gas. Since the Second Law stated that all energy in a system will diffuse, then it could be assumed that the gas molecules would spread out equally to fill the entire space allotted. This would suggest that all areas of the test tube would have a uniform temperature, since heat resulted from the ceaseless random motion of molecules.

Maxwell then postulated that since the direction and velocity at which molecules travel are random, it was *possible* that all of the fastest-moving molecules could wind up in one end of the test tube. This would then cause a momentary temperature spike by the *spontaneous concentration of energy* where all the molecules were gathered—a direct contradiction to the Second Law's foundation that energy always disperses.

Maxwell thus demonstrated that the Second Law was only *probabilistically* true, or true only "most of the time." In doing so, he proved that the majority of physical laws can never be absolutely precise.

"People often cite Maxwell's proof that the Second Law of Thermodynamics is only probabilistic rather than absolute as evidence that chance exists," Tversky responded. "But I would postulate that randomness is only the *appearance,* not the reality."

Forsythe raised his eyebrows at Tversky's bold statement. What he was proposing was almost beyond comprehension. They both knew what he meant, but Forsythe had to state it aloud, if only to hear it said.

"So you believe that the velocities and directions of electrons are *not random?*"

"If you truly believe in Heisenberg's theory that *anything* is possible," Tversky said, "then you must also accept the *possibility* that the movements of electrons are *not* random."

"But if the movements of electron particles aren't random, then what lies behind them?"

"Does it matter?" Tversky asked.

"Of course it matters," Forsythe said with a wave of his hand.

"Why?"

Forsythe stared at his old colleague, unsure of what to say. "What do you mean, *why?*"

"I mean," Tversky said, leaning forward in his chair, "why does it matter *what* is responsible for the movement of electrons? It could result from organized particles smaller than quarks that have yet to be discovered, or energy flow from a nonlocal reality—hell, it could even be that electrons are sentient. My point is that it doesn't matter *why* the movement is not random, only that it is *not* random."

"But the controlling variable behind electrons' movement—"

"Is a very interesting concept, but outside the purview of my research."

Forsythe took a long, slow sip of his coffee, mulling over Tversky's statements. "But you still haven't explained Heisenberg's 'flawed' reasoning."

"I don't have to. If you accept the fact that electrons move with some sort of purpose, then you must also accept that a force exists which exerts that purpose. Don't you see? If that undiscovered, as-yet-immeasurable force exists, then it is *possible* there are ways to observe an electron without the use of a light wave."

Forsythe couldn't help but stare at the man.

"But your logic is both circular *and* paradoxical. You're saying that because anything can happen in a probabilistic universe, that the universe could be deterministic rather than probabilistic! You're using Heisenberg's Theory of Uncertainty to *disprove* Heisenberg."

Tversky merely nodded. His arrogance was astonishing, and yet there was a bizarre fluidity to his ideas that was strangely compelling. Still, Forsythe didn't want to let on that Tversky was actually beginning to convince him.

Clearing his throat, Forsythe said, "And I'm supposed to accept these heretical hypotheses because . . . why, exactly?"

"I'm not asking you to accept them at face value, only to believe that they *could* be possible."

"Based on what?"

Tversky's eyes shone. "Faith."

"Not the most compelling of arguments, you have to admit."

Tversky shrugged. "Look, James, I'm no salesman. I'm a scientist. But I'm telling you I'm right. I saw it. If you were there, then you would understand."

"But I wasn't there."

"But I *was*."

Forsythe shook his head. "I'm sorry, but that's just not good enough. I can't allocate resources without proof. I can't—"

Tversky slammed his fist on the desk. "Why the hell not? Science used to be revolutionary. It used to be practiced by poor geniuses working out of their basements around the clock because they had a theory that the way the universe worked was different from the way those around them *believed* it worked. They had vision. And they had courage *in* their vision." Tversky stood up and leaned in to Forsythe. "I'm begging you—for once try not to be a bureaucrat and try to be a scientist."

Forsythe reclined in his chair. "I *am* a scientist. The only difference between you and me is that I live in the real world and understand the constraints. I'm smart enough to work *within* the system instead of whining about it. You're telling me to have courage . . . well, I ask you—where is *your* courage? What have you done that was so goddamn risky in your pursuit of science?"

Tversky was struck dumb. Forsythe wasn't sure if it was out of fury or speechlessness, but he didn't care. Either was fine with him.

"I thought so." Forsythe stood and opened his office door. "If that's all, I have a very busy schedule today. I welcome you to come back and re-present your theories—when you have some proof."

"I will get proof," Tversky said with a flat conviction. "Although when I do, I doubt I'll be coming here with it." Tversky spun around and briskly walked down the hall.

Forsythe turned to the guard at his door and added, more than a little self-satisfied, "Please make sure Dr. Tversky finds his way to the exit."

"Yes, sir," the soldier responded, and quickly took off after his charge. Forsythe stood in the now empty hallway a moment longer and then reentered his office. It wasn't until he closed his door that a smile crept across his face. He felt confident that his jibes had adequately lit a proverbial fire beneath Tversky's ass. As he already knew of Tversky's "secret" tests on his Alpha Subject, it wasn't a stretch to think that Forsythe's taunts would push Tversky to take even more risks than he had thus far.

Now all Forsythe had to do was sit back and watch. If Tversky's next experiment blew up in his face, then Forsythe could focus on other projects. But if Tversky was right . . . well, then Forsythe would instruct Agent Vaner to swoop in and do what she did best. After that, he could take over where Tversky left off.

And science would be none the wiser.

Jasper was already gone when Caine awoke. There was a Post-it stuck to the couch that read *Doing errands, be back L8R.* Caine didn't know what errands his brother had to run, but he didn't worry about it. Despite his slight mental instability, it was becoming clear that Jasper could take care of himself. The person in trouble was Caine.

He could barely get his mind around what had transpired the night before. It seemed so unreal. He decided to make some coffee; he always thought better on caffeine. As he listened to the sound of the liquid tinkling into the pot, he noticed the red light on his answering machine blinking angrily. He pressed "Play" with tired resignation. A second later Vitaly Nikolaev's silky voice filled the room.

"Hey, Caine, it's Vitaly. Just wanted to check on how you were feeling. Why don't you swing by the club? I'm worried about you."

"I'll bet you are," Caine said to the metal box. The other five messages were hang-ups. It had been the same story on his cell's voice mail. It was now Tuesday; he had owed Nikolaev eleven grand for two calendar days. Since Nikolaev charged 5 percent interest a week, Caine now owed $11,157. He was seriously fucked.

On the way home from the hospital, he'd emptied his checking account. His entire net worth of $438.12 was less than a week's worth of interest. He had to figure out what to do about Nikolaev. Caine attacked the problem the way any good statistician would—by analyzing the probabilities and outcomes of every scenario to determine the best course of action.

Unfortunately, he had only two choices: pay or disappear.

But because of his seizures, disappearing was not an option. There was no way he could go on the lam and still stay on the experimental drug. He had to check in twice a week for blood work, and he had only twenty pills, just enough for ten days. Even if he found a way to outrun Kozlov, he could never outrun his seizures. No, he had to stay in Dr. Kumar's study, if only to know that he'd tried.

So he had to pay—either that or make peace with Nikolaev. Maybe he could work off the debt. Caine shook his head even as the idea popped into his mind. Work it off as what? A button man? Not likely. He sighed. There was no way around it—he had to get the money.

But how could he earn the cash? The first answer was fairly obvious: the same way he'd lost it—gambling. He unconsciously fingered the thin wad of cash in his pocket. He could hit one of the other clubs with his $400 stake and try to turn it into something. It wasn't out of the realm of possibility.

If he lucked out, he could win a couple grand by morning. Of course, if he lost, he would be even deeper in the hole. Plus, if it got back to Nikolaev that Caine was playing at another club, the Russian would not be happy.

What about Atlantic City? He could hop a bus to AC, maybe pick off a few tourists at the Hold 'Em tables. He would definitely win if he played conservatively; the problem was that it would take too long. The surefire losers played only low stakes—three-six or five-ten—plus, there was always at least one bona fide shark at each table. With such small betting, Caine could only eke out twenty to thirty bucks an hour. Not bad cash, but at that rate it would be too little too late. Even if he played for a sixteen-hour stretch, he'd only clear between $320 and $480; at that rate he'd have to win 116 days in a row.

No, casino gambling was definitely out. As for playing at

another poker club, Caine decided to keep that option in his back pocket for the time being. The other alternative was to get a job, but there was no way he could get a regular job fast enough. Not in this economy and not with his résumé, which had a giant gap of inactivity. He could just picture the interview now:

"So, Mr. Caine, what have you been doing since 2002?"

"Well, I was a shut-in for a few months because a couple times a week I tend to see things, and then I start convulsing. But since last September I've been frequenting Vitaly Nikolaev's club—I play a mean game of Texas Hold 'Em. Oh, yeah, that reminds me: Could you advance me eleven grand? I need to pay off the Russian mob before they kill me."

Or maybe he could get some kind of research gig from one of the professors. It was a good idea, but probably better in theory than in practice. Those jobs were always competitive, and there was no way he could get paid in advance; plus, the pay was chicken feed. The only big bucks came from the private sector, which was why all the top professors doubled as consultants on Wall Street.

Suddenly Caine had an idea—he could ask his old dissertation adviser to hire him on one of his consulting projects. If Caine pledged his soul, then maybe Doc would let him do his analytical grunt work. Hell, if he was lucky, Doc might even give him some money up front. He looked at the clock—it was a few minutes past ten.

Doc usually taught a 10:30 A.M. statistics class at Columbia. He ran that class rather than a graduate seminar so he could maximize his time on research rather than preparing high-level lectures. Like most professors, Doc loathed teaching, although no one would ever guess after watching the great show he put on for the undergrads.

A quick call to the registrar confirmed that today was Doc's first class of the semester. If Caine hurried, he could catch Doc before class began. He grabbed his leather jacket, and the bottle of white capsules fell out of his pocket, reminding him that it was time for his next dose. As he dumped a pill into his palm, he couldn't help but wonder if last night's audio hallucination had been real, sparked by this experimental drug.

He was scared to take another pill, but he was too scared not to. He dry-swallowed the capsule before he lost his nerve and then walked out the door. As he ran down the stairs, he thought he was forgetting something, but he couldn't figure out what the hell it was. He felt the knowledge dance at the tip of his consciousness, just out of reach. Caine let it go, knowing that it would come to him eventually.

Things like that always did.

Twenty-seven minutes later, Caine took a deep breath and stepped into the classroom. He picked a seat in the back and sat down. His heart was hammering, but so far he didn't feel like he was going to pass out. He could do this. It was just a room. It's not as if he was lecturing. He would be fine as long as he just sat here.

At the front of the class, Doc grabbed a piece of chalk and scrolled in huge letters:

PROBABILITY IS BORING

A few students laughed. "Anyone disagree?" No one did. "Okay, now that we've got that out of the way, let me reassure you that this class is going to be well worth your time, because in this class we're not going to talk about probability theory. We're going to talk about life. And *life* is interesting. At least mine is—I've got no idea how yours is shaping up.

"Probability theory *is* life—just put to numbers," he continued. "Let me give you an example. I'll need a volunteer from the studio audience. Hands." Several shot into the air. Just then the door at the back of the classroom slammed shut, and all eyes turned to look at the late arrival. The frat boy was already slinking over to a seat, a baseball hat nearly obscuring his eyes. Doc walked briskly to the back of the room and grabbed his arm.

"This is what I call a mandatory volunteer." Doc held up the frat boy's arm like a referee holding up a prizefighter's. "What's your name?"

"Mark Davis."

Doc spun around, grabbed a computer printout off his desk, and handed it to Mark. "What is that?"

"Uhhh . . . looks like a class roster."

"Exactly. Now, tell me, how many students are listed there?"

Mark paused a minute, then looked up. "Fifty-eight."

"And are birthdays listed next to the names?"

"No."

"This is going to be fun," Doc said conspiratorially to the class before turning back to Mark. "Would you say you're a betting man?"

"Sure."

"Excellent!" Doc clasped his hands together. He reached into his pocket and counted out five crisp one-dollar bills that he showed to the class like a magician about to perform a trick. "I'll bet you five big ones that at least two people in this classroom have the same birthday. What do you say?"

Mark looked at the class and then back at Doc with a smirk. "Yeah, I'll take that bet."

"Fantastic. Let's see it."

Mark furrowed his brow in confusion.

"The money, the cash."

Mark shrugged but reached into his pocket and extracted a crumpled five-dollar bill.

Doc snatched it out of his hand and slammed it onto the table. Then he turned to the class and smiled, pointing his thumb back to Mark. "Sucker," he said. The class laughed, and Mark reddened. "If Mark knew anything about life—that is, probability—then he would have known that he just made a very bad bet. Does anyone know why?"

No answer.

"All righty, more volunteers, then." No one made a move. Then Doc spotted Caine. He tried to sink lower in his seat, but it was too late. "We have a special guest in class today. One of my best Ph.D. students—David Caine. David, raise your hand." Caine reluctantly put up his hand, his throat dry. The rest of the class turned to stare at him. "I call David 'Rain Man' because he's the only guy in the department who doesn't need a calculator. Care to help me out, David?"

"I assume I don't have a choice?" Caine asked, trying to ignore the fact that his heart felt like it was about to burst through his chest.

"Not really, no," Doc replied.

"Well, then I'd be honored." The class chuckled. Caine forced his heart to slow down. Just like riding a bike. He could do this.

"Excellent," Doc said, clasping his hands together. "What are the odds that you and I have the same birthday?"

"About 0.3 percent."

"Please explain to us mortals how you got that answer."

"It's 1 divided by 365."

"Exactly. Since each of us was born on one of the 365 days during the year, then there is exactly a 1-in-365 chance that you and I were born on the same day." Doc ran around to the board and scribbled

$$1 / 365 = 0.003 = 0.3\%$$

"Everyone get that?" There was a ruffling of papers and a couple of grumbles as everyone realized it was time to take notes. "Okay, had I asked if you wanted to bet that we *didn't* have the same birthday, you would have said yes, right?"

"Right."

"And that would be a smart move; you'd probably win. I was born on July ninth. When were you born?"

"October eighteenth."

"There you go. There was only a 1-in-365 chance that our

birthdays were the same, and a 364-in-365 chance that they were different. Now tell me the odds that you have the same birthday as *anyone* in this room, including me."

Caine thought for a second, and then looked up. "That's 14.9 percent."

"Correct. Please explain."

"If you want to calculate the odds that I *will* have the same birthday as one of the other 59 people in the classroom, you first need to calculate the odds that I *don't* have the same birthday as anyone else, which is 364 over 365 to the 59th power. It's the same as calculating the probability that I don't have the same birthday as another student multiplied by itself 59 times."

Doc scribbled as Caine spoke.

$$\begin{aligned}\text{Prob (different b'days than all)} &= (364 / 365)^{59} \\ &= 85.1\%\end{aligned}$$

"So," Caine continued, "since the probability that I *don't* have the same birthday as anyone else is 85.1 percent, then the probability that I *do* have the same birthday is 14.9 percent."

$$\begin{aligned}\text{Prob (same b'days)} &= 1 - \text{Prob (diff. b'days)} \\ &= 100\% - 85.1\% \\ &= 14.9\%\end{aligned}$$

"Perfect," Doc said. "Everyone still with me?" Various heads nodded around the classroom as the students finished copying Doc's math into their notebooks.

"Okay, let's back up. Knowing that you and I don't have the same birthday, what's the probability that *both* you and I won't have the same birthday as anyone else?"

Caine cleared his throat. "First you calculate the probability that I don't have the same birthday as anyone else—which we already know is 85.1 percent—then you calculate the odds that *you* don't have the same birthday as everyone else, already taking into account that we don't have the same birthday."

"Whoa, that's way too fast," Doc said dramatically. He

threw his piece of chalk across the room to Caine, who caught it instinctively. "Can you come up here and show me what you mean?"

Everyone turned to look at him. His hands were sweaty, and his heart was really pounding now, but somehow he forced himself to stand. As he walked down to the front of the class, each step seemed like an eternity. And yet the closer he got to the board, the more confident he became. Until finally he was there, standing in front of the class just as he'd always done. He quickly blinked his eyes, but the world stayed focused. Dr. Kumar's drug was working. He was back where he belonged.

"Um, okay," Caine said, turning to the class. "Like I was saying, we already know that Doc and I don't have the same birthday. To calculate the probability that neither one of us has the same birthday as anyone in the class, you have to first calculate the probability that Doc doesn't have the same birthday as anyone else.

"I'll do that the same way I calculated that I don't have the same birthday as anyone else, except that this time I'll use 363 as a numerator and 364 as a denominator, because I already know that he and I have different birthdays, so I have to eliminate a day. Then I raise the fraction to the 58th power instead of the 59th power, because I only have to compare him to 58 people in the classroom, not 59, because I'm excluding myself.

"Thus the probability that Doc doesn't have the same birthday as anyone else in the class is 85.3 percent."

$$\text{Prob}_{\text{Doc}} \text{ (different b'days than all)} = (363 / 364)^{58}$$
$$= 85.3\%$$

Caine turned back around to face the class. For a sickening moment, he had a flash of palm-tree hands and felt his stomach flip. He squeezed his eyes shut and then opened them. He was all right. The palm trees were gone. He took a deep breath and continued.

•

"So if you want to know the probability that neither of us has the same birthday as anyone else, you must multiply the two probabilities together."

Prob (Caine & Doc different b'days than all)
$= \text{Prob (Caine diff)} * \text{Prob (Doc diff}_{\text{given diff Caine}})$
$= (364 / 365)^{59} * (363 / 364)^{58}$
$= (85.1\%) * (85.3\%)$
$= 72.5\%$

"The probability that neither Doc *nor* I have the same birthday as anyone else is 72.5 percent. Hence, the probability that either Doc or I *do* have the same birthday as someone else is 27.5 percent."

Prob(C&D same b'days) = 1 – Prob (diff b'days)
$= 100\% - 72.5\%$
$= 27.5\%$

"Everyone following along?" Doc's sudden interjection surprised him. Caine had almost forgotten that it wasn't his class. "Great," Doc said when everyone nodded. "Okay, last question: What are the odds that *any* two people have the same birthday?"

"Well," Caine said, turning back to the board, "assuming you don't know our birthdays are different, you just repeat the same calculation I did to determine whether you and I had the same birthday right down the line for every student in the class, each time subtracting one from the numerator."

Prob (no two b'days the same)
$= (364 / 365) * (363 / 365) * (362 / 365)$
. . .
$* (308 / 365) * (307 / 365) * (306 / 365)$
$= 0.006$
$= 0.6\%$

"Since there's only a 0.6 percent chance that *no one* has the same birthday, then there's a 99.4 percent chance that at least two people *do* have the same birthday."

Doc clapped his hands together slowly. He turned around and pocketed the pile of bills on the table, then slapped Mark on the back. "Thanks for the money, Mr. Davis. You can sit down now."

"Hang on a second," Mark protested.

"What's on your mind?"

"Just because your buddy said I'm wrong doesn't make it true."

"Ah, a disbeliever. Are you saying that you don't believe in probability theory?"

"Not 100 percent of the time," Mark said with a smirk.

"Blasphemy!" Doc shouted, holding his hands to the heavens like a gospel preacher. "My brothers and sisters, we have a disbeliever in our midst! Help me save this man's soul! Everyone who was born in January, stand up."

Four students rose from their seats. "Count off the date of your birth, starting from the back."

None had the same birthday. Mark's smirk widened. Doc merely shrugged. "I would wipe that grin off your face if I were you. It's going to look really dumb in a second." Doc turned back to the class. "Okay, Januarys, have a seat. Februarys, stand up and count off."

This time five students stood up. Again none had matching birthdays. He got the same results for March, April, May, and June. Mark grew more and more smug. That is, until it was time for the Julys to count off.

A skinny engineering student: "July third."

A tall jock with a crew cut: "July twelfth."

"Hey, me, too! July twelfth!" exclaimed a tiny Asian girl in a pink T-shirt.

Doc smiled broadly, opening his arms wide and taking a deep bow. "I rest my case."

Mark scowled and sat back down.

"So what's the moral of the story? First, the larger the

sample, the larger the probability. In other words, with enough observations, anything can—and will—happen, no matter how improbable. If we had a class of, say, ten people, then Mark might not be going home a loser, because then the odds of two people having identical birthdays would be . . . Rain Man, help me out."

Caine closed his eyes for a few seconds, then opened them. "Only about 12 percent."

Doc smiled. "Correct. So where was I? Oh, yes, the second moral of the story." He looked directly at Mark. "Probability theory *never* lies. Believe in it, for it is the one true God."

Doc did a miniature bow, and a few people actually clapped. He beamed. "Okay, now let's review the reading."

Caine took that as his cue to return to his seat. As he walked up the aisle, he felt a surge of joy. He had done it. Even though two Swords of Damocles called epilepsy and Vitaly Nikolaev still hung over his head, for that moment Caine didn't care. For a few minutes, he had taught a class. For the first time in nearly eighteen months, Caine suddenly believed that maybe he could get his life back. If only he'd known sooner, he wouldn't have waited so long to enter Dr. Kumar's clinical trial.

Forty-five minutes later, Doc finished up his lecture. "Class dismissed. See everyone on Wednesday. Perhaps if we're lucky, Mr. Caine will see fit to join us again."

Although most of the students quickly scrambled out of the classroom, Caine watched as a few goody-goodies swarmed around Doc to question him about the lecture. Once the crowd dispersed, Caine approached his old mentor.

"It's great seeing you again, Caine." Doc slapped him on the shoulder. "You know, we really should take our show on the road."

"I'm not sure people would actually pay money to see it."

"Are you kidding? Fifty-eight students, each of whom is paying $14,000 tuition for four courses just did. That's . . ."

Caine blinked his eyes. "$134.62 per student, per class."

"Exactly!"

"Cool," Caine said. "Then my half for today's lecture comes to $3,904. Can you write me a check?"

The white truck with the famous blue-and-orange block letters killed its engine directly across the street from Sam's Diner. The FedEx truck was one of forty purchased by a shell corporation wholly owned by the National Security Agency. However, except for its exterior, the vehicle bore little resemblance to the shipper's other trucks; it was now outfitted with a powerful engine as well as military-grade surveillance equipment.

None of the truck's three passengers carried any identification except for the fake name tags on their stolen uniforms. Steven Grimes was the team leader. He was one of the top surveillance experts in the country, although he hardly looked the part, with his greasy black hair and ghostly white skin.

When he was at the Surveillance Center, he sat in a large leather captain's chair, from which he could see ten monitors and had access to five keyboards. But out in the field, things were stripped down; he had only three screens, two keyboards, and a tiny metal stool drilled into the floor. Yet it was in the truck that he thrived, as Grimes was really a field geek at heart.

More than anything, he loved to watch. When it came to voyeurism, Grimes was the master. Despite his lack of formal education, he was an electronics genius and, thanks to having a felon for a father, an expert burglar. These two skills enabled him to build tiny homemade cameras and install them wherever he saw fit, which he began doing as a sophomore in high school in the girls' locker room. After getting kicked out of school, Grimes decided that he wanted to be a professional watcher, so he applied to the NSA. Although his first application was summarily rejected, he was able to change HR's mind after he hacked into the NSA network and wrote a personal note to the director of cryptography, which appeared on the man's screen when he logged in.

Grimes was hired the following day, and the next eight years were a voyeur's wet dream. He was given his own electronics lab and a nearly infinite budget to buy spy toys. The only things he didn't like about his job were the bureaucratic bullshit and his boss, Dr. James Forsythe. Forsythe—or, as Grimes liked to call him, Dr. Jimmy—was a royal pain in the ass, worse than all the other military jackoffs put together.

Up until recently they had maintained a mutually beneficial, albeit acrimonious, relationship. But that was before Grimes had lost everything thanks to Forsythe's stock tip from hell. If it weren't for Dr. Jimmy, Grimes would still have over $200,000 in the bank. But two months earlier, Grimes had invested everything in philoTech because Dr. Jimmy told him Senator Daniels was sponsoring a major defense bill that would guarantee the company a huge government contract.

When the news about the bill hit the wire a few weeks later, the stock went through the roof, skyrocketing from its fifty-two-week low of $20¼ a share to 101½. Instead of cashing in, Grimes doubled his stake, as he knew that the government contract was triple Wall Street's expectations. He was primed to make a fortune, but then Daniels woke up dead and everything went to hell. No more Daniels, no more defense bill, and no more contract for philoTech. And all that was before the accounting scandal hit the front page.

In the first hour of trading, the stock lost 98 percent of its value and Grimes was wiped out. His initial stash was now worth less than ten grand. But did Forsythe share his pain? No fucking way. That asshole had cashed out the second the stock broke triple digits and made a mint.

And there was nothing Grimes could do about it. Worse still, sticking with Forsythe was the only chance he had of making his money back, so here he was, doing the little man's bidding. Just then his phone beeped, and he slapped a button on his console. The MP3 he'd been listening to was replaced by Dr. Jimmy's annoying voice.

"Do you have audio yet?" Forsythe asked without so much as a hello.

"Don't get your panties in a bunch, Dr. Jimmy," Grimes said, enjoying the sniggers from the other guys in the truck. "Augy is working on it. We should be on in a couple of minutes."

"Fine," Forsythe growled. "Make it accessible through the Ethernet once it's done."

Dr. Jimmy clicked off, and Grimes returned his attention to the monitor, which showed some old dude in a diner. He wondered what was so important about Tversky that Dr. Jimmy wanted Grimes's team to watch the guy eat his lunch.

Doc's favorite diner had a large neon sign above the door, which advertised its "World-Famous Burgers and Soup." Caine had always thought that was an odd combination, as he could never remember eating burgers and soup together, but they did have great food. While Doc caught him up on the latest journal articles, Caine worked up the courage to ask his old professor for a job. But he was nervous. There was something about Doc that seemed . . . different. He had nearly taken off the waitress's head when she screwed up their drink order. It wasn't like him.

Caine figured it was just his imagination making excuses and was about to push himself to ask. Unfortunately, before he could pop the question, a man walked in and looked expectantly at Doc, who immediately waved him over. The man was Doc's physical opposite, dressed prim and proper in a gray three-piece suit and dark red bow tie. Caine recognized him as Doc's on-again, off-again research partner, but he couldn't remember the man's name.

"You remember David, right?" Doc asked the man, neglecting to introduce him.

"Of course, nice to see you again," the man said. He shook Caine's hand with all the firmness of a wet fish, staring as if Caine were an animal in the zoo.

"So what's on your mind?" Doc asked his colleague. "You look pissed."

Bow Tie Man ran a hand through his thick hair and grumbled. "Just having a bad day. I had an argument with someone about Heisenberg. Gave me a headache."

"Tell me about it," Doc said, momentarily thoughtful. "I've never been a fan myself. What about you, Rain Man?"

"Huh?" Caine asked, surprised that Doc had pulled him into the conversation. "Oh, I don't know . . . Heisenberg never made much sense to me."

"Really?" Doc asked, eyes sparkling. "What didn't you understand?"

Caine could have kicked himself. He had forgotten about Doc's insatiable appetite to explain complex phenomena. Over the years Caine had spent hours trapped in Doc's office as the professor waxed poetic on everything from the big bang to chaos theory.

Caine looked over at Bow Tie Man for help, but he was already staring down at the menu, oblivious to the conversation at hand. Finally Caine said, "I guess what I never understood is why physicists believe that a particle doesn't have a singular position just because they can't figure out where it is. It's not like it can be in two places at once."

"Actually, in a way it can," Doc said, clearly happy to have steered the conversation toward something he could lecture about. "Physicists have been able to use the double-slit experiment to prove it."

"Okay, I'll bite," Caine said. He knew there was no stopping Doc now, so he figured he might as well learn something. "What's the double-slit experiment?"

"Imagine that you shone a light through a slit in a piece of paper onto this plate. What would you expect to see?"

Caine shrugged. "A bar of light, I guess."

"Exactly." Doc spread a thin line of ketchup across the middle of his empty plate. "The photons of light that make it through the slit will hit the plate and create a solid bar." He paused to take a drink of his water. "Now imagine that you shone a light through a piece of paper that had *two* slits. What would you see then?"

"Two bars of light."

"Wrong," Doc said. "You would see a series of blurry bars and shadows, like this." Doc spread more lines of ketchup across the plate parallel to the first one and then smudged them with one of his fries. "If you think of light as a wave, this pattern isn't that surprising, since you can imagine the different light waves interfering with each other on the other side of the paper on their way to the plate, thus causing this blurry pattern.

"Even if you think of light as what it is—a series of particles—you can still explain the pattern, since every photon has its own frequency, so they could also interfere with each other to create the blurry pattern on the plate."

"Okay, so it's explainable. What's the big deal?" Caine asked.

Doc held up his finger. "I'm about to get to that. Recently some physicists developed a light source that only emits *one* photon at a time, and they replicated the experiment. And guess what? They got the *exact same* interference pattern on the other side."

Caine furrowed his brow. "How could there be an interference pattern on the other side if only one photon goes through the slit at a time? What's it interfering with?"

"Each individual photon interferes with *itself* on the other side of the paper because it passes through both slits simultaneously during the experiment." Doc smiled triumphantly.

"How?"

"Because the photon, which was previously thought of as a particle, is *also* a wave. When there's only one slit, it acts like a particle, but when there are two slits, it acts like a wave. The reason is that the photon simultaneously has the properties of both a particle *and* a wave. This is known as 'particle-wave duality.'

"Essentially, all matter is two things, with different properties, in different locations, all at the same time, until it is measured."

"But that doesn't make sense," Caine said.

"Welcome to quantum physics," Doc said, munching on another fry.

Bow Tie Man finally perked up. "If you really want to blow his mind," he said to Doc as if Caine weren't there, "then tell him about Schrödinger's cat."

Caine held up his hand. "Really, that's okay—"

"Come on, it will just take a minute," Doc said. "Quick and painless, I promise."

"All right," Caine said with mock reluctance. "Last one." Caine had forgotten how much fun it was just to sit around and talk without wondering whether the guy next to you was bluffing. For the second time that day, he had allowed himself to forget about his problems and lose himself in the moment. It felt nice—even if they were talking about quantum physics.

"Despite the fact that Erwin Schrödinger was one of the fathers of quantum physics, he realized how illogical the field was, especially when it was applied to the real world. So he proposed a philosophical problem about his cat right about the time Heisenberg was completing his Uncertainty Principle.

"Essentially it went like this: Imagine that you had a radioactive atom that vacillated between two states—'excited,' during which time it gives off surplus energy, or 'unexcited,' during which time it lies dormant. Quantum physics tells us that once we *observe* the atom, it will be in either one state or another, but as long as we *don't* observe it, it's essentially in two states simultaneously—just like the photon in the previous example was in two places at the same time.

"Schrödinger's philosophical problem is this: What would happen if you put a cat into a box with a bottle of cyanide gas, a radioactive atom, and a robotic hammer programmed to swing when it detects energy? If the radioactive atom is excited, then the hammer will swing into the bottle, which will release the gas, and the cat will die. But if the radioactive atom is unexcited, then the hammer will stay put, and the cat will live.

"However, until you open up the box and *observe* the atom, it is neither excited nor unexcited, but some probabilistic combination of the two. So the question is this: While the box is closed, what happens to the cat?"

Caine thought about it for a moment. "I guess . . ." His voice trailed off, and then he smiled. "Oh, I get it—since the atom is theoretically in two states at once, so is the cat. It's simultaneously both alive *and* dead—that is, until you open the box and observe the atom, at which point the cat definitively enters into one state or another."

Doc smiled. "There you go. And you said you didn't understand quantum physics."

"The point, obviously," Bow Tie Man interjected, now directing his attention toward Caine, "is that even though quantum mechanics is technically correct, it's even more illogical than it seems when you try to apply it to the real world rather than to invisible subatomic particles."

"So are you saying you don't believe in Heisenberg?" Doc asked Bow Tie Man.

"Do you?" Bow Tie Man countered.

Doc shrugged. "For the most part, I believe what I see with my own two eyes. Everything else is just theory." Then he turned his attention back to Caine. "I'm sorry, you were about to ask me something before we got sidetracked."

Caine picked at one of Doc's fries, suddenly embarrassed to be asking for help, especially in front of a third party.

"Well, I'm in a bit of a jam. . . ."

"Oh," Doc said, concerned. "What is it?"

"I have a . . . cash-flow problem."

"You know I'd give you your teaching fellowship back in a heartbeat, but after your . . . um, troubles, the department head would never let me. Not this semester, at least. But there's always next year."

"Yeah, I know, it's just that my cash needs are a bit more immediate." Caine felt mortified, worse still that Doc's friend wasn't keen enough to excuse himself. He just stared down at Caine as if he smelled something very ripe. Caine did his best to ignore the bow-tied biostatistician and rushed forward. "If you have any private research projects that you need some help on, even if it's grunt work, I'll do it. I'm a bit desperate."

Doc stared at the ceiling for a second, lost in thought. When he returned his attention back to Caine, his face was not hopeful. Slowly he shook his head.

"If there was any way I could help you, I would. But right now I just don't have anything."

Caine tried to keep from slumping down in his chair, but it was hard to do.

"I'm sorry," Doc said.

"That's okay," Caine said, thinking there was nothing even *remotely* okay about his situation. "I knew it was a long shot. Don't worry, I'll think of something."

Caine glanced down at the table so he wouldn't have to look into Doc's eyes. He slid the last french fry across the plate, scooping up ketchup from Doc's double-slit illustration. As he lifted the fry to his lips, a glob of ketchup dripped off the end and fell to the plate, splattering minuscule lines of red around its point of impact.

As Caine watched, he felt time slow.

. . .

The lines of red thicken, stretching out to the edges of the plate. The tiny drop is now a crimson puddle, growing, pulsing with life. It grows to such a mass that it begins to overflow, splashing onto the table, spraying red droplets into the air.

(92.8432 percent chance)

They fly in slow motion toward the faces of Doc and his colleague, tracing lines across their foreheads and cheeks, creating giant splotches on their shirts. The drops burn through their clothes and skin. Now the two doctors are bleeding; their dark red blood runs down their faces and spurts from their chests.

(96.1158 percent chance)

Caine stands, unable to catch his breath. Doc's mouth forms words, but there is no sound. His throat is filled with blood, which bubbles over his lips. Caine feels like all the oxygen is sucked from the room. He gasps, but there is nothing, only emptiness and an intense pain in his skull.

(99.2743 percent chance)

It's happening. Another seizure. But this doesn't feel like any other seizure. He has other visual hallucinations, but nothing like this. Nothing even close. He wishes he can scream, that he can stop what is happening, but he cannot—

Everything stops.

Doc, his friend, the other patrons are all still as statues; the blood hangs in the air like shimmering drops of red rain. And then, slowly, things start moving. But something is wrong. It takes Caine a moment to realize that everything is moving backward.

(98.3667 percent chance)

The red drops rush back toward their source. Wounds narrow and heal, but not before expelling tiny shards of glass, firing past Caine's face toward the giant window that is now a gaping hole in the wall.

(94.7341 percent chance)

They move quickly as the twisted grill of the pickup truck appears from nowhere and begins backing out of the diner over their table. The truck is gone; the tiny chunks of glass join together like a giant jigsaw puzzle and fuse to re-create the plate-glass window.

. . .

Caine gasped.

Doc and his friend were as they were before—intact, unbroken. Caine looked down at the plate, and the pool of blood was gone, replaced by a tiny glob of ketchup. He opened his mouth in shock, and the fry slipped between his fingers and fell to the floor.

"David. David?" It was Doc, the usual mirth-filled look on his face replaced with worry. "Are you all right?"

"Huh?" Caine said, shaking his head as if he were waking from a nap. "What happened?"

Blood . . . so much blood.

"You spaced out for a few seconds." Doc stared at Caine.

Caine blinked rapidly and returned Doc's stare, but all he could see was the blood streaming down his face. Slowly Caine reached out his shaking hand. Doc didn't move. Caine braced himself, expecting to feel the wet, sticky, unmistakable sensation of blood. But when his trembling fingers touched Doc's face, all he felt was the beginning of a five o'clock shadow. The blood was gone.

"Rain Man?" Doc said, softer this time, as if he were afraid to wake a sleeping tiger in the next room. Suddenly Caine understood. The truck. The truck had driven through the window and killed them all. Had? No, not had. Everything was so mixed up, jumbled in his brain. Not had—would. The truck *would* drive through the window. The only question was whether they would still be sitting here when it did.

. . .

(94.7341 percent chance)

. . .

"We have to move," Caine whispered hoarsely.

"What do you mean?" Doc asked.

"The truck . . . the blood," Caine said, aware of how unintelligible he sounded. "We're going to die unless we move."

"Okay, David, sure," Doc said, his voice assuming the reassuring tone people reserve for the unstable. "Let me just pay the check, and then we're gone. Cool?"

Caine shook his head. "No. Not cool. We have to go now!" he exclaimed, his voice rising, knowing—that was the right word, wasn't it?—*knowing*. Because he knew, somehow he knew, that there was a 94.7341 percent chance they had only ten more seconds to live.

"I think you need to take a deep breath and relax," Bow Tie Man said, wrinkling his nose. "You're causing a scene."

Caine closed his eyes and tried to think. Everything was so confusing, so out of whack. Was he having a schizophrenic break? It all seemed so real, but that's what Jasper had said it would be like. Still, the screaming in his brain told him he now had less than five seconds. In a split second, Caine decided on his course of action. He opened his eyes and stood up.

Four seconds left.

He shot out his hands and grabbed both of the old professors, one by each arm. He pulled them both to their feet.

Three seconds.

Caine stepped backward into someone—

. . .

She's a waitress, her name is Helen Bogarty, she lives in a five-story walk-up on Thirteenth Street, she decides to adopt a Chinese baby girl.

. . .

—dragging Doc and his friend with him.

Two.

"Hey!" the waitress screamed as four porcelain coffee mugs crashed to the floor. Caine didn't care. After the accident, neither would she.

"Down!" Caine screamed, pulling them all to the floor.

One.

The air was filled with sound—metal and flying glass. Caine didn't see this, as his eyes were squeezed shut, but he knew it. He could picture the scene as if it were a movie clip that he'd watched a million times. The thousands—19,483 to be exact—of glass shards in the air, the grille of the Chevrolet Silverado Z71 jutting through the hole, their table crushed beneath its tires, destroyed when the truck came smashing down after jumping up over the curb.

And then everything changed. It was different. The particles of glass flew through different trajectories, as they were robbed of the soft flesh they had buried themselves in before . . . but it wasn't before. It was now. But not *this* now. Another now. A now that would have happened but didn't.

It was then that Caine passed out. If he were sentient during that first second of unconsciousness, he would have understood everything. But he wasn't, so instead he felt nothing—and that was good enough . . . for now.

Smoke.

That was the first thing Caine sensed as he struggled back to consciousness. The smoke burned his lungs, stung his eyes. He could feel the heat all around him. Then he felt someone drag him through what remained of the restaurant. He could see light behind his closed lids, the air cool and clean, as his savior lowered him to the ground.

Caine sucked in a short, tentative breath and was relieved to discover he could once again breathe. He coughed and drank in the fresh air.

"David, are you all right?"

Caine squinted up at the silhouette above him. It was Doc. "Yeah, I think so." Doc reached out his hand and helped him into a sitting position. Caine looked around. He didn't see Bow Tie Man anywhere. "Where's . . . ?"

"I'm fine," Doc's friend said, walking over. "Thanks to you."

"Huh?" Caine's head was still spinning.

"If you hadn't made us move, that truck would have killed us." The professor tilted his head slightly and lowered his voice. "How did you know?"

Caine stared at him; the professor's hair was askew, and his perfectly tailored tweed jacket was badly singed. Caine didn't know what to say. He closed his eyes, trying to remember. The images that came to him were a tangled web, flashes edited together like a bad music video. Ketchup. Blood. Glass. Truck. Death.

"I . . . I don't know," Caine said, suddenly wanting to vomit. He struggled to his feet. When he heard the shriek of sirens, he decided it would be best if he weren't there when the police started to ask questions. "I have to leave." He turned to go, when he felt a strong grip on his arm.

"David, I think we should talk about what just happened," the professor said.

When Caine stared into the man's eyes, he didn't like what was there. "Nothing happened. I just saw the truck out of the corner of my eye. That's all. Now, let me go." Slowly Bow Tie Man released his grip on Caine's arm, but the look in his eyes did not change. Caine turned to Doc. "I'll call you later."

He turned to Bow Tie Man. "Good-bye, Professor."

"David, you can drop the formalities and just call me by my first name—it's Peter."

Caine didn't bother to respond. He just walked away.

Caine didn't know how long he spent wandering through the city. He zigzagged down the streets and avenues, letting the traffic lights choose his next direction. As he walked, the events at the diner replayed in his mind over and over.

There was no rational explanation. But that wasn't exactly true, was it? There was one very rational, plausible explanation, but he just didn't want to admit it: The antiseizure medication had pushed him over the edge—he was going insane. This was all part of a schizophrenic break, an incredibly realistic hallucination.

But it *had* happened. One look at his charred clothing proved that, didn't it? But what if that was a delusion, too? What if he was aimlessly wandering the city in perfectly clean clothes that he only *thought* were stained with smoke? Didn't that make more sense than . . . ? He didn't want to let himself even think it. Oh, hell, why not? Just form the word—precognition.

So that's what he was faced with.

Which was more plausible—that he was insane or psychic? He had to get ahold of himself. He needed to talk to someone. Crossing the street, he flipped open his cell phone. The display told him that he had missed the last three calls. In truth, he hadn't "missed" them at all, just avoided them.

Who do you call when you're going insane? Only one good answer to that one. Caine scrolled through his address book, selected the appropriate name, and then pressed "Talk." The voice on the other end answered after only one ring.

"Hi, this is Jasper, and this is my beep." *Beep.*

Caine thought about leaving a message but decided

against it. What would he say? *Hey, Jasper, I'm losing my mind. Call me back.* He snapped his phone shut, and it immediately started vibrating. He looked at the display before answering it, just in case it was Nikolaev again. It wasn't. He didn't know the number, but he recognized the extension—it was someone from Columbia.

"Hello?" Caine answered hesitantly.

"David, I'm glad I caught you. It's Peter."

Caine was silent.

"Listen, I'll cut right to the chase. I think I have an opportunity that might interest you. It would be worth two thousand dollars."

Caine stopped short. "Did you just say two grand?"

"Yes."

"You've got my attention."

"I'm currently doing a study, and I think you might be a good candidate. . . ."

Caine stared up at the ceiling and counted backward from a hundred. He hated needles, but it was worth it—in about ten minutes, he would be $2,000 richer. The lab tech removed the hypodermic from Caine's arm and replaced it with a piece of gauze.

"Just hold that there for about a minute," she said absently as she labeled the three vials of blood. Caine did as he was told, glad the day's events were almost over. He couldn't remember ever having had so many tests, even when he was first diagnosed with epilepsy. Four MRIs, three CAT scans, a urine sample, and one blood test. Peter had been very cagey when Caine asked what he was studying, but Caine didn't press the man despite his curiosity. The only thing that mattered was that he was paid in cash.

Once Caine had gotten off the phone with Peter the day before, he'd called up Nikolaev and cut a deal—Vitaly agreed to lay off the heat, and Caine agreed to pay him two grand a week for seven weeks—$14,000 in total. Caine had no idea where he was going to get the second installment, but what

Nikolaev didn't know wouldn't hurt him. All Caine needed was time. Given enough of it, he'd figure a way out.

An hour after his final blood test, Caine walked into Chernobyl; Nikolaev and Kozlov were waiting. Kozlov glared down at Caine, as if wishing for a reason to attack. Caine tried to ignore him and focus on Nikolaev.

"Hello, Vitaly."

"Caine, so glad you're back on your feet," Nikolaev said with an open smile. "But you look pale, no?"

"Just a long day," Caine said, still feeling slightly faint from the five-hour medical exam.

Nikolaev nodded. Caine knew that the man couldn't care less how he was feeling, as long as he got paid. Nikolaev put a strong hand on Caine's shoulder. "Let's go in the back and talk."

Caine followed Nikolaev down into the cellar, bending over as he descended the tight staircase, with Kozlov close behind. Once inside the *podvaal,* Caine blinked a few times to adjust his eyes to the dim light. There was a game going on in the corner, mostly regulars. He nodded at them and got a few nods in return from the ones who had already folded.

Caine entered Nikolaev's cramped office, which had just enough room for a couch, a tiny desk, and a swivel chair. He sat down on the couch, which was covered with scores of cigarette burns; Nikolaev sat behind the desk. Kozlov stood, leaning his massive frame against the wall, as if he were holding up the building.

Without waiting to be asked, Caine removed a thick wad of cash and counted out twenty one-hundred-dollar bills. Nikolaev picked a bill at random and held it up to the light to look for the watermark. Once he was satisfied, he folded the stack and made it disappear into his jacket pocket.

"Sorry about your apartment," Nikolaev said, "but it's just business."

"Of course," Caine said, as if it were a common business practice to steal a man's television, VCR, and stereo.

Nikolaev leaned forward, palms flat on his desk. "So where are you getting the cash to pay me back? I only ask because I am . . . concerned that this installment is both the first and the last."

Caine stood and smiled, not missing a beat. "Don't worry, I've got everything covered."

Nikolaev nodded. Caine didn't think the man believed him, but it didn't matter. Either Caine would come up with another two grand in a week or Kozlov would break his arm. It was that simple. Nikolaev stood and shook Caine's hand, his grip just a little too tight, his eyes cold and sharp.

"Would you like to stay for lunch? On the house."

"Thanks, but I already ate," Caine said. The last thing he wanted to do was hang around Nikolaev's one second longer than he had to. "Maybe next time."

"Sure," Nikolaev said, "next time."

Dr. Tversky read through Caine's medical file for the fifth time. He practically had it memorized, but he still felt compelled to read it again, focusing in on Caine's dopamine levels and the chemical analysis of the experimental antiseizure medication. It was all right there. Caine's physician had stumbled onto the triggering agent without even realizing it. All Tversky had to do now was tweak his current formula and then . . .

He was reluctant about trying the new medication on Julia before running an animal trial, but the clock was ticking. She'd said it herself: Every second that passed was one in which the shaky balance of her brain chemistry could change, and he would lose his chance. The mistake wasn't in action, but in *in*action. He had to start now.

He returned to the file, reading it over again to make sure he hadn't missed anything. He would have only one chance, so he needed to be absolutely certain it would lead to success. If it did, he would know what moves he should make next. In fact, he would know more than that.

He would know everything.

"Are you ready?" Mr. Sheridan was so excited he looked like he was going to burst out of his cheap suit. The Powerball publicity rep's giant plastic smile made Tommy sick to his stomach.

Just nerves, that's all. You're nervous because you're about to be famous.

But Tommy knew that wasn't true. He'd felt like vomiting from the second he awoke, hours before he even knew he was going to be on TV. The acid sloshing around in his belly was due not to his impending fame but rather to his dreamless sleep the night before.

There'd been a time when he viewed his dreams as a curse, when he would have given anything for a night to pass without being haunted by the giant glowing numbers. But now he realized that without them he was empty, alone. He tried to shake the feeling.

It makes sense that they stopped. I don't need them anymore. I won.

He knew that was true, but it didn't make him feel any better.

"Come on, let's go," Mr. Sheridan said with a wide grin, slapping Tommy hard on his back. Tommy followed Mr. Sheridan out the door and onto the miniature podium that the Multi-State Lottery Association had set up for the occasion. He stared out at the crowd of photographers, but before he got a good look he was blinded by scores of flashbulbs, all of which seemed to explode simultaneously, quickly followed by the whirring and clicking sounds of the cameras.

Tommy put on his best smile, suddenly glad the makeup woman had spent twenty minutes covering up his zits. Mesmerized by the lights, he nearly jumped when he felt Mr. Sheridan's hand on his shoulder.

". . . Our winner is a twenty-eight-year-old cashier living in Manhattan. He is now worth over 247 MILLION DOLLARS!" Mr. Sheridan's already enormous smile somehow grew even larger. "That is, until Uncle Sam takes out *his* piece." All the reporters laughed politely. "Now, without further ado, I'm happy to present Mr. Thomas DaSouza!"

Mr. Sheridan took a step to the side and pulled Tommy in front of the bouquet of microphones growing out of the podium. More flashbulbs popped as reporters shouted out his name. Mr. Sheridan leaned in front of Tommy.

"Please, one at a time." He looked around the crowd and then pointed. "First we'll hear from Penny, then Joel."

A platinum blonde in a bright red pantsuit popped up from her chair with a smile. "How does it feel to be a multi-millionaire?"

Tommy looked over at Mr. Sheridan, who nodded at him, motioning to the microphones. Tommy bent down slightly, trying as best as he could to speak into the entire nest. "Pretty cool." Laughter.

"How did you choose your numbers?" a balding man shouted out.

"I dreamed them." The second the words left his mouth, he knew it had been a mistake, but it was too late. The reporters all shouted in unison.

"One at a time, one at a time!" Mr. Sheridan yelled over them. "Curtis, Bethany, Mike, and then Bruce."

A large black man stood up to get Tommy's attention. "How long have you been having these dreams?"

"Almost all my life, I guess."

"What were they like?" asked a woman who'd had one too many face-lifts.

Tommy closed his eyes for a moment, remembering the giant floating orbs. "They were beautiful."

For the next fifteen minutes Tommy was asked everything from "Do you believe in God?" to "Are you a Republican or a Democrat?" Tommy answered the questions he knew and stammered "I don't know" to the ones he didn't. By the time Mr. Sheridan cut off the reporters ten minutes later, Tommy felt like he was flying.

He was happy. For the first time in as long as he could remember, Thomas William DaSouza felt happy. But as he rode home in the limousine provided by the nice folks at the Multi-State Lottery Association, he couldn't help but wonder about his dreams—and what his life would be like if they really were over.

Nava tried to pull up Tversky's photo, but there was nothing there. Grimes must have been updating the images on the server; she would have to check back later to see what her prey looked like.

Next she reviewed his personal information. Twice married, twice divorced, Tversky lived alone in a modest one-bedroom. Although the first marriage had ended because of "irreconcilable differences," his second wife had charged Tversky with mental cruelty and adultery, citing an affair with one of his students.

Such an affair shouldn't have been too surprising to the second Mrs. Tversky, considering that she, too, was a former student and probably the reason Tversky's first marriage had ended. Nava made a note to have Grimes run a check on all of Tversky's female students' phone records to determine which one he was sleeping with now. From what Nava had heard about Grimes, he would enjoy prying into their sex lives.

Although she probably wouldn't need the information, Nava was a firm believer in being overprepared. If she had to kidnap Tversky, knowing every detail of his personal life could be useful in unnerving him.

Next she turned her attention to his résumé. He finished college at the age of nineteen, graduating with honors from Caltech with a B.S. in mathematics and an M.A. in biology. He did his doctoral work on the East Coast at Johns Hopkins, where he received a Ph.D. in biostatistics before his twenty-fourth birthday. After that, his résumé was a "who's who" of top schools—Stanford, Penn, Harvard, and then Columbia. Along the way he earned research grants from the NIH, WHO, CDC, and, not surprisingly, the NSA.

Nava shook her head. Another genius who thought he could change the world with the help of his government. Yes, they gave him money, but in the end he became just another political tool. She, too, had been naïve once, a weapon of her own native government. But through a fortunate turn of world events, that had all changed over a decade ago.

Her free-agent status was ironic considering her communist upbringing. She doubted that Dmitry would have approved, but would he have blamed her? She doubted that, too. It didn't matter. Dmitry Zaitsev was long since dead, as dead as Tanja Aleksandrova was—the little girl she'd once been before becoming Nava Vaner.

Changing her identity had been like putting on a new pair of jeans. At first it was uncomfortable—stiff in places, too loose in others. But over time it melded to her so completely it became like a second skin. After a while she began to forget Tanja altogether, until she was nothing more than a distant memory, like an old friend she hadn't seen since childhood.

Now Nava was no one. No loyalties, no family, no country, no consequences. She'd been living this way for so long she'd forgotten what it was like to really feel. Nava wanted to change that, but she knew it was impossible unless she got out. She would again start a new life, but this time she would do it right. The only thing standing in her way was Dr. Tversky and his Alpha Subject.

She had to figure out the subject's identity in the next thirty-six hours. If she couldn't piece together enough information from the file, then she would be forced to tail Tversky. If that didn't work, she would have to extract the information forcibly. However, once she went down that path, she would have to hold the doctor captive until she acquired the Alpha Subject. Either that or kill him. Neither option was attractive.

There had to be an easier way, some type of clue in his notes that would lead Nava to the Alpha Subject's identity. It was there—she'd just have to find it. For the next three hours, Nava pored over the thousand-plus-page file, searching for an answer. Just as she was about to give up, she found what she was looking for:

> The Alpha Subject was then administered 5 mg of phenytoin (1 mg for every 10 kg of body mass).

That was it. If the dosage was 1 milligram for every 10 kilograms of body mass, then the Alpha Subject weighed approximately 50 kilograms, or 110 pounds. Nava smiled. Of course—the Alpha Subject was a woman. After reading through Tversky's philandering history, she should have known. Probably someone in his lab. Grabbing her coat, Nava rushed out of her office, on the hunt for a 110-pound female grad student.

With a giant gut, pocked skin, and thick matted hair, Elliot Samuelson didn't have much of a social life and thus spent almost all his waking hours in the lab. He was exactly what Nava was looking for. She found him at a hot-dog stand just outside one of Columbia's science buildings.

Under normal circumstances, Nava would have developed a relationship with Samuelson over a period of weeks, slowly extracting the information she needed without raising any suspicion. However, today she had no time for subtlety. Instead she assumed the identity of a private investigator working on behalf of one of Tversky's ex-wives. At first Elliot had been reluctant to answer Nava's questions, but once she slipped him a hundred, she could barely get him to shut up. After listening to him list all the physical attributes of nearly every woman in the lab, Nava finally interrupted.

"Are there any petite women? Say around a hundred and ten pounds?"

"Hmmm," Elliot thought out loud as he scratched his arm. "There's Mary Wu, she's kinda small. Although I haven't seen her around lately because she's been in Cambridge coauthoring some article with a muckety-muck at *Hahvahd.*"

Nava mentally crossed Wu off the list of grad students Grimes had given her. According to Tversky's files, he had been experimenting on the Alpha Subject at least twice a week for the past three months. Elliot continued.

"Candace Rappaport and Marla Parker are both tiny, but Candace is engaged and I heard Marla is a lesbian."

Even though Elliot had eliminated the two women, Nava did not. In her experience being engaged didn't rule out affairs, and she put no stock in Elliot's lesbian theory. She went through the remaining names, but according to Elliot no one else fit the bill. Nava was about to leave when Elliot stopped her.

"Wait, there's someone else."

"Oh, really?"

"Yeah. Technically she's not part of our lab because she's an NYU student, but she's been working up here on an exchange program for the past couple years. Anyway, she's tiny, like five-one or five-two, but I don't think she's your girl."

"Why is that?"

"I dunno." Elliot shrugged. "She's just weird. Especially lately. Like, the last couple weeks, she's always wearing a baseball cap. I know it bugs her, because she's always scratching her head and adjusting it so that it doesn't get in the way when she uses the microscope, but she never takes it off."

"Anything else?" Nava asked, her mind spinning. Although the girl could just have a bad haircut, Nava suspected a different reason for her sudden affinity for hats.

"Nothing else, except for the rhyming."

Nava froze. Tversky had written that the Alpha Subject had exhibited a few signs of schizophrenia, including disorganized speech—specifically, rhyming.

"What do you mean?" she asked.

"Lately she'll be talking and she'll say something like 'Hey, I'm going to get some lunch-*crunch-hunch-punch.*' It's fucking weird."

Nava acted uninterested, despite the fact that her heart was galloping in her chest. She didn't want Elliot to remember her being so focused on the girl the same day Nava intended to make her disappear.

"I'll check her out anyway, even though she's probably not the right girl," Nava said. "What was her name again?"

When Julia caught sight of herself in the mirror, she jumped—momentarily terrified that some hideous stranger had sneaked into her bathroom.

It's only me. That's what I look like now. Remember?

She bit her quivering lip. Though she had never been vain, Julia had always thought her hair, albeit mousy and unmanageable, was her best feature. Now it was all gone. She traced her finger across her bald scalp, which was covered with sharp brown stubble.

She could see the eight circles that Petey had drawn on her head to mark where to insert the leads. In the center of each dark blue circle was a tiny red puncture mark. She gently poked at one and winced. It was still sore from the night before. Julia sniffed loudly, holding back the tears. The voice in her brain she recognized as her conscience railed at her.

How could he do this to you?

—He doesn't do anything that we don't both want.

Are you kidding? Look in the mirror! Did you want *to shave your head? Did you* want *him to make you look like a human paint-by-numbers?*

—Stop it. He loves me, and I love him. Besides, we're so close to the end—

The only thing you're close to is getting killed. Already the drugs have messed with your system so much you sleep half the day. You hardly eat anymore, you're emaciated. Stop it, before it's too late. I'm begging you—

—NO. I finally have someone, and I'm happy. Why can't you just leave me alone?

Julia closed her eyes and chased the self-doubt from her mind, repeating over and over, *He loves me. He loves me. He loves me.*

Once she felt more like herself, she opened her eyes and put on her wig. It didn't look exactly like her old hair, but it was close enough. She'd been wearing it for two weeks, and so far nobody had noticed. Except for Petey, no one ever looked at her. Not really.

As Julia left her apartment and hurried across the street,

she passed by a tall brunette smoking a cigarette. Disgusting. She never understood smokers, especially beautiful women like that. Why they insisted on such self-destructive behavior was beyond her. She looked at her watch—2:19 P.M. She would have to run if she wanted to be at the lab in time.

Petey didn't like to be kept waiting.

Nava smoked the last of her cigarette, then crushed it beneath her boot. She decided to let Julia Pearlman get half a block ahead before following her. Nava wasn't worried about being spotted—the girl looked way too frazzled to pay any attention to her surroundings. Besides, it wasn't like Nava was doing any long-term surveillance. The second she had an opportunity, Nava would grab her.

She followed Julia for seven blocks and watched from across the street as Julia entered the ten-story building that housed Tversky's lab. After flashing her ID at the security guard, Julia disappeared from sight. Nava waited a few minutes before following her into the building. She sauntered up to the guard, putting on her most flirtatious smile.

"Excuse me, I was supposed to meet my girlfriend twenty minutes ago, but she hasn't shown up. Is there another way out of the building?"

"No, ma'am," the guard responded, trying to suck in his gut. "Except for the emergency exits, the only way out is to come by me."

"Thanks," Nava said. "I must have missed her."

Nava exited through the revolving door, crossed the street, and bought a fresh pack of Parliaments from a newsstand. Keeping her eyes on the building, she tapped out a cigarette. After the first rush of nicotine hit her bloodstream, she let herself drift. She knew she was in for a long wait, but Nava didn't mind—she'd found the Alpha Subject.

Any doubts she had were dispelled as soon as Nava caught sight of the bad wig beneath Julia's baseball cap. It all made sense. If Tversky was constantly monitoring Julia's brain waves, then he would want to insert the electrodes at the same point each session. The easiest way to do that, of course, was to shave her head.

When Julia left the lab, Nava would follow her, force her into the van she had parked down the street, and turn her over to the RDEI, along with the disk containing the unedited version of Tversky's research. Then Nava would catch the next flight to São Paolo, change IDs, get on another plane to Buenos Aires, and disappear. It was that simple.

All she had to do was wait until Julia left the building. After that, everything would take care of itself.

Even though Caine pretended he was just taking a walk, he knew it was a lie. By sundown he found himself on Mott Street across from Wong's Szechwan Palace, staring at the restaurant's flashing neon sign that featured yellow noodles piled high in an oversize red bowl. He felt his wallet, which held everything he had. He could do it. He knew he could. If he just slowed down his play and took a breather whenever he felt like he was going to tilt, he could win.

Of course, that's what he had told himself before he'd walked into Nikolaev's and lost eleven grand. But that was different. A onetime, low-probability event. Incredible bad luck like that meant he was due for some good luck. Simple regression to the mean. He exhaled a long, deep breath.

Caine didn't want to gamble, but he had no choice. In six days he owed Nikolaev another $2,000, and the little money Caine had wouldn't be enough to stop Kozlov from putting him in the hospital. If he could just win $267 a day for the next six days, he'd be able to pay the next installment and still have $40 left over for food. Caine had been on much better streaks before. Back when he was an addict, he once won over three grand in a marathon Hold 'Em game that had lasted thirty-six hours.

When he was an addict.

Funny. Like he wasn't an addict now. Right. Besides his Gamblers Anonymous sponsor, he wasn't fooling anyone. And Caine probably wasn't even fooling him—not that he really cared. Thanks to Nikolaev, Caine had finally learned his lesson. He was getting out, right after this. If he just played smart, he would be fine.

Once he worked off his debt, he'd quit for real. He would go to five meetings a day, whatever it took. Caine nodded to himself, agreeing with his plan. Feeling nervous but confident, he crossed the street and walked into the restaurant. The girl who worked out front barely looked up as he breezed by. Caine navigated through the noisy kitchen to the back room.

Even though the club seemed pretty sketchy, Caine knew that Billy Wong's was one of the safest places in the city. Everyone knew that Billy's brother was Jian Wong—the *dai lo dai,* or chief—of the Ghost Shadows, the largest and most ruthless Chinese gang in New York. Along with the Flying Dragons, the Ghost Shadows controlled everything in Chinatown, from drugs and prostitution to gambling and loansharking. Yeah, Caine was perfectly safe.

"Long time no see!" Billy Wong announced when he spotted Caine on the other side of the steel-reinforced door. Despite his Chinese heritage, Billy's accent was all Brooklyn. "C'mon in!" he said, wrapping his arm around Caine's shoulders.

"Good to see you, too, Billy," Caine said, finding to his surprise that it was.

"You have cash?" Billy asked casually, as if he wanted to know the time.

"Billy, you know me," Caine said.

"Yes, and I also know Vitaly Nikolaev. Word is that you're into him for twenty large."

"It's down to twelve, including interest, and I've got it covered."

"Of course you do," Billy said, eyes sparkling. "But I

gotta tell you up front that I won't be able to extend any credit. Nothin' personal."

Caine nodded, the gravity of his situation pressing at his lungs. No love was lost between Billy and Nikolaev; in fact, they openly despised each other. So if Billy knew that Caine was into Nikolaev, everyone in town must also know. He would have to win his way back to the plus side strictly on his own bankroll.

"I'm feeling lucky today, Billy. I won't need any credit."

Billy threw back his head and laughed. "Of course not!" He clapped Caine on the back. "So how much are you cashing in?"

Caine reached in his pocket and removed his entire roll—$438. He counted it all out except for $20—enough to get a few shots at Cedar's just in case things didn't work out so well. Billy gave Caine his chips and then led him over to the table, even going so far as to pull out his chair.

When Caine sat down, the rest of the players looked up expectantly, hoping to see the cherubic young face of some rich Wall Street type with a fat wallet who was new to the scene. They were disappointed when they saw Caine. Even though most of the men didn't know who he was, one look at the circles beneath his eyes and his washed-out face told them everything they needed to know: He was no rookie; he was one of them. Maybe he was good, and maybe he wasn't, but he was no fish.

The men gave Caine a perfunctory nod and then returned to their cards. Caine watched the hand play through, hoping to learn a tiny bit about the players before they dealt him in. The pot went to a bird-faced man in the corner who bet hard on the deal and then got everyone out after the flop. He smiled a crooked grin as he raked the chips, stupidly flashing everyone his pair of queens.

Judging from how quickly everyone got out when Birdface was betting, Caine judged him to be a show-off who rarely stayed in unless he had something good. Now all Caine had to do was figure out who the hell everyone else was, get some good hands, play cool, and win. The second he was up $267, he would stop. He wouldn't get carried away, he wouldn't push his luck—he would just stand up and leave.

Piece of cake.

CHAPTER twelve

Tversky watched Julia's EEG readout, his hands trembling. He had already been so close in his own research that it had taken him only a few hours to synthesize the necessary serum to stimulate simultaneous brain-wave maximization. He stared down at Julia's limp form, sprawled out on the table. It had been almost ten minutes since he'd given her the last injection. At this point her brain chemistry should be almost identical to Caine's. Now all he could do was wait. All the theories and puzzles that had led him to this point bounced around his mind. Einstein's Theory of Relativity. Heisenberg's Uncertainty Principle. Schrödinger's Cat. Deutsch's Multiverse. And, of course, Laplace's Demon.

None of the famous thinkers except for Laplace would have thought this was possible. Of course, none of them had seen what he had seen. They weren't in that diner. And hadn't Maxwell proved that the laws of physics were not absolute? What would he have said about Tversky's theory? Infinitely improbable, but not impossible?

Suddenly Julia turned to him. Her eyes were still closed when she began to talk, her voice low. "What is that terrible smell?"

The smell was unlike anything she'd ever experienced. It was so powerful that Julia didn't think the word "smell" was even appropriate.

This must be it. This must be the beginning, the aura. Julia's heart skipped a beat in her chest. She knew she had to focus, but the smell was overpowering, clawing at her nose, eyes, and throat. The remains of her lunch suddenly flooded her mouth; she coughed up the chunky liquid, savoring the bitter taste as it flowed across her tongue, grateful for the momentary distraction from the smell.

She rolled off the table and crashed to the floor. She could hear Petey shouting something, but he was so far away. She pushed herself onto her hands and knees, her face inches from the yellowish puddle of vomit. Although her eyes were squeezed shut, she could still see the congealing pool below her. Behind closed lids, her pupils traced the movements of every bacterium, every molecule.

She could feel her consciousness slipping away. Was this it, or was she passing out? No, she couldn't let Petey down. She had come so far—she couldn't let go without an answer. She had to concentrate. Her clouded brain tried to obey, but it couldn't; desperately she tried to grasp the question that had brought her here, to this place. And then she could see it . . . and she knew.

. . .

It is more than complicated, because it is infinite. It is eternity, stretching out in all directions at once, a twisting road so convoluted that it resembles a plane rather than a path. But the plane is not alone—at every intersection among the quadrillions of nodes that make up its surface is another plane, expanding at impossible angles, twisting and turning, folding in on itself over and over again.

. . .

Julia was screaming. The mind-numbing pain filled her entire being. Her back arched as her head shot up, then slammed into the floor. It was then that she heard the Voice. She knew the Voice from another time. It was one among a trillion she now knew, but she knew this one in a different way.

The Voice was whispering to her. It promised that it would let her go if only she looked at a tiny piece of the great eternity. Just one piece, and then it would all be over. Just one piece.

. . .

So she looks. Since everything is everywhere, wherever she looks, it is there. Sorting it out from everything else is the challenge. And then she sees it, right there . . . but it isn't singular, rather a million, a billion. So many are the same, but so many are different, from the extreme to the minute.

She can write a thousand books on the When *that she wants to know. And yet there is no time. No time . . . funny. Here there is in fact no time, but there, back in the* When *she is from, she knows that her time is running out. There in the* When, *she has time only to tell him what to do.*

. . .

Julia lifted her head to speak her message. Her voice was faint. Petey bent his ear so close to her mouth that his hair tickled her face. As she spoke,

. . .

she can see the planes shift in response, the everywhen *changing. And finally it is the* everywhen, *shifting and molding to conform to the shape of her flowing words that tears apart her sanity. It is more than she can take, the* everywhen *evolving before her eyes, and her at the center. Too much, too much, too . . .*

. . .

Julia felt herself exhale, thinking, no, not thinking, knowing—

. . .

for she can see herself now, in the middle of the everywhen—*that her time is almost over.*

. . .

She needed to hold on. There was still so much for her to do. She hoped that she would have time. And then,

. . .

because Julia wishes it, She shows her the way to help make it so.

. . .

Julia fell limp in his arms, and Tversky shivered. He felt for a pulse. It was there. Weak, but there. He pulled back one lid and then the other, but all he saw was white. Julia's eyes had rolled back into her skull. He gently slapped her face to try to rouse her, but he knew it was pointless.

Every instinct cried out that she was gone. He put her back on the table and reconnected the EEG leads that had been dislodged in her fall. At first he thought the electrodes had been damaged, but then he realized the truth—there was no brain activity. Nothing. The consciousness that had been Julia Pearlman had vanished; her heart still beat weakly in her chest, but her mind was destroyed.

Tversky desperately looked around the lab, trying to figure out what to do. He wanted to sit down and catch his breath, but he knew there wasn't time. How was he going to explain this? His skin was instantly covered in a cold sweat, and he started to hyperventilate.

He looked at the clock on the wall—11:37 P.M. The janitorial staff came through around midnight—only twenty-three minutes. He had to think. He could call an ambulance. She was still alive; maybe they could save her. But one look at Julia told him this wasn't an option. Her skull was still covered with pen marks. And if she died, there would be an autopsy. They would know.

The medical examiner would detect the chemicals in her blood. It wouldn't take a genius to figure out Tversky's involvement. Simply calling would guarantee that he would become a suspect. He wanted so desperately to run out of the lab as fast as he could, but there was the security guard. He would remember Tversky's leaving so late at night.

Christ. What had he been thinking? He'd always been so careful—why hadn't he made a contingency plan? He stared at Julia, hatred in his eyes. The fucking cunt was going to die right here in his lab and ruin everything.

Twenty-one minutes.

Tversky ran his sweaty hands through his hair and began pacing around the room. There was no way he could pull this off. He was fucked. On the eve of the most important scientific discovery on the planet, he was going to prison.

Twenty minutes.

Time was passing too fast. He needed a way out. He needed . . . a window. He raced over to the window and heaved. It groaned in protest, but he was able to force it open. Holding on to the frame, he leaned outside and craned his neck to look down at the alleyway six stories below. It could work. If he was smart and didn't panic, he could make it work.

He hurried over to the sink and filled his hands with the industrial-strength pink cleaning solution. He had to wash the marks off her head. As he scrubbed her scalp, he made a mental list of all the other things he needed to do . . .

Eighteen minutes.

. . . before the janitorial staff arrived. Once she was clean and he'd mopped the vomit off the floor, he would have to hide the data—the video recording, the EEG readouts, his notes—everything had to be copied and then erased. Finally in control of his breathing, Tversky took a step back to view his handiwork. The pen marks were gone. Unfortunately, there was nothing he could do about the tiny red welts. Perhaps if her skull were crushed in the fall, the sores might be overlooked. He could only hope.

He hoisted her body up over his shoulder and carried it across the room. He had positioned it against the window frame when he heard the sound. A long, low moan. He stared at her face, looking for some sign that she was back but there was nothing to see except her slackened jaw.

Nine minutes.

For a moment he froze, realizing that once he completed this final act, there was no turning back. And then she moaned again. It was a quiet, horrible sound. Tversky would have thought it was impossible for any noise to be filled with so much sadness. Her voice sounded like the mewling of a dying animal.

Eight minutes.

He couldn't take it. He would go mad if he had to listen to that sound any longer. Using all his strength, he heaved her body out the window. A second later there was a crash followed by a loud smacking sound. And then nothing. Tversky exhaled a huge sigh of relief.

Tidying up the lab and burning his data onto a CD should take only a few minutes. He would be out before the cleaning crew arrived and then home a half hour after that. He couldn't wait to review the videotape. She had said so much he was barely able to take it all in, although one part kept repeating itself over and over in his mind.

"Kill him," Julia had whispered. "Kill David Caine."

PART II

MINIMIZING ERRORS

Penetrating so many secrets, we cease to believe in the unknowable.
But there it sits nevertheless, calmly licking its chops.

—Henry Louis Mencken, author

Sometimes I've believed as many as six impossible things before breakfast.

—The White Queen, monarch in Wonderland

CHAPTER thirteen

Nava raced across the street when she heard the crash. It was too dark to see what had fallen, but she had a sickening suspicion it was a person. As Nava entered the alleyway, she was taken aback by the stench of rotting meat. She covered her nose with her hand and pushed through the ring of torn-open garbage bags that surrounded the Dumpsters, ignoring the scratching and squeaking sounds from the rats that darted out of her path.

Then she saw the body. The woman was naked and entirely hairless, except for a small tuft of pubic hair. Her limbs bent back at unnatural angles, giving her the appearance of a mannequin. The only sign she'd once been alive was the long gash across her stomach that was still leaking blood.

Nava gently turned the dead woman's head. Even though her face was twisted in anguish, there was no doubt as to her identity. It was Julia Pearlman—the Alpha Subject. Nava's heart sank. The RDEI would not accept yet another missed deliverable. Without the Alpha Subject, they would either have Nava killed or turn her over to the SVR.

Immediately Nava felt a wave of guilt, realizing she hadn't stopped for a second to mourn the poor dead girl. How had things gotten so fucked up? When had she become so cold that she could think of only herself? But even as she questioned herself, the part of Nava's brain dedicated to self-preservation kept working, desperate to find a way out.

She removed a tissue from her pocket, wiped it against

Julia Pearlman's wound, then wrapped it in a piece of plastic torn from a trash bag. She hoped that maybe a blood sample would appease the RDEI until she thought of something else. Then she heard a sound that made her heart stop.

The dead girl was talking.

Julia said what she needed to say.

Now it was finally time to rest.

Now. The word rolled over in her mind; it seemed so foolish. She remembered how important it had all seemed, but that time was over. In 3.652 seconds there would be no more *Now.* Only the pure and beautiful *everywhen.* And in the *everywhen,* there was no smell. If nothing else, for that, she was grateful.

Julia took one final, shuddering gasp and opened her eyes.

Caine was up $360 in less than four hours. Almost $100 more than the $267 he'd planned. He knew he should get up and walk away, but he just couldn't. Instead he told himself the same old stories: He was on a roll. He was in the zone. And, of course, the mother of all gamblers' lies: *The second the cards go against me, I'll quit.*

But then he lost a stupid $80 pot; his trip tens got beat by a river straight. And then he did exactly what he promised himself he wouldn't do—he tilted. He was so pissed about losing the $80 that he refused to fold the next five hands even though his cards were crap. He knew he was playing like shit, but he couldn't stop. His large pile of chips, built up over hours of conservative playing, disappeared in less than thirty minutes.

After he lost the last of his stake, Caine stood up silently and left. Out on the cold street, he jammed his fists into his pockets to keep warm. His sole twenty-dollar bill rubbed against his knuckles, mocking him. He didn't even feel like using it for its intended purpose—to get drunk.

Instead he took a circuitous route home, embracing the cold during his two-hour walk, ripping into himself the entire time. How could he have been so fucking stupid? It wasn't enough that he was into Nikolaev for twelve grand, but he had to gamble away his last $400 on top of that?

Absently Caine wondered if Peter had any more experiments he could participate in.

Outside his brother's apartment building, Jasper checked his watch for the fifth time that minute—12:19:37—seven hours since David went to the card room. The Voice said that they were coming soon. Jasper had wanted to bring his gun, but the Voice said no, so he left the weapon lying on the coffee table.

He checked his watch again, just in time to see the digital readout change to 12:20:00. It was almost time. Despite the cold, Jasper was sweating profusely, anticipating the beating he was about to endure. He had taken beatings before, but they'd all been at the hands of orderlies at Mercy and ended with a blissful injection of Thorazine. He had never been in a street fight, and there sure as hell wasn't going to be any pharmaceutical treat tonight.

But the Voice said he had to do it to protect David, so here he was.

They're coming now. Relax. It will all be over soon.

Just then a black Town Car pulled up to the curb, headlights blazing. The driver barreled out of the Lincoln without bothering to kill the engine. A second later he was standing in front of Jasper, glowering down on him. Jasper had just enough time to remember the giant Russian's name when Kozlov punched him in the stomach. The air whooshed out of his lungs, and Jasper doubled over. Kozlov forced him up, grabbing him by the hair, and slugged him in the jaw. The world went black.

When the blackness faded, Jasper's face was being crushed in between the freezing sidewalk and Kozlov's boot.

"Vitaly wanted me to give you a message, Caine. He said for you to remember that your money isn't for gambling, it's for *paying*. If you have extra money, you pay Vitaly. You don't blow it with the Chinks, eh?"

Kozlov's boot pressed harder onto his skull, until Jasper realized he was supposed to speak.

"Okay, okay! I got it!"

"Good."

Kozlov lifted his boot, and Jasper swore he could feel his skull pucker out. Then Kozlov felt around Jasper's pockets until he found a wallet, but the Russian threw it back at him in disgust when he found only a single dollar bill. The Voice had warned Jasper to clean out his wallet before the encounter.

Kozlov bent down close to Jasper's face. "I will see you in five days," he said, and punched Jasper in the mouth for good measure. Jasper's head bounced off the sidewalk, and he slipped into unconsciousness.

Tversky didn't let himself exhale until he heard the click of his dead bolt. He'd made it. He dropped his duffel bag on the floor and collapsed into a wingback chair. Closing his eyes, he tried to process everything that had happened in the last thirty minutes. His mind raced, stopping for a moment to inspect one detail and then speeding back down his personal timeline to absorb another.

He tried to center himself. Everything had happened so fast. He needed a drink. He went over to the liquor cabinet, poured himself four fingers of single-malt scotch, and took a long swig, savoring the feel of the liquid as it burned down his throat. He polished off the rest while standing, then quickly refilled his glass. When he finally returned to his chair, the world had taken on a warm glow.

"Better," he said aloud. "Much better."

After he finished his second glass, Tversky slid the videocassette into his VCR. On the way back to his chair, he took another refill. Half a bottle later, he aimed the remote at the black rectangular box with a wobbly hand and pressed "Play."

He watched himself on the screen, transfixed by the bright image. He said the time and the date and then introduced the Alpha Subject (it was easier for him this way, to think of her as just another part of the experiment, rather than as a person—as a person he'd murdered), who was already unconscious on the table. Then he injected her with what he now knew would be her final dosage.

Her EEG played out in the corner of the screen, the four lines gently rising and falling. At first only the theta waves rose with any intensity, while the others languished like soft ripples in a pond. Then the EKG began beeping excitedly and all of the waves spiked, moving up the graph like a tidal wave. He slowed the VCR, his eyes glued to the screen, trying to understand where he'd gone right—or wrong.

But there was nothing to see. Just an EEG graph that should have been impossible and the image of a woman whose eyes were moving so quickly behind her closed lids they looked like they might burst. Then she vomited and rolled off the table in a quick jerk, out of camera range. The image on the screen was now static, showing only the empty metal table.

He pressed "Play" to return the video to its normal speed so that he could once again hear her last words. He turned up the volume. Surrounded by the hissing of the tape, her voice, barely a whisper, took on an eerie quality. She spoke for exactly three minutes and twelve seconds, her speech speeding up and slowing down as if she were talking to him while riding a roller coaster.

Some segments were entirely incoherent, but others were incredibly lucid and included detailed instructions for every possible scenario. After the sixth time through, he turned off the television. The room was suddenly quiet, but the Alpha Subject's first few words rushed to fill the silence in his mind.

Kill him. Kill David Caine.

He had hoped her instructions had been anything other than what they'd seemed. But now, after listening to her hoarse whisper over and over, there was no denying it. If he wanted to obtain the knowledge, then he had no choice but to do as she had instructed.

He stumbled over to his desk and logged on to the Internet. Once the page loaded, he typed the query beneath Google's colorful logo; 0.63 seconds later the screen listed the first 10 of 175,000 hits. He clicked on the seventh link, just as Julia had instructed. The front page of the site read:

> Information contained on this site deals with activities and devices that may be in violation of various federal, state, and local laws. The webmasters of this site do not advocate the breaking of any law and bear no liability. Our files are for INFORMATIONAL PURPOSES ONLY.
>
> Please click ENTER if you have read and agree with the terms and conditions explained above.

Tversky hurriedly clicked the hyperlink. When the screen reloaded, he began to read.

Nava collapsed into her black Aeron chair, which bounced gently as it adjusted to her weight. She flicked on her desk lamp, which illuminated her workstation in a soft white light and cast the rest of the darkened office deeper into shadow.

She pressed her thumb against the square glass panel. There was a quick flash of light, and her thumb glowed a rosy pink. The flat screen flashed two words.

> FINGERPRINT CONFIRMED

She was in. She didn't bother reading any of the latest data downloads from Tversky's laptop. Instead she navigated through the system until she reached the application commonly known as the "Phone Book."

The program was hooked in to every government database, including the Central Intelligence Agency, Federal Bureau of Investigation, Social Security Administration, Citizenship and Immigration Services, and, of course, the

Internal Revenue Service. If the man Julia Pearlman had spoken of existed, the Phone Book would know.

As Nava wasn't sure of the spelling of his name, she keyed in multiple entries.

LAST NAME: cane, cain, caine, kane, kain, kaine
FIRST NAME: david
CITY: new york city
STATE: ny

She hit "Enter" and waited while the computer searched its databanks. She didn't have to wait long.

SIX MATCHES TO SEARCH QUERY

1. Cane, David L.—14 Middaugh Street, Brooklyn, NY
2. Cain, David P.—300 West 107th Street, Manhattan, NY
3. Caine, David M.—28 East 10th Street, Manhattan, NY
4. Caine, David T.—945 Amsterdam Avenue, Manhattan, NY
5. Kane, David S.—24 Forest Park Road, Woodhaven, NY
6. Kain, David—1775 York Avenue, Manhattan, NY

SUBMIT ANOTHER SEARCH

Nava zeroed in on the second and the fourth entries, as both addresses were within a six-block radius of Columbia University. She clicked "Cain, David P." There was a brief pause, and then the screen filled with information. Nava's eyes ran down the page, looking for something that jumped out at her, but there was nothing. Just an average New Yorker with an overpriced apartment and too much debt.

She skipped the next record and proceeded to "Caine, David T." Her eyes widened when she saw he was a student at Columbia. He must be the one Julia had told her about.

She stared at his passport picture. David T. Caine stared back at her, his eyes hard, a hint of a smile at the corners of his lips, as if he knew she was watching him.

She paged through the rest of his file, memorizing the information as she went. When she was finished, she returned to his photograph.

"Why are you so important, Mr. Caine?" she asked, wishing she'd had more time with Julia. Suddenly she heard soft footsteps padding along the floor. Someone was coming. Nava barely managed to clear her screen when Grimes emerged out of the darkness. He took a huge bite of the Granny Smith apple he was holding and sat down across from her. He flashed her a yellowish smile as he chewed.

"Waaanna 'ite?" he asked, holding out the piece of fruit to her.

"No thanks," Nava said, trying to mask her revulsion. "I already ate."

His cheeks puffed out, and then he swallowed with an audible gulp. "Suit yourself." He took another bite, this one even larger than the first, and continued eating. He leaned back and put his bare feet on her desk.

"Can I help you?" Nava asked.

"Maybe. Who knows?" Grimes answered between chomps.

This guy was unbelievable. "Let me put this another way: What do you want?"

"Nothing. Just burning the midnight oil like you, and I thought I'd say hello."

"Hello," Nava said.

Grimes took another bite, chewing with his mouth open as he stared up at the ceiling. It was clear he wasn't going to take the hint.

"Well, if there's nothing else, I'm going to get back to work," Nava said.

"Sure, no problem," Grimes said, although he made no move to leave. Nava gave him a withering look. "All right, all right, I'm going. Christ, just trying to be social." He got up and started walking away but stopped midstride. "By the way," he said, turning around, "how did you know about David Caine?"

Nava kept her poker face. "What do you mean?" she asked calmly.

"Well, you were looking at his file just now, weren't you?"

"You think this . . . why?" Nava asked.

"I *think* it 'cuz I *know* it, babe," Grimes said as he took another bite. "I tag all the files I'm working on so I know who accesses them and when they do it."

"Why were *you* working on the David Caine file?" Nava asked coyly.

"Dr. Jimmy—I mean, Forsythe—wants all the information we got on Caine before you grab him tomorrow."

Nava was confused. She let her hand fall against her leg, fingering the gun in her ankle holster. She resisted the urge to ram it against his temple. Nonchalantly she said, "I was unaware that I would be 'grabbing' anyone tomorrow—much less David Caine."

"Well, it's not official yet, but I know how Dr. Jimmy thinks. He's gonna want Caine in-house ASAP."

"Why?"

Grimes looked at her like she was an idiot.

"Because he's the Beta Subject." He took one last bite of his apple and chucked the core toward her garbage can. It bounced off the rim and landed on the floor. Grimes made no move to pick it up.

"I infected Tversky's computer with a worm the other day," he said with more than a hint of pride, "so that whenever he permanently deletes a file that's been backed up somewhere else, his computer automatically e-mails it to me. Tonight I hit the mother lode. Looks like Tversky did a clean sweep through all his data folders around midnight. Most of the stuff I already had, but one of the new files contained an entire medical workup of David Caine, and identified him as the Beta Subject.

"Since I haven't shown the info to anyone, I was wondering how you knew."

"Physical surveillance," Nava said, as if that answered all his questions.

"Oh, you saw him meet with Tversky, huh?" Grimes asked, impressed. "I dig the spy stuff. Cool. Anyway, since Dr. Jimmy has had such a bug up his ass about not knowing who the Alpha Subject is, I'm sure he'll want to snatch the Beta Subject quicker than yesterday."

Nava nodded.

"Oh, well. Gotta get back to my 'puter. I got a Halo tournament starting in five minutes. Later." Without waiting for a response, Grimes walked off into the darkness toward another pool of light farther down the hall. Nava ran a hand through her thick hair. If Grimes was right about Forsythe, then things had just gotten much more complicated.

She wished she had more time to figure out what to do, but the clock was ticking. She quickly accessed the blueprints to Caine's apartment through the New York City Department of Buildings, grabbed her coat, a knapsack, and a large black duffel bag, then headed for the door. Once on the street, she hailed a cab.

"945 Amsterdam," she said to the driver. The cab accelerated sharply, pushing her back into the seat. Nava checked her gun and closed her eyes. They were roughly a hundred blocks from his apartment. She had at least fifteen minutes to make her decision.

As Caine approached his building, he saw a homeless man sprawled on his stoop. He felt for the man, at least in part because Caine suspected he himself would be living on the street before long. When he reached the steps, he bent down, gently turning the man over onto his back.

"Hey buddy, are you all ri—" The words died on his lips when he saw the man's bloody face. It was his own. For a second, Caine felt his sanity stretch away, and then it came flying back like a rubber band. He wasn't looking down at himself but at Jasper.

"Jesus Christ. Jasper, what the hell happened?"

"I bumped into one of your Russian friends." Jasper coughed, wiping the blood from his nose. "Vitaly says hi, by the way."

"Oh, man, I'm so sorry."

Throwing one of Jasper's arms over his shoulder, Caine led his brother to the door. He fumbled his key into the lock and helped Jasper up the steps, hoping there weren't any more surprises waiting for him inside.

On a rooftop across the street, Nava lowered the night-vision goggles from her eyes as Caine carried the stranger to his door. There was something familiar about the man; she just couldn't place it. The blood on his face made it difficult to discern his features. She whipped out the tiny digital camera, which was also equipped with night vision, and snapped a few shots, focusing in on the stranger's face. She would analyze them later.

She then turned her attention to the tripod she'd set up earlier. She looked through the scope, aimed it at the fifth-story window, and waited for the light to turn on. After watching the dark glass for nearly a minute, she began to wonder if she had the right apartment, but then she spied a tiny ray of light.

Caine must have just opened the door; the light was coming from the hallway. He would be in her sights within seconds. Nava tensed her shoulders in anticipation.

After Caine pushed open the door and turned on the light, the two brothers stumbled into the apartment. Caine grabbed the doorknob for support, preventing them from falling to the floor.

"Come on, Jasper. We're almost there."

Jasper grunted, and his right eye fluttered open. His left tried but failed—it was already swollen shut. He came back to life momentarily and staggered the last few steps, collapsing on the couch. Caine leaned against the doorway, listening to his brother's labored breathing.

Once he caught his own breath, Caine went to Jasper and carefully unbuttoned his shirt, trying to assess his injuries. Although there was a dark bruise on his brother's chest, there were no fractured ribs; his face was where the real damage was done.

His left eye was dark purple, the cheek torn open in a few places and crusted with blood. His nose was swollen and bloody, although it didn't appear broken. Finally there was a nasty bump on the back of Jasper's head that had swelled to the size of a jawbreaker.

Caine went into the tiny alcove that served as his kitchen. He filled a bowl with warm water, grabbed a roll of paper towels, and returned to clean his brother up. Once he washed away the blood, Jasper didn't look quite so terrible. He still looked like he'd gone a round with Mike Tyson, but not like he was going to die in the immediate future.

Caine thought about taking him to the hospital, but he knew that there was nothing a doctor could do for Jasper that Caine couldn't—except prescribe better pain meds. What his brother needed was a good night's rest, not a five-hour wait in the ER.

"Hey," Jasper mumbled, making Caine jump.

"How are you feeling?"

"Not great, but probably better than I look," Jasper said, sitting up and throwing his legs over the side of the couch.

"Whoa, where do you think you're going?" Caine asked, holding Jasper's shoulders.

"To the bathroom. You want to watch?" Jasper asked, pushing away Caine's hands. He stood and almost fell over, grabbing Caine's arm for support.

"How about I just help you get there?" Caine asked.

"Sounds good."

Caine waited outside while his brother did his business. A

few moments later, Jasper opened the door. He still looked terrible, but at least he was grinning a bit—or trying to.

"I looked in the mirror, and I changed my mind—I feel pretty much exactly how I look." Jasper cautiously touched the back of his skull. "You got any good drugs?"

Caine shook his head. "Nothing stronger than Advil. Unless you want some experimental antiseizure medication."

"I'll stick with the Advil."

"Wise choice." Caine walked past his brother into the bathroom. "How many you want?" he asked, holding up the bottle.

"How many you got?"

Caine shook out four tablets, and Jasper dry-swallowed them like a pro. Caine helped him over to the couch, where they both sat down. "So you mind telling me what you got into tonight?" Jasper asked.

"Nothing I can't get out of," Caine said, hoping his words sounded more confident than they felt.

"I guess that's why the Russian played patty-cake with my face."

"He thought you were me, huh?"

"Yeah."

Caine looked down at his fingers, not sure how to ask the next question. "So . . . did he mention why he wanted to beat the shit out of me?"

"Something about not hanging around with Chinks."

"Shit." He couldn't believe that Nikolaev had found out so quickly about the game at Billy Wong's. Another one of the players must have dropped the dime on him. "Christ, I'm sorry, man."

Jasper waved his hand. "You didn't mean for it to happen."

"Yeah, but still. It might be best for you to get out of town for a bit. New York isn't a supersafe place for me these days—or people who look like me."

"I was thinking the same thing. I'll leave for Philly tomorrow." Jasper scratched his nose gingerly. "Why don't you come with me?"

"I wish I could, but I need to stay here for Dr. Kumar's tests. So far I think the new antiseizure drug is working."

Jasper shook his head. "You need to get out of town."

"I can't." Caine stood up, running his hands through his hair. "I won't be able to have a life unless I get control of my seizures. This is my last chance."

"You won't have a life if that guy kills you either."

"Gee, I hadn't thought of that," Caine snapped.

"Look, I'm just trying to help."

Neither brother said anything for a moment. Finally Caine broke the silence.

"I'm sorry, Jasper. I'm just up against the wall here. Under normal circumstances I would be able to figure out the money situation, but with everything that's going on with my health, not to mention . . ." Caine let his voice trail off. He didn't want to talk about what had happened at the diner. "I don't know, I just feel like I'm losing it."

Caine slumped down into a chair. He suddenly felt completely overwhelmed. Looking into his twin's battered face, everything seemed too real.

"Let's get some sleep," Jasper said, closing his eyes and spreading out across the couch. "Who knows? Maybe the answer will come to you in a dream. Stranger things have happened."

"Yeah," Caine said, thinking back to the diner. "They have."

After she heard the heavy-breathing sounds of sleep, Nava removed her headphones and began dismantling the directional microphone while she planned her next move. She could wait until the two men left the apartment, but it was still four hours before dawn.

She considered getting some shut-eye and resuming her surveillance at daybreak, but something was bothering her. She had a hunch that the identity of Caine's friend was important. So, instead of returning home, she went back to the STR lab one last time.

Once she was at her workstation, she uploaded the digital images of Caine's strange visitor. There were nine in total, each from a slightly different angle, as the man had been moving when Nava had snapped the photos. She zoomed in on his face in each picture, but the images were dark, blurry, and distorted.

She pressed a few keys, and the facial-recognition software worked its magic; the nine individual pictures merged into one three-dimensional image of a man's face. Slowly the nose took shape, as did the eyes and the bone structure. One eye was badly swollen; the face was covered in blood. Another few keystrokes eliminated the blood, replacing it with light pink flesh that matched the rest of his face. It started to look familiar.

She boxed off the swollen left eye and replaced it with a mirror image of the right. Then she shrank the obviously swollen nose. When she was finished, she pivoted the face so that it was staring directly at her. At first she thought she'd made a mistake—but after a quick double-check, she realized she had not. The man in the doorway was David Caine's doppelgänger.

Then it hit her. She pulled up Caine's file, and there it was, plain as day: a twin brother. Nava's mind raced as she calculated how she could make this unexpected piece of information work to her advantage. She doubted that Grimes had reviewed the file carefully enough to note that David Caine had a twin. If she was wrong, then her subterfuge would be caught quickly. But if she was right . . .

She had to make a choice—wait and possibly lose her initiative or make her move and risk exposure. In times like this, she always trusted her instincts. As she saw it, all choices could result in negative repercussions; the trick was to analyze the risks and minimize them. They could never be eliminated—not entirely.

Nava decided she had to act.

Although she didn't have clearance to edit the NSA master file, Nava knew there was another way. A few months before, she had bribed one of the system administrators at Social Security to issue her an ID and password so she could create false aliases. It had been nearly six weeks since she'd used the illicit password, but it should still be valid.

She accessed the Social Security database and pressed "Enter." The screen went black. For a second, Nava thought the system had been swept clean and her password eliminated. She imagined a silent alarm being triggered, security doors crashing down, and armed men running to her terminal. But instead she was greeted with a menu.

She pressed F10 to edit the data on the Social Security master file. It only took five minutes. When she was finished, she returned to the NSA database, selected Caine's file, and instructed the computer to update his record. The screen flashed *WORKING* as it accessed the source databases it used to create its files. Thirty seconds later the screen refreshed.

All the data was the same with the exception of one field. It was done. If Grimes pulled a backup file from last night's data dump, he would see what she had done, but it didn't matter. If things reached that point, she would already have the head start she needed. She left to go back to David Caine's apartment for the second time that night.

She knew that, one way or another, it would be the last.

James Forsythe was beyond mad.

He was furious. The only reason he didn't crucify Grimes on the spot was that he still needed him. Forsythe forced himself to close his eyes until he could control his emotions. He concentrated on his breathing. In. Out. In. Out.

"You feelin' okay, Dr. Jimmy?" Grimes asked, unconsciously picking his ear.

"Dr. Forsythe. *FOR-SYTHE,*" Forsythe said through gritted teeth, opening his eyes.

"You know I'm just kidding around." Grimes smiled. "Look, I'm sorry I didn't wake you up last night, but I didn't know."

"You didn't think I wanted to be notified when the scientist we were observing *disappeared?*"

"Technically he hasn't disappeared—they just haven't been able to find him since they started looking."

"But they started looking *three hours ago.* And on *your watch.*"

Grimes shuffled his feet. "Look, I don't know what you want me to say. What's done is done."

Forsythe was about to respond, but then he realized that the idiot was right. There would be time to exact his revenge later.

"Okay, fine." Forsythe sighed and leaned back in his chair. "Tell me everything you know. From the beginning."

Grimes clicked his PDA and began reading. "According to the police report, sometime between eleven P.M. and twelve A.M. a grad student named Julia Pearlman died. Evidently the girl took a flying leap from a sixth-story window.

She was found naked in a Dumpster by some homeless guy at around two. The medical examiner hasn't determined the cause of death, but the preliminary finding is a severed spinal column. So far they're treating it as a suicide, although they haven't ruled out homicide yet."

"And they think Tversky might have been involved?"

Grimes nodded. "They want to talk to him, since she jumped from Tversky's lab, and a bunch of other students said she and Tversky often worked late together."

Forsythe gasped, suddenly putting the pieces together. "She was the Alpha Subject."

"Yeah, looks that way. I got a download from his computer when he tried to erase the hard drive. He was testing out a new chemical compound on her right before she bought it. Seems like he developed it from a guy he tested in his lab yesterday who exhibited similar . . . ah, abilities. He calls him the Beta Subject."

"Christ," Forsythe said, "another unknown subject."

"Actually, we figured it out. His name is David Caine."

Forsythe perked up. "How do you know his identity?"

Grimes smiled. "When I saw that Tversky had all these new test results come in, I cross-checked their ID number with the accounting department. On the same day, they cut a check to David T. Caine with the same reference number."

"Wait a minute—you said '*we* figured it out.' Who's *we?*"

Grimes's smile turned into a frown. "Agent Vaner, although she was kinda vague about how she did it. Spy shit, I guess."

"Where is she now?"

"Last time I checked, she was outside his apartment."

Forsythe was happy to have at least one piece of good news. "All right. Have her keep tabs on Caine, and in the meantime locate Tversky."

"Aye-aye, Cap'n Jimmy." Grimes clicked his heels together, spun around, and left.

Relieved to be alone, Forsythe turned his attention to Tversky's final lab notes. Even incomplete, they were amazing. Although his evidence of Caine's ability was anecdotal, the chemical analyses seemed to support his theory. Also, Pearlman's EEG readings were unlike anything Forsythe had ever seen. Less than a minute after she'd been injected with the compound, all the Alpha Subject's brain waves had spiked in perfect synchronicity. Even though Tversky's experiment had killed the girl, the scientific implications of the study were revolutionary.

Although it would be easier to proceed with Tversky working for him, it wasn't necessary. What he really needed was to run more tests on David Caine. However, if Tversky's theories were right, then Caine would be a very dangerous man to bring in. Forsythe consulted his Rolodex, picked up his phone, and dialed. After he sat on hold for nearly five minutes, the man he needed came on the line.

"Good morning, General," Forsythe said, sitting up straight in his chair. "I need to ask you for a favor. . . ."

As Caine walked across the street, carefully balancing two cups of coffee and a bag of bagels, he got the feeling something was about to happen. Ignoring it, Caine tried to focus on the music flowing from his earphones. Whenever he was stressed, he always used his Walkman as a retreat. He flipped around, checking out the more eclectic stations, but ultimately ended up with classic rock, catching the end of "Comfortably Numb" before the Jefferson Airplane began singing about Alice's choice of pharmaceuticals.

Then the smell began to fill his mind.

Oh, no.

He stopped short, causing a tall man on a cell phone to smack into him. Caine stumbled forward, dropping one of his coffees and bumping into an obese black woman wearing a blue dress and carrying two oversize sacks of groceries. The woman veered to her left but lost her balance, and the grocery bags tumbled to the ground, scattering oranges and apples across the sidewalk.

The fallen fruit caused even more chaos. A bald man in a

tight white tank top spilled his Frappuccino all over an elderly woman wearing a bright yellow blouse. An Asian woman in a purple skirt fell and broke two nails. A beefy construction worker dropped his toolbox on the foot of a sharp-dressed businessman, breaking his big toe and ruining his Gucci loafers.

In a heartbeat Caine had changed the course of their day. The bald man would buy another Frappuccino. The elderly woman would need to go home and change. The Asian woman would need another manicure. The construction worker would have to hire a lawyer to defend himself from a suit brought by the businessman, who would miss the day's staff meeting while he waited in the emergency room for someone to take care of his toe.

Each of these changes would cause more changes. Caine could see them all spreading out before him, like a rock thrown into a quiet lake, rippling out into the distance. He couldn't quite put his finger on it, but Caine knew that something was wrong. Then he realized—none of this was supposed to happen.

The bald man was supposed to go to the gym and meet a man who would become his friend and then his lover. The construction worker was supposed to have another son, but the stress of the businessman's lawsuit would lead him to a divorce. The businessman was supposed to die in two months, but his doctor would discover a heart murmur during his impromptu visit, which would lead to preventive surgery that would save him from having a fatal heart attack. The elderly woman was supposed to fall and break her hip on her way to the subway, but now she'd be fine. The Asian woman was supposed to attend a business lunch that would have led to a promotion.

The images flashed across Caine's mind in an instant, and then they were gone. He felt like his own heart was about to burst. Sweat poured down his face. He realized that his eyes were closed, so he slowly opened them and tried to unclench his fists. Deep breaths, just take deep breaths, try to understand what had just happened. Was it intuition? Prescience? No, no. It was just a crazy waking daydream, a bizarre riff on the game he used to play with Jasper when they were kids. They would pick people at random and predict what was going to happen to them later that day.

Deep breaths, deep breaths. Yes, that was it. Just a waking daydream. Already it was beginning to fade. He turned around as the businessman began screaming at the construction worker—and then there was only blackness. Cool blackness.

. . .

Throbbing. It felt as if his skull expanded and contracted with each beat of his heart. He opened his eyes. He was flat on his back, looking up at a circle of faces surrounding him.

"I think he's coming around," said a pudgy blonde.

"You okay, buddy?" a dark face inquired.

Caine began to struggle to his feet, but a pair of strong hands pushed him back to the sidewalk.

"Don't let him get up. He coulda snapped his spine," commanded a man from the back of the crowd.

"Just relax, buddy." It was the dark face, which seemed related to the arms holding him down. "The paramedics are on their way."

Caine closed his eyes again. All the talking faces were making him nauseous. The blackness was better, and so he retreated back into its familiar cave.

Go ask Alice. When she's ten feet tall.

"Well?" Forsythe's voice crackled in his earphone.

"We're reviewing the feed now, but it looks like he just collapsed in the middle of the sidewalk," Grimes responded, turning to look at the bank of monitors in front of him. The one in the lower-right quadrant was looping through the incident. He had already watched it ten times, but he was still enraptured.

"Tell me exactly what happened."

"The target stopped short, and this guy bumped into him,

which made the target knock into this *huge* fat broad, and then she dropped a sack of fruit everywhere. A bunch of people tripped over her shit, and then the target looked around, grabbed his head, and just went down."

"Is he all right?"

"Peachy keen, although he's probably got a whopper of a headache. Someone called an ambulance, but the target wouldn't go with them. I listened in on their radio frequency, and the EMT said that he seemed fine, at most a mild concussion."

"Watch the video a few more times, and let me know if you catch anything else. In the meantime stay on him."

"Roger, Roger." *Airplane!* was one of Grimes's favorite movies, and he loved to quote it, especially when he was mocking Dr. Jimmy. Grimes could tell that it had riled him, since Dr. Jimmy didn't respond for a full ten seconds. Grimes bet that if he played back the call, amplified the volume, and cut out the background noise, he'd be able to hear the good doctor cursing under his breath. He'd definitely check that out later.

"So where is he now?"

"He's walking back home. We're following him with the truck, and Vaner is on the ground. I've also got a couple satellites looking down, and we have a directional mike trained on his apartment. Don't worry, Dr. Jimmy, we've got it covered."

"Let Vaner know that an assault team is on the way to assist in the acquisition."

Grimes let out a low whistle. An assault team? This was going to be good.

Caine tossed a bagel wrapped in tinfoil at his brother and dropped the *New York Post* on the coffee table. "Onion with cream cheese, lightly toasted."

"What, no coffee?" Jasper asked.

Caine contemplated saying, *I had another vision, passed out and spilled your coffee all over the sidewalk.* But instead he said, "Sorry, I forgot."

"No worries," Jasper mumbled, mouth already full of dough. He chewed thoughtfully, then swallowed. "So did the sandman bring you any solutions?"

"Afraid not. The only thing he brought me was a day closer to having to pay Nikolaev two thousand dollars that I don't have."

"Too bad you're not this guy," Jasper said, picking up the newspaper.

The front page read POWERBALL MILLIONAIRE!!! in large block letters that hovered in the air above a man holding a giant check for $247.3 million. Caine didn't know why he'd even bought the paper, as usually he read the *Times,* but when he saw the headline, he couldn't resist.

"Holy shit . . . it's Tommy DaSouza," Jasper said, holding up the picture so Caine could see. "Remember, from the neighborhood?"

"Wow, I didn't even recognize him," Caine said, staring at the picture. Tommy was at least thirty pounds heavier than when he'd last seen him. "Are you sure it's really him?"

Jasper flipped to the story and then began nodding. " 'Thomas DaSouza, twenty-eight, still lives in Park Slope, only five blocks away from where he grew up.' "

"That's great for him, but it still doesn't help me."

"What are you talking about? That kid used to worship you. He followed us around the playground for a year after you saved his ass that time."

Caine shrugged, remembering how he'd intervened one day when a particularly mean bully had been picking on Tommy. "That was a long time ago, Jasper."

"Yeah, but you were always a good friend to Tommy. Hell, if you hadn't tutored him in algebra, he probably would have dropped out of high school."

High school. Back then Caine couldn't wait to graduate. Now he'd give anything to return to that simpler time. He and Tommy had had a lot of fun back in the day. But after graduation they'd drifted apart. Tommy got a job, while

Caine started college. After a couple years, Caine found that he no longer had so much in common with his old friend.

"I haven't talked to him in almost five years."

Jasper grabbed the cordless phone off the end table and pitched it to his brother. "I would say now's a good time to renew the friendship."

"What do you want me to do? Call him up and say, 'Hey, Tommy, congrats on the lottery, could I borrow twelve grand?' No way." He tossed the phone back to Jasper.

"Fine," Jasper said. He pressed the "Talk" button and began dialing. Two seconds later Jasper said, "Brooklyn. Thomas DaSouza." He wrote down a number on a sheet of paper and pushed it and the phone across the coffee table toward his brother. Caine stared at it as though Jasper had passed him a dead rat.

"Look," Jasper said, "if you don't do it, I will. What's the harm? The guy just won more cash than he could ever spend, and you're about to get killed if you don't come up with a measly twelve thousand dollars. If he says no, you're no worse off. If he says yes, you're home free. There's no downside."

"What about my pride?" Caine asked.

"Worry about your pride *after* you pay off the Russian mafia," Jasper said. "Now, make . . . the fucking . . . call-*maul-fall-wall.*"

Even though Jasper's rhyming gave Caine a sinking feeling in the pit of his stomach, he knew that his brother was right. Reluctantly, Caine picked up the phone and dialed the number. An impatient voice picked up on the first ring. "Yeah?"

"Tommy DaSouza?" Caine asked.

"Look, whatever it is you're selling, I don't want any, okay? I'm obviously in the phone book, so just put your catalog in the mail and I'll call you if I'm interested. G'bye."

"Wait, I'm not selling anything!" Caine said, suddenly desperate, realizing that this might indeed be his only chance. "Um, it's David. David Caine."

There was a moment of silence when Caine thought that Tommy was about to hang up. Then, "Wow, Dave! How the hell are you?"

"Funny you should ask," Caine said, raising his eyebrows at his brother as he switched the phone from one ear to another. "That's kind of why I called. . . ."

"You got the money?"

Tversky nearly jumped. He turned around, but the only other person in the alley was a skinny little kid. He couldn't have been much older than twelve, although the Yankees cap turned to the side made him look even younger.

"You got the money or not, old man?"

"You're Boz?" Tversky asked in surprise.

The kid laughed. "You kiddin'? Boz ain't gonna meet some cracker he never heard of before. I'm Trike."

"I was told I was meeting with Boz."

"Yeah? Well, guess what? Meetin's canceled. Now you meetin' wid *me.*" The kid's hands disappeared into his oversize pockets. "Lemme see the money or I'm Audi."

Tversky removed a white envelope from his coat pocket, struggling to steady his trembling hands. Trike tried to snatch the money, but Tversky held it just out of reach. "First let me see what I came here for."

Trike smiled up at him, showing two gold teeth. "Sure thing, Gramps," he said, and extracted a brown paper bag from one of his pockets. Tversky glanced around to see if anyone was watching, but the street was deserted. He took the bag from Trike, surprised at how heavy it felt.

"Now gimme the fuckin' Benjamins."

Tversky handed Trike the envelope. The kid licked his finger, did a quick count, and then stuffed the money down the front of his pants. "Nice doin' bidness with you," he said before disappearing down the alley, leaving Tversky alone. Tversky stowed the brown paper bag in his satchel and quickly walked toward Broadway.

He didn't dare remove the bag until he was safely back in

his dingy motel room. He had left his apartment right after he'd watched the video. Julia had told him to relocate here, so that's what he did.

Once he had drawn the blinds, he placed the bag in the center of the bed. Swallowing hard, he reached inside and touched the smooth plastic cylinders. They felt cool against his sweaty fingers. Breathing deeply, he slowly pulled the shotgun shells out of the bag one by one. He stacked them neatly in a row. There were ten in all. For a minute he just stared at them, wondering how it was that he got to this place, this time.

But it was too late to go back now. After what happened to Julia—after what he *did* to Julia—it was far too late. He had to see this through. He checked his watch; he still had a few hours until six. If David didn't show, he could assume that Julia had been wrong. But he didn't think that would be the case.

So far everything had come to pass as she'd said it would—everything from where to sit at the diner to how to find the pint-size gun dealer. If she had foreseen all of that correctly, there was no reason to believe that the rest of what she predicted wouldn't also happen. He had no choice now.

But that wasn't true, was it? He didn't *have* to do what she had instructed. He could change his mind, choose a different path. But even as he wished there were another option, he knew that he wouldn't take it. He was sad that he must try to kill David Caine in order to get what he wanted. But he would do it.

It was too late to go any other way.

CHAPTER fifteen

Nava input the ID number and clicked "Find." The words on the blue screen were instantly replaced with a street map of New York City that featured two blinking dots—one represented Nava's current location and the other was Caine's. The global positioning system was working perfectly.

She'd tagged Caine's leather jacket with a microdot earlier that morning. Now all she had to do was wait for his twin. Once she tagged Jasper Caine, she could use him as a decoy for Grimes while she made her move on David Caine. After that, Nava could disappear.

She looked at her watch. It was nearly eleven o'clock. If Jasper didn't exit the apartment soon, she was screwed. As she stared across the street, a FedEx truck stopped in front of her, obscuring her view. The driver leaned across the seat and opened the passenger-side door.

Nava climbed into the truck and slammed the door shut. Once inside, she slid open the panel between the cab and the storage area and walked through. Grimes and his partner barely looked up when she entered, as both were typing furiously at their respective keyboards, their eyes darting among the three flat-screen monitors that were mounted in front of them.

There was no place for Nava to sit, so she stood and waited until Grimes was through. After about a minute, he held out his hand, even though he didn't deem it necessary to turn around.

"Give me your PDA. I've got to update some info."

Without thinking, she gave Grimes the metallic pad. The second it was out of her hand, she realized her mistake, but it was too late. He inserted it into a vertical slot on his console and pressed a button. A New York City street map replaced the image on Grimes's central monitor.

"Oh, great, you already marked him. I'll send his coordinates to the entire surveillance team." His fingers flew across the keyboard. "There. Now everyone knows where the target is in case you miss him."

"He's a target now?" Nava asked.

"Yup." Grimes spun around on his swivel chair. "Dr. Jimmy officially green-lighted the op this morning. You're on tactical; there's an assault team on the way."

"What?"

"See for yourself," Grimes said, pointing to the rightmost monitor and the auxiliary keyboard. The first commando's dossier was already on the screen. As the NSA didn't have any combat personnel, she expected that the additional operatives would be surveillance geeks who happened to be certified on a few firearms.

She was wrong.

NAME:	Spirn, Daniel R.
UNIT:	Special Forces
RANK:	Lieutenant
WEAPONS:	Pistol (9mm, .45 cal, .38 cal), M16A2/M4A1, Shotgun (12-gauge), M24 sniper rifle, M203 grenade launcher, M249 squad automatic weapon, hand grenade, AT-4, M240B machine gun, M2 HB machine gun, MK-19 grenade machine gun, mortar (60mm, 81mm, 120mm), pyrotechnics, M18A1/A2 claymore mine, mines (general),

	TOW missile, Dragon, recoilless rifles (RCRL—84mm, 90mm, 106mm), AT-4, light antitank weapons (LAW)
UNARMED COMBAT:	aikido, choi kwang-do, hapkido, judo, jujitsu, muay thai, tae kwon do

Nava paged through the other three soldiers' files. With the exception of Gonzalez, who was the demolitions expert, all had similar training and had been in the field—several on classified missions. Nava exhaled. This was going to make things much more complicated. She looked over at Grimes.

"Don't you think this is a bit overkill? Four combat operatives to grab one civilian?"

"What can I say?" Grimes shrugged. "Dr. Jimmy's freaked. He doesn't want anything to go wrong."

"How did he get access to special-forces guys?"

"I dunno, called in a few favors, I guess, same way he got you. He's pullin' out all the stops on this one." Grimes grabbed a Gummi Worm from a plastic bag between his legs and offered it to her. Nava shook her head. Unfazed, Grimes stuffed it in his mouth. He began talking between chews. "They'll be here in a few minutes. After you do your meet and greet, Dr. Jimmy wants you to snatch him."

Grimes's terminal started beeping. He turned around and pressed a button. "Yeah? She's right here, hang on." He took off his wireless headset and handed it to Nava. "It's Forsythe."

"Doctor?"

"Agent Vaner, I just wanted to make sure that Mr. Grimes has given you all the information you need."

"I believe so, sir. As I understand it, I'm to lead the team to acquire Mr. Caine and bring him to the STR lab."

"Correct. I want you in charge, as this needs to be low-profile. The men that will be joining you aren't known for their subtlety; unfortunately, they were all that I could get on such short notice. I'm hoping you can keep them in check."

"I'll do my best, sir."

"Good. Use every precaution when dealing with Mr. Caine—he's more dangerous than he appears."

"Understood," Nava said, wondering exactly what Forsythe meant by that.

"Good luck, Agent Vaner."

"Thank you, sir." There was a click, and the line went dead. Nava took off the headset and was about to hand it back to Grimes when she noticed he was already wearing one.

"I always bring a spare," he said with a grin. "Dr. Jimmy's a real pansy, huh? *'Use every precaution when dealing with Mr. Caine,'* " he said, carefully articulating every word, just like Forsythe. Nava wasn't sure whether she was more surprised that he had eavesdropped on her conversation or that he had admitted it so proudly.

"Should be a piece of cake, right?" Grimes asked obliviously. "You guys can just bust down his door and grab him."

Nava exited the truck without responding. The problem was, Grimes was right. His plan of attack was the best—simple and direct, with no risk from the environment—and if the special-forces operatives were any good, they would know that, too. Once the NSA captured Caine, she would never have another chance to get to him.

She had to figure out a way.

Once they realized who Tommy was, the branch manager got on the phone. He even called Tommy "sir." Tommy didn't think anyone had ever called him "sir" before. Sir Tommy. He liked the sound of that.

Maybe now that he was rich, he should go by "Thomas." Nah. He could never imagine saying, "Hello, I'm *Thomas.*" He had done fine with "Tommy" his whole life, and "Tommy" he would stay. He picked up the phone and called Dave to tell him the good news.

"I don't know how to thank you," Dave gushed.

"I said I would pay you back one day, didn't I?" Tommy

asked, grinning. "If it wasn't for you, I would have gotten pounded on a daily basis in middle school. Plus, I never would have passed Miss Castaldi's class. I really owe you."

"I don't know about that, but . . . well, this is just above and beyond. I don't know what to say."

"You don't have to say anything, man."

"So I guess I'll see you at six."

"Yup. Lookin' forward to it."

Dave thanked him another two times before Tommy was finally able to get him off the phone. He felt great. Better than great—incredible. He had never been able to help anyone before. But now he was the man, paying off his debts. From this point on, things would be different. He was going to do things, big things. He was going to make a difference.

His phone rang again, but he let his machine pick it up. It was another saleswoman. This one wanted to be Tommy's financial planner. She began rattling off a laundry list of things Tommy needed to get figured out—estate planning, stock portfolio, life insurance, tax shelters, trustees for his will—*BEEP*. His machine cut her off.

Tommy glanced at the clock on the wall—he had only a couple hours to go to the bank and travel into Manhattan. Dave had volunteered to come to Brooklyn, but Tommy wanted to go into the city and party.

He went into the kitchen to get his coat, still grinning. Dave had always been such a good friend to him. Tommy hoped they wouldn't lose touch after this. Dave was just the kind of guy Tommy needed—smart and decent, someone who wouldn't take advantage. Suddenly that gave Tommy an idea.

He grabbed a piece of paper, wrote a long note, and then stuck it to his refrigerator with a magnet shaped like a football. He knew it was a pretty weird thing to do, but now that he was a multimillionaire, he had to think of these things. Had to be responsible and stuff.

Looking at the note made him feel good, like when he

told Dave that he'd help him out. Yeah, things were finally gonna be different. He couldn't wait for the rest of his life to begin. Tommy put on his coat and headed out. He would have to hurry if he was going to make it to the bank in time—although something told him that the branch manager would keep the bank open no matter what time he showed up.

Tommy was a big man now. A big man with big plans.

Jasper's face was still a bit swollen, but he looked a hell of a lot better than he had the night before.

"You sure you want me to leave town?" Jasper asked. "I mean, assuming Tommy comes through, then all the bad guys should go buh-bye, right?"

"That's the theory."

"So then why do you want me to take off?"

"I don't know," Caine lied. Although Caine didn't *know,* he did have a feeling that things were going to get a whole lot worse before they got better. "I just think it would be a good idea if you hit the road."

"Okay, then." Jasper got up and put on his old army jacket. It was covered with dark brown splotches. Caine was about to comment when he realized they were dried blood. Caine lifted his leather jacket off the chair and tossed it to his brother.

"Your coat looks like crap. Take this."

Jasper looked at his brother's expensive jacket in surprise. "You serious?"

"Yeah. I want you to have it. Consider it a consolation prize for last night's boxing match."

"Thanks, bro," Jasper said, excitedly switching his coat for his brother's. "What do you know? It fits."

"What are the odds?"

Caine grinned. It felt like the first smile to cross his face in an eternity. He threw on an old trench coat and locked the door behind them. The twins slipped behind identical pairs of shades and headed down the stairs. As they walked out of the building, neither paid any attention to the white FedEx truck or the black van next to it.

"Hold position," Nava instructed as she watched the two brothers exit the building.

"But, ma'am, we have a clear shot—"

"Hold position. That's an order, Lieutenant."

"Understood."

Nava stamped out her cigarette and followed the twins. As she walked down the block, she wondered what to do next. She had managed to stall Grimes by explaining that she didn't want to grab Caine in front of any witnesses who knew him, such as his houseguest. However, the second Jasper left his brother's side, she wouldn't be able to stop her men from grabbing David.

"Shit, Caine and his friend sure do look a lot alike," Grimes blurted over her earpiece. "They're like twins."

"Cut the chatter," Nava barked. The last thing she wanted Grimes to do was jog something in his own memory.

"Whatever," he muttered.

"Just focus on the target," Nava said. "The other one is irrelevant."

"Which one *is* the target, ma'am?" Spirn asked.

Nava suddenly saw her opportunity. As long as the brothers were together, the men wouldn't be able to tell which one was wearing the GPS transmitter, since it was accurate only within one meter. For a split second Nava considered identifying Jasper as his brother, David. In the scuffle she was confident she could knock out the transmitter. By the time they figured out they had Jasper, she would be able to make her move on David and get away.

But since she had used their proximity as the reason they couldn't strike before, there was no way she could backtrack now. If only she'd managed to tag both of them as she'd planned, then she could lead them to Jasper. If—

She peered at the man she had thought was David Caine. Around the periphery of his dark sunglasses, she could see a slight discoloration. She looked at the other brother, just to make sure. His face was clean. For some reason David had switched jackets with his brother, which meant that the transmitter was on *Jasper,* not David.

"I need to get a closer look," said Nava, already formulating a new plan. She kept walking, waiting for the brothers to cross the street. They slowed at the next intersection. When the light turned green, the twins stepped into the street and began to walk toward her. Although they tried to let her slip between them, Nava made sure to stumble into David.

"Oh, sorry," she said, grabbing him by the elbow with one hand while squeezing his shoulder with the other.

"No problem," he replied.

She nodded and kept walking. "Target is wearing the black leather jacket."

"Copy, black leather jacket."

"As soon as they separate, move on my command," Nava ordered.

"Understood."

At the next intersection, the two brothers paused. They spoke for a moment, hugged briefly, then parted. David crossed the street, while his brother rounded the corner. This was it.

"Close in. Michaelson, head him off. Brady, right flank. Gonzalez, pull the van up alongside when we move in. Spirn, you're with me." All her men fell into position, walking quickly. Dressed in civilian clothes, they blended with the pedestrians on the busy Manhattan street.

"Position." Michaelson was two meters in front of Jasper.

"Position." Brady was a meter to Jasper's right.

"Hold," Gonzalez said. "I've got a little traffic, hang on."

The team all kept close to the target while Gonzalez maneuvered the black van around a double-parked cab, then drove past the team and pulled over about ten meters in front of the target. "Position."

"We go when the target's one meter from the van. Spirn

and I will make the approach, Michaelson and Brady, hang back in case he tries to run."

As Nava closed in behind Jasper, she removed a thin metallic cylinder from her pocket. She would have to move fast. If he blurted out that David was his twin, then it was all over. Nava quickened her pace as Jasper approached the van. She was almost close enough to touch him. Over Jasper's shoulder she could see Michaelson leaning against a parked car three meters away.

Nava reached out and grabbed Jasper's biceps. "Excuse me, Mr. Caine?"

Jasper turned, confused. "Yes?"

Nava quickly flashed a fake badge. "Could you step over to the van, sir? I need to ask you a few questions."

Jasper looked at Nava and then at Spirn. "Um, sure," he said, stepping to the curb, his back to the van.

"Thank you, this will just take a second," Nava said. Without another word she jammed the cylinder into his thigh. Jasper's eyes widened, and he let out a quick "AHHH!" Spirn tightened his grip on Jasper's arm to make sure he couldn't flee, but it was unnecessary. Two seconds after Nava's hypodermic ripped through Jasper's jeans and punctured his skin, the benzodiazepine hit his bloodstream.

The sedative worked almost instantaneously. Eyes that had been filled with shock a moment before became dreamy and relaxed. Nava shot a look to Michaelson, and he nodded. None of the other pedestrians had noticed.

"Mr. Caine, we're going to need you to come with us," Nava said, holding Jasper's arm to make sure he didn't fall. He opened his mouth to speak, but all that came out was a long, unintelligible slur. She and Spirn helped him walk to the back of the van. Spirn popped open the door and lifted Jasper inside, while Nava did her best to shield them from any passersby.

She climbed in after them, as did Michaelson and Brady. Both looked disappointed that the target hadn't resisted. Brady slammed the door shut, and Gonzalez hit the gas.

Nava spoke into her microphone: "We have the target, coming into base now."

"Understood. I'll let Dr. Jimmy know the good news."

Nava leaned forward. "Gonzalez, let me off on the next block."

"Aren't you coming with us?" Michaelson asked, confused.

She shook her head and faked a yawn. "I was doing recon all night. I'm heading home. Spirn, you have command. Coordinate with Grimes once you get to the lab."

The lieutenant nodded. When the van pulled to a stop, Nava opened the door and jumped out, casually lifting her knapsack from the floor of the van and throwing it over her shoulder. She slammed the door shut and gave it a quick tap. Once the van was out of sight, she removed her PDA.

She typed in the new GPS ID number and waited as the device connected to the satellite. A familiar map with two blinking lights replaced the text. David Caine was two kilometers away, heading west. It was 5:37 P.M. She had only twenty-three minutes.

She thought about hailing a taxi, but at this time of day, it was quicker to run.

Tversky pointed the video camera down at the rusty Chevrolet. It was a chilly night, so there weren't many people around, although, due to some construction project, there were several trucks and a couple barrels of gasoline amid the scaffolding that covered his building. He adjusted the lens so he had a clear view of the sidewalk. Perfect. Now all he had to do was wait. He tried to tell himself that whatever happened would be for the best, but he knew that wasn't the truth.

He wanted—no, not wanted, *needed*—David Caine to show up. If he did, then it would prove that Tversky had been right all along—and, more important, that everything else Julia had predicted would come true. If Caine didn't show, well . . . Tversky sighed and shook his head. He couldn't think of that. Not now. He had to focus.

He snapped open the leather case and examined the electronic mechanism. Although he'd tested it at least ten times that afternoon, he was still worried something would go wrong. He tried to cast those thoughts aside, thinking instead about the events that had led him here. His research. The incident at the diner. His discovery. Forsythe's rejection. Julia's vision.

Each event was a link in the chain, bringing him to this moment. He wondered what the probability of such a series of events was. One in a thousand? A million? A trillion? Such a thing could never be calculated. That was the beauty in life—anything was possible, everything infinitely unlikely, yet among all the improbable events, something must always be chosen, something must occur.

Suddenly a man carrying a large metallic briefcase stepped onto the small video screen as he walked by the large oil truck double-parked a few feet from the Chevy. Tversky's heart immediately quickened as he waited for the man to turn so that he could see his face. Tversky wiped his trembling hands on his pants, never for a moment taking his eyes off the man on the screen. Carefully he touched the surface of the keypad.

Slowly the man turned, revealing his profile. Tversky exhaled, disappointed. It wasn't Caine. His face was pudgy and covered with acne scars. He looked eager, as if he were waiting for someone. Tversky hoped, for the man's sake, that he would not be staying long. It would be a shame if he got caught in the explosion.

"I think we have a problem, sir," Lieutenant Spirn's hard voice rumbled through Grimes's earpiece.

"Wonderful. Care to enlighten me?"

"The man we just snatched. His name isn't David Caine—it's Jasper Caine."

"Huh?"

"He started mumbling something about David. I thought it was weird, the guy talking about himself in the third person, so I checked his wallet. According to his license, his first name is Jasper. When I asked him who David was, he said it's his brother."

Grimes punched the inner wall of the FedEx truck. "Shit!"

"What should we do, sir?"

"Hang on a sec."

Grimes's fingers flew across the keyboard as he accessed Caine's file. He scrolled down to the "Family Relations" section. No listing of a Jasper Caine. In fact, no listing of any siblings at all. Weird—although he'd only glanced at the file once before, he could have sworn something had been there. Grimes had an odd feeling in the pit of his stomach. On a hunch he ran a trace on the last edit made to the file.

The only change that had occurred was a data refresh. Unfortunately, he couldn't tell which fields had changed from his terminal in the FedEx truck. He clicked on the sat-phone and was instantly connected to one of the geeks in his department.

"Yo." It was Augy.

"Hey, it's Grimes. I need you to pull the last backup file on Caine, David T.; ID number Cat-Delta-Tiger-6542."

"No sweat, hang on."

After a minute Augy came back on the line. "Just fired it off to you. Should be in your box now."

"Got it." Grimes double-clicked the paper-clip icon and scanned the file. His eyes grew wide. Someone had altered the file; David Caine *did* have a sibling—a twin brother named Jasper. "Okay," he said, heart pounding, "run a system log of all the data-refresh requests. Shoot it to me when you got it nailed."

"Sure thing."

Grimes clicked off. Seconds later his computer pinged, letting him know that he had mail. Grimes opened the file, shocked at what he saw. The hacker had successfully masked his ID with a fake username, but Grimes recognized the computer terminal code. It was Vaner's. He replayed the last fifteen minutes in his mind. How she had ID'd the target and then drugged him up right before separating from the team. He wasn't sure what it meant, but he was sure of one thing—Forsythe was gonna have a fucking *cow.*

He flicked a switch to connect to Spirn. "Lieutenant, I just confirmed that your guy is the target's brother."

"Understood. What do you want me to do?"

Grimes's mind raced. Forsythe was going to flip no matter what, but he'd go even more ballistic if they were transporting an innocent civilian.

"When will the drugs wear off?" Grimes asked.

"They'll probably last another twenty minutes, and then he'll sober up. He'll be a bit groggy and probably have one hell of a headache, but other than that, he'll be fine."

"Okay. Dump him."

"Sir?"

"You heard me!" Grimes barked, sweat running down his back. "Pull over at the next park bench and leave him there."

"Understood," Spirn said calmly, although Grimes sensed some displeasure beneath the soldier's tone. Grimes didn't care. Fuck him. Five minutes later the black van was racing away from the alley where they'd dumped Jasper, the FedEx truck close behind. Grimes pressed the speed-dial button and heard his boss's voice in his ear.

"Houston," Grimes said, "we have a problem."

Nava's cell phone buzzed on her hip. The call was coming directly from Forsythe's office. She must have been made. She turned off the phone and concentrated on the task at hand, wondering how long it would take before they picked up her trail.

Then she realized they already had.

Grimes would have sent a signal to the phone and worked a trace before letting Forsythe call, which meant they already knew where she was. She had to move fast. It would be bad enough if she lost Caine, but if she got arrested, then she would be out of options.

She turned the phone back on, which instantly began ringing. Ignoring it, Nava stepped into the street with her arm raised, knowing that her fate rested in the hands of the first cabbie to pull over.

"Did you get the trace?" Forsythe demanded.

"Yeah. We lost the signal for a second, but now it's coming in strong, moving south at thirty-five miles an hour."

"Can you link the tracking signal to the satellite feed?"

"Already done," Grimes said. "She's in a cab. It just got onto the West Side Highway."

"Send the team to intercept."

"They're on their way. They should nail her in the next few minutes."

"As soon as they have Vaner, let me know."

Forsythe severed the connection and began to pace back and forth in his office. He wondered if Vaner knew something that he didn't. If she did, then David Caine probably was exactly what Tversky thought he was. And now they'd lost him. But at least they hadn't lost her. When he was through with her, she would regret her betrayal. Dearly.

CHAPTER sixteen

Abdul Aziz was only mildly surprised when the man driving the black van slapped a flashing siren on his dashboard and waved for him to stop. He should have known that the woman was in trouble when she gave him the hundred.

The cabbie quickly glanced at his bizarre passenger and then returned his eyes to the road. After he pulled over, three men jumped out of the van and surrounded his cab, guns drawn. Aziz could see the traffic slow down to get a peek at the arrest.

"Both of you. Step out of the car and put your hands on your heads. Now!"

Aziz didn't need to be told twice. He knew what the police did to people of his skin color under the best of circumstances. Never mind this. Moving in slow motion, he unlocked his door and pulled the handle. He stepped out of his cab and raised his hands high above his head.

"Get down on your knees!"

Aziz did as he was told. The instant his right knee connected with the pavement, a pair of rough hands pushed him face-first into the ground while another whipped Aziz's arms behind his back and cuffed them. A boot pressed down on his neck, pushing his cheek into the gravel.

"What the fuck?"

"Where the hell did she go?"

"Oh, shit!"

A few seconds later, a man yanked him up by his hair. "Where did you drop off the woman?"

"Nowhere," Aziz replied. He grunted as a boot connected with his abdomen.

"I'm not fucking around. Now I'll ask again: Where did you drop her off?"

"Please don't hurt me! I'm telling the truth!" Aziz gasped. "She never got into my cab! She just gave me the—"

"Sir!" a voice called out, cutting Aziz off. "I think you better look at this."

The hand released his hair, and Aziz smacked his chin on the pavement. He could taste blood in his mouth. Before he could move, the hand was back, again yanking his head up.

"This? Is this what she gave you?"

Aziz stared at the small silver phone the man held in his hand.

"Yes. She put it in the backseat and told me to head downtown and drop it at an office building on Broad Street. Did I do something wrong?"

Caine had a sudden instinct to flee—just hop a cab to La Guardia, take the next flight to anywhere, and never look back. It would be so easy, just leave it all behind. Start over, somewhere new, where the people didn't know his name or what a mess he'd made of his life.

But like all escapist fantasies, it was impossible. There was nowhere on earth he could go to outrun his illness. Wherever he went, the time bomb in his brain would travel with him. Caine swore that if Dr. Kumar's drug worked long term, he would take a good, hard look at his life and start making serious changes. But before he could do that, he had to take care of a few things, which meant paying off Nikolaev and never setting foot in a poker club again.

He sighed and began walking toward the old record store where he and Tommy used to hang out whenever they came into Manhattan. When he rounded the corner, he could see that Tommy was already there.

Good old Tommy, always on time. He was dressed in a worn New York Giants winter coat, probably the one he had in high school. He was leaning against an old Chevy and holding a large metal briefcase. Caine's salvation. He wondered if it was worth the price of his self-respect but knew he'd already made that decision.

When Tommy turned around and Caine saw the smile cross his face, he couldn't help but return his old friend's infectious grin. Caine gave a little wave and quickened the pace to cover the distance that separated them. When he reached Tommy, he held out his hand, and the two grasped each other for a moment before letting their arms fall back by their sides. Caine suddenly had a feeling of déjà vu mixed with dread, but he put it out of his mind. Tommy was here with the money.

What could go wrong?

Tversky's breath rushed out of his lungs when he saw David Caine. Julia had been right. Even though he'd expected it, he now realized that until that moment he hadn't truly *believed* it. But now the proof was standing fifty feet below him.

If the rest of what Julia predicted came to pass, he would have what he needed. With trembling fingers, Tversky punched in the six-digit code. The device was now activated. He'd been both surprised and horrified at how easy it had been to construct the remote-controlled pipe bomb. The instructions on the Internet had told him everything he needed to know. He was able to purchase all the equipment he needed from Radio Shack. Everything, that is, except gunpowder, which came from the shotgun shells he'd bought from Trike.

He double-checked the three video cameras trained on the sidewalk around the car. Each was wired to his laptop. He watched his screen like someone watching a movie, knowing that the good part was just around the corner. He surprised himself by whispering an apology.

"I'm sorry, David. I wish there'd been another way."

He checked his watch. Ten more seconds. He breathed

evenly, hoping that if the explosion killed David, it would be quick.

From across the street, Nava clicked the safety off her gun as she watched Caine accept the briefcase from the man in the Giants coat. She strained her ears to hear what they were saying, but the bug in the GPS transmitter suddenly squealed a high-pitched whine.

She wanted to ignore the anomaly, but all her training and instinct kicked in. This was something important. Powerful electric transmissions like that did not randomly shoot through the air. They had a purpose. She replayed the sound in her brain as she scanned the nearby scaffold-covered buildings. Then she saw him.

Standing on the rooftop almost directly above her was a man holding a box with a thin antenna. A feeling of dread grew in the pit of her stomach. Whatever the man had turned on was probably in Caine's vicinity. Then she saw it—a small, dark shape hidden beneath the Chevy. It couldn't be a coincidence. Julia's message, Caine's meeting, the man with the remote, the package.

There was only one thing it could be.

"BOMB!"

Caine looked over at the woman screaming across the street and again felt an incredible sense of déjà vu. Without thinking, he took a step back from Tommy and held the briefcase in front of him like a shield. Suddenly there was an enormous rush of heat and a powerful sound that gripped his heart and made his hair stand on end.

Caine was lifted off his feet as a jet of fire erupted from the sidewalk. He was flying through the air, spinning around, arms outstretched like a cartoon Superman slapped by a monstrous hand. He landed hard, slicing his palms before his left knee smashed into the sidewalk, halting his slide.

He lay on the ground, trying to breathe. Everything hurt.

He rolled over onto his back and tried to sit up, ignoring the burning pain in his hands. The street had been transformed into an inferno. He squinted through the thick, black smoke pouring out of a hunk of twisted metal at the intersection, half a block away. He could make out three distinct shapes within the blaze, although they were rapidly melting into one giant lump. Several smaller fires crackled at the outskirts of the primary explosion, fanning back and forth.

"*Tommy!*" Caine yelled. His eyes burned with smoke. He tried to stand, but as soon as he put weight on his left leg, the bones in his shattered kneecap ground together and he collapsed. The world went black. When it swam back into focus, he was lying on his side, clutching his ruined knee with bloody hands.

He felt the next explosion a half second before he heard it. The red-hot air rushed by his face, and the sidewalk hiccupped as the world once again filled with an apocalyptic roar. He twisted his neck to look up the street.

Another car had exploded, raining down fiery shards of metal and glass. He shielded his face as the fragments crashed around him. When he looked up, a license plate was buried in the sidewalk inches from his head. He had to get the fuck out of there. His luck wouldn't hold up forever, and the next metallic fire shower would probably kill him.

Again he tried to get to his feet, this time keeping all his weight on his right foot and using a nearby hydrant as a crutch. He was almost standing when he caught his left foot on the curb, viciously twisting his knee.

The pain was unlike anything he'd ever experienced, as if his leg were being twisted off like a piece of taffy. Soaked with sweat, he bit his tongue hard enough to draw blood and forced himself to look down.

At first he was confused—Caine looked at his right foot, then back at his left. The sight almost made him pass out; he could feel his consciousness begging to slip away, but he refused to let it, biting deeper into his tongue, a river of salty blood filling his mouth.

His left foot was turned 180 degrees, facing his back. There was no way he'd be able to get down the block like this. He would have to turn the leg around. His stomach lurched at the thought, filling his mouth with acid, burning his lacerated tongue. He spit onto the sidewalk, a phlegmy mixture of bile and blood.

Caine hopped over to the wall of the building, groaning in pain at each step as his twisted leg smashed down on the sidewalk. He fell against the building just as a wave of nausea and dizziness washed over him. He looked down at his leg, but the sight no longer had any effect; he was going into shock.

Another car exploded with an ear-shattering roar. More metal rained down as Caine covered his head. When he opened his eyes, he saw that a bumper had wrapped itself around the hydrant he'd just been leaning on. He pressed his back hard against the wall and tried not to think of the pain; he reached down with both his hands and in one quick motion twisted his leg back to its normal angle.

Agony.

Pure, unadulterated agony. Sweat clouded his vision, making it seem like he was looking out at the street from the inside of an aquarium. The car in front of him caught fire. Caine could only stare, hypnotized. The fire spread out across the plush black leather seats, a lazy old cat stretching her legs. Then the flames took on a life of their own, licking the steering wheel, the dashboard, the roof. The steering wheel started to melt, folding over itself while the seats liquefied beneath his gaze, losing their shape, their being.

Suddenly,

. . .

The car in front of him explodes. It flies apart in slow motion. Pieces of shattered glass speed from the window frames in every direction as forty-seven tiny cuts lacerate his face, his arms, his legs. The doors rip from their hinges, hurtling metal shards through the smoke like miniature missiles. One turns in the air and flies parallel to the ground toward Caine's midsection.

The sharp edge cuts into his flesh, slicing through his stomach like butter. Even in slow motion, it happens so fast that it's painless. That is, until it rips through his spinal column. An electric pain shoots through his back with the force of a javelin attached to a freight train.

His eyes open so wide that he worries for an instant they will burst from his skull; he hears the sickening crunch as the metallic missile continues its trajectory. As the shard hits the brick wall behind him, it contorts and ruins what is left of his internal organs, which disintegrate in its path.

Caine dies.

The first blast had triggered a chain reaction unlike anything Nava had ever seen, as the fire spread like a tornado of flames, spurred on by the oil truck parked across the street. Nava started toward the spot where she'd last seen Caine, but she could no longer make him out through the smoke.

She tried to get to him, but three unidentifiable vehicles, each in a different stage of destruction, blocked her access. The first was an amorphous melted frame, like a piece of chocolate left in the sun. The second glowed white hot but still bore the dark silhouettes of seats and wheels. The last was a pillar of fire, a completely unrecognizable hunk of twisted metal.

She scrambled to find a way through the wreckage, but a wall of flames blocked every route. She paced back and forth like a caged lioness, looking for a way to get to Caine, but unless a bridge fell from heaven, there was no way she would reach him in time.

Caine opened his eyes and took a giant gulp of smoky air. He immediately coughed it up. He had died, but now he was alive. What the hell had happened? He looked down at his torso—it was intact, but his knee was still a shattered mess. The car in front of him was still in one piece, although he could see a few flames beginning to make their way across the seat.

He must have blacked out . . . or had another vision. But

it seemed so vivid, so real. He remembered the metal slicing through his stomach and the indescribable pain as it shattered his spine. Christ, maybe he was crazy. Maybe—

Flames spread across the car in front of him. Watching them was hypnotic. Déjà vu all over again. He squeezed his eyes closed, attempting to shake off the feeling. Vision or no, if the car exploded, he would die. He tried to move away, but a fresh bolt of pain rushed through his knee. He couldn't. If he was going to get out of here, he'd need a miracle, and he'd need it fast.

Caine had never been religious, but he figured it was never too late. He closed his eyes to pray and discovered something totally unexpected—he could still see.

. . .

The fire, the street, and himself caught in the middle, broken and bleeding. He watches himself hurling a silvery—

. . .

Another explosion rocked the street, ripping Caine out of his trance. Suddenly he knew what to do. Without thinking, he reached out and closed his hand over the handle of the metal briefcase. With all his strength, he pulled back his arm and whipped it forward, releasing the silvery

. . .

—rectangle.

The case falls from the air and crashes down onto the hood of a parked car next to the one in front of him. Caine falls back against the wall, ready to accept his fate when the car explodes. As the roof lifts up, the metal briefcase shoots across the street like a Scud missile. It ricochets off the building and skids beneath an SUV, fiery sparks in its wake, triggering another explosion as the sparks ignite the pool of gasoline. The SUV lifts off the ground and slams into the building's scaffolding.

The chain reaction starts.

A silvery object shot through the air, and then the SUV exploded, smashing into the building with a tremendous crash, as bricks and pieces of scaffolding showered down onto the sidewalk. If Nava hadn't known better, she would have sworn someone had just fired a rocket-propelled grenade. A metallic groan cut through the air, making her wince. She looked up, but there was nothing to see except for the giant fire escape snaking up the building.

There was so much smoke, and the fire escape seemed to sway slightly from side to side. She heard another groan. Nava stared more closely, and then she gasped. The vertical ladder looked like it was swaying because it *was* swaying.

When the explosion pulled down the scaffolding, some of the fire escape's supports were probably destroyed. That, combined with the heat, must have weakened its structure. Another groan, this one louder. It looked like it was going to collapse any—

With a final shriek of tearing metal, the fire escape ripped from the building and swung down toward earth.

Time cycles through a loop.

The same fire escape keeps crashing to the ground. It lands in the middle of the fire and begins to melt.

(loop)

Caine throws the briefcase. The car explodes. The briefcase ricochets off the building. Fiery sparks ignite the gasoline beneath the SUV. Another explosion. The scaffolding crumbles. The fire escape falls and breaks into two pieces on impact.

(loop)

Caine throws the briefcase. The car explodes. The briefcase ricochets off the building. Fiery sparks ignite the gasoline beneath the SUV. Another explosion. The scaffolding crumbles. The fire escape falls and abruptly stops; still attached to the building, it hangs in the air, pointing to the sky at a forty-five-degree angle.

(loop)

The images speed up, his brain barely able to interpret

what he sees before the loops. Again and again Caine sets in motion the chain of events that cause the fire escape to crash down until finally it falls . . . right.

Nava narrowly avoided the fire escape as it smashed onto the street with a deafening boom. The metal latticework miraculously remained in one piece, with only a slight bend where it traversed the row of flaming trucks. Nava stared at the ladder for a moment in disbelief. Then she realized: She had her bridge.

She peeled off her thin overcoat and, with a quick slash of her dagger, ripped off three long strips of fabric, wrapping a piece around each hand and one around her mouth and nose. Ignoring the fire beneath it, she climbed atop the fire escape and crawled across the broken metal.

Already it had begun to heat up, but her torn jacket protected her hands. She moved quickly toward the apex, glad for her training climbing Gora Narodnaya in the northern Urals. The smoke and the sweat that poured off her brow made it nearly impossible to see, but she kept moving, feeling her way along the fractured staircase. Stopping, she hunched down, gripping the hot metal struts with her wrapped hands and staring forward. She was three feet from the peak of the fire escape. Her objective was on the other side of the wall of flames.

She looked for a safe place to jump down, but there was nothing. Fires raged on either side; the only possible path was forward. She looked again, searching for a way. She wasn't sure but thought she could see the other side of the bridge behind the firewall. It was beginning to glow, but it wasn't on fire yet. It was the only way.

She resisted the urge to take a deep breath, as the air was black and sooty. She crouched, directing all her strength to her calves, and jumped forward, arms outstretched.

The world skips.

There is a beautiful gymnast.

She climbs the fire escape and jumps through a wall of twenty-foot flames; reaching out to grab a section of white-hot metal, she misses. She falls onto the fiery husk of a truck, screaming in pain.

(loop)

He throws the briefcase. The chain reaction ensues. The fire escape falls, creating a bridge. The gymnast climbs the fire escape and trips before attempting the jump; flailing, she falls off the metal bridge into a roaring gasoline fire.

(loop)

He throws the briefcase. The chain reaction ensues. The fire escape falls, creating a bridge. The gymnast climbs the fire escape and jumps through the flames, performing a forward handspring off a section of white-hot metal as one of the trucks explodes, sending metal shards tearing through her body.

(loop)

Caine watches the woman die a hundred times. A thousand. A million. And then—

Although the metal shifted beneath her sudden push, Nava got off a clean leap. Once in the air, she straightened, her body rigid. The flames heated her arms, her stomach, her legs . . . and then she was through. She opened her hands wide, waiting for them to connect with the metal on the other side. And then—

She closed her hands around what felt like a rod of fire and held on. Loosening her grip slightly, she let her body weight twist her hands around the rod, bending backward as she did so, and then released. She flew forward and down feet-first. The drop was just three meters; she'd be all right as long as she didn't land on a piece of jagged metal.

She fell onto solid ground and instantly dropped into a crouch. Before she had time to catch her breath, Nava heard a metallic groan. She took off in a sprint, weaving her way through remnant pieces of burning steel. Once clear, she glanced over her shoulder and saw the fire escape collapse into the flames.

Nava kept running.

The gymnast was now running toward him, having survived her trial by fire. Caine wondered if he was already dead and whether the woman was some type of angel.

"Can you walk?" the angel asked, suddenly in front of him.

Caine stared at her. What does one say to an angel? She didn't wait for an answer. Instead she bent and threw him over her shoulder. Caine yelled at the jarring pain that ripped through his ruined knee, but the angel took no notice and began to run.

Caine watched as the car behind them exploded, as he had known it would. This time it happened in real time, not slow motion. The glass shattered, and shards of razor-sharp metal flew from the car and smashed into the wall. Only this time Caine wasn't standing in front of it.

He would have died had the angel not snatched him away. His knee twisted again, sending waves of electric pain through his body. Now that he was in the arms of the angel, he didn't need to hold on to his consciousness anymore.

So Caine let go.

CHAPTER seventeen

Caine felt heavier as he went limp, but Nava kept moving. She knew she was running on pure adrenaline; if she stopped, she might pass out. She had to get them to safety.

Without slowing, Nava ripped the tiny GPS transmitter from Caine's shoulder, the one she'd attached just an hour before, and tossed it into the fire. Now there would be no way Grimes could track them. The only question was, where could they hide?

She couldn't go back to her apartment, and Caine's was also not an option. So was hot-wiring a car, as he was bleeding badly. She needed to find a place where she could treat his wounds. She looked up at the green street sign, her mind turning.

The apartment where she'd met Tae-Woo was only a few blocks away. She didn't know whether the RDEI used it on a regular basis or just that one time. If there were more than two agents there when she arrived, she would be committing suicide. Caine moaned over her shoulder. She didn't have a choice—she would have to risk it.

She kept moving. Just three more blocks. There were few pedestrians on the street, but those she passed were hardcore New Yorkers and knew to mind their own business. No one stopped the beautiful brunette carrying a man with the bloody leg over her shoulder. Either there was a good explanation or they sure as hell didn't want to know.

By the time she reached the building, she was exhausted.

Her back and shoulders throbbed beneath Caine's weight as she climbed the five flights of stairs. She dragged her way up to the last story, pulling her body up the final steps by sheer force of will.

Nava laid Caine on the floor in the hallway and quietly approached the apartment. Holding her SIG Sauer 9-millimeter with both hands, she stepped back and kicked open the door. She swept the dark room just as she had a few nights earlier, but this time it was deserted. Nava heaved a sigh of relief and dragged Caine inside.

Once the door was closed behind them, she felt along the wall for the light switch. When the naked bulb hanging from the ceiling came to life, she saw that the room was as she had left it. Stark walls, dirty hardwood floor, tiny kitchen, yellow refrigerator. Nothing out of order. She let go of the breath she'd been holding and emptied her knapsack on the floor.

Her first concern was security. She jammed some putty both above and beneath the door. It would be a bitch to remove when they left the apartment, but for now it would prevent anyone from kicking it in. Next she turned to examine Caine. He looked terrible.

His face was white as a sheet, and his shirt was plastered to his chest with perspiration. Both hands were red and raw, but after a quick inspection she assessed that the lacerations were just flesh wounds, nothing serious. The real problem was his left leg, which was a bloody mess. She used her dagger to slice his jeans along the seam.

Although his calf was covered with blood, it appeared fine except for a few scrapes and bruises. The source of the blood was his knee. She felt gently with her hands to confirm what she suspected: His entire kneecap was smashed. She could see the whitish yellow cartilage exposed beneath his torn flesh.

She unwrapped her hands and spread the remnants of her jacket across the floor. Not the most sterile environment, but it would have to do. She removed various scalpels and syringes from her field kit. She was about to inject Caine with 100 milligrams of Demerol when she remembered Forsythe's words: *For this mission assume that anything is possible and everything is probable.*

The likelihood was small, but still . . . She cursed under her breath. She couldn't take the chance. Putting aside the syringe, she cracked a vial of smelling salts and waved it beneath Caine's nose. He batted it away unconsciously for a couple of seconds before his eyes flew open. She stared at him, person to person, for the first time.

Despite his weakened condition, his eyes were fierce and defiant, a deep emerald green. He quickly turned his head left and right to get his bearings before returning his gaze to Nava's.

"Who are you?" he coughed.

"My name is Nava. I'm here to help you, but I need to ask you a couple of questions—"

"Help me how?" Caine tried to sit up, but Nava pinned his shoulders. His legs scraped against the floor, and he winced. "My knee . . ."

Nava nodded. "Are you allergic to Demerol?"

"Can't have it," he gasped.

"What about—"

"No," he said, breathing heavily, "I can't have anything. I'm . . ." His eyes fluttered, and he gritted his teeth. "I'm on an experimental medicine. I can't take any other drugs because . . . because of the possible interactions."

"Shit," she muttered beneath her breath. "I need to stop the bleeding and set your leg. This will hurt."

Caine nodded. "Do what you have to do. Just no drugs."

"Okay," she said hesitantly. She was about to begin when suddenly her own exhaustion descended upon her. She dug another syringe out of her field kit and jabbed herself in the thigh. Her heart jumped a beat as the methamphetamines rushed through her blood. Suddenly wide awake, she took a scalpel off her makeshift tablecloth and made the first incision.

"Where is he?" Forsythe was furious.

"We're looking everywhere, but I'm telling you, he just disappeared," Grimes told him for the fiftieth time.

"Tell me again what happened."

"After I realized Agent Vaner had duped the assault team, I ran a trace on all her GPS transmitters, since I figured she must have used another one to tag the real target. Then I pulled the feed."

Grimes replayed the surveillance video from one of the NSA satellites 150 miles above the earth's surface, time-coded 18:01:03.

"Okay, here's David Caine," Grimes said, pointing to the top of a man's head on the screen. "You can see here how the other guy hands him a briefcase."

"Do we know who he is or what they were meeting about?" Forsythe asked.

"He could be the pizza-delivery guy. How the hell would I know? It's only been an hour since this all went down."

Forsythe glared in silence until Grimes continued. "Anyway, twenty seconds after the exchange, this car explodes. But if you look at it with infrared"—Grimes froze the image, then backed up a few frames and zoomed in on a small square next to Caine's feet—"you can see that it's not the car that explodes but this box.

"When I saw that, I widened the scope." The image zoomed out. Then Grimes focused in on a dark form on top of a building. "Although I can't be one hundred percent positive, it looks to me like this guy has some sort of remote control."

"Are you saying . . . ?"

"That someone tried to blow up David Caine. Yeah, that's exactly what I'm saying."

"Christ," Forsythe said, his composure slipping for a moment. "Was it Vaner?"

"No, but she might have been there." Grimes pointed back to the screen, which was inching forward on slo-mo. "The original explosion seemed to set off this Rube Goldberg chain reaction. Due to all the construction, there were a ton of trucks parked on the street, along with a couple barrels of gasoline for refueling. Not a good thing to have lying around in a fire."

One after the other, the trucks silently exploded on the monitor.

"That's when she appears." Grimes paused the image on an overhead view of a woman. "Unfortunately, we never got a clear shot of her face. It could be Vaner, but it also could be my mom. It's impossible to tell." He clicked another button, and the video continued.

"See? She just races around the corner, like a bat out of hell."

"Maybe she was running away from the fire," Forsythe suggested.

Grimes shook his head. "No way, José. She's running *toward* the fire. Unless this chick is a total pyro, I'd say she was heading for our boy." Grimes touched the screen with his finger and drew an invisible line from the woman to the subject, who was leaning against a wall halfway down the block.

"Then what?"

Grimes shrugged his shoulders. "I dunno. The last image we have is of the woman running toward this line of burning trucks. After that, there's too much smoke to see anything."

"What about infrared?"

Grimes turned in his chair to face Dr. Jimmy, as if to say, *Don't tell me how to do my job.* "Gee, why didn't I think of that? Oh, yeah, I already did. Because of the heat from the fires, the infrared was useless. By the time the smoke cleared, they were both gone."

"What about the GPS transmitter that Vaner was using?"

"It went dead a couple minutes after the explosion."

Forsythe was silent for a beat before deciding this was somehow Grimes's fault. "No one—I repeat, *no one*—goes home until you've found the subject. Understood?"

"Whatever," Grimes sighed.

Forsythe marched out of the room, slamming the door behind him.

Grimes followed him with his eyes. "Asshole."

"Tommy," Caine gasped. "He's dead, isn't he?" Caine asked the woman.

"I don't know," she said, but he knew she was lying. Avoiding his eyes, she continued mending his knee. It was almost a relief; the sheer physicality of the pain helped to dull the shock of Tommy's death. He felt a tremendous guilt. If Caine hadn't called him, Tommy never would have been there. He would have just kept living his life. And now . . . now he was dead.

"He was thrown in the opposite direction from you after the explosion. He could have made it. You did." The woman met his eyes. "I'm sorry about your friend. But if you're going to survive this, you have to put him from your mind. At least for the time being."

He glared at her. Who was she to tell him not to grieve? He felt suddenly overwhelmed with emotion. Guilt, confusion, gratitude, sorrow, fear, anger. Each washed over him like a wave, crashing down and then retreating to make room for the next. He took a deep breath and wiped his nose.

The strange woman was kind enough to give Caine his dignity; she pretended to stare out the dark window while he blinked back his tears. After he collected himself, she returned to mending his knee. For some reason it no longer seemed to hurt as badly.

"What did you do?" he asked.

"A regional nerve block. It should lessen the pain, at least while I repair the cartilage damage."

He stared at her for the first time. Caine didn't think he'd ever seen a woman in better physical shape. Her form-fitting black tank top exposed the taut muscles of her shoulders and arms. Her stomach was flat as a board, her legs long and powerful, without an ounce of fat.

Her skin was flawless, a deep olive hue; she had strong dark features, long chestnut brown hair tied back in an efficient ponytail, revealing a face that would have been beautiful if she'd smiled. But instead her mouth was a tight horizontal line, her brown eyes cold and empty.

"Who are you?" he finally asked.

"My name is Nava Vaner."

"No, I mean . . . who are you? Why did you save me? What do you want?"

"That's a more complicated question." Nava sighed, wiping her forehead on the back of her wrist. "I'm not even sure I can answer for myself."

Caine was silent for a moment. And then he said one word: "Try."

As Nava stared at David, she felt an intense desire to tell him everything. She'd been alone for so long, living the lie so well that she'd almost forgotten the truth. To tell him was a risk, yet somehow it felt like the safest thing she could do. The voice in the back of her mind, the one that had kept her alive all these years, screamed at her to lie.

But her gut told her that everything would be okay if she would just tell him. And then there was Julia. So far everything she'd said had come true—and she had told Nava that David Caine was the one person she could trust. Nava continued to clean out his wound as she thought.

He seemed to understand. He didn't push her or try to fill the silence with useless chatter. Instead he waited, gritting his teeth against the sharp bolts of pain as she gently picked pieces of metal and shattered glass from his flesh. Finally she looked up at him. She was ready.

"I lied to you," she said, her voice steady. "My real name is not Nava Vaner, although it's the one I've used for over ten years. When I was born, my parents"—she paused, surprised at the wave of emotion she felt just thinking about them—"my mother named me Tanja Kristina." Nava took a deep breath, finally ready to tell her story.

"I was twelve years old when she died."

CHAPTER eighteen

"There was a plane crash," Nava said. She remembered that night as if it were yesterday. "We were all supposed to go on a family trip. It was going to be my first time on an airplane, but the week before, I had a nightmare . . . so I refused to go.

"My father stayed home with me, but my mother and sister got onboard." Nava paused. "They never came back."

"I'm sorry," Caine said. Nava nodded, silently accepting his condolence. She was surprised at how much it hurt to talk about, even after all these years. But in a way it felt good to unburden herself, even to a stranger. Somehow it felt honest, the first human interaction she'd had in years that wasn't based on a web of lies.

"The first month it was like a bad dream. I kept expecting to come home and see my mother in the kitchen, but . . ." She stopped as her voice caught. "But every day was the same. She was still gone. . . . I was still alone."

"But your father—"

"My father died that day, too, in a way," she said bitterly. "After the crash he was never the same. It was like living with a ghost."

Nava remembered that first year when her name was still Tanja, alone in the house with her father. He never forgave himself for not keeping his wife and daughter home. But instead of blaming himself, he blamed Tanja. And so Tanja lost not only her mother and sister when the terrorist's bomb ripped apart the plane, but her father as well.

Every night she asked God why He took them away. Then she would cry. She would cry because they were gone, because her father no longer hugged her and because her mother would never again kiss away the monsters. But most of all she would cry because secretly, deep down inside, she was glad it had been them and not her. And for that she could never forgive herself.

"Ah!" Caine exclaimed, gritting his teeth.

"Sorry," Nava said. She'd been so lost in her thoughts that she had inadvertently jogged his knee. She wiped at her eye. "Do you really want to hear all this?"

"Yes," Caine said, eyes thoughtful. "I think it's important."

Nava nodded, realizing that it was. She continued her story.

"I was angry. I was twelve years old, and I was looking for someone to blame. Then one night I overheard my father talking on the phone with one of the party leaders. It was then I discovered that Afghan terrorists had been responsible for the plane crash.

"The next day I took a bus to Moscow and marched down to Lubyanka Square to visit the KGB." Despite her bitterness, Nava smiled ever so slightly, remembering herself as Tanja—the scared little girl who wanted to kill terrorists. She wondered how things would have turned out had she not overheard her father. Probably she never would have met the man who became a second father to her. His name was Dmitry Zaitsev, and he taught her much during the next few years. Including how to kill.

One day, a few weeks after being turned away from Lubyanka, Tanja was walking home when a powerful arm suddenly wrapped around her chest, another around her neck. She turned wild, kicking and clawing with the ferocity of a cornered mountain lion. The arms squeezed tighter.

She didn't know that even from that first moment, Dmitry was testing her, to see if Tanja's bravery would evaporate when she was faced with death. But she did not shrink from the attack; she fought harder than ever, smashing her head back into the unseen man's chest again and again until he made her world grow dark.

When she awoke, her left wrist was handcuffed to a wooden bedpost in a tiny studio beneath the shadow of the Kremlin. Once she became aware of her surroundings, she leaped from the bed, almost tearing her arm out of her socket. She immediately went to work on the cuffs, but it was no use. The man allowed her a few minutes to absorb the futility of her situation before he spoke.

"Relax."

Tanja spun around to confront him, her face a mask of hate. She took a deep breath and spit. Her saliva landed on his shoulder.

He looked down at it then back at Tanja, smiling. "Good aim."

Tanja said nothing, although she unclenched her jaw slightly.

"My name is Dmitry. What's yours?"

Tanja folded her right arm across her tiny chest.

"Let me help you. Your name is Tanja Aleksandrova. Your mother and sister were killed three months ago when an Afghan rebel's bomb blew up their plane." The blood drained from Tanja's face. "I am KGB—I fight those terrorists. A friend told me you wanted to fight as well. Is this true?"

Tanja stared at him, searching his cold eyes. Then, slowly, she nodded.

"Good. If you want to help, you have to promise to do whatever I say."

"That depends on what you want me to do."

"Fair enough," Dmitry grunted. "If you had agreed to do whatever I said, I would have known you were a fool or a liar. I am glad you are neither."

"I'll be glad when you let me go," she said, rattling her handcuffs.

"If I do, will you at least agree to hear me out?"

She nodded.

Dmitry walked to the bed, mindful to stay out of kicking range. He twisted his key in the lock and released her. Tanja snatched back her arm and massaged her red, swollen wrist.

"That is your first lesson: Make sure the cuffs are tight, or else whoever you're holding may slip away."

Tanja didn't say a word. But neither did she run. She was curious.

"Now for lesson number two," Dmitry leaned forward and gently plucked a bobby pin from her hair with one hand and snapped the cuff back on her wrist with the other.

"Hey!" Tanja exclaimed. "You promised to let me go!"

"And you promised to hear me out," Dmitry said, holding the pin before her eyes. "As I was saying . . . lesson number two: how to pick a lock." For the next ten minutes, Dmitry explained the inner workings of a locking mechanism and showed her how even a simple hairpin could be used as a key.

Once he had finished his demonstration, he handed the pin back to Tanja. She immediately went to work. Although it took her several attempts, eventually she heard a click, and the cuffs clattered to the floor. She looked up beaming, the smile on her face the first in months.

"Very good, Tanja. Now tell me about your father," Dmitry commanded.

"His name is Yegor—"

The palm of Dmitry's hand smashed into Tanja's cheek so hard that she fell off the bed.

"Lesson number three: Never tell anyone anything." Dmitry raised an eyebrow. "At least, nothing that is true."

Tanja stood up slowly, rubbing the side of her face, which was already glowing a faint red.

"That's enough lessons for today. If you want to learn more, meet me in the alley tomorrow after school. If not, then forget this. Whatever you decide, never tell anyone about what happened today, especially not *Yegor*." Dmitry mocked her with his eyes. "Not unless you want more than a slap on the face."

"Hold that here," Nava said as she tied a tourniquet around Caine's thigh. He grimaced but did as she asked. She knew how much this must hurt and was impressed by his high threshold of pain.

"Keep talking," he said, sweat pouring off his brow. "Give me something to think about besides . . ."

"All right," Nava said, remembering the months following her first encounter with Dmitry. "We met in the alley every day after school. We would walk around the streets of Kitai Gorod, and Dmitry would teach me about Russian history. Whether he told me about Peter the Great conquering Estonia during the Northern War, Lenin's socialist revolution, or modern Marxist philosophy, I couldn't get enough. Now when I look back, I realize he was indoctrinating me with party propaganda. But then . . . well, then I believed every word. He was like a father and teacher rolled into one, and I his most eager student.

"Eventually he taught me how to spy. He started slowly at first, quizzing me about the people we would pass along our walks. What color was the fat woman's dress? How many children did she have? What was the mustached vendor selling from his cart? I was a natural and quickly learned how to absorb the world around me. Dmitry was impressed, and within six months he was sending me into taverns to eavesdrop on party members the KGB suspected of disloyalty.

"Once Dmitry decided that I had 'the gift,' he began to have others teach me as well. That's when I learned to steal."

Nava had to retie his tourniquet, and Caine suddenly let out a gasp, but he quickly cut it off through gritted teeth. "Don't stop," he said, his knuckles white. "I want to hear."

Nava nodded and continued repairing his knee as she resumed her story.

"My teacher's name was Fyodor," Nava said, remembering the dark little man with thick eyebrows. He didn't speak much, and at first glance he seemed totally unremarkable. He was the type of man you would forget the second he entered the room. However, it was his innate ability to blend into his surroundings that separated him from other men. Walking by Fyodor was as memorable as walking by a brick wall. Except, of course, a brick wall didn't steal your possessions as you passed.

In the late afternoon, as the Muscovites returned home from work, Fyodor and Tanja would walk among them. At the end of the day, they would duck into an alley, and Fyodor would open his satchel and reveal the fruits of his labor—wallets, rings, watches, money clips, and any number of items that he lifted while walking with his favorite pupil. Over time he taught Tanja his skills.

"But why did he teach you to steal?" Caine asked.

"Fyodor said a spy's most important skill was to be able to get things you weren't supposed to have from places you weren't supposed to be. In truth, being a spy is no different from being a thief. It's all about stealing. But while a thief steals jewels, a spy steals secrets.

"So Fyodor taught me to be a master thief. First he taught me how to pick pockets. Then how to pick locks. Padlocks, dead bolts, combination locks, car locks, and everything in between. Fyodor never met a lock he couldn't open in less than twenty seconds. I wasn't as skillful, but at the end of a few weeks, I could open most locks within a minute or two.

"When I turned fourteen, Dmitry decided that I should study with the KGB full-time. By then my father and I barely spoke, so when I told him I was going away, I think . . . I think he was grateful. Having me around was only a reminder. Without me in the house, he could pretend that he'd never had a family."

Nava stopped. Caine, sensing her sadness, helped her to press on. "So you went to spy school?"

"Yes," Nava said with a hint of a laugh. "I went to 'spy school.' It was called the *Spetsinstitute.* I was part of a pilot program with ten other gifted children. I had classes eight hours a day, seven days a week. First there were languages. Although they taught everyone English, because of my dark complexion the party decided I should also learn Hebrew and Farsi so that I could work in the Middle East.

"I also learned about technology, politics, history, communism, sociology, and anthropology. After class I would spend four hours with my combat instructor, who taught me *Systema,* Russian martial arts."

Each night after training, Tanja would eat dinner and limp back to her room, battered and bruised, where she would study for three hours before passing out for her nightly seven hours of sleep before starting all over again. The first few weeks, Tanja would wake feeling mentally and physically exhausted, but there was never any time to rest, so all she could do was press on. The classes were difficult, but they were nothing compared with her combat sessions.

Nava smiled, remembering Raisa—the statuesque beauty with porcelain-white skin and long jet-black hair. Weighing only 55 kilograms herself, Raisa was used to fighting men who were more than double her size, and did so with deadly precision.

Raisa was part of the Russian special forces, also known as the *Spetsnaz.* For months Tanja practiced punches, kicks, chokes, and holds. The more skills she mastered, the harder Raisa attacked her. Once Tanja learned how to defend herself against a single opponent, Raisa forced her to spar with two and three attackers at the same time.

Her training was relentless, and Tanja was forced to develop her own style, to move unpredictably to fend off continuous attacks from every conceivable position. As soon as Tanja felt comfortable with hand-to-hand combat, Raisa moved on to armed combat.

That was where Tanja first encountered the weapon that would grow to be her favorite—a small, curved, seven-inch *kindjal* dagger from Dagestan. Raisa taught Tanja how to slash a man's Achilles tendon so he could no longer walk, where to stab a man to sever his spinal cord, and, of course, how to thrust up into the scrotum and twist the blade to completely incapacitate him.

"Once I learned the *Systema* and how to hold my own with a dagger, they sent me to the firing range."

Mikhail, her lanky weapons instructor, insisted that she understand the mechanics of every piece of artillery and the physics behind its action before taking a single shot. He taught her the difference between an automatic (loaded with a magazine or clip) and a revolver (each bullet had to be manually loaded). She learned it was necessary to cock the hammer manually before shooting a single-action revolver, while a double-action revolver would do it automatically. She discovered that a gun's caliber was simply the measure of the diameter of its bullets, such that a .38-caliber had shells with a diameter of 0.38 inches. Moreover, she learned that larger-caliber bullets traveled more slowly but caused more damage.

She memorized the benefits of a 9-millimeter semiautomatic pistol—high-velocity bullets, relatively quiet shot, near-perfect accuracy, little recoil, and a large magazine—as well as its weaknesses—shallow-penetrating wounds that didn't draw a lot of blood, higher likelihood of jamming.

Tanja learned the three ways a bullet could bring a man down—blood loss, head trauma, or penetration of a major organ like the heart or lung. This led to other lessons, like how if she wanted to kill a man with a .22, she should aim for the head, because a low-caliber bullet was powerful enough only to penetrate the skull but not exit, so once inside, it would bounce around and scramble the victim's brain. When using a .45, a shot to the torso would be fatal, as a .45 slug was strong enough to blow a man's organs out the six-inch exit wound it would tear through his back.

She learned that hollow-tipped bullets were concave at the end so that they could scoop up organs as they penetrated the body and that a Glaser safety slug was simply a copper cup filled with liquid Teflon and a lead shot, sealed with a plastic cap. Upon impact the cap would disintegrate, maximizing the energy transfer to the contents. The Teflon and lead shot would then expand out, increasing the probability of hitting a major artery. This also meant that the bullet wouldn't ricochet or exit the body, making it a "safe" round for everyone except the target.

Lastly, Mikhail taught her about the different models. The Austrian Glock, the German Heckler & Koch, the Swiss SIG Sauer, the American pistols—Smith & Wesson, Colt, Browning—the Italian Beretta, and, of course, the Russian Gyurza and Tokarev.

It was only then, after she had learned more than she ever thought there was to know about guns, that Mikhail handed her an old-style single-action Russian Nagant. After Tanja carefully loaded the 7.62-millimeter cartridges into its seven-chamber cylinder, she fixed her stance, aimed, cocked the hammer, and pulled the trigger. The recoil was so strong it knocked her off her feet and she toppled over, landing hard on her backside.

That was the only time she ever saw Mikhail laugh. "And *that,*" he said, "is the difference between book learning and field training."

Angry, Tanja picked herself up and took another shot. She never fell down again.

As with her other studies, Tanja picked up weaponry extremely quickly, mastering pistols of all calibers before moving on to other artillery. First there were the machine guns; Uzis, Browning M2HBs, and M60s all left her arms feeling rubbery, like they were infused with Jell-O. Next there were the shotguns, like the Baikal MP-131K and the Heckler & Koch CAWS, which left a dark bruise on her shoulder from its powerful kick. Finally Mikhail taught her how to calculate distance, wind speed, and drag so that her shots from the Dragunov sniper rifle always found their home.

Nava paused. She'd finished splinting his leg. Caine was bathed in sweat.

"That should do it," she said, staring down at her handiwork.

"Thanks," he said.

Nava nodded, suddenly feeling shy, wondering why she felt so comfortable with this man she hardly knew.

"So then what happened? What do they do for a final exam at the *Spetsinstitute?*"

"I had to kill a man," Nava said flatly. "He was a terrorist—an Afghan rebel named Khalid Myasi."

"And did you?"

"Yes," Nava said. "I put two bullets in his chest and one in his head. Just like I had been taught." She remembered that moment with perfect clarity. Three tight explosions as each bullet sped from the muzzle. Myasi's dying scream, cut short as the blood welled up in his throat. The numb feeling that spread through her chest as she stood over his lifeless body.

It wasn't like she'd imagined. She was not filled with triumph, nor was her desire for vengeance diminished. But the KGB didn't care. They had successfully transformed her into a killer, and they were anxious to make use of their new weapon.

Sometimes they would have her play the part of a schoolgirl, other times a teenage prostitute. Mostly they used her for surveillance work, although when the situation called for it, the seventeen-year-old Tanja was asked to kill. And she did.

As Tanja was fluent in Hebrew, Farsi, and English, on her eighteenth birthday the party decided to send her to Tel Aviv. She lived there for nearly a year before Zaitsev instructed her to assassinate Moishe Drizen. The soft-spoken Mossad agent was the first man Tanja murdered whose death she questioned afterward.

For all the others, the reasons had been obvious. They had

been enemies of the party, murderers in their own right. But Drizen was different. After conducting the pre-op surveillance work, it was obvious to Tanja that he was neither anti-Russia nor pro-terrorist. In fact, he was an antiterrorist operative himself.

But when Tanja asked Zaitsev what Drizen had done to deserve death, his only answer was, "Do not question the party."

And so Tanja did what she'd been trained to do—she slit Drizen's throat in an alleyway. She hadn't known it at the time, but that had been her last test. The next day Zaitsev told her she was finally ready for deep cover in the United States.

Tanja was assigned a host family of fellow Russians whom the party had sent to America twenty years earlier. Their cover was that of Israelis who'd decided to move to the States to raise a family. Shortly after they arrived, the couple gave birth to a baby girl. They named her Nava.

Nava led a very ordinary life up until May 7, 1987, when she mysteriously disappeared. Denis and Tatiana Gromov—then known as Reuben and Leah Vaner—were beside themselves. Afraid to contact the police for fear of drawing attention to themselves, Denis Gromov asked his KGB handler for help. Zaitsev told him that he would use all his resources to locate the seventeen-year-old girl. But in the meantime could they do him a favor?

Fearing for their daughter's safety, the Vaners did as Zaitsev asked. They moved out of their small bedroom community in Ohio to a Boston suburb, leaving behind the life they had created. A month later they learned that their daughter was safe in Russia and that she would remain safe as long as they "adopted" Tanja. The next day Tanja arrived at the Vaners'. It was then that Tanja Kristina Aleksandrova ceased to exist and a new Nava Vaner was born.

The Vaners did their part, letting their adopted daughter live in their home while they taught her how to be an American. After summer was over, the new Nava went to high school. When it came time to apply to college, Nava did very well, gaining acceptances to six universities across the country. Zaitsev thought it would be best for her to attend the University of Southern California, as it was the "most American." Four years later she graduated magna cum laude with a B.A. in Arabic and a minor in Russian.

When the Central Intelligence Agency received her application for a field position, they were ecstatic. After conducting a full background search, including interviewing her friends from high school and college as well as her parents and neighbors, they offered her a spot in their elite Clandestine Service training program.

After all, Nava was the perfect candidate.

During the next two years, Nava underwent intensive training. Although her fellow recruits struggled to absorb combat, weaponry, and foreign culture, Nava sailed through. Never had her Langley instructors seen anyone with so much "natural" talent. And so, for the second time in her life, she was selected to kill for her country.

But by that time Nava didn't know which country was hers.

Although she had grown up in Mother Russia, living in the United States for six years had opened Nava's eyes to Western culture in a way that her sessions at the *Spetsinstitute* never had. Suddenly Nava wasn't so sure of where her loyalties lay. She found she had lost the drive to spy for Russia. Still, she did not have any great desire to spy for America either.

However, no more than a month after she began working for the CIA as a Middle Eastern antiterrorist operative, the unthinkable happened—eight senior party officials attempted to take over the government of the USSR. Each day she scanned the *International Herald Tribune* in shock as she read more accounts of how Gorbachev's vice president, Gennady Yanayev, had assumed control of the USSR, along with KGB Director Vladimir Kryuchkov, Soviet Prime Minister Valentin Pavlov, and Defense Minister Dmitry Yazov.

But then the people revolted. Led by Boris Yeltsin, they

took back the Kremlin, and the "Gang of Eight," including Kryuchkov, were arrested. Nava knew that her world had changed when she saw the statue of Felix Dzerzhinsky, founder of the secret police, toppled in front of KGB headquarters. She sent a message to Zaitsev, asking him what she should do.

After four months of waiting, Nava learned through CIA channels that Dmitry Zaitsev, her teacher, mentor, and adopted father, was dead, killed by his own hand. Without his beloved KGB, he saw no reason to live. Nava was devastated, but, as she had done before, she pressed on.

And still she waited. When no one from the SVR—Russia's newly emerged espionage unit—contacted her by the first anniversary of the failed coup, Nava realized that she had been "misplaced." The few people in the KGB who had known her true identity were dead, and there had never been any formal records of her status.

For the first time in her life, Nava was free to do whatever she wanted. But all she knew was how to kill, so she stayed in the CIA. During the next five years, she assassinated so many terrorists she lost count. But however many she murdered, she was never able to wipe away the guilt for having lived when her mother and sister had died. She knew that for every man she killed, she saved countless lives, but it was never enough to fill the emptiness she felt.

Even so, she carried on her own personal vendetta. Thus, on a blistering summer day in 1999, when the CIA had decided not to terminate one of the terrorists she'd been tracking, Nava decided to ignore her orders. With some support from the Mossad, she executed the man herself. When it was through, she was surprised when the Israeli government paid her for the service that she would gladly have done for free.

And so started another chapter in her career—selling secrets and running covert missions for whoever wanted to eliminate the terrorists America did not wish to kill itself. At first she worked only for the Mossad, but over time she gained notoriety in certain circles and was hired by the

British MI6 and the German *Bundesnachrichtendienst* to take care of their nastier citizens.

Nava was very good at what she did and was paid handsomely for it. But after five more years, she was burned out, which was why she agreed to do one more mission and then disappear to a place where neither the CIA nor the SVR would ever find her. The mission was to find an Islamic terrorist cell that the North Korean RDEI wished to destroy.

Unfortunately, that didn't work out as well as she'd planned.

When Nava finished, she calmly lit a cigarette and exhaled a long trail of smoke. Caine didn't know what to say. Her tale was so far-fetched he almost believed it. No one would ever tell such a preposterous story unless it were true. And whether it was despite or because of their trial by fire, he already felt an intense connection with her.

But then reality settled upon his shoulders. The *Spetsinstitute.* Terrorists. Rogue agents. He couldn't believe that he hadn't seen the truth earlier.

"Christ," Caine muttered under his breath. "It's happened."

"Excuse me?"

Caine squeezed his eyes shut, willing her to vanish, but when he opened them, she was still sitting next to him.

"Are you all right?" the illusion asked.

"You're not real."

"What?"

"You're not real. None of this is real—it can't be. I'm having a schizophrenic break. It's the only rational explanation."

"David, I assure you—"

"NO!" Caine said, suddenly raising his voice. "This is *not real.* You're part of some delusion."

"What are you talking about?"

Caine just stared back at her, not sure of what to do. What was it that Jasper said? He furrowed his brow and blinked rapidly, trying to remember.

Try to make smart decisions within whatever world you create. Eventually you'll find your way back to reality.

Okay. He could do that. Just go with the flow. If he couldn't snap back to reality, then he would just ride it out. Jasper's advice was solid; the best way to avoid doing something crazy in the real world was to be as sane as possible in the illusionary one. And if somehow this *was* reality—even though it couldn't be; he knew that for sure—then at least he would be making rational decisions.

Comforted by his pragmatic analysis, Caine looked over at Nava again, wondering what he should say. The answer immediately popped into his head—whatever he would say if this *was* the real world. Caine opened his mouth, pausing for a moment as he realized the absurdity of the situation, but he could think of nothing else to do.

"Uh, I'm sorry, I was just feeling . . . um, not myself for a moment."

"Are you all right?" the illusion—*Nava, she said her name was Nava*—asked.

"Yeah, I'm okay." Caine said, still feeling odd but rapidly coming to grips with his new mental state. He pressed on, trying to find his way back to sanity. "So that's an incredible story, but it still doesn't explain how you know my name. And why you saved me."

Nava's face clouded, upset. "There was . . . a woman. She told me about you—who you were, where you would be, everything. And the precise time of your death, unless I was there to save you."

Her answer was more confusing than illuminating. "That still doesn't explain how this woman knew about me. Or why you decided to save me."

"To be honest," Nava said, "my original plan wasn't to save you but to kidnap you."

"To hand me over to the RDEI?" Caine asked.

"Right."

"What changed your mind?"

"The girl. She knew . . . she knew my name. My *real* name. And she knew about . . . she knew things that were impossible for her to know, unless the professor's theories were right."

Caine felt chilled. "What professor? What theories?"

"The one who ran those tests on you two days ago."

Caine felt his heart grow cold. Nava nodded. "The NSA has had him under surveillance. They intercepted some data which suggested he had recently made progress toward . . . his goal."

"What was his goal?" Caine asked, although part of him already knew the answer.

"He was convinced he had found a way to predict the future."

Caine felt sick. This delusion was starting to seem all too real. Again Jasper's words echoed in his mind.

It doesn't feel like anything at all. . . . That's why it's so fucking scary.

His brother had been right, for Caine had never been so scared in his life. He suddenly had a whole new respect for his twin.

"Are you okay?" Nava asked.

Caine ignored the question and instead asked one of his own. "This theory . . . does it have a name?"

"Yes," Nava said. "Laplace's Demon. Does that mean anything to you?"

Caine nodded, but his mind was elsewhere, trying to put the pieces together.

"I skimmed all of his abstracts at the STR lab," Nava said. "Most were about physics, biology, and statistics, but at the end there was an entire section about Laplace's Demon. I didn't have time to read it in depth, but it seemed like he was talking about the occult."

"Not the occult," Caine said. "Probability theory."

Nava looked at him blankly. "I'm not following you."

Caine sighed, not sure where to begin or why it was even necessary to explain this to a hallucination that was merely an extension of his own subconscious. But maybe that's what *he* wanted—an explanation to himself. Caine looked past Nava, trying to think of the best way to explain it. Despite the fact that he had studied Laplace's works for years, he didn't quite know where to begin so he just started to talk.

"In London during the early 1700s, there was a French statistician named Abraham De Moivre. As statistics was still in its infancy, De Moivre was able to support himself by calculating odds for local gamblers.

"He did this for about ten years, then wrote a book about his theories called *The Doctrine of Chances.* Even though it was only fifty-two pages long, it was one of the most important math texts of its time, as it laid the foundation for probability theory, which he explained through problems dealing with dice and games.

"The thing is, despite what the title of the book seems to imply, De Moivre didn't *believe* in chance."

"What do you mean?" Nava asked.

"De Moivre believed that chance was an illusion. He hypothesized that nothing ever happened 'by chance'—every seemingly random event could actually be traced back to a physical cause." Nava looked confused, so Caine resorted to his old probability standby—when in doubt, talk about coins.

"Okay," he said, grunting as he gingerly reached into his pocket and removed a quarter. "If I flip this coin, you'd say that whether or not it comes up heads or tails is pure luck, or *chance,* right?"

Nava nodded.

"Well, you would be wrong. If you were able to measure all the physical factors that go into a coin flip—the angle of my hand, its distance from the ground, the force that I use to toss the coin into the air, the wind currents, the composition of the coin, et cetera, et cetera—then you'd be able to predict with a hundred percent accuracy a flip's outcome, because the coin is subject to the laws of Newtonian physics, which are absolute."

Nava paused to light a cigarette as she considered his words. "I may be a bit out of my depth, David, but isn't it impossible to measure all those factors perfectly?"

"For people? Yes, it is," Caine said. "But just because we can't measure the factors doesn't mean the result of the coin flip is determined by chance. It only means that we, as human beings, don't have the ability to measure certain facets of the universe. Hence, events may *appear* random even though they're entirely determined by physical phenomena.

"This school of thought is called *determinism.* Determinists believe that nothing is uncertain; everything that happens is a consequence of some earlier cause, even if we don't know what that cause is."

"So walking down a busy street and bumping into a friend isn't chance?" Nava asked.

"No," Caine said. "Think about it. You never go anywhere randomly, do you? Wherever you go is a direct result of physical, emotional, and psychological forces. The same is true for everyone else. So even though an event like 'randomly' bumping into a friend may *seem* like chance, it isn't.

"Imagine a computer that could see into your mind and muscles as well as your friend's. If the computer also knew all the environmental conditions of the world in the minutes or hours leading up to your meeting, it would be able to predict when, where, and how you would meet. Hence, the ever-popular 'chance meeting' is not chance at all—it's predictable fact."

"But in the real world," Nava said slowly, "a 'chance meeting' *is* unpredictable."

Caine shook his head. "No, it's not. Because there is no such computer, we cannot predict such an event, but that doesn't make the event *unpredictable,* it just makes us *unable to predict it.* See the difference?"

Nava slowly nodded as everything clicked into place.

"That's nice in theory," said Nava, "but it just doesn't work in the real world."

"Well, De Moivre would have disagreed with you. He used physical data all the time to predict seemingly unpredictable phenomenon, including the date of his own death."

"How did he do that?" Nava asked.

"During the last few months of his life, De Moivre noticed he was sleeping fifteen minutes longer every night. As he was a determinist, he carried that knowledge to its eventual conclusion—that if he continued to increase his sleep time at the same rate, then on the night he was 'scheduled' to sleep for twenty-four hours straight, he would die. He predicted that date would occur on November twenty-seventh, 1754. And when that day came, just as he predicted, De Moivre died."

"That hardly proves his theory," Nava said skeptically.

"No, it doesn't. But you have to admit there is something interesting about a man who thought everything could be predicted if the right measurements were taken and was then able to find a measurement to predict his own death," Caine said, suddenly feeling somber. Neither spoke for a while, and then Caine continued.

"Anyway, De Moivre's *Doctrine of Chances* served as a foundation for the work of another very famous French mathematician named Simon-Pierre Laplace."

As Caine said the name, he suddenly remembered the stuffy, wood-paneled room at Columbia where he used to teach honors seminars. Although it had been more than a year since he'd lectured about the eighteenth-century statistician, he could still remember the class.

"Like most of us in this room, Laplace was misunderstood by his parents," Caine said as he paced in front of the board.

"Although his father wanted him to become either a soldier or a priest, Laplace decided on a life of academia. So when he was eighteen, he went to the academic epicenter of France—Paris. There he got a job teaching geometry to cadets at a military school, including a little kid named Napoleon Bonaparte, who I believe went on to do some pretty extraordinary things."

Caine got a slight chuckle from the twelve students crowded around the table.

"Then, in 1770, Laplace presented his first paper to Paris's prestigious Académie des Sciences. After that, it was clear to everyone that he was a mathematical genius. And so he dedicated the rest of his life to two fields—probability and astronomy. Almost thirty years later, in 1799, he merged the two fields when he published the most important astronomy book of the time—*Méchanique Céleste,* or *Celestial Mechanics.* Not only did the book contain an analytical discussion of the solar system, but it also included new methods for calculating planetary orbits.

"However, the reason *Méchanique Céleste* is still viewed as important today isn't because of Laplace's astronomical findings but because Laplace was the first person to apply probability theory to astronomy. He showed that multiple observations of the location of a star tended to conform to the bell-shaped curve that De Moivre had described in *The Doctrine of Chances.* Quite simply, by using probability theory, Laplace was able to predict planetary positions and was better able to understand the universe."

"What do you mean by 'multiple observations of the location of a star'?" asked a pale student with dark, lanky hair.

"Ah, good question," Caine said, walking to the board. "Back then one of the biggest problems with astronomy was that everyone took their measurements by hand. And, because people make mistakes, the data wasn't clean. Twenty different astronomers would each record the position of a star and get twenty different answers.

"However, Laplace took those twenty different observations and graphed them. When he did, he saw that the positions were in the shape of a bell curve like this." Caine pointed to a chart of a normal distribution on the wall.

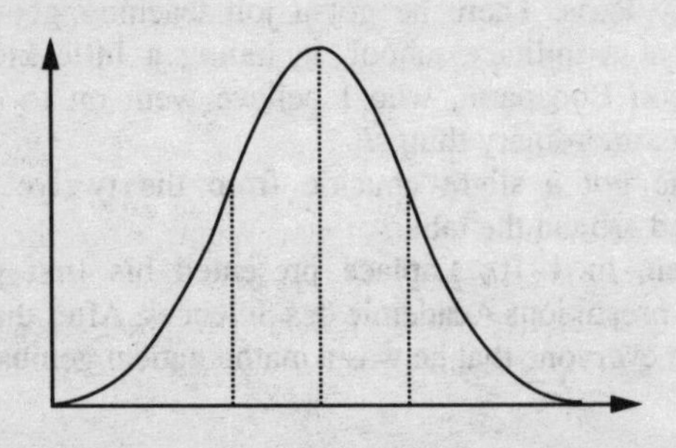

"When he saw that, he said, 'Aha, if the observations are in a normal distribution and the tip of the bell curve shows the sample's *probable* true value, then the tip is probably the true position of the star.' Seems somewhat obvious now, but at the time it was revolutionary. This was the first example of how someone applied probability theory to another discipline. Laplace said that even though it was impossible to know the precise location of the star, it was possible to know the star's position with a certain degree of probability."

Caine stopped, just to make sure that everyone was following along.

"But Laplace didn't stop there. In 1805 he published the fourth volume of *Méchanique Céleste,* where he developed a new, philosophical approach to physics. He theorized that every phenomenon in nature could be understood by studying the forces between molecules. He used this new theory to study everything from air pressure to astronomical refraction, again by using probability tools like bell curves to measure different phenomena.

"Laplace's crowning achievement came in 1812, when he published *Théorie Analytique des Probabilités,* or *Analytical Theories of Probabilities.* It was there that he fleshed out the method of least squares and the importance of minimizing errors—"

A chubby student named Steve poked up his hand. "I don't follow."

Caine remembered that because his seminar was cross-listed as a history class, there wasn't a statistics prerequisite. As there were three other history majors in the seminar, he needed to explain what he meant by minimizing errors. He scratched his head, trying to figure out where to begin.

"Do you know the difference between *statistics* and *probability?*"

Steve and the other nonmathematicians shook their heads.

"Okay. *Probability theory* is the study of so-called 'chance' events, like throwing dice or flipping a coin; *statistics* refers to the measurement of 'actual' events, like birth rates and mortality rates. In other words, probability theory is used to derive equations that *predict* statistics."

Although Caine thought he saw a lightbulb appear above Steve's head, he wasn't sure about the other two, so he reverted to his old standby.

"Let's start with a simple example. Say I'm going to flip a coin four times in a row. How many heads do you think I'll get?"

"Two," Steve said.

"Why?"

"Because heads comes up half the time, and half of four is two."

Caine nodded. "Essentially what you just did was use probability theory to predict a statistic—the number of heads. Whether you realized it or not, you created an equation to solve this problem." Caine wrote down:

H = Number of heads flipped
F = Number of coin flips
Prob(H) = probability of getting a head when flipping a coin.

How many heads do you predict in four flips?
H = Prob(H) * F
H = 0.5 * 4
H = 2

"Even though we know that the most likely outcome of four coin flips is two heads and two tails, do you think the number of heads will be exactly two every time?"

"No."

"Correct. In fact, *most* of the time there *won't* be two heads."

Steve looked confused. "Wait, didn't you just say that two heads is the most likely outcome?"

"Yes, I did."

"Then I don't understand. Won't there be two heads at least half the time?" he asked.

"No. There are sixteen possible outcomes when you flip a coin four times in a row. Let me show you."

H = Number of heads flipped
T = Number of tails flipped
n = # of possible outcomes in four coin flips

H = 0 ➔ TTTT (n = 1)
H = 1 ➔ HTTT, THTT, TTHT, TTTH (n = 4)
H = 2 ➔ HHTT, HTHT, HTTH, THHT, THTH, TTHH (n = 6)
H = 3 ➔ HHHT, HHTH, HTHH, THHH (n = 4)
H = 4 ➔ HHHH (n = 1)
Therefore,
n = 1 + 4 + 6 + 4 + 1
n = 16

"You see? Of the sixteen different possibilities, only six will result in two heads and two tails. Hence, ten out of sixteen trials, or 62.5 percent of the time, there *won't* be two heads. So I'll ask you again—if I tell you that I'm going to flip a coin four times in a row, how many heads do you think I'll get?"

Steve stared at what Caine had written on the board and furrowed his brow in concentration. "I would still say two."

"Why would you say two when I just showed you that you're going to be wrong 62.5 percent of the time?" Caine asked.

"Because any other number I pick, I'll be wrong more than 62.5 percent of the time."

"Precisely," Caine said, snapping his fingers. "If you said either one head or three heads, you would be wrong 75 percent of the time, and if you said either zero heads or four heads, you would be wrong 93.75 percent of the time." Caine smiled. "By choosing two heads, you chose the answer that *minimized* the probability of being incorrect. That is the foundation of all probability theory—minimizing errors.

"Even though the outcome of the flips is likely to be some other number besides two heads, your original equation

H = 0.5 * F

"is still valid, because it *best* describes the phenomenon. Another way to check this is by graphing the data. As you can see, there's a natural bell curve, and the tip of the bell curve reflects the natural tendency of the phenomenon.

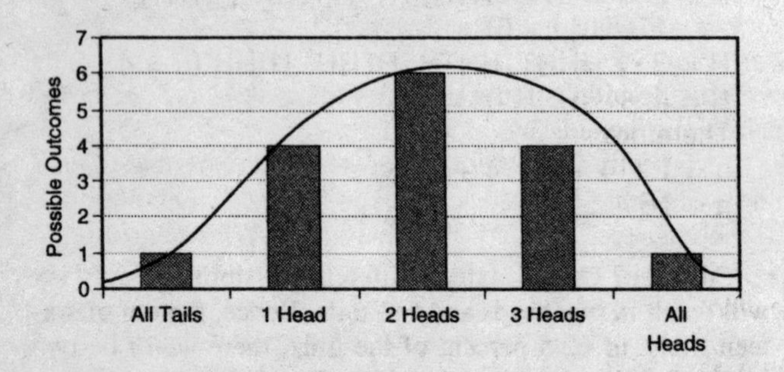

"What Laplace did was roughly the same thing, except instead of predicting the number of heads, he used thousands of astronomical observations and developed equations to predict planetary orbits."

"Okay, I get it," Steve said, "but I still don't understand why it's important."

"It's important because it demonstrates how probability theory works. Laplace showed that the best way to predict reality *isn't* to calculate the right answer but to figure out what answer will be the *least wrong*. In the coin example, even though the likelihood of getting two heads in four flips is only 37.5 percent, the likelihood of getting any other number of heads is even less likely—hence, your prediction of getting two heads is the *least wrong* and therefore the *most right*.

"That's why Laplace could predict the orbits of the planets

while others could not. He developed equations that minimized the differences in all the astronomers' data and was therefore able to determine planetary orbits that had the lowest probability of being incorrect."

"And thus the highest probability of being right," Steve said.

"Exactly," Caine said, pleased that Steve seemed to understand. "The important thing to note is that through this method, as well as others in probability theory, you can never be absolutely certain of anything, as the goal of predictive equations becomes to *minimize* errors, not to *eliminate* them."

"Why wouldn't you want to eliminate errors?" a dark-haired girl named Colleen asked.

"Technically you would. However, it's impossible to entirely eliminate errors, because you never have enough information necessary to create a perfect predictive equation."

"Why not?"

"Think of polls you read in the paper before an election—they're never 100 percent correct, because it's impossible to poll every voter. However, by surveying a small sample of people across different socioeconomic strata, pollsters are able to develop equations to predict with a certain degree of probability which candidate will win. That's why you always see that the polls are only accurate within one or two percentage points—because poll results are probabilities, not certainties.

"You see, probability theory gives scientists the freedom to assume an answer is 'right' even when they're not 100 percent sure, because probability theory states that when the chances of being wrong are minuscule, you have probably discovered the truth."

Caine was silent for a moment to let everything sink in, then continued.

"So that brings us to Laplace's most controversial theory, which was often called his 'demon.' Two years after he published *Théorie Analytique des Probabilités,* he wrote *Essai Philosophique sur les Probabilités,* or *Philosophical*

Essay on Probabilities. In it was his second-most-famous quote." Caine referred to his notes and read Laplace's quote aloud.

> Given for one instant an intelligence which could comprehend all the forces by which nature is animated and the respective situation of the beings who compose it—an intelligence sufficiently vast to submit these data to analysis—it would embrace in the same formula the movements of the greatest bodies of the universe and those of the lightest atom; for it, nothing would be uncertain and the future, as the past, would be present to its eyes.

"In other words," Caine continued, "since Laplace believed that the universe was deterministic, he surmised that if someone understood all the laws of physics and knew the position of every subatomic particle in the universe at a single moment in time, then that someone would know everything that ever happened and would be able to perfectly predict all future history."

"But it's impossible to know everything," Colleen said.

"Nothing is impossible," Caine said, "although certain things are infinitely improbable." He took a sip of his Coke as everyone absorbed his words. "Scientists now refer to his theory as Laplace's Demon."

"Why is it called his demon?" Steve asked. "Because it plagued him?"

"No, that's a common misconception," Caine said. "It didn't plague him at all, because Laplace was convinced he was correct. After he died, scientists adopted the phrase 'Laplace's Demon' to describe an omniscient intelligence that was capable of knowing everything in the present, and therefore would know all that had happened in the past and all that would happen in the future."

"Sounds like God," Colleen said.

"Yeah," Caine said, musing. "Something like that."

Nava made him a splint while Caine finished an abridged version of his lecture. After he was through, Nava was quiet for nearly a minute before breaking the silence.

"David," she said, "the scientists at the STR believe *you* are Laplace's Demon."

Caine shook his head. "That's crazy. Laplace's Demon isn't a real thing. It's not an entity; it's a theory. Laplace's Demon is just a phrase used to describe an all-knowing intelligence that can predict the future."

He paused, his head spinning. "Besides, Laplace's Demon was proved impossible in the early 1900s."

"How?" Nava asked.

"A physicist named Werner Heisenberg showed that subatomic particles don't have a single position until they are observed."

Nava raised her eyebrows, to which Caine responded, "Don't ask—it's quantum physics, it's not supposed to make any sense."

"Okay, fine. But why does that make Laplace's Demon impossible?"

"Because, if subatomic particles have multiple positions at the same time, then it is impossible for any intelligence—even an omniscient one—to know the precise position of every particle since they don't have exact positions. And, since that knowledge is a requisite to predicting the future, the future is impossible to predict. Hence, Laplace's Demon is impossible.

"Besides," Caine said, "I don't know everything and I can't predict the future."

"What about the diner?" Nava countered.

Caine felt himself grow cold. "How do you know about that?"

"The NSA was watching." Nava leaned forward. "I saw what happened, David. I saw you pull everyone out of the way a second before the truck plowed through that wall. If that's not predicting the future, then what is?"

"Look, I don't know what happened in that diner. Call it

intuition, hell, even call it precognition. But that doesn't make me an omniscient intelligence." Caine ran a hand through his unruly hair. "Christ, if I knew everything, you think I would owe the Russian mob $12,000? Nava, I can't even predict the next card, never mind all future history."

But even as Caine heard his words, he realized they weren't entirely true. Hadn't he known the explosion was going to kill him unless he could figure a way out? Hadn't he thrown the briefcase that started the chain reaction that allowed Nava to reach him in time? Caine didn't know what to think besides the impossible.

It was suddenly even clearer to him that all this was a delusion. Perhaps this mental exercise was working . . . maybe he was getting close to finding his way back to sanity. Already he felt more focused, more alert. He decided to push forward.

"Okay, let's say I am . . ." Caine paused. "What you say I am. What do we do?"

"Whether you are or not, we have to move." Nava motioned toward a patch of sunlight on the floor. "It's almost nine. If we stay here too long, they'll find us."

"Which 'they,' exactly?" Caine asked.

"FBI, NSA, RDEI—take your pick," Nava said solemnly.

He nodded. It didn't matter anyway. It was all a dream. He might as well follow Nava's instinct and move. She squatted beside him and put his arm around her shoulders.

"Put your weight on me and try to stand." Caine did as she asked, trying to help by using his right leg as she heaved him off the floor in one fluid motion. She was even stronger than she looked. He put some weight on his left foot, and the room got dark and fuzzy.

"Whoa!" Nava grabbed him with her other arm, holding him tightly to her body. The world swam back into place.

"What happened?" Caine asked.

"You almost passed out," she said. "If I let go now, do you think you can stand?"

Caine gently put his weight on his left foot again and nodded. Slowly she released him from her embrace and stepped back. Although Caine wobbled slightly, he managed to remain standing. Another dizzy spell washed over him, but he closed his eyes and rode it out, holding on to the refrigerator for support.

"Do you think you're going to pass out again?"

"I don't think so." He tentatively hopped a couple of steps forward. "Although I don't think I can make good time without a crutch or something."

She nodded. "Agreed. I'll be right back." She opened the door and left the apartment, and he heard a sound like kindling being chopped.

"Here, try this," she said, returning with a makeshift walking stick. He carefully took it from her hands, trying to avoid the jagged edges.

"Yeah," he said, "this will do."

"Ah," Caine said on his way down the stairs, gesturing toward the three missing spindles in the railing, which now served as his splint and cane. Nava just nodded and helped him maneuver the narrow staircase. As they reached the ground level, she steeled herself for whatever awaited them outside as she pushed through the front door.

Nava held her breath for an instant—if somehow the NSA knew they were here, it would happen now. She wondered whether she'd feel the bullet drill into her forehead.

Nothing.

All she felt was the rain on her skin. It was coming down hard, plastering Nava's clothes to her body, chilling her to the bone. She briefly looked up at the sky, a slate-gray backdrop punctuated with heavy black clouds. She was still alive—not a minor accomplishment. Now that they'd survived their first hurdle, Nava assessed their situation.

The NSA would want to keep this operation as quiet as possible, especially given that there had been at least one fatality. However, if they genuinely thought Caine was some "omniscient intelligence," they wouldn't let him slip through their grasp without a fight. She looked at her watch: 9:03 A.M. Caine had been off their radar for almost fifteen hours. If Forsythe hadn't called in reinforcements yet, he would do so soon.

The first order of business was to get out of New York City, the focus of the manhunt. She toyed with the idea of leaving the country but didn't want to risk being subjected to post-9/11 airport security. That left three other means of egress: car, bus, or rail.

She could easily steal a vehicle, but she feared going through any toll booths—they would be watching. She and Caine could take a subway out of the city and hot-wire a car in one of the outer boroughs, but again she feared the cameras in the subway stations. If an assault team cornered them underground, there would be no escape.

She didn't like the idea of taking the bus, as it was vulnerable to traffic and could easily get stopped in a roadblock. She knew that a train could also be stopped, but at least it was big enough to provide someplace to hide if it was boarded.

She rubbed her head, unsure of what to do. Normally she was so decisive, but there was something about Caine that unnerved her, made her question herself. She tried to shake off her uncertainty.

Caine, sensing her indecision, looked over at her. Their eyes locked, and he did something very odd: He squeezed his lids shut as if he'd been blinded by a bright light.

She grabbed his arm. "David, what's wrong?"

For a moment he didn't respond. It was as if his consciousness had left his body. And then suddenly he was back. His eyes opened, and he gasped for breath.

"David, what happened?"

"Nothing," he said, wobbling a little on his feet. "I'm fine." And then, "We need to get out of the city."

"I know," Nava said. "The only question is how."

"Train," Caine blurted out. "We need to take the train."

"Why?"

"I don't know, but that's what we need to do."

"Are you sure?"

"Yes, " Caine said, clearly frustrated, "but don't ask me why."

"Okay, but first we need to get you a new wardrobe." She pointed to his torn pant leg and the naked knee beneath. The flesh that surrounded the bloody bandages had turned a deep shade of purple.

"Good point," he said. "You could probably use some new

things yourself." Nava looked down at her own bloodstained pants. As quickly as Caine could manage, she led him to an army/navy surplus store two blocks away. Ten minutes later they left the store in their new clothes.

Nava wore a bomber jacket over a tight black tank top, her long brown hair hidden beneath a green bandanna. Caine wore a baggy pair of camouflage pants and a used army jacket to cover his wounds. He had traded in his homemade walking stick for a black cane with a silver snake-head handle worn smooth. Despite the rain, Caine slipped on a pair of five-dollar sunglasses. The two of them didn't look good, but at least they no longer looked like the walking wounded.

Nava raised her hand and flagged down a nearby cab.

"Where to?" the driver asked in a thick Indian accent.

"Penn Station," Nava replied. "The quicker the better."

Forsythe paced back and forth in his office. Caine had been missing for almost fifteen hours. Fifteen fucking hours. Forsythe couldn't believe he'd slipped through their fingers. It was Grimes's fault. Forsythe should never have allowed that pimple-faced little turd to run the surveillance team.

It wasn't too late to call in a new tactical commander, but once Forsythe made the call, there would be no turning back. He decided to hold off until he got an update from Grimes. He walked out to the Surveillance Center, a large round room with no overhead lighting. All the illumination came from the hundred glowing monitors, three for each workstation. The desks fanned out in concentric circles, with Grimes at the center. He was sitting in an oversize leather chair, surrounded by plasma screens and keyboards.

"Have you made any progress?" Forsythe barked.

Grimes spun around, glaring. He ran his hand through hair that was even greasier than normal. He had dark circles beneath his eyes, and two new pimples bloomed on his chin. "He's dropped off the map. No calls to or from his cell, and he hasn't been back home since the incident.

"I checked his e-mail, but there's been no activity. I fed his voiceprint into the mainframe and compared it against all calls made from the tristate area in the last fifteen hours. No matches. Then I checked his known friends in the city. There's no evidence he's made contact of any kind."

Hands clasped behind his back, Forsythe stared at the floor. "Have you been able to determine whether the woman at the explosion was Vaner?"

Grimes nodded. "I reviewed the satellite photo again. Although we didn't record an image of her face, we have a great shot of the top of her head as well as one of her hand."

"And?" Forsythe hated when Grimes dragged it out like this. He would never just say what he knew; he always forced his audience to follow along.

Grimes pointed to one of his monitors, which showed a bird's-eye view of a woman. "I compared the hair color and skin pigmentation from the satellite to our own security tapes from yesterday. It's a perfect match for Agent Vaner." He pressed another few buttons, and her dossier appeared on the screen.

"Did you know that she was responsible for the assassinations of more than two dozen members of Al Qaeda, Hamas, and the PLO—"

Forsythe cut him off. "I'm familiar with her background. The question isn't *who* but *why*."

Grimes took a sip of coffee and shrugged his shoulders. "Guess you'd have to ask her. Maybe she's still answering to the CIA."

Without bothering to respond, Forsythe stormed into his office and slammed the door. He had to remain calm. He closed his eyes and counted to ten. When he opened them, he sat down and picked up the phone.

After explaining the situation to Doug Nielsen, the CIA's current DDO—deputy director (operations)—Forsythe heard the man sigh.

"Heck, I don't know what to tell you, James," Nielsen said in his slow southern drawl. "Vaner was one of our best. Quite frankly, I'm shocked that something like this has happened."

"And you had nothing to do with this?"

"I've got news for you, James," Nielsen said, ire creeping into his voice, "the CIA's got bigger fish to fry than muckin' around in one of your science projects." Forsythe was about to snap back, but the contempt in the DDO's voice made him realize that Nielsen was telling the truth.

Now it was Forsythe's turn to sigh. "Okay. How do I find her?"

Nielsen snorted. "You don't."

"That's not acceptable."

"Well, it'll have to be, friend. You don't have the manpower to—"

"I don't, but *you* do."

Nielsen was silent for a moment. Then he said in a low voice. "What do you expect me to do? Send over an assault team like General Fielding?"

"How did you know—"

"It's my *job* to know, James. Same as it's my job to know that, according to Senator MacDougal, in about three weeks you are out of a job."

Forsythe's fingernails dug deep into his palm. If MacDougal was mouthing off, then no one would help him. He was at a loss. Fortunately, Nielsen was not.

"Listen, James," Nielsen said, "I still may be able to help. All I ask is that you remember this when I retire. If you do, then I'll let you slide."

"Slide on what?"

"All the laws you've broken. Not to mention that little venture-capital nest egg you've been collecting on the sly." Forsythe's mouth went dry. It seemed there was nothing Nielsen didn't know. All Forsythe could do was go along.

"I would be grateful for any assistance you could provide," he finally said.

"Good."

Forsythe could practically hear Nielsen's self-satisfied smile on the other end of the phone.

"Here's my advice: First I'd call up Sam Kendall. I don't think he's heard the news of your impending change in status, and if you don't tell him, neither will I. Kendall should be able to spare some resources, along with his natural gift at making nice with the local authorities."

"Excellent suggestion, Doug. Thank you." Forsythe wasn't optimistic about the extra manpower that the executive assistant director of the FBI would give him, and he knew that Kendall's diplomacy when dealing with police was notoriously poor, but it was better than nothing.

"Anything else?"

"Well, if you really are serious about finding Vaner and your lost boy, I know a tracker you could use. He used to be in the FBI, but now he's Joe Citizen. Off the record, he's done some excellent freelance work for us. I'm sure he would help you out. For the right price, of course."

"Of course," Forsythe said, his mind already racing. "What's his name?"

Nielsen paused. "Martin Crowe."

"As in *the* Martin Crowe?"

"You want to find them, don't you?"

"Of course, but—"

"Then you best get on the horn with Mr. Crowe pronto. Time's a-wastin', James."

Forty minutes and a thousand dollars later, Forsythe was face-to-face with Martin Crowe—the most frightening man he'd ever met.

Crowe kept his dark olive face inscrutable as he silently listened to Dr. Forsythe. He found that it was better to allow stories to be told in a long narrative—interruptions often made people lose their train of thought, leading to the omission of critical details. Whenever he had a question, he made a mental note and continued to listen. After ten minutes

Forsythe finished his fantastical tale about the rogue CIA agent and the man she'd kidnapped.

"Have you left anything out?"

Forsythe shook his head. "No. That's everything."

Crowe stood up and held out his hand. "It was nice meeting you."

"Wait," Forsythe said, shooting out of his chair. "What about the job?"

"Dr. Forsythe, I'm successful because I take great pains to make sure I'm never surprised. That's what keeps me alive. I will not engage in an operation unless I know what I'm up against. And right now I don't."

"What are you talking about? I've told you everything."

"No you haven't," Crowe said simply.

Forsythe looked indignant. "Mr. Crowe, I assure you—"

Crowe slammed his fist down on the desk, stopping Forsythe in midsentence. "Don't insult me, Doctor. I know I'm being lied to. Now, if you want my help on this, you'll tell me the *real* reason David Caine is so important to you."

Forsythe's jaw worked as he decided what to do. When he finally began to speak, Crowe sat back down. Once Forsythe was through, Crowe slowly nodded, assessing the situation. It was clear that Forsythe believed everything he'd said, but Crowe was still skeptical. This "demon" that Forsythe had described couldn't be real. If it was, that would mean man had no free will, and that was something Martin Crowe could never accept.

He was open-minded enough to believe that maybe Caine had some paranormal abilities or precognitive powers. But anything more than that was simply impossible. Still, if Caine had even half the gift Forsythe had described, the mission could prove very difficult.

That, combined with the rogue CIA agent, gave Crowe a very bad feeling. If anything happened to him, there would be no one to take care of Betsy. But then again, if he didn't come up with some cash, Betsy wouldn't last much longer, with or without him.

Despite the risks, Crowe knew that if the money was there, he didn't have a choice. "My rate is $15,000 per day, with a $125,000 bonus when I acquire the target—$250,000 if it takes less than twenty-four hours. Nonnegotiable."

Forsythe gagged for a moment but then squeaked out a response. "I can pay that amount."

"Good." Crowe stood up and extended one of his powerful hands. This time Forsythe took it and gave it a quick shake. Crowe met his eyes briefly before Forsythe turned away. Crowe didn't like what he saw there, but it didn't matter. His days of fighting for the good guys were long behind him. Now the only thing he fought for was Betsy. All his ethics were on hold as long as she needed him.

As Crowe contemplated the mission before him, the adrenaline in his veins began to work its magic. The feeling reminded him of when he first became a G-man, back when there was a clear line between right and wrong.

Before he met Sandy.

Before they had Betsy.

And before she got sick.

Ever since he could remember, Martin Crowe had wanted to serve his fellow man. His mother had always hoped he would do so by becoming a priest, but Martin knew he was far too aggressive to be a clergyman. So, instead of seminary school, Crowe attended Georgetown Law, thinking that the adversarial nature of the justice system would provide a natural home for his combative personality.

However, when it came time for graduation, Crowe chose to enroll in the FBI instead of taking a job at the U.S. Attorney's Office. Once he began training at Quantico, he never looked back. Crowe sailed through with ease, reveling in the intense competition that he'd missed since his days as a college athlete.

Driven by an intense desire for justice, he proved to his superiors time and again that he was a true rarity: an exceptional agent with absolutely no outside interests who could work fifteen hours a day, seven days a week, for months at a time without showing any signs of fatigue.

He was willing to do the lowliest grunt work and the worst stakeouts, indifferent to whether he was stationed in Milwaukee or Miami. Whatever the Bureau threw at him, he did it with precision and excellence. And when it came time to make an arrest, Martin Crowe was first through the door, gun outstretched.

During the first few years, there was nothing more important than his job. Then he met a fellow agent named Sandy Bates, and everything changed. After a whirlwind three-month romance, Martin Crowe proposed. A year and a half later, Sandy gave birth to a beautiful little girl. During Betsy's baptism Martin Crowe cried the only tears of his adult life. He had never been happier.

Becoming a family man gave his work new meaning, and although he no longer enjoyed traveling for weeks at a time, he knew he was making the country a safer place for his wife and daughter. And then one day his life came crashing to a halt. He could still remember Sandy's choked voice when she told him that Betsy had been diagnosed with juvenile myelomonocytic leukemia. Suddenly Crowe's world was transformed into a very scary place, where evil was measured not by the penal code but by cancer cells and blood counts.

He had finally come face-to-face with an adversary he couldn't bring down, and he was powerless to do anything except watch as it devoured his little girl. Sandy quit her job at the Bureau to take care of Betsy, while Crowe worked overtime to try to make up the financial slack. Unfortunately, however much he worked, it wasn't enough, especially when he discovered that his health insurance didn't cover many of the experimental procedures Betsy's doctors wanted to try.

Within six months they had spent all their savings, but Betsy was still dying. Crowe found himself up against the wall, slowly going out of his mind. He should have taken a leave of absence, but he needed the money, so instead he volunteered for extra shifts.

That was how he got on the Duane case.

"Big Daddy" Duane had abducted and killed seven children, keeping them for a week before mailing each one back in pieces to the grieving parents. The media had nicknamed him the "FedEx Killer" (much to the express shipper's chagrin), and Crowe swore to himself that one way or another, he would bring the man in.

When Crowe joined the team, they were searching for Bethany O'Neil, a six-year-old from Falmouth, Massachusetts, who'd been snatched from the park four days earlier. The clock was ticking, and everyone knew it. Then they caught their first break—Stephen Chesterfield, one of the perverts Duane often chatted with online, was busted in a routine pedophile sweep. However, after twenty-four hours of interrogation, the federal agents in charge of the investigation couldn't break him.

So they called in Martin Crowe.

All the cameras were turned off, and Chesterfield was left alone with Crowe behind a locked door in a soundproof room. It was there, staring at Stephen Chesterfield, knowing that another little girl's life was on the line while his own little girl lay dying in a hospital, that Crowe finally snapped.

He emerged after an hour with Big Daddy's location scrawled on a bloodstained piece of paper. The other agents didn't ask what Crowe had done. They didn't want to know. All they wanted was to get Big Daddy before he started mailing the O'Neil kid back to her parents.

Two hours later, they burst through the door of the pedophile's log cabin, where they shot and killed Big Daddy Duane. Supposedly he had a gun, even though no weapon was ever recovered. However, while the two arresting agents basked in glory, the media ripped Crowe apart for violating Chesterfield's civil rights.

Had Chesterfield been just any perp, they could have swept the whole incident under the carpet. Unfortunately for Crowe, Stephen Chesterfield was the brother of a U.S. prosecutor, so when he was discovered bruised and beaten, someone had to pay. After photos of Chesterfield's bloody face were leaked to the media, headlines blasted Martin Crowe, citing him as the poster child for all that was wrong with law enforcement. The *New York Post* gave him a nickname—"Black" Crowe—and the moniker stuck. He was immediately terminated from the FBI and indicted.

Eight months later Crowe's attorney pointed the finger at every other agent in the field office, in a desperate attempt to show reasonable doubt. Crowe probably would have gotten the max—ten years in a federal penitentiary—had it not been for the O'Neil family, who attended every day of the trial. They sat directly behind Crowe, so that whenever the jurors looked at the man accused of being a sadist, they also saw the beautiful girl he had saved. It took the jury only three hours to come back with a verdict.

Not guilty.

Despite the acquittal, the strain of the trial had ruined what was left of his life. When it was all over, Crowe found himself unemployed, uninsured, penniless, and on the brink of a divorce. All that would have been terrible enough, but it paled in comparison with what was happening to Betsy, who was fighting an impossible battle—one she would surely lose without an expensive bone-marrow transplant. Although the doctors had yet to find a match, Crowe promised that when they did, he would have enough money to pay for the procedure.

And so he became a mercenary. He knew that most of his employers were conducting illegal activities, but he didn't care. All his religious, ethical, and philosophical beliefs were irrelevant as long as Betsy was sick. Although he had done some immoral things in the last few months, he'd managed not to kill anyone. He told himself that was something he would never do—not for any amount of money.

But in his heart he knew he would cross that line, too, if by doing so he could save his only daughter. It was merely a matter of time.

There was something about Crowe's dead eyes that gave Forsythe the chills. Afraid to interrupt the man while he was thinking, Forsythe pretended to study his computer screen. Crowe steepled his fingers and balanced his chin on their tips. After what seemed like an eternity, he looked up and began giving orders.

"They'll be headed out of the city. Airport security is too risky, so they'll drive or take a train. If they left the city last night, we're screwed. If not, maybe we'll get lucky. Do you have agents covering Penn Station?"

Forsythe perked up, glad he could answer the question in the affirmative. Nielsen had been right—Kendall hadn't been aware that Forsythe was going to be replaced, and thus he'd been willing to assign a few men to assist in the manhunt.

"There are FBI agents monitoring every platform at Penn Station as well as patrolling the terminals at Port Authority."

Crowe shook his head. "Covering the bus station is a waste of resources. No trained agent would ever trap herself on a bus. Who's responsible for communication around here?"

"Grimes."

"Get him."

Forsythe summoned Grimes into his office. The second he walked in, Crowe took charge.

"Pull the men at Port Authority and have them double up at the train station."

"Anything else?" Grimes asked.

"Yes," Crowe said quietly. "Get me a list of every single person the target knows within a five-hundred-mile radius. Monitor all their communications until we catch him."

"You think they'll be that stupid?"

"If Vaner was running the show, I'd say no, but we can't know that for sure. When civilians are on the run, they typically go to someone they can trust. If we have any hope of catching him, it will be through his friends. Or family.

"Now," Crowe said, turning his attention back to Forsythe, "tell me about his twin."

Caine was about to ask Nava where they would go from Penn Station, but then he remembered this was all a dream. For a moment he'd almost forgotten, going along with the delusion as if it were reality. Did it really matter where his dream self was headed? He thought it didn't, but then a tiny voice in the back of his mind disagreed. But where should he go? As soon as he asked the question, the answer popped into his head. It was so obvious. Again his brother's words guided him.

Try to find ways to anchor yourself, places to be safe or people to be safe with.

He should go to Jasper in Philly. If he could direct his delusion toward the one person that could help him, maybe he could find a way out. Convinced this was the best course of action, Caine let himself sink down into the vinyl seat and watched the city stream by his window. The DJ on the radio announced that it was 9:47 A.M. before Jim Morrison began crooning "People Are Strange." As the song ended, Nava began giving Caine instructions.

"When we enter the train station, keep your head down. There are cameras in the ceiling. When we're standing still, just pretend to be reading this." She thrust a soggy newspaper from the floor of the cab into his hands. "Understood?"

Caine nodded.

"You go first. I'll be right behind you," she said. "If there's trouble, take off. Do not wait for me. I can take care of myself. The important thing is for you to disappear."

Nava slid a cell phone into Caine's pocket. "If we get separated, add 'one' to the last digit of the first number on speed dial—anyone answers besides me, assume I'm dead. Hang up and run. Clear?"

"Crystal."

After exiting the cab on Thirty-fourth and Eighth, they rode down the escalator in silence. Once underground, Caine limped toward the Amtrak trains. He had gone this route a hundred times and knew the stores he passed even as his eyes studied the floor in front of him. All the while he could feel Nava's presence behind him.

He stopped beneath the enormous schedule board in the center of the station, resisting every natural instinct to look up.

Nava's breath touched the back of his neck. She mumbled aloud, "The next train is in eight minutes, headed to Washington; we take that."

Perfect. Philly was on the way to D.C. Once on the train, Caine felt confident he would be able to sell Nava on going to Philadelphia. If he couldn't, he'd ditch her—assuming that it was possible to ditch a delusion. After a few more minutes, a staticky voice announced that Train 183, the 10:07 to D.C., was arriving on Track 12.

Nava firmly grasped Caine's elbow, turned him in the direction of the flowing crowd, and nudged him forward. Like a cork in Niagara Falls, Caine was carried toward the platform below.

Agent Sean Murphy always got stuck with the shitty assignments. Sometimes he felt like he had a Post-it stapled to his forehead that read *Please put me on irrelevant stakeouts.* He couldn't believe he had to stand on Track 12 all fucking day looking for someone who was probably already in Mexico. He glanced down at his paper again, which showed a five-by-eight grid of computer-generated images. Twenty were of David Caine, the other twenty of Nava Vaner. Each was pictured in any number of disguises.

Caine with a beard, no mustache. Caine with a mustache,

no beard. Vaner wearing spectacles. Caine wearing spectacles. Vaner with short hair. Vaner with long hair. Caine bald. It was all so stupid. The most important pieces of info were height and weight. Height couldn't be changed, and weight was difficult to fake. However, most suspects concentrated on disguising their face, which was a waste. Their eyes always gave them away.

People on the run had a look that reminded Murphy of the pet rabbit he had as a kid. Whenever it was time to clean Bugs's cage, the pitiful animal hunkered down in the corner, its eyes darting around with a naked fear that made Murphy want to puke. He hated that stupid rabbit. His mom made him take care of it so that he'd learn to be responsible, but all he really learned was that he hated rabbits.

Murphy watched the river of people, searching their faces. He'd seen a thousand passengers since 7:00 A.M. As it was still morning, 50 percent of them had the glazed look of people who'd rather be sleeping. Another 40 percent just looked annoyed; New Yorkers felt like they owned the world and were surrounded by idiots. Only 10 percent actually looked happy, excited about their upcoming trip. Anywhere else in the country, that 10 percent would be 60 percent. But this was New York—land of the free, home of the pissed.

More eyes streamed by. Bored, tired, closed, pissed, pissed, bored, pissed, half-lidded, exhausted, bloodshot . . . They kept coming and coming. Every once in a while, he'd glance back down at his sheet and then up at the sea of pissed humanity.

"Got anything, Murph?" His earpiece crackled, startling him out of his fugue.

He tilted his chin and spoke into the mike on his lapel, not even trying to hide the action. In the early days, when every mission seemed like he was fighting for Truth, Justice, and the American Way, he had done everything by the book. But after seventeen years of stakeouts in bus stations, train stations, airports, public restrooms (those really sucked), parks, and hotels, the novelty had worn off—as had the finer points of training.

"Nuthin'. You?" Murphy asked.

"Nada."

Murphy opened his mouth in a wide, silent yawn. Eyes, eyes, eyes. Christ, this was a fucking waste of time. No way David Caine would show up here. He looked at his watch. Another hour, and then he could take a break. He fingered the pack of cigarettes in his pocket longingly, fantasizing about that first drag as he watched the eyes roll by.

Nava made him in a second. He broke all the rules, making no effort to blend. He was big and bulky, probably about six-two, 240 pounds with a steel gray crew cut, wearing a blue blazer in a pitiful attempt to conceal his shoulder holster.

He was even holding a piece of paper, which no doubt bore Caine's likeness. The agent hadn't spotted them yet, as he was only inspecting the passengers as they reached the platform. Another mistake. Just twelve people separated them from the agent. Nava cursed herself for following Caine's suggestion of taking the train. She should have carjacked a tourist, thrown him in the trunk, and driven to Connecticut to regroup.

Ten people left.

She leaned forward to whisper in Caine's ear. "Move aside, and whatever I do, follow me." Before Caine could turn around, she firmly pushed him aside and squeezed next to him. Caine followed her lead and hopped backward onto the stair she had just vacated.

Four people left.

Amazingly, the agent didn't notice Nava and Caine's switch. Pathetic. Although she knew she should be grateful, she was irritated at the man's incompetence. America's intelligence force might be massive, but, for the most part, it was poorly trained.

Two people left.

Nava, eyes supremely confident, put on a big fake smile and held it. Assuming they were only looking for Caine, her plan should work. If they were looking for her—and if the agent was as fast as he should be—they were screwed.

One person left.

Nava arched her back, leading with her breasts, and stared at the agent with a sensual gaze. If he was KGB, he would have looked to the man behind her wearing sunglasses despite the gloom. But he wasn't. In that moment he was barely an intelligence agent. He was just a horny guy.

His eyes raced across her body, pausing at her breasts, but when his gaze reached her face, his eyes faltered. She had to move before he could react. Pretending to stumble, she fell toward her would-be attacker, allowing him to catch her in his arms. Then she quickly ran her hand up his chest and ripped the mike off his lapel in a swift jerk.

"Hey, you're—" He stopped speaking when he felt the pressure on his groin.

"Don't move," she whispered, keeping the smile plastered to her face. "What you now feel is the tip of a seven-inch blade. Unless you want to feel the rest of it, gently put your arms around me like we are embracing, and take two steps backward toward the wall. Very slowly."

The agent did what he was told. People streamed by the apparent lovebirds, completely oblivious of the dagger at the man's groin.

"How many are with you?"

"Look, Vaner—"

Nava made a quick jab with her dagger, pricking his thigh. "How. Many?"

"Okay, okay," he said, trying to retract his pelvis, but his back was to the wall. "There are ten others in the station."

"How many on this platform?" She tilted her head up, as if to give him a kiss. She could smell the cigarettes on his breath.

"One other."

"Describe him."

He hesitated for an instant, so she reminded him what was at stake.

"Jesus!" he hissed. "I'll tell you, just be careful with that thing. He's about five-ten, thin, probably a buck-sixty. Blond hair, cut short like mine."

"Who do you work for?"

"CIA," he answered too quickly; he was lying.

"Okay." She turned her head and rested it on his chest so she could speak to Caine out of the side of her mouth. "Get the blue *pen* from the bottom zipper compartment and put it in my hand." She turned back and looked up at the agent as Caine rummaged in her knapsack. "Hey, look at me."

The agent reluctantly obeyed. She saw fear in his eyes.

"Don't worry. You'll live."

Caine put the three-inch plastic tube in her left hand, and Nava jabbed it into the agent's thigh. The blue cylinder collapsed, triggering the spring mechanism that released the needle. His muscles tightened as the syringe pierced his flesh. Five seconds later, after the benzodiazepine rushed through his veins, he went slack, a dull smile on his face. Dropping the now empty plastic tube, Nava put the palm of her left hand on his chest to make sure the agent didn't fall.

"What's your name?"

"Sean Murphy." He spoke as if he were in the middle of a dream.

"How do you feel, Sean?"

"Sleepy." As if to emphasize the point, he leaned his head back and closed his eyes.

"Sean. Sean!" Nava sheathed her blade and gave Murphy a quick shake.

He opened his eyes with a start, looking down at her in confusion. "I want to sleep."

"I know. I just need one favor, okay?"

"Okay," he mumbled into his collar, like the world's biggest four-year-old.

"If anyone wakes you, just tell them you were tired and took a quick nap after the train left. You never saw me. You must have fallen asleep."

"Right. Never saw you." He blinked his eyes rapidly, as if trying to prevent them from closing on their own. "Can I sleep now?"

"Just one more question. Who do you *really* work for?"

He mumbled something as his eyes slowly closed. Nava gripped his shoulders tighter in frustration. He'd be out in ten seconds whether she gave him permission or not. "Who do you work for?"

Nava bent her ear to Murphy's mouth, as his voice was but a whisper. "F . . . B . . . Iiiiiiii." His head dropped onto his chest, and a line of drool dripped from his lips. Nava closed his mouth and gently propped him against a support in the wall.

"Attention, passengers: Train 183 to Washington, D.C., now arriving on Track 12."

Nava pulled her knapsack off her shoulder and removed another plastic tube, identical to the first except this one was yellow. By now she could hear the *CLANG, CLANG, CLANG* of the bell as the train pulled into the station. She quickly glanced around for any voyeurs, but everyone was jostling for the best spot on the platform. She turned to Caine, who wore a look of horror.

"Is he . . . I mean, did you . . . ? "

"He's not dead. If I killed him, they'd know where we were going." She pulled the tiny plastic bud out of Murphy's ear and placed it in her own with one hand and reattached his lapel mike with the other.

Just then it crackled to life. "Check in, Murphy."

"Here," Nava said gruffly into the mike, camouflaging her voice.

"See anything?"

"Nope."

"Yeah, me neither. I think you were right—this is a waste of time."

"Yup." Nava knew that if she kept her answers to one syllable, she'd be safe.

"Okay. Talk to you again in five."

" 'Kay." Nava waited another five seconds and then returned the earpiece to the agent, adjusting the volume control on his battery pack to the maximum output.

"Attention, passengers: All aboard for Train 183 to Washington, D.C., which will be departing from Track 12 in two minutes."

Nava injected Murphy's thigh with the second syringe—flumazenil mixed with amphetamines to counteract the BZD. Then she spun around and grabbed Caine's arm, pulling him into the queue of people. A minute later they were on board as the train pulled away from the station.

Nava exhaled a deep breath as the train picked up speed, heading out of the city. She wondered if they had truly escaped, but she knew they wouldn't have to wonder long. They would know soon enough.

"Tickets!" the stout woman shouted as she shuffled through the aisle. "Please have your tickets ready. Tickets!"

Nava pushed some twenties into Caine's hand. "Buy a one-way to Washington."

When the ticket taker reached Caine, he did as Nava had instructed. He didn't react when Nava bought a round-trip to Baltimore. "If anyone asks, I didn't want her to think we were traveling together—it might buy us some time."

"So we're both going to Baltimore, then?" Caine asked.

Nava shook her head. "No. We're getting off at the next stop."

"Why Newark?"

"I want off this train before they get back on our trail."

"Do I get a vote?"

"No. This is the safest option."

Caine drew a deep breath. He had to take control of the delusion. If he could get to Jasper, then he would be safe. "I want to go to Philadelphia."

"Why?"

"My brother lives there." The second the words left his mouth, Caine knew it had been a mistake.

"That's exactly why we *shouldn't* go there. It's the first place they'll look."

"Who's 'they'?"

" 'They' is the FBI and whoever else the NSA has employed to bring you in," she whispered, lowering her voice, "or haven't you been paying attention?"

"But I need to get to Jasper."

"You can't now. Can't you understand that?"

"None of this makes any sense!" Caine erupted, causing several other passengers to turn their heads.

"Keep your voice down," Nava hissed through clenched teeth. All around, ears strained to hear them. She leaned back and whispered in Caine's ear. "Not here. It's too public."

"Fine," Caine whispered. "But I'm still going to Philly."

"No you're not. You need me, David, and I'm telling you that going to Jasper is suicide. Please trust me."

Caine opened his mouth to argue but knew there would be no changing her mind. He closed his eyes, trying to figure out what to do. He knew that Philly was the right move, and he needed Nava to go with him. If this were real and he truly was Laplace's Demon, he should already know whether he would get to Philly. Either that or he would be able to figure out how to make everything come out the way he wanted. But instead all he could come up with was to hide in the bathroom.

He scoffed at himself. His plan was hardly that of an omniscient intellect. He let his mind drift, trying to figure out what to do, but nothing came except the repeated image of himself standing in the bathroom, dialing—

Suddenly he opened his eyes, sucking in his breath in a loud gasp. Nava instantly turned toward him, her face worried.

"David, are you all right?"

Her voice seemed a million miles away. He looked down at his watch. It was 10:13:43. If he was going to make it, he needed to get to the businessman in exactly thirty-eight seconds. Abruptly he stood up.

"Where—"

"The restroom," Caine said, answering her question before it was complete.

She eyed him suspiciously and then stood up, gripping his elbow. "I'll help you get there."

"Sure," Caine said, mentally counting the seconds. He didn't need to rush. He still had plenty of time. He carefully took a step forward, exaggerating his limp. Nava paid no heed, as Caine knew she wouldn't. He continued forward as if in a dream. He felt like he was navigating through a maze he'd walked through a million times before.

At the end of the car, the door slid open and a thirty-something businessman walked through, right on schedule. He was carrying a cardboard tray of food in both hands. Caine couldn't see what was in the tray, but he knew anyway—a Coke-filled plastic cup, a bag of Doritos, and a tuna sandwich. The man kept coming. Caine stopped for a moment, pretending to lose his balance. Nava grabbed his arm to prevent him from a fall that never would have happened. Caine thanked her and took another step forward.

Now he and the man were almost on top of each other. Caine turned sideways to let him pass just as the train lurched to the left. Then Caine stumbled forward, bumping into the man, causing him to spill his Coke.

"Christ, watch it!" the man yelled, roughly pushing Caine away from him.

"Sorry, my fault," Caine said as he continued toward the restroom, Nava in tow. Once he was safely behind the closed bathroom door, Caine removed the cell phone that he had pulled from the businessman's belt clip. He closed his eyes, trying to remember the number he'd heard four days earlier.

Once he extracted it from his subconscious, he began dialing.

Jennifer Donnelly kept one hand on the wheel of her Ford SUV as she fished around in her purse looking for the phone. Her stupid cell always rang at the worst times. She looked down just as a Mini Cooper darted in front of her. Startled, she jammed on her brakes. A second later a silver Lincoln rammed into her bumper, sending Jennifer's SUV skidding across the intersection until it smashed against the guardrail.

She was slammed back against her seat; the airbag had inflated so quickly that Jennifer felt as if someone had punched her in the face. She sat in a daze until the warm, wet sensation between her legs brought her out of it.

"Oh my God," she said, squeezing her thighs together as if that could stop what had happened. But it was too late.

There was a flush, and then Caine stepped out of the bathroom.

"Come on, let's sit back down," he said, a little too quickly.

Nava felt that he was up to something, but she didn't know what, so she silently followed him back to their seats. They would be in Newark in less than five minutes. She couldn't wait to get off the train. She had a bad feeling the NSA was on to them. If the agent she'd knocked out remembered their encounter, they could be speeding right into a trap.

Nava looked around the car, already planning their escape. If she were running the counter-op, what would she do? Wait until they walked out and take them on the platform? Board the train at the station and do a search? No. She'd stop the train about a mile outside the station and board there. That would be the best way to control the situation: Even if they tried to run, there would be nowhere to go.

But that's what *she* would have done. She wasn't running the op. Americans were. And in America they worried too much about innocents and hostages. They would be more concerned about what the headlines would say the next day than about the outcome of the mission. So that meant . . . what? They wouldn't board the train, fearing a standoff.

They'd want to surprise them, leaving the station in a "controlled" environment.

She started to formulate a plan.

Bill Donnelly was watching the track unroll before his speeding train when the cell phone in his overalls began to buzz. He knew that everyone mocked his outfit—denim from head to toe, including his short-brimmed cap—but he figured that train conductors *should* wear overalls. He fished out his phone, keeping both eyes on the tracks.

"Yyyellow," he answered. The smile of amusement at his favorite greeting disappeared when he heard panting on the other end of the phone. "Sweetheart, is that you?"

"Yes, it's me." His wife's voice was weak. "There's been an accident."

"Are you all right? What about the baby?"

"My water just broke." She paused, breathing deeply. "I'm going to the hospital."

"But you're not due for another six weeks!"

"Bill, I need you. Are you almost home?"

"Ah, jeez . . . we're right outside of Newark, but I'll step on it, sugar pie."

She yelped in pain. "Please, Bill. I'm . . . I'm scared. I can't do this again . . . not alone. . . ." She broke down in tears.

"Hey, hey," he said softly, "everything will be all right, honey. I'll be there quicker than you can say, 'It's a boy.' "

She sniffed softly, her tears subsiding. "Promise?"

"I promise I will be right there beside you, holding your hand, when that baby comes into the world."

"Okay. I'm gonna go to the hospital now. The ambulance is here. I love you."

"I love you, too." There was a brief click, and then she was gone.

He remembered his last trip to the delivery room two years ago. He'd been working late and didn't make it to the hospital on time. No big deal, he'd thought. There was nothing to see anyway the first couple hours. His sister had had three children, and the shortest time she'd spent in labor was twenty hours. He hadn't thought ninety minutes would make a difference. But he'd been wrong.

The labor was short, and the baby—little Matthew William—was stillborn. Bill had always felt guilty about not being there those first few moments when Jennifer was lying alone in the recovery room. When he finally arrived with a box of cigars, she spit in his face. It had taken them a full year of counseling to get back to some semblance of normalcy. Three months after that, she learned that she was pregnant again.

He often wondered if it had been a mistake to try for another child. The stress of the second pregnancy almost destroyed their marriage. But somehow they made it through. He had even arranged to go on unpaid leave so he would be in town when it was time. What was it that they said? The best-laid plans . . . always fell apart. Something like that. He couldn't believe it. It wasn't supposed to happen this way. Not again.

He looked at his watch and then at the schedule. They were supposed to do routine maintenance in Trenton, which would take twenty minutes. Plus the café car needed to be restocked—another ten minutes. What could he do? Nothing. But then he thought of his wife, Jenny, all alone in that room . . . the same hospital where they'd lost Matthew.

Bill sighed. He knew what he had to do. It was worth losing his job. He turned around and locked the door. He shifted into high gear, increasing their speed. Then he picked up the microphone, took a deep breath, and pressed the button.

"*Attention, passengers: We regret to inform you that we will be skipping the following stops: Newark, Metropark, Princeton Junction, and Trenton.*"

Several passengers grumbled, unsure of what was happening.

"*We at Amtrak regret any inconvenience this may cause you. Next stop, Thirtieth Street Station, Philadelphia.*"

At the last sentence, a mild riot of angry commuters erupted around Nava, but she paid no heed. She knew they wouldn't do anything more than write a nasty letter the next day, if that. Instead she focused her attention on Caine, who was staring out the window.

"What did you do?" she asked.

Caine turned to look her in the eye. "I don't know what you're talking about."

"Bullshit," Nava hissed. "You caused this, didn't you?"

"You're paranoid," Caine replied.

"You're lying."

Caine didn't respond. He just turned back to the window. She didn't know how, but somehow he'd made this happen. When she had first read Tversky's theories regarding Laplace's Demon, she hadn't believed them. Not really. That's why she'd been so willing to turn Julia over to the RDEI.

At the thought of the North Koreans and the price she must have on her head for defying them, Nava shivered. She tried not to focus on her own desperate situation and returned her attention to the man next to her. Nava thought it was possible he might have *some* paranormal ability, but still . . . There was quite a difference between predicting the future and controlling it.

Nonetheless, the fact that their train was not stopping until it hit Philadelphia—what were the odds of that? What could possibly have caused the conductor to skip the next four stops? She shook her head in denial. It didn't make sense. Tversky had written that Caine wasn't consciously in control of his abilities. Although, after what had just happened, Nava wasn't so sure. She knew to trust her instincts, and right now her instincts were screaming at her.

She looked again at Caine. But this time her look wasn't one of speculation. It was of fear.

Grimes put Fitz and Murphy on the box so Crowe could hear. Fitz did most of the talking, although Murphy interjected a few times, mostly to make himself look good—or at least less stupid for falling stone-cold asleep against a wall. When they were through, Grimes looked up at Crowe.

"What do you think?"

"I think a sudden bout of narcolepsy is rather abnormal. Especially for a forty-three-year-old male with no history of any extraordinary medical conditions," Crowe said solemnly.

"But what does it mean? Think Caine and Vaner are on the train?" Grimes loved this part. Surveillance was cool, but chasing down targets, trying to find them in the myriad of fish-eye lenses across the country, now, *that* was kick-ass. And Crowe knew his shit; that was for damn sure.

"Tell me about the train. Anything unusual about its journey so far?"

"Hang on a sec, lemme check." Grimes cracked the Amtrak firewall in less than a minute. One of his plasma screens now showed a map of the eastern seaboard, a vein of railroad tracks running along the coastline. "Whoa . . . this is interesting." Grimes turned up the volume on his headset. "Seems like the conductor went nutso and decided to hijack the train. Something about his wife having a baby and needing to get to Philly ASAP. Man, that guy is *sooo* fired."

Crowe leaned forward, suddenly interested. "Can you search the Amtrak database and determine how many times an employee has hijacked a train?"

"Sure thing." It took Grimes only a few seconds to find the proper menu item and get the data. "Here it is. In the fifteen years that they've tracked the info, it's only happened eighteen times."

"Calculate the probability."

Grimes thought it an odd request, but Crowe was the man. "Let's see, assuming they've had the same schedule for the last fifteen years, and since they run 100 trips per day, that'd be 36,500 trips per year, multiplied by fifteen years would give you"—Grimes plugged the numbers into his keypad—"547,500 trips. And since there were only eighteen hijackings, that'd make the probability 0.003 percent or about one in 30,000."

Crowe punched his fist into his palm with satisfaction. "It's Caine. He's on that train."

"You want me to call in the cavalry?"

"Wait." Crowe held up his hand. "How long before the train reaches Philadelphia?"

"Let me check, hang on." Grimes maneuvered through the menus back into the arrivals database. "They're going to arrive in about forty-seven minutes." He grinned. "They're running a bit ahead of schedule."

"Do we have a chopper on the roof?"

"Yup." Grimes nodded. "Fueled and ready. Want me to call the pilot?"

Crowe was already running down the hall toward the elevator. Grimes took that as a yes.

He was five thousand feet above the city within four minutes. At 130 miles per hour, they should arrive just ahead of the train. If they got lucky with the winds, they might even beat it. Crowe pressed a button on his headset.

"Grimes, I want you to get every available agent from the Philadelphia field office to converge on that train. Make sure they all have computer-generated images of both Caine and Vaner. . . ."

Grimes listened intently for another minute as Crowe spelled out his plan. Oh, yeah. David Caine would soon learn what being hunted was all about.

Caine couldn't pinpoint the exact moment he awoke. The gentle rocking motion, back and forth, the *click-clack, click-clack* of the train put time in a perpetual loop as the feeling of déjà vu once again swarmed around his mind. Adrift in a sea of cotton, he struggled to consciousness. He yawned before opening his eyes.

Then it came rushing back to him. Again he felt the dull ache of guilt over Tommy. . . . He never should have died. It was all Caine's fault. If only he had stayed away from the *podvaal,* then none of this would have—

No. This wasn't real. The explosion, the woman, the crazy phone call—none of it. He had to keep moving forward. If he could just get his dream self to Jasper, then everything would be okay. He looked over at Nava. In another life he would have been overjoyed to run off with such a gorgeous woman. But in this life—this dream—they weren't running away from everyday problems but from killers.

"Attention, passengers: We will be arriving in Thirtieth Street Station in five minutes. Again, we apologize for any inconvenience the schedule change may have caused. Thank you for your understanding."

Caine felt another wave of déjà vu and suddenly knew he had to get to the café car. There wasn't much time.

Nava wondered if Caine had finally snapped. One second he was fast asleep, and the next he was dragging her to the café car, urging her to hurry. When they got there, he bought ten bags of chips. Before she could comment, he started to rip them open with his teeth as he hobbled over to the end of the car.

He pushed the flat black panel on the door, and it slid open, allowing Caine to step through onto the hinged metal floor that joined the café car with the one behind it. Through the small gaps in the floor, she could see the tracks racing by. That was when Caine bent down and started pouring chips through the gaps. When Caine emptied the last bag, he discarded it at his feet along with the others.

"Are you crazy?" Nava asked.

"Yes, Nava," Caine said. "I think I am."

"Why did you just do that?" Nava pressed.

"I . . . I'm not sure," Caine stammered, a faraway look in his eyes.

Nava felt cold. "Do they know we're on this train?"

"Yeah . . . I think so." Caine nodded.

If this were a normal op, she'd run through her contingency plans, but today she was flying without a net. What about using Caine? Somehow he'd managed to bring them to Philadelphia, hadn't he? But she worried that pushing him to use his . . . abilities . . . could have disastrous results. Then she thought again about what they were walking into and decided it was worth the risk. She turned and stared into Caine's emerald green eyes.

"David, I want you to imagine us escaping the train station uninjured."

"Nava, I don't think it works that way."

"But you don't *know,* do you? Come on. Pro athletes visualize a game before they take the field. Soldiers picture the battle before they deploy. Please, David, humor me." Then, after a moment, "Trust has to start sometime."

Caine looked like he wanted to protest, but then he nodded. "You're right." He closed his eyes just as the intercom crackled to life.

"Attention, passengers: We are now arriving at Thirtieth Street Station, Philadelphia. For those of you getting off,

thank you for traveling with Amtrak, and enjoy your stay in the City of Brotherly Love."

A black-and-gray spotted pigeon swooped down from the dark sky and landed on the tracks seconds after the metal beast rumbled away. She pecked at the broken pieces of fried potato that littered the ground. She had to get what she could before the rest of the flock came. Suddenly she heard a squeaking sound and turned to see five furry creatures scurrying toward her. Without hesitating, she shot into the air.

She wasn't aware of the giant roaring bird until it was too late.

They were cutting it close. Crowe listened to the FBI team over his headphones. He had no idea how the hell Forsythe had gotten interagency assistance so quickly, much less how he'd gotten the feds to report in to the NSA. As Crowe was the NSA's point man, he was effectively the SAIC—special agent in charge. Someone at the Bureau would probably lose his job when it got back that Crowe had been handed the reins, but he didn't have time to worry about that now. The train was pulling into the station in ninety seconds.

He should be there in time to supervise the assault. The helicopter began its descent just as it started to rain, making his stomach lurch. He held on to his belt and leaned back in his seat. Suddenly the helicopter halted in a gut-wrenching jerk, and they began to climb again, banking sharply to the left.

"What the hell was that?" Crowe yelled over the thunderous blades. The pilot ignored him and struggled with the stick for a moment, trying to right the helicopter.

"I think a bird flew into the tail rotor!" He flipped a few switches and then resumed their descent, this time much more slowly. "I'm having problems steering, sir! I'm going to have to set her down in that parking lot!" The helicopter jerked again, this time forcing them into a steep dive before the pilot regained control.

"Just get us down safe!" As the helicopter pitched back and forth, Crowe yelled into his microphone, "Has this ever happened to you before?"

"Never, sir!" the pilot replied as the chopper closed in on the ground.

Crowe didn't believe in coincidences. He didn't know how, but somehow David Caine had caused this. For the first time in his life, Martin Crowe wondered whether he was the hunter or the prey.

If he wanted to get to Jasper, then Caine needed Nava, which meant he had to trust her. Eyes closed, he tried to focus on their escape. He held the picture of himself and Nava driving away, losing their pursuers in a sea of black. Over and over he repeated the scene in his mind.

He felt the way he did whenever he watched the March Madness tournament, staring at the television screen, gripping his beer, wishing—no, *willing*—the foul shot to be good. He would watch the player warm up, all the while rooting for him to make the shot, feeling as if he wished hard enough, if he *pushed* hard enough, he could somehow make a difference.

As the train pulled into the tunnel, Caine became hyperaware of his surroundings—the squealing of the brakes, the rhythm of the wheels running across the tracks, the flickering of the car's fluorescent lights as they entered the belly of the station. He felt it all happening. He was truly in the moment—more so than he'd ever been in his life.

Yet he also felt as if he were watching himself from the outside. His double was in . . . a car? Yes, a big black car, speeding away. Nava was at the wheel. A familiar face floated between them. His double viewed the *Now* as the past. Caine tried to read his future self's mind, to reach into his memory and ask, *How?* but nothing came.

His mind left his doppelgänger and returned to the present: working, wishing, willing himself and the world around him to make what he wanted become a reality. He knew it was *possible*—he just had to make it *probable.* But he didn't know what to do, so he just kept on thinking, focusing, *willing.*

"David! David!" Nava snapped her fingers in front of his eyes. Caine blinked rapidly and tumbled back into the present; the feeling of pushing into a new reality retreated to the back of his mind. In one instant it was crystal clear. In the next it was just a distant memory, as if he had suddenly woken from a surreal dream. After a few seconds, even the memory was gone.

"Are you okay?" Nava asked. Her fingers were digging into his biceps. He had the feeling this wasn't the first time she'd asked him that.

"Yeah . . . what just happened? Did I black out?"

Caine wanted to ask more questions, but just then the doors slid open.

Nava leaned into him, speaking softly. "They'll want to take us in a controlled area, to lower the chances that we'll hurt someone. We should be safe on the platform as long as they think we don't suspect anything. When we step off the train, don't look around and don't look nervous. Just follow my lead. Ready?"

"Ready as I'll ever be." Although Caine had used the expression before, only now did he understand what it meant: *No fucking way am I ready, but let's hit it.*

Nava gripped his hand and gave it a reassuring squeeze as they stepped off the train. Suddenly Caine thought that going to Philly might not have been such a good idea after all.

The helicopter set down a mile from the train station in an empty corner of a bank parking lot. The landing was rough, but Crowe didn't care; he was out of the chopper in a second, standing in the pouring rain. It was coming down with a vengeance, soaking him instantly.

He ran for the nearest car, a black Honda Civic, and smashed a rear side window with a sharp blow from his S&W. A spiderweb of cracks bloomed from the point of impact. He thrust his elbow into the center, and the glass broke away.

Once behind the wheel, he slicked back his hair, wiped the water from his eyes, and reached beneath the dashboard. He got the engine to turn on the second try, and he squealed out of the parking lot, nearly colliding with a teenager wildly waving his arms. Probably the car's owner.

"Status!" Crowe barked into his headset.

"Sir, the target has been located," the team leader responded.

"Is he alone?"

"No. Target is accompanied by Vaner." Shit. Despite the fact that everyone *thought* she was with him, *knowing* she was had an impact. On the helicopter ride, he had briefed the Philly team about Vaner. She was dangerous. Although it was preferable she was captured, that goal was secondary to acquiring Caine uninjured. When Crowe gave his next order, he rationalized that it didn't matter, that she was a traitor, but his conscience wasn't fooled by his lies.

"If necessary," Crowe said, "use deadly force to stop Vaner."

"Copy, deadly force on Vaner."

Crowe tried not to think about his last command and instead focused on the mission. "Team One, are you in position?"

"Affirmative on One."

"Team Two?"

"Two in position, sir."

Crowe blew through a red light as he thought through the scenario to come. "Team One, you're a go."

"Team One: Go," the team leader echoed in his earpiece. With any luck, it would be over by the time Crowe got to the station. The problem was, he knew that with Caine as their adversary, luck wouldn't be on their side.

There was a limited risk of being dropped by a sniper; besides that, the positives of being underground were zero.

There was no way out except for the double doors that led to the escalators at either end of the platform—unless they wanted to use the empty track across from their train. The track ran beneath the station for about a hundred meters, beyond which Nava could see a misty daylight.

She considered the option, but it would leave them totally exposed. The only choice was to go up the escalator, an almost equally dangerous alternative. If agents were waiting at the top, they'd walk right into their midst like cattle to the slaughter. Nava scanned the crowd on the platform.

No one seemed to pay them any special attention, but if the agents were good, that's the way it would work. She eliminated the obvious sheep—moms, kids, and the elderly. That knocked out 40 percent of the people milling around. Not enough. Again she considered the tracks.

Nava felt a sudden urge to grab Caine, jump down, and make their escape. But as much as she hated it, she knew that their best chance was to surround themselves with innocents on the escalator. It would be easier to make whoever might be gunning for them. She looked over her shoulder and spotted a young mother trying to control her twin girls while maneuvering an infant in a stroller. Perfect.

Nava slowed her pace so the family would catch up to them. She gave Caine's arm a quick squeeze; he slowed as well. She continued scanning the crowd for telltale signs. A couple of young jocks were checking her out, but their stares were sexual in nature, not professional. An athletic woman a few feet away looked like an agent, but she was loaded down with three shopping bags. Nava began to think that maybe they had lost their pursuers after all . . . when she spotted him.

There—the man dressed in worn jeans and an old sweatshirt, ripped slightly at the neck. He didn't match the clothes. His hair was cut short and neat, and he had a perfectly trimmed mustache. A quick glance at his too-new sneakers eliminated all doubt.

He was watching them out of the corner of his eye, but

now that Nava had him made, his surveillance was obvious. She leaned into Caine and stole another look at Mustache Man, who was now staring over Nava's shoulder. She followed his gaze and met the eyes of a young woman in a business suit. The woman was good; she controlled herself, waiting a few seconds before returning to her newspaper. But Nava spotted the bulge of a sidearm before her *Philadelphia Inquirer* obscured it.

"Mustache in the sweatshirt, seven o'clock. Blonde with newspaper, two o'clock."

Caine nodded; to his credit he kept his eyes focused forward. He was learning. Nava took a deep breath. She knew they cared only about Caine, which meant she was expendable. She paused for a second, and then calm descended. No reason to panic; she would live or die, same as always.

She slowed her pace, managing to sidle up next to the mother of three, keeping the children between Caine and Mustache Man. With her left flank covered, she focused her attention to the right. They were almost on top of the female agent, the crowd slowly pushing them forward. Caine would pass within a meter of the agent in seconds.

Nava turned and saw Mustache Man was making his move, heading directly toward them. The escalator was less than three meters away. The woman turned a few degrees to her right and adjusted her stance, preparing for a fight. If the agents were going to grab them on the platform, this was their last chance.

And it looked like they were going to take it.

Caine saw nothing special about the woman in the business suit, but if Nava said she was one of them, he accepted it as fact. He stayed aware of her proximity as he continued toward the escalator. Six feet. He wanted to slow down, but the crowd didn't allow it. Three feet. And then he was next to her. She smelled of perfume. He was so close he couldn't resist looking directly at her through his dark sunglasses.

She gave him a flirtatious smile. She didn't seem dangerous. At another time he might have been attracted to her clean good looks and what Jasper used to call a "corporate porno fantasy body." Caine smiled back, forgetting for a second that he was a wanted man. Then he saw a glint of something in her right hand. It looked like an oversize silver pen.

Caine watched her, transfixed. Then he realized that the pen was actually the same type of spring-loaded syringe that Nava had used back in New York. Suddenly the agent jabbed it toward him.

. . .

The needle pierces his flesh and—

(loop)

She jabs the syringe toward him; he tries to block her arm, but he misses. He feels a stab of pain, and—

(loop)

He swings his injured leg toward the needle's trajectory, deflecting the attack and—

. . .

The hypodermic hit home right above his knee, burying itself in his wooden splint. As the needle snapped off, the woman grabbed Caine's arm, pulling him off balance. For a second he tried to stay standing, but it was no use, so he did his best to make the fall count. He leaped forward, smashing his shoulder into her chin.

She tumbled backward, dragging Caine down with her. She pivoted as she fell and landed on her side, facing him. He was about to push her away when he felt the muzzle of her gun press into his stomach.

"I don't want to kill you, but if you move I will shoot," the woman said. "If that happens, you'll wish I *had* killed you."

Caine believed her. Suddenly a woman screamed, and the crowd transformed from a mindless herd into a pack of scared animals. Someone stepped on Caine's injured knee. Excruciating pain shot through his leg, and he convulsed in agony.

Then he heard the gun explode.

CHAPTER twenty-three

Nava watched the female agent go for Caine, but knew she wouldn't kill him, so Nava concentrated on Mustache Man, who *was* trying to kill *her.* He charged forward, hand reaching for his holster, pushing past the other passengers. Nava recognized the look in his eyes, as she'd worn it herself a thousand times. He was a professional. He would not stop unless he *was* stopped. Nava pointed to his pistol and screamed at the top of her lungs.

"OHMYGODHE'SGOTAGUN!!!"

She didn't need to say it twice. It was a phrase every city dweller half expected and fully dreaded hearing. Instantly the crowd became a frenzied mass of hysteria. Everyone was in everyone else's way, too many people surging toward the double doors leading to the escalator.

As luck would have it, the pair of jocks decided to be heroes, rushing at Mustache Man, momentarily pinning his arms in place between them, but they were no match for the trained agent. He smashed his elbow into the gut of one of them and punched the other in the face, breaking his nose. They both would have crumpled to the ground if there'd been room. Instead the mob carried away their limp bodies.

Undeterred, Nava pushed toward the agent. He saw her coming and prepared to meet her. He extended his gun arm, and instantly a small circle cleared around him, as those between him and the doors pushed forward even harder, while those behind jumped into the tracks and ran for the daylight.

"On the ground, federal agent!" he barked.

Nava didn't pause; he probably knew she wouldn't but acted out the play nonetheless. He pulled the trigger. She saw it but could do nothing except grit her teeth and keep moving. Amazingly, there was no gunshot. Confusion registered on his face, and then he realized his gun had jammed. But by then it was too late; she was upon him.

She came in fast and low, grabbing his gun hand and forcing it to the ceiling. Anticipating her move, he was quick with a left hook to her chin. She saw the fist out of the corner of her eye and was therefore able to do something that common sense said was a very bad idea.

However, Nava was no longer relying on common sense but on her fighting instincts, drilled into her by the KGB's best hand-to-hand-combat experts. Before his left hook connected, Nava turned toward the blow and bowed her head. His fist smashed into the top of her skull, the hardest bone in the human body. She felt like she'd been hit with a sledgehammer, but she knew from the crunch his hand made upon impact that it hurt him a hell of a lot more than it did her.

The agent grunted, and Nava's arm sprang forward like a serpent, grabbing hold of his wounded hand. She twisted hard and squeezed, snapping his wrist like a twig as she ground his broken fingers together. Before he could counter, she ripped the gun from his other hand and smashed it across the bridge of his nose. The agent went down, smacking his head against the concrete floor. He was out cold.

Without pausing, she scanned the crowd for other threats but found none. Now that Nava had the pistol, she created a pocket of space wherever she went, as the mob desperately tried to escape her path. She spotted Caine lying on the floor holding on to the female agent, who had a gun at his stomach.

Nava assessed the situation in an instant. She didn't hesitate before she pulled the trigger.

The second Caine heard the shot, the world stopped.

. . .

Caine is instantly covered in blood. The agent's face disintegrates, replaced by a gaping hole, a bloody gray omelet beneath. Every muscle in her body goes limp; her gun clatters to the ground between them. And—

(loop)

She is alive before him, and the bullet tears through her neck, her jugular pumping blood into the air like a geyser. And—

(loop)

Over and over she dies, like watching the Zapruder film of the Kennedy assassination in a continuous loop. As he stares in horror, time slows even further, so that he can see the bullet penetrate her flesh. Usually it enters through her eye socket, but sometimes it tears through her jaw, showering Caine with shards of broken teeth.

A few times he feels the searing pain as the bullet crashes through his own skull, but those sensations are mercifully quick—when the lead shot enters his brain, he snaps back to the beginning of the reel. At last the movie begins to change, as Caine realizes what he must do. With all his strength, he forces her forearm up and—

. . .

—as the bullet smashed through her wrist, its trajectory altered 12.3 degrees to the left and the lead shot buried itself into the wall. Before Caine could react, a shadow swooped down and slammed the agent's head into the floor, knocking her unconscious.

"Let's go," Nava said, pulling him to his feet, "we don't have much time."

The platform was nearly empty, leaving them totally exposed. The gunshots had driven some of the crowd down to the tracks, racing through the tunnel toward the misty daylight. Nava discarded the agent's gun and reached for his arm.

"Hang on!"

Before Caine knew what was happening, she'd picked him up, thrown him over her shoulder, and jumped onto the tracks. They landed hard, but somehow Nava didn't lose her footing. Instead she used their momentum to swing Caine off her shoulder and back to the ground.

Within seconds they merged with the frantic crowd as they hobbled toward the light at the end of the tunnel.

"Shots fired! I repeat, we have shots fired!" Crowe's earpiece screamed.

"What happened? Is anyone down?" He was still a half mile away, and the mission was going to shit. "Team One, answer me, goddamn it!"

"This is Team One. Neither of the agents on the platform is responding."

"Get down there!"

"Impossible, sir. There's a mass of people coming up the escalator. Some injured. We can't get down until they clear out. We think the target is still on the platform."

If the two agents weren't responding, they were either incapacitated or dead. Crowe had never lost an agent under his command. The thought that it might have happened now was like a punch in the stomach. He wanted to stop, to think, but he knew any hesitation could result in more loss of life. He was the commander. He had to lead.

No way in hell would Vaner stay on the platform and wait for more agents to converge on her position. Crowe pictured the layout. They had disabled the elevator and blocked the stairs, leaving the escalator as the only exit. He doubted Vaner would risk it, even given the crowd of scurrying people. The only other way out was . . .

"The tunnel! They'll try to exit along the tracks!" he screamed as he blew through another red light, sideswiping a white BMW without slowing down. "Cover the two tunnel exits!"

"We can't get adequate coverage of both the station and the tunnel!"

"Right now you don't have shit for coverage, period! Leave a two-man team covering the escalator. Get everyone else to the tracks. Now!"

"Understood."

"One more thing," Crowe said, measuring his words. "Take Vaner out. No more chances. If you ID her . . . kill her."

A few squealing rats scampered from their path as they tried to keep pace with the mob. Caine ignored the creatures, instead concentrating every ounce of energy on not falling down. As they neared the lip of the tunnel, Nava and Caine slowed to a stop. Although it was midday, the light was dim, the sky dark with storm clouds. She scanned the perimeter, but the rain was falling in thick sheets, making it nearly impossible to see.

Outside, their progress slowed even further. With an embankment on either side, they were forced to move along the slippery tracks and the muddy earth beneath. A few people slipped and fell. Some stayed down, calling out for help or holding their hands over their heads, shaking with hysterical sobs. Others struggled back to their feet and kept stumbling forward, covered with mud like zombies from a B movie.

Suddenly the crowd in front of them stopped. Ahead was a makeshift roadblock of police officers. Caine and Nava hung at the back of the crowd. Nava untied her ponytail and let her long, wet hair fall in her face, lest anyone recognize her from the platform. Fortunately, with all the chaos, no one paid them any heed.

"People, please quiet down and listen," shouted a squat police officer through a megaphone. *"Everything is going to be all right. We just need to check IDs."*

The officers then directed them to form three queues. Once cleared, the passengers would be escorted up the muddy embankment. Although a couple of loudmouths began to complain about being forced to stand in the pouring rain, most were too shell-shocked to do anything besides follow directions.

Caine glanced at Nava; her hand was in her pocket. With her jacket soaked, he could see the outline of a gun grasped in her hand. He knew this wasn't real, that this was all a delusion, but . . . what if he was wrong? He had to stop her.

As his mind raced, he closed his eyes. Suddenly he knew what to do.

"Before you shoot anybody else," Caine said, "I've got a plan."

"You've got thirty seconds," she said. "I'm listening."

"First," Caine said, "I'm going to need a gun."

Although they were near the back of the crowd, there were still almost fifty people behind them and another thirty more loitering inside the tunnel, trying to stay dry. Slowly Caine and Nava walked back through the rest of the passengers, searching their faces. Caine hoped he was doing the right thing. He reasoned that anything was better than letting Nava open fire again in the middle of the crowd.

Then Caine spotted him. The guy was perfect. Caine motioned to Nava, and she nodded, making her way toward the mark. She sidled up to the dark-haired man and smiled. The man smiled back, staring at Nava's soaked top, which was plastered to her chest.

The smile disappeared when Caine pushed a gun into the man's side. Terrified, the man turned to Nava for help, but she also removed her gun, which she held to his gut.

"Come with us," Nava said. "Slowly." Nava walked alongside the man; one hand held his arm, the other her gun, hidden beneath his sports jacket. Caine followed. When they reached the comforting darkness of the tunnel, they huddled around him.

"Give me your wallet," Caine instructed.

"You're fucking robbing me?" the man asked incredulously. "I can't believe this! First somebody goes nuts and starts shooting, then I get fucking *mugged?*"

Nava nudged his groin with her pistol. "The wallet," she commanded.

"Okay, okay." The man dug around in his coat pocket, withdrew a black Gucci wallet, and handed it to Caine.

Caine pulled out his ID. "Richard Burrows. Do you go by Rick or Rich?"

"Rick," he said angrily.

"Okay, Rick. Is this your family?" Caine asked, waving at a picture of Rick with a pretty blonde holding a baby. Rick stared venomously at Caine and nodded. Nava flipped open her cell phone and punched in a number. After a few seconds, she spoke.

"It's me. Go to—" Nava paused and looked at Rick's driver's license—"4000 Pine Street. Break into the house. There's a blonde and an infant. Take them to the safe house. If you don't hear from me in the next hour, kill them."

As Nava clicked the phone shut, Caine watched Rick's reaction. His face bore a bizarre expression, somewhere between anguish and fury, although Caine also sensed a quiet resignation beneath.

"What do you want?" Rick pleaded. Before Nava had a chance to answer, Caine took over, knowing he could deliver the lighter touch to the poor man he'd chosen to terrorize.

"Let me tell you what we don't want," Caine said. "We don't want to hurt your family. Do you believe that?"

Rick nodded slowly, his lip quivering. He certainly didn't look like he believed it, and that was just fine. Caine hated himself, but he knew that as long as Rick thought his family was in danger, he would do anything they wanted.

"If you do exactly as I say, your family will be fine." Caine paused, staring directly into Rick's eyes, knowing that he was about to cross a line. "But if you don't, then it will be *you* who killed them, not me. Understand?"

Rick nodded again. Suddenly Caine wanted to take it all back, to tell the man there was no one at his house, that his wife and son were safe. But he couldn't. He had already gone too far. He tried to console himself that none of this was real, but that part of his mind was slowly fading away as his delusion took on a life of its own.

Pushing away such thoughts, Caine turned back to Rick and carefully explained his plan. Rick protested, but Caine reassured him that everything would work out fine if he did as Caine instructed.

"Now give me your hand," Caine said. Rick held out a trembling palm, and Caine pressed the gun into it. Rick stared down as if the pistol were a live grenade. "Put it in your pocket." Rick tried, but his hands were shaking so much it took three attempts before he was able to slide it home.

Caine pointed to the shortest of the three lines. Rick looked over, then back at Nava. She lowered her weapon. He started walking forward, like a man on death row.

Once he was out of earshot, Nava gave Caine an impressed look. "You did well."

"Yeah—so well I almost gave him a heart attack."

"You had no choice."

Caine stared back at her. "There's always a choice." But even as the words left his mouth, Caine recognized his own hypocrisy. He wondered when his humanity had slipped away.

They silently waited in line five meters behind Rick. Ten minutes passed. From Nava's standpoint, it looked like the longest ten minutes of Rick's life. To the trained eye, everything the man did revealed his slow-boiling terror. He was constantly shuffling his feet, uncomfortable in his own skin. However, his naked fear didn't worry her.

What worried Nava was that every thirty seconds or so, Rick glanced back at his would-be attackers with a pleading, fearful look. That look froze Nava to the core. If the agents doing the checks were good, they would spot Burrows's behavior and the game would be over.

Under the circumstances Caine's plan was probably their best chance. A part of her trusted it on its merit, but another part, a part that was growing stronger as she started to truly *believe,* trusted that whatever Caine planned out would come to pass.

"Next." Agent Sands stayed on his toes. They had received a radio communication that Hauser and Kelleher were both on the way to the hospital. Whoever had taken them out had to be good.

Sands still couldn't believe what Caine and Vaner had done to them. He hoped to God that if Caine was in line, he'd get to bust him. If that happened, Caine might accidentally smash his face into Sands's fist a few times on his way to HQ. Sands smiled at the thought. If he caught Caine, the man would be in a world of hurt before he transferred custody.

"Next!" he yelled again. He knew it was hard to hear in the driving rain, but the guy in line had to have noticed that Sands had waved the last woman through almost a minute before. The guy nervously looked over his shoulder.

Sands's radar went up as the guy trudged over to meet him; everyone else had run beneath the tarp to escape the pouring rain. But this guy walked slowly between the two wooden sawhorses, his eyes focused on the ground as if he were walking through a field of land mines. None of the six policemen milling around seemed to notice, but what else could you expect from city cops?

When the guy got closer, Sands could see that he was absolutely terrified, his skin the color of old paste. He kept moving his hands—into his pockets, to his side, at his hips—as if he were trying to look casual. If there was one thing Sands knew, it was that innocents didn't try to look casual. Especially innocents waiting in the rain.

Although the man's features were slightly different from David Caine's picture—the nose a bit too thick, the eyes a dark muddy brown—they weren't so far off that Sands was convinced. Especially since the rest of his physical characteristics were a match—five-eleven, about 180 pounds. Sands adjusted his stance, ready for a fight.

"Where are you coming from today, sir?" Sands asked, never taking his eyes off the guy's face.

"Uh . . . I . . . New York. I'm coming from New York," the guy stammered. He looked down at his feet.

"Can I see some identification?"

The man nodded and nervously reached into his coat pocket. Sands's muscles tightened. *If he pulls out a gun, I'm gonna drop him, one shot to the head. Fuck what Crowe says.* Instead the man removed a thin black wallet and handed it over with a trembling hand.

Sands flipped it open and looked down at the name, trying to read while keeping one eye on the man in front of him. His name was David—*holy shit.* In one fluid motion, Sands dropped the wallet, unholstered his weapon, and, gripping it with both hands, leveled the muzzle at David Caine's head.

"On your knees, hands on the back of your head! *NOW, FUCKHEAD, NOW!*"

Caine was frozen, a deer in headlights. Then he fell backward, dropped by a vicious club to the knee administered by Martin Crowe, who was suddenly by his side. Sands pulled back his leg and kicked Caine in the gut as hard as he could. His foot sank into the man's flesh like it was made of pudding.

Caine coughed up a wad of blood.

"That was for Kelleher, you worthless piece of shit."

Sands leaned over and grabbed the guy's hair, turning his muddy face toward him, again mentally comparing it to the photograph of Caine. Not a perfect match, but in his experience people didn't always look like their mug shots. Yeah, it was Caine. He quickly frisked him and found the gun. The same gun that had shot Hauser and Kelleher.

Sands pulled back his fist and punched Caine as hard as he could. Blood spurted from his nose, which flattened with a sickening crunch. Sands was about to deliver another blow, but a strong hand caught his arm. He turned, and Crowe gave him a solemn look. He had allowed Sands his payback, but that was it. Sands nodded and lowered his fist. He leaned down, pulling Caine's hair hard until he opened his eyes.

"You shot a friend of mine, you stupid fuck," Sands spat into Caine's whimpering face. "You're gonna fry, you know that?" The man just squeezed his eyes shut again and began bawling like a baby. They were all big men until they were caught. Then the wusses just cried for their mommies. Sands pushed the fucker's head back into the mud and stood up.

"All yours, Crowe."

Nava allowed herself to feel a modicum of relief as the two agents dragged Rick Burrows away, but then her heart sank. She had hoped that once they'd found "David Caine," the feds would end their search, but instead they instructed the remaining women to stay in line. Nava silently cursed beneath her breath. Their luck had finally run out.

"You've got to go," Nava said.

"But you'll get caught."

"That remains to be seen. If I *am* identified, I've got a much better chance of escaping if I don't have to worry about you."

Caine started to protest, but Nava cut him off.

"David, there's no time to argue. They're still looking for me, which means soon they'll start questioning your doppelgänger. When that happens, it won't take long before they figure out their mistake.

"Now, listen: Go to the worst part of the city and check yourself into a motel. Pay cash. Do *not* contact Jasper. Meet me in the lobby of the Philadelphia Art Museum at noon tomorrow. If I'm not there by five past, then you're on your own."

Caine said nothing for a few seconds, blinked his eyes, and then nodded.

"I'll see you soon," he said. Without another word, he turned to make his way up the mucky incline.

Caine didn't look back. He needed to get to the top of the embankment as fast as possible. Unfortunately, his bad knee didn't make his task easy. Suddenly he felt a strong hand on his elbow. He glanced down and saw the dark blue police uniform.

"Hey, buddy, need some help?" the portly officer asked.

There was no way Caine could refuse, so instead he said, "Uh, sure, thanks."

"No sweat," the officer said, gripping Caine's elbow even tighter as he led him up the hill. Their pace was slow but steady. Soon they were only ten slippery feet from the street.

Caine dug his shoes into the mud and pushed forward, bracing himself for what was to come.

Crowe didn't feel comfortable until he double-checked all the restraints. Only then did he unclench his jaw. He stared at Caine, quivering in the seat bolted to the van's floor. He knew that with Vaner still on the loose, he should get Caine back to New York ASAP, but Crowe held off. Despite the fact that Forsythe could care less what happened to Vaner, Crowe couldn't just cut and run. She was dangerous and needed to be caught.

Besides—something was wrong. He couldn't believe that this was the man who'd helped to incapacitate three agents.

"Where is Vaner?" Crowe asked Caine for the third time.

Caine didn't respond. As before, he continued to cry, dry sobs catching in his throat. His hands were trembling so badly now that his ring rattled against the armrest—*rat-a-tat-tat, rat-a-tat-tat.* Crowe cocked his head, his eyes focusing on the ring finger of the man's left hand.

Crowe's heart stopped. David Caine wasn't married. It could be part of the disguise, but . . . Crowe grabbed the trembling hand, and the man jerked with fright, clearly anticipating some physical abuse. Crowe wrestled with the wedding band for a moment before he was able to remove it. Once it was off, he stared at the naked digit. The spot where the ring had been was lighter than the rest of the finger. The band was no disguise. His stomach dropped.

"You're not David Caine."

The man just sputtered and cried. Suddenly it all made sense. Why it had been so easy; why this man was such a whining coward. Crowe pulled out his Smith & Wesson 9-millimeter and pressed it against the man's head, gripping his captive's chin with the other hand. Crowe could see Betsy alone in her hospital bed. Without the money there was no way he could save her. He wouldn't let her down. He *couldn't* let her down.

"Look at me. *LOOK AT ME!*"

The man opened his eyes, tears streaming down his cheeks.

"You have five seconds to tell me what's going on. If you don't, I will pull this trigger and splatter your brains all over the back of this van. If you think I'm bluffing, look in my eyes and you will see that I am not.

"Five.

"Four.

"Three."

Their eyes met—Crowe's cold and determined, the man's quivering and terrified.

"Day ulled a un on ee," he sobbed. *They pulled a gun on me.* "Day ed day'd ill ii ife an ii vaaaeeee." *They said they'd kill my wife and my baby.*

"Jesus Christ." Crowe kept the gun leveled at the man's head. "When? Where??"

"Ust ow. In ine." *Just now. In line.*

Crowe pushed by the man and blew through the doors in the back of the van, roaring into his headset, "All teams! Acquired target was a decoy! Repeat: Acquired target was a decoy! Lock down! Now!"

Nine feet. Eight. Seven.

Caine allowed his heart to slow. He was so close. Just another few steps, and he could dispatch the cop. Through the rain he could see cars speeding by now, barely slowing to check out the police cruisers on the side of the road.

Then, midstep, the officer stopped as his walkie-talkie began to scream.

Nava hung back at the end of the line, trying to determine the best course of action. There were still four women in front of her. She considered taking one of them hostage, but that would only force the feds' hand, and with no cover to protect her, it was suicide.

There were only three FBI agents left at the checkpoint, along with six police officers. She had survived worse mismatches—barely. There was still a chance she wouldn't be recognized and her fake ID would get her through, but she doubted it. Suddenly the three agents froze, almost in unison.

When the first started to reach for his gun, Nava knew that David's ruse had been penetrated. A red haze fell over the world as she whipped out her Glock and began to fire.

Caine yanked his arm out of the policeman's grasp, pulling the officer off balance. Before the cop had a chance to compensate, Caine swung his staff in a wide arc toward the man's skull.

Nava focused her attention on the FBI agents, as she knew they were better marksmen than the police. With surgical precision she squeezed off three quick shots. Before the echo from the first reached her ears, the bullets were slicing through the rain toward their intended targets.

Chaos erupted as the agents went down, each with a bullet in his right shoulder. The remaining women in line scattered, screaming hysterically, while the policemen ducked for cover.

Before any of them could collect their wits, Nava broke into a run, scrambling up the slippery embankment toward Caine, just as he smashed the end of his walking stick across a cop's head with an audible crack. The blow was strong enough to knock them both off their feet, and the two went down in a tangle of arms and legs.

Nava climbed past the cop, who was lying flat on his back, blood oozing from a gash above his right ear. He was out. She reached down, pulled Caine to his feet, and dragged him up the last few steps of the muddy hill to the street.

They needed a car.

Police cars were everywhere, but they appeared to be empty. A few other passengers were walking in the breakdown lane about twenty feet ahead of them, oblivious to what had just happened. Caine looked over his shoulder and immediately wished he hadn't; six cops were racing up the embankment, their guns drawn.

He estimated that he and Nava had fifteen seconds to disappear before the shooting continued. Nava was good—hell, she was fucking great—but he didn't think she could take on six armed cops. Moreover, Caine didn't want her to try; part of him was afraid that she *could* take them on but would kill them all in the process. There was only one way out.

"Give me a gun," Caine said. Nava didn't hesitate. Apparently the request didn't sound as ridiculous to her ears as it had to his own.

Without hesitating, Caine limped into the middle of the rainy street, waving his gun in the air. A red VW bug squealed to a halt, skidded off the road, and smashed into the guardrail. A Ford Mustang swerved around him in a dark blue blur, a sheet of water spraying up from the tires. Momentarily blinded, Caine wiped the water from his eyes as a black Mercedes barreled down on him.

He pointed his gun at the windshield. It was a bluff, but it worked. The driver screeched to a stop six inches from

Caine's broken knee. As the windows were tinted, Caine couldn't see the man behind the wheel.

Nava raced toward the car and opened the door. She pulled out the driver by his neck and thrust her gun in his face. Despite the heavy artillery, the man seemed very calm. He looked past Nava and stared directly at Caine.

"Rain Man?"

"Doc?" Caine asked incredulously.

Nava shot Caine a look.

"You know him?"

Caine nodded dumbly.

"Fine, get in the car," she barked. Nava shoved Doc in the passenger seat as Caine slid into the back. He'd barely shut the door before Nava floored it. Caine heard a horn blare and turned around just in time to see a compact slam into a minivan.

They kept accelerating, Nava effortlessly passing all the cars in their path. After a couple minutes, she seemed to decide they were temporarily out of danger and slowed to eighty-five miles per hour. As Caine looked over at her, with Doc's familiar form between them, an incredible feeling of déjà vu came over him.

"Why are you in Philly?" Caine asked Doc.

"I was giving a talk at Penn," Doc said, more than a little flustered. "More important, what the hell are *you* doing here . . . with *that?*" Doc motioned to Caine's weapon, which lay motionless in his lap. Caine sighed. He was about to explain what was going on when Doc's cell phone began ringing.

"Don't answer that," Nava commanded.

"No," Caine said in a faraway voice, "I think you should."

Doc clicked a button and held the phone up to his ear. "Hello?" Caine vaguely heard a voice on the other end as he watched Doc's face transform from dazed to stunned. "Um, yes. Hold on." Doc held the phone out to Caine. "It's for you."

Nava gave Caine a questioning look as he took the phone.

"Hi," Caine said calmly; he was the only one in the car who wasn't surprised. "Yeah. We're all right. . . . Yeah . . . Meet at that place we watched the Knicks win that finals game. We'll get there as soon as we can." Caine snapped the phone shut and handed it back to Doc.

"Who was that?" Nava asked, her eyes watching him in the rearview mirror.

"It was Jasper. We need to get back to Manhattan."

"What?"

"Trust me," Caine said. "I think I finally know what I'm doing." He leaned back and closed his eyes. He would need to rest if he was going to be ready for what was next.

After the EMT said Williams would be okay, Crowe grabbed Williams by his collar and slammed him up against the ambulance.

"What the hell happened?"

Officer Williams was still dazed. Dried blood had formed a bizarre geometric pattern on the side of his face. "Ah . . . well, I was helping Caine up the hill, and—"

"You were *what?"* Crowe asked in disbelief.

"Yes . . . well, it was just that . . . I mean, I did help him, but you see, I didn't know that it was *him* when I was, you know, helping. . . ." Williams's voice petered out beneath Crowe's wilting stare. He cleared his throat and continued. While the cop tried to explain himself, Crowe turned away in disgust. He couldn't believe they'd been so close, only to lose them at the last moment.

This was why Crowe hated large-scale manhunts. Due to the sheer number of agents and cops let loose, there were bound to be careless errors, which was how the bad guys got away. He much preferred the solo hunt. One man tracking another. He looked at the mashed minivan in the middle of the street and wanted to throw his hands up in the air.

The drivers involved in the accident said that a man and woman had carjacked some poor sap. Problem was, neither remembered the make of the stolen car. The one in the Hyundai said it was big and dark blue; the Voyager's owner said it was small and dark green. The statements were useless. The only thing the two drivers agreed upon was that it was a dark color, which in Crowe's experience probably meant the car was bright yellow. They had nothing.

He looked up at the light gray sky. The rain had finally stopped, but the air was still moist. Unfortunately, the storm hadn't dissipated fast enough for their satellites. A quick call to Grimes confirmed what Crowe already knew in his gut: The cloud cover had prevented any useful surveillance.

He took a deep drag from his cigarette and stared at the orange ember at its tip. He held the smoke in his mouth for a few seconds before exhaling it in one long breath. The cloud slowly drifted up and over the road, disintegrating into the atmosphere. He let his mind wander as he followed the smoke with his eyes.

If he were Caine, what would he do now? He had to think like a civilian. First, he'd want to stay alive, and judging from Vaner's résumé and her latest bit of handiwork, Caine would probably trust her with that end. Second, he would want to get back to his normal existence. He'd be afraid to go to the cops but wouldn't want to spend the rest of his life on the run. So he would do . . . what? He'd seek solace in a friend—or a brother.

But where was his twin? Crowe couldn't believe that Grimes had let Jasper Caine go after Vaner pulled the bait and switch. Had Crowe been running the operation, he would have *used* the twin. But now it was too late—Jasper Caine was as lost as his brother. Crowe had a couple of agents watching Jasper's Philadelphia apartment in case anyone showed up, but he didn't have his hopes up.

He stubbed out his cigarette and stared at the sky. The two

brothers couldn't hide forever. Eventually they would surface. And when they did, Crowe would be there.

Next time there would be no mistakes.

It took the rest of the two-hour drive for Caine to fill in his old mentor about Jasper, Nava, Forsythe, Peter, and Laplace's Demon. As Caine spoke, Nava mentally reviewed their situation. When she first read Tversky's files, she'd thought them science fiction. But in the alley Julia had begun to change Nava's mind.

Still, Nava hadn't been convinced that Caine could do everything Tversky thought he could. But now—after their "luck" at the train station and "accidentally" meeting up with Doc—Caine had to be at least partially responsible, even if he didn't know how he was doing it. She didn't know the limits of Caine's abilities, nor did she want to find out. She was afraid of what might happen once he discovered how to use his powers.

Her thoughts drifted to the time when she first saw elephants at the circus as a child. There were three of them, and each six-ton beast was kept from wandering away by a thin piece of rope tied around one of its massive ankles. This confused Nava. She remembered asking her father why the animals didn't just break the ropes.

"It's all in their mind," her father explained. "When elephants are babies, they are tied to posts with heavy steel chains. During those first few months they learn that no matter how much they struggle, the chains are unbreakable."

"But ropes are so much weaker than chains," Nava replied. "The elephants could easily break them."

"Yes. But the trainers don't use ropes until the elephants learn that escape is impossible. You see, Nava, it's not the ropes that prevent the elephants from escaping—it's their minds. That's why knowledge is so powerful. If you think you can do something, even if you shouldn't be able to, often you can. And if you think you can't, you never will, because you won't even try."

That was Caine in a nutshell. He'd once been bound by a chain, and now the chain was gone, replaced with a tiny rope. He had already discovered that sometimes he could stretch the rope. But when he discovered that the rope could be broken—had already *been* broken, in fact—then what? Nava shivered.

What would happen when Caine realized that the normal rules didn't apply to him?

"The Real Me" by The Who came on the jukebox, and Roger Daltrey's lion's roar filled the East Village tavern: *"Can you see the rrrrreal me? Can ya? Can ya?"*

Jasper sipped his Coke and nervously watched the door. Every time it opened, he shielded his eyes from the bright sunlight that streamed into the dimly lit bar. For the first few moments, those who entered were just silhouettes. It was only after the doors clicked shut that he was able to make out their features—and determine whether they worked for the government.

The conspirators were everywhere; he knew that now. He could feel them watching him, trying to pry into his mind, but he wouldn't let them. If he stayed one step ahead, he and David would beat them. Until now he'd done what he could to keep David out of their clutches, yet Jasper knew that soon it would be David who had to save Jasper. But that was okay. That's what brothers were for—to protect each other.

Jasper finished his soda and began working on the ice cubes, crunching them between his teeth. The curvy waitress noticed his empty glass and sauntered over.

"Another Coke, honey?"

"Yes-*guess-mess-less,"* he said, doing his best to lower his voice during the rhymes. The waitress gave him a look and then retreated back to the bar. Jasper let out a long breath. It was almost time. So close he could taste it . . . hell, he could almost *smell* it. But it wasn't like the other smell. This smell was good, clean and pure. It was the smell of victory. Of vindication.

He'd been right all along, and they had locked him away. Far, far away, because they were afraid of the truth trapped in his mind. But now . . . now the truth was free. *He* was free. He finally understood what the Voice had been trying to tell him all these years. It was so obvious; he didn't know why he hadn't seen the answer earlier. But now he knew. And soon David would know, too.

Only a week ago, David would have resisted. He would have given Jasper that fearful look. When David gave him that look, Jasper felt like he could hear his brother mumbling under his breath, *Please not me . . . don't let this happen to me.* Jasper used to hate that look, but over time he grew to understand it. He didn't blame his brother; if the situation had been reversed, Jasper would have acted the same way.

The waitress returned with his Coke (sans smile) and Jasper downed the glass in three long swallows. The carbonated soda water burned his throat, but he didn't mind. It was so good he couldn't help himself. Ever since he'd seen the truth, everything felt good—the ridged lines of graffiti carved into the wooden table; the smooth, wet chill of the glass beneath his hand; even the dank, pungent, beer-soaked air in the bar—it was all so perfect, so real, so *now.*

The door swung open again, and Jasper squinted into the bright light. Three dark figures entered. The first was the woman. The Voice had told him about her. She would be a strong ally, but right now she was still dangerous, uncertain. Next was a man with bushy gray hair. That would be David's old adviser, Doc. Jasper had met him once before. He'd liked him. He was smart. He would understand.

Finally he recognized the unmistakable form of the last entrant. It was the other him that existed outside himself. David, his twin. After the door swung closed, Jasper met his brother's eyes. They were wilder than he remembered, darting back and forth with a cagey paranoia before locking into Jasper's gaze.

He had seen eyes like David's many times before, but they'd all been within the white-and-gray walls of the various mental institutions Jasper had frequented the last three years. Jasper nodded to himself, relaxing for the first time since his reawakening four days earlier.

His brother was finally ready.

PART III

LAPLACE'S DEMON

Quantum mechanics demands serious attention.
But an inner voice tells me that this is not the
true Jacob.
The theory accomplishes a lot,
but it does not bring us close to the secret of the
Old One.
In any case, I am convinced that He does not play dice.

—*Albert Einstein, twentieth-century physicist*

Evidently God not only plays dice, but plays
blindfolded,
and at times throws them where you can't see them.

—*Stephen Hawking, twenty-first-century physicist*

Caine spotted Jasper and felt a huge rush of relief.

He had finally navigated through this nightmarish delusion. Caine felt certain that now everything would be okay. Jasper would know what to do, how to lead him out of the darkness and bring him back to sanity. Jasper had made the journey before. He would know the way.

Jasper stood, and Caine enveloped his twin in a tight embrace. "You have no idea how good it is to see you," Caine said, still holding on to Jasper.

"Actually, I think I might," Jasper said into his ear. "Welcome back-*hack-mack-rack.*" Jasper slapped him on the shoulder, and then the twins separated and sat down. Caine slid into the booth directly across from his brother. Nava sat to Caine's right, Doc next to Jasper.

Before Caine could speak, the waitress descended upon them. They all quickly ordered drinks, more to get rid of her than out of any desire for sustenance. As soon as the waitress was out of earshot, Jasper turned to Nava. "Don't worry, there aren't any conspirators in here. We're safe." Then he leaned forward, lowering his voice. "They'll be coming soon, but there's still time to tell David what he needs to know-*row-mow-toe.*"

Nava shot Caine a questioning look.

"It's okay," Caine said, wondering if he believed his own words. Despite his previous confidence that only Jasper could bring him out of his fugue, now that he saw the crazy look in his brother's eyes, Caine wasn't so sure. But he had to try. "Jasper, I—"

"David, I'm sorry, but I'm not going to tell you what you want to hear. All this," Jasper said, sweeping his hand in a large arc above his head, "is *real.* So is everything that happened to you in the last twenty-four hours. I know it seems crazy, but once you're on the other side, you'll understand."

"What are you saying?" Caine felt his mouth go dry. "That Laplace's Demon is real, too?"

"Yes and no," Jasper said.

Caine felt exasperated. Jasper had been right on one count—he wasn't telling Caine what he wanted to hear. Caine closed his eyes and started rubbing his temples. This wasn't happening. He needed to get out. He needed to wake up. There was a loud slam, and Caine's lids snapped up. Jasper's fist was planted in the middle of the table; a few people sitting at the bar turned to see what was happening. Nava looked furious, and Doc just looked stunned.

"David, *you have to listen.* Open your mind to what I have to say; give me ten minutes. After that, if you still think I'm crazy—or that you're crazy—then you can do whatever you want. But at least give me time to explain."

Caine wanted to resist, but the pleading look in Jasper's eyes convinced him to do what his brother asked. "Okay," he said, trying to open his mind to the horrific possibility that everything that had happened to him since he took Dr. Kumar's experimental drug was actually real. Just then the waitress returned with their drinks—two Cokes for the twins, a Red Bull for Nava, and a coffee for Doc. As Caine wasn't sure when he would have another opportunity to take his medication, he quickly downed a pill.

"Okay," Jasper said once the waitress had left. "You asked me whether or not Laplace's Demon was real and I said yes and no. Let's assume for the moment that the answer was an unequivocal yes and that you were the physical manifestation of Laplace's Demon."

"If that were the case," Caine said, "then I would literally know everything—which I don't."

"But if you did know everything, you'd be able to predict the future, right?"

"Yes, but I thought Heisenberg proved—"

"Fuck Heisenberg," Jasper said with a wave of his hand. "I'll circle back to that. For now just answer the question: *If* you were Laplace's Demon *and* you knew everything, *then* you would be able to predict the future. Yes or no?"

"Yes," Caine said, feeling exasperated, "but even if I did know everything, my brain would still need to process all that information, which is impossible."

"Right again," Jasper said with a smile.

"But if it's impossible, how could I be Laplace's Demon?"

"Because," Jasper said, "you don't need the ability to process the information; you just need to be able to access it. Think about it this way: If you wanted to talk to someone who only spoke Japanese, what would you do-*moo-goo-too?"*

"I don't know . . . use a Japanese-English dictionary, I guess. Either that or hire an interpreter."

"Exactly," Jasper said. "You wouldn't need to be able to speak Japanese as long as you had access to some tool that allowed you to translate your thoughts *into* Japanese. Essentially you would outsource the information processing, either to a person or to something else, like a dictionary."

"Okay," Caine said hesitantly. "I see where you're going, but I don't understand how you can compare translating a language to processing all the data in the universe."

"Why-*cry-dye-lye?"* Jasper asked.

"Because even if you could access the data, there isn't an intellectual force on the planet, be it man or machine, capable of processing that amount of information."

"That's where you're wrong," Jasper said. "There is."

"What is it?"

"The collective unconscious."

Caine stared at his brother, trying to understand. He remembered from his college days that a German psychologist named Carl Jung had developed the theory of the collective unconscious in the mid-1900s, but besides that, he was pretty fuzzy on the details. Jasper saw the look of confusion on Caine's face and began to explain.

"Okay, let me back up. Consciousness as we know it, is intermittent. Most people sleep an average of eight hours a day, meaning that we spend at least one-third of our life in an unconscious condition. Jung believed that the conscious mind, at least in part, is driven and affected by the unconscious.

"Jung classified the unconscious into three separate categories. The first category includes personal memories that you can extract voluntarily, such as the name of your fourth-grade teacher. You don't have it at the tip of your tongue, but you can probably pull it out of your unconscious if you try hard enough."

"Like long-term memory."

"Yes-*guess-less-mess,*" Jasper said, nodding vigorously. "The second category consists of personal memories that *cannot* be extracted voluntarily. These are either things you once knew but can no longer remember or something like a childhood trauma that's been repressed. These memories were all in your conscious mind at one point in time, but for some reason they got buried so deep that you can no longer access them.

"The third category is the collective unconscious. Its contents are completely incapable of becoming conscious because they have *never* been in your conscious mind. Essentially, the collective unconscious contains knowledge that has no known origin-*bin-din-sin.*"

"Like what?" Nava asked.

"A newborn baby knows how to suck when presented with a nipple and how to cry when she's hungry. A fawn takes its first steps seconds after it's born. When fish eggs hatch, the babies are born knowing how to swim. The list goes on and on. All creatures in nature are born with complex physical skills and knowledge about themselves and the world around them, without a known source."

Caine furrowed his brow. "But I thought that knowledge is programmed into our DNA."

"That's what *biologists* believe, not physicists—and so far not one biologist has been able to answer the question as to where the *original* instructions come from."

"I'm not sure I follow you."

"Think of it this way: Since all life on the planet evolved from simple one-celled organisms, that means the instructions we're all born with had to be *learned* before they could be coded. There was a *first* baby that had to *learn* to cry, a *first* fawn that had to *learn* to walk. But everything scientists know about biology suggests that learned experiences are *not* passed down to offspring."

"Okay," Caine said, "so if the biology can't explain it, how can physics?"

"Many physicists—and psychologists—believe that living creatures' inherent knowledge *did* in fact originate in the conscious mind—just not their own." Jasper took a long drink from his Coke before he continued. "Okay, you know that modern physicists believe that matter exists as waves rather than as specific points in time and space, right?"

Caine's head was spinning. "Barely."

Jasper sighed. "This would be a lot easier if you had studied physics instead of statistics."

"It's not like I could have anticipated this conversation eight years ago when I was picking a major."

"Actually, you could have, but I'll get to that," Jasper said. "Now, where was I?"

"You said nothing exists at a specific point in time and space."

"Right-*might-sight-tight,*" Jasper said. "You see, until the early 1900s, everyone still believed in what's now called classical physics, which was formulated in 1687 by Isaac Newton when he wrote *Principia.* The most important tenets of classical physics were Newton's laws of motion, which stated that the motion of bodies was determined according to the action of forces upon them.

"These laws were used to explain everything from planetary orbits to a car's acceleration. Essentially Newton believed that God had set up the universe in an ordered fashion with certain immutable laws. This belief even seemed to reflect itself in society as a whole, as capitalism spread and the world changed to obey the so-called laws of supply and demand."

Jasper, clearly excited now and in full lecture mode, began increasing his pace. "Then, in 1905, Einstein developed his Theory of Special Relativity, which stated that everything was relative. Einstein proved that position, speed, and acceleration, which Newton thought existed as absolutes, actually existed only in *relation* to something else. More important, he proved that time itself was relative."

"Now in English, Jasper." Caine looked down at his watch. "And you've only got five minutes left."

"Um, okay-*may-lay-say,*" Jasper said. "I'll speed it up.

"Einstein said two things: First, the speed of light is constant no matter where you are or what you're doing," Jasper counted off on his index finger. "Second, the laws of physics are perceived as the same for any two observers who are moving at a constant speed relative to each other.

"This means that if you and I are on a train that's accelerating, we'll see the landscape in the same way, but if you're on the train and I'm standing still alongside the tracks, we'll see the landscape differently. That's a pretty big oversimplification, but you get the point."

Caine nodded, remembering how the trees had passed in a blur on his way to Philadelphia.

"Now, if I were on a rocket ship that was traveling close to the speed of light, which is 186,000 miles per second, something weird happens. Relative to your point of view, time for me would *slow down.* When I got off the rocket ship, I would be younger than you.

"When Einstein proved this, he showed that even *time* was relative. Then he went on to show that energy and mass were intrinsically linked—the faster a body was accelerating, the more its mass would seem relative to a body at rest-*best-rest-test.*"

"Give me an example," Caine said, in hopes of slowing down his brother enough for himself to catch up.

"Sure. When you're sitting in an airplane that's taking off, your body is pushed back against the seat, right? Almost as if you were—"

"Heavier," Caine finished, understanding.

"Exactly. However, once the plane reaches its cruising altitude and stops accelerating, you feel normal again. This is where $E = mc^2$ came from; E is energy, m is mass, and c is the speed of light. Since c is a constant, that means when energy increases, so does mass. Thus, if you're sitting on a plane when it takes off, as it accelerates, you have a greater amount of kinetic energy than your immediate environment; hence, on a *relative* basis, it seems like your weight increases."

"Okay, I get it," Caine said. "But what does this have to do with waves?"

"Well, as I said before, Newton thought that all matter had a precise location in space and in time, but once Einstein showed that everything was relative, physicists realized that matter has neither an absolute location nor even an absolute age. This caused a revolution that led to the development of *special relativity,* which studies the emission and absorption of energy by matter.

"This, in turn, led to the prediction and later discovery of the elementary particles that are the building blocks of all matter, known as *quarks.* Even though physicists have proven the existence of twelve different types of quarks—*up, down, charm, strange, truth, beauty,* and their antiparticles—"

"Hang on," Caine said, holding up his hand. "Those are the names of the building blocks of matter?" Caine looked over at Doc, who had been uncharacteristically silent during

Jasper's lecture, for confirmation as to whether his brother had completely lost his mind.

Doc nodded. "He's right, Rain Man. That's what they're called."

"Okay," Caine said, rubbing his head. "Keep going."

"Right. So anyway, even though there are twelve different types of quarks, all matter in our reality only consists of *up* and *down* quarks and another quarklike elementary particle called a *lepton.*" Jasper took a breath. "The important thing to understand is that quarks and leptons aren't really matter."

"Then what are they?" Caine asked.

"Energy. You get it? According to quantum physics, matter *doesn't really exist.* What classical physicists *thought* was matter were just compounds of elements, which were made up of atoms, which were made up of quarks and leptons—aka, energy. Hence, matter is really energy." Jasper paused to let what he'd said sink in before continuing. "Now, guess what else is made up of energy."

Caine connected the dots. Suddenly Jasper's convoluted explanation was all tying together. "Thought," Caine said.

"Exactly. All conscious and unconscious thought is created through neurons firing off electrical signals in the brain. You see? Since all *matter* is energy and all *thought* is energy, then all matter and thought are interconnected. That's where the collective unconscious comes from—the shared, connected, unconscious mind of every living creature that ever was, is, and will be-*me-see-tee.*"

"Okay," Caine said, trying to wrap his brain around what his brother had just said. "Even if I can buy that there actually is a metaphysical manifestation of the collective unconscious, I still don't understand how it can span time."

"Because time is relative," Jasper said. "Think about it. The only thing that's faster than the speed of light is—"

"The speed of thought," Caine finished, the final piece clicking in.

"Right—specifically, *unconscious* thought. And since time slows down as particles approach the speed of light relative to those standing still, you can think of the unconscious mind as eternal; hence, it's literally timeless."

Caine nodded. In a crazy convoluted way, what his brother was saying almost made sense. He looked at Doc for another sanity check and was surprised to see that his adviser was nodding.

"How did you put this all together?" Doc asked.

"Philosophy." Jasper grinned.

"Explain," Doc said.

"All Eastern religions and philosophies are founded on the belief that the universe is energy, which is now backed up by quantum physics. Also, they all believe that everyone's minds are essentially one with the universe, which made me think of Jung's collective unconscious.

"Buddhists believe that everything is impermanent. The Buddha taught that all the suffering of the world comes from people's desire to cling to objects and ideas instead of accepting the universe as it flows, moves, and changes. In Buddhism, space and time are seen as merely reflections of states of consciousness. Buddhists see objects not as things but as dynamic processes participating in a universal movement that is constantly in a state of transition. Translation: They see matter as energy, just like quantum physics suggests.

"Taoists also believe in the dynamic movement of the universe; *Tao* means 'the way.' They see the universe as a system of energy—called *chi*—that is constantly changing and flowing; as such, they believe that the individual is only an element in the whole universe, or a part of that energy. Their doctrine is the *I Ching,* also known as *The Book of Changes,* and it teaches that stability can be achieved only when harmony is reached between *yin* and *yang,* which are seen to be opposite but related natural forces in the universe. This, too, reflects quantum physics, because it states that everything is made up of particles bound together by subatomic energy."

Now Caine's head was really spinning. "But all those philosophies are thousands of years old. How is it that they all founded their teachings *before* the discovery of quantum physics?"

"Through the collective unconscious," Jasper answered. "Remember—it's timeless, which means that thought flows *back* through time as well as forward. Great thinkers, philosophers, scientists, they're all said to be 'ahead of their time' because they make huge intuitive leaps. Some people call it genius, but what is genius except incredible insight? Don't you see? So-called geniuses are just people who can better access the collective unconscious than the rest of us-*fuss-muss-suss.*"

Doc sucked in his breath, staring at Caine. "That's how you were able to know that we had to move at the diner. You must have accessed the unconscious mind of your future self."

Caine shook his head. It was all too much. "Even if I believed that everyone's unconscious was somehow linked, how is it that I'm able to access the collective with my conscious mind?" After Caine heard himself voice the question, he suddenly knew the answer. "Oh, my God . . . it's the seizures, isn't it?"

"I think they're the symptoms, not the cause." Jasper explained. "Since everyone draws off the collective unconscious, there must be something in our brain that can tap in to it. I think there's something about your brain," Jasper said, pointing to Caine's skull, "specifically your temporal lobe, that allows you to connect into the collective unconscious in a way that others can't. Up until recently when you did, it overloaded your brain; hence you would have a seizure and blackout—thus entering the unconscious for real-*deal-meal-seal.*

"I think that Dr. Kumar's experimental drug has somehow 'fixed' your brain so that you're able to simultaneously connect to the collective unconscious *and* stay conscious yourself, allowing you to see the future."

"But what I don't understand is how it works from a physics perspective." Caine paused, gathering his thoughts.

"I mean, Laplace stated that you must know *everything* to predict the future, but Heisenberg said that nothing has a true position in nature, so it's impossible to know everything. Therefore, predicting the future is impossible, and an omniscient intelligence like Laplace's Demon can't exist, can it?"

"I haven't figured that out yet-*bet-get-net,*" Jasper admitted, before quickly adding, "but that doesn't mean my theory is wrong."

No one spoke for a minute as Caine tried to process everything Jasper had said.

"There's one way to find out," Doc said.

"How?" Caine asked.

"Look into the future," Doc answered.

"I don't think that's a good idea," Nava said, surprising Caine. She'd been so quiet until that point, he'd practically forgotten she was there.

"Why?" Doc asked.

"What if it's dangerous?" Nava asked as she lit a cigarette.

"Dangerous for whom?" Doc asked.

"All of us," Nava said, blowing smoke into the air. "Especially David."

"Why?" Doc asked again.

"What if he's not able to get back? What if he puts his mind into the collective unconscious and gets trapped? You said it yourself—it's timeless. He could submerge himself in the collective unconscious for a few seconds and return only to find that his body had died of old age."

Caine felt his stomach drop. He hadn't considered those possibilities. Part of him longed to go there. But another part was suddenly terrified. As he contemplated his options, he realized two things. The first was that Jasper's ten minutes were up. The second was that he no longer thought this was all a delusion.

It was impossible—he simply didn't know enough physics to have dreamed it up himself.

"W*hat the fuck did you think you were doing?"*

Forsythe held the phone away from his ear. He made sure to breathe before answering the FBI executive assistant director, who was furious about the debacle at the train station.

"Sam, obviously I had no idea it was going to go down like that—"

"Don't fucking 'Sam' me!" Sam Kendall shouted into the phone. "You told me that you needed a few men to detain a *civilian*—there was no mention of a rogue CIA agent!"

"Sam . . . um, I mean . . ." Forsythe stumbled. He didn't know how Kendall had found out about Vaner so quickly.

"Don't bother, *James.* I know you rooked me. Congratulations. Who put you up to it? Nielsen?" Forsythe didn't try to interject; he just let the man rant. "Yeah," Kendall growled, more to himself than Forsythe. "Well, *fuck* him and *fuck* you. And then you have the *balls* to pull Martin Crowe into the mix? It's a fucking miracle somebody didn't wind up dead!"

Kendall paused to take a breath before continuing his tirade. "Plus, I just heard that MacDougal is going to replace your ass next month. Let me tell you, after the stunt you just pulled, consider yourself replaced *now.*"

Forsythe's fingers tightened around the phone. "You don't have the authority—"

"Who the fuck do you think I am?" Kendall was screaming now. "I'm the executive assistant director of the FBI, and believe it or not I have some pull in this town! I talked to Senator MacDougal about this morning's escapade, and we *both* agreed that it would be best if you resigned *today.*

"You've got thirty minutes to pack up your shit before I have the MPs escort you out. Been nice knowing you, asshole." Kendall slammed down the phone so hard the sound echoed in Forsythe's ears.

Forsythe was stunned. He wasn't ready yet. Yes, Tversky's work had shown a great deal of promise, but what if it didn't pan out? He'd thought he would have at least another month to mine the STR database and use the NSA's resources before heading out on his own. Now he had nothing. Nothing except Tversky and his "demon"—and he didn't have even that. Forsythe took a moment to collect himself before asking Grimes to come to his office.

"Steven, I don't know how to say this, but . . ." He paused, letting Grimes think the worst before delivering his lie. "We've been fired. Today is our last day."

"What? I mean, I knew you were toast, but . . . why me?"

"It was political," Forsythe said. "But maybe it's a good thing for both of us."

"What do you mean?" Grimes asked, scrunching up his face.

Forsythe tried to think of the best way to tell him. He didn't want Grimes to know he'd been planning to jump ship without him for the past six months. He already had the research lab set up and $10 million in the bank. All he lacked was a complete staff of scientists. He'd planned on recruiting from the private sector rather than draft any of STR's "government talent," but now there was no time.

And he wasn't about to give up on poaching more research from STR's backyard. Since Grimes hadn't actually been fired, his security codes would stay active until someone realized Forsythe's deception—by then he should have all the information he needed. As much as Forsythe hated to admit it, Grimes was essential.

"I was planning on saving this as a surprise, but . . ."

Forsythe spent the next fifteen minutes explaining his plan to Grimes, stressing the fact that only Forsythe knew that Grimes had been fired, hence Grimes should keep it quiet.

When he was through, Grimes rubbed his pimply chin. "I want equity."

"What?"

"You heard me," Grimes said. "If you want me to join you, I want a piece of the pie."

"How much?" Forsythe asked, clenching and unclenching his fists beneath the desk.

"Ten percent."

Forsythe let out a slow whistle. He didn't have time to argue, and he knew that Grimes would be completely infantile about negotiating his share. Forsythe made up his mind in an instant.

"Steven, if I owned the entire enterprise, then I would gladly give you 10 percent. But the VCs already own 80 percent." The lie rolled off Forsythe's tongue like oil; although the venture capitalists were vultures, they had demanded only a 35 percent equity stake for their $12 million—$2 million of which he had already spent setting up the lab. "How about this: I'll offer you 10 percent of what I own."

"That's only 2 percent," Grimes sniffed.

"It's a fair offer, Steven." Forsythe kept his face solemn.

"Make it 3 percent and you got a deal," Grimes said.

"Done."

Grimes held out a sweaty hand. Forsythe shook it and quickly wiped his palm on his slacks.

"Excellent," Forsythe said, anxious for his relationship with Grimes to return to employer-employee. "Now, get Crowe on the phone."

"Sure thing . . . *partner.*" Grimes flashed him a large, yellow-toothed smile before leaving the office. Eighteen seconds later the red light on Forsythe's phone started flashing. He took a breath and picked it up.

"Mr. Crowe, it's James Forsythe," he said. "There's been a change of plans. . . ."

After Crowe clicked off, he let his mind go blank as he continued staring at the sky. The sun was finally peeking through the clouds, and a rainbow appeared. Betsy had always loved rainbows. Whenever she saw one, they would get in the car and drive around, looking for the pot of gold.

His eyes misted. Betsy had been so proud of her daddy. He wondered what she would say if she saw him now. He knew from Forsythe's car-salesman-like pitch that nothing good could come from what he wanted Crowe to do, but the money was too much to pass up.

If Forsythe still wanted him to bring Caine in, Crowe would figure out a way to do it. He paged through his cell's phone book until he found what he was looking for. Jim Dalton's number glowed blue against the white backdrop of the screen.

Crowe had promised himself he would never work with Dalton or his thugs again after the mercenary had tricked Crowe into providing security for a drug dealer. But then again, what was another broken promise? Besides, it wasn't as if the other mercenaries he knew were any more upstanding. The fact was, if Crowe could keep Dalton's violent streak under control, there was nobody better.

With a slight pang of resignation, Crowe pressed the "Talk" button. Dalton picked up on the first ring.

"Marty, what's shakin'?" Dalton said.

"I've got a job, and I need some backup," Crowe said.

"When?"

"Now."

"Shit, I wish I could help, but I got a guy in town who needs me to do a couple of errands for him. How 'bout next week?"

"It can't wait," Crowe said, pinching his brow. "How much does an errand boy make these days?"

Dalton paused for a second before answering. "Thirty for five days' work."

"Is that for you or the whole crew?"

"Just me. Rainer, Leary, McCoy, and Esposito are each pullin' in fifteen apiece."

He figured Dalton was lying, but Crowe didn't care. It was Forsythe's money.

"My employer will pay the four of you one-fifty for the week," Crowe said. "You can divide it up however you like."

Dalton whistled. "What are you into, Marty?"

"Nothing worse than usual. Are you in or out?"

"What's the job?"

"Some recon, a snatch, and then maybe some guard duty."

"Who's the target?" Dalton asked suspiciously.

"No one who'll be missed. Just a civilian."

"Why the big money? Sounds like this is something you could do all by your lonesome."

"He's got a bodyguard."

"And?"

"And," Crowe said, starting to get irritated at all the questions, "she's ex-CIA, covert ops. Very tough."

"*She?*" Dalton laughed. "Okay, you need me and the boys to deal with your lady friend, then we can probably help you out. But I want the cash up front."

"No way. Half up front, half after we acquire the target."

Dalton was silent for a moment, but Crowe wasn't worried. He knew that Dalton would take the deal.

"Okay," Dalton said, as if he were doing Crowe a favor. "Where's the job?"

"Not sure right now, but probably tristate area."

"You want me to meet you somewhere?"

"No," Crowe said, his mind working. "Just get the boys together along with the usual hardware; then sit tight and stay sober."

"Got it," Dalton said.

"When I've got the location, I'll call you."

"No problemo. Nice to do business with you again, Marty."

A minute after Crowe hung up, his phone buzzed. Dalton hadn't wasted any time in sending his account number. Crowe forwarded the message on to Grimes, along with instructions on how much money to wire. With that done, he headed back to his apartment to crash. It was too early to sleep, but he'd try to grab a nap while he had the chance. He had the feeling it was going to be a long night.

As he drifted off, his mind returned to the upcoming mission. He was confident that wherever Caine was, Grimes would find him. It was only a matter of time. And when he did, Crowe would bring him in—probably killing Vaner in the process.

There was nothing he could do now except wait.

Caine stared down at his Coke. "I should have ordered a stronger drink."

"Are you going to try . . . ?" Doc asked.

"I don't know," Caine said. "Even if I wanted to, I'm not sure how I would do it."

"I still think it's too dangerous," Nava said. "As long as we're on the run, it's too risky."

"You didn't have a problem with me doing it on the train," Caine countered.

"That was different." Nava said. "Besides, I didn't know the risks."

"But what if they're tracking us right now?" Caine asked. "Maybe it's too risky *not* to try."

Nava frowned, absently stabbing out her cigarette.

"He's got a point," Doc said.

"Try, David. The Voice—" Jasper cut himself off. "I mean, I think it's time."

Caine eyed his brother. Jasper still hadn't told him everything—like how he knew to call Doc right after Caine had carjacked him—but Caine knew there had to be a reason.

After Jasper's physics lecture, however, everyone seemed to forget that David wasn't the only Caine brother who seemed to be exhibiting unnatural abilities.

It made sense, though. They were identical twins, which meant that if David Caine could do something, odds were Jasper Caine could as well. Caine didn't know whether that meant he should have more or less confidence in his brother. But when he looked into Jasper's eyes, his decision was clear.

"I'm going to try," Caine said. Despite the conviction in his voice, he was afraid. All his other problems—his academic career, his seizures, Nikolaev—suddenly seemed trivial compared to what he was about to do. What if Nava was right? What if he got trapped forever, lost in some timeless void? Would he go insane? Or maybe he was already. . . . No. He wasn't insane. He'd never been delusional—just too afraid to admit the truth.

He took a deep breath. He had to put his fear aside and do this before it was too late. Right. Just like when he'd put his fear aside and become a shut-in, hiding from his friends, his students, his life. No, that was different. He didn't have a choice then. Didn't he, though? Looking back, he saw what a coward he'd been. Well, he wasn't going to be a coward anymore.

He closed his eyes, and . . .

CHAPTER twenty-seven

. . .

Nothing happened.

Caine could still hear Mick Jagger singing on the jukebox in the background. He could still feel the hard wooden seat beneath him and the dull throb of his knee, which pulsed with every heartbeat. He could still smell the stale scent of day-old beer mixed with sweat that pervaded the bar. The only difference was that before he closed his eyes, he could see, and now he could not.

He let out a long exhale and tried to slow his breathing. What had he been thinking in the diner? He couldn't remember; one minute he was eating a fry, and the next Doc and Peter were covered in blood.

There were six quick clicks.

At first Caine thought the sound was coming from somewhere else, somewhere inside him, but when the waitress began talking, he realized it had only been the sound of her heels.

"You guys need another round?"

"Could you come back later?" Doc asked. "We're right in the middle of something."

"Sure thing."

And then suddenly the blackness faded away, as if someone had slowly turned up the lights. Caine still had his eyes squeezed shut . . . but he could see. And there was more than just sight before his eyes—there was knowledge.

. . .

The waitress is a tall redhead with a low-cut black top and too much makeup. Her name is Allison Gully, but everyone calls her Ally. The heavy eye shadow is there to hide the bruise that Nick Braughten gives her. She wants to leave him but she is afraid.

Because Caine's party doesn't order drinks, she walks back to the bar and flirts with Tim Shamus. He's new, and she thinks he's cute. When Tim is at home that night, he fantasizes about her. He paces around the apartment. He finally falls to sleep at 4:00 A.M. *When he wakes, the sun is high overhead.*

Tim is late. He races to his car, a black '89 Ford Mustang. On his way to work, he cuts off Marlin Kramer as he blows through a red light. Marlin is having a terrible day. He honks his horn at Tim, and, in his frustration, he makes a wrong turn. He gets stuck in traffic and misses his plane to Houston. Matt Flannery is waiting on standby and takes Marlin's seat next to Lenore Morrison. They talk the entire flight. When they land, he asks for her number. She blushes for the first time since . . . she is fifteen and kisses Derek Cohen at the movies.

Matt and Lenore have sex on the third date. They use a condom the first few times but then decide it's safe not to. But it's not safe. Lenore is HIV-positive. Matt is diagnosed with AIDS. He dies alone in the hospital, instead of marrying Beth Peterson and having two children and three grandchildren.

. . .

or

. . .

Caine orders a drink. Ally walks back to the bar ten seconds later than if there hadn't been a drink order. On her way, Aidan Hammerstein and Jane Berlent finally catch her eye and order two shots. Ally tells Tim to hurry up and pour. There's no time to flirt. Ally delivers Caine's drink along with Aidan's and Jane's Alabama Slammers. The alcohol puts Jane over the top. She's drunk. Instead of going home, she and Aidan decide to paint the town red. What the hell, it's her birthday. She's twenty-five.

She keeps drinking while . . . Tim Shamus falls asleep just fine at 2:00 A.M., he wakes up on time, and Marlin Kramer catches his flight . . . On Jane's way home, she stops off at the Korean deli and buys a pack of Marlboro Lights. It's her first cigarette since . . . she's twenty-one, vomiting up two enchiladas and a chicken taco. The smoke mixes with the smell of her partially digested dinner. She vows never to smoke another cigarette again. She never does. She lives to be ninety-seven years old. Seth Greenberg, the favorite of her six great-grandchildren, cries at her funeral.

. . . but now at twenty-five she does smoke. It tastes great in the cool night air. She wonders why she ever quit. She never quits again. Aidan can't stand the smoke. It leads to a fight. He has an affair with Tammy Monroe, his secretary. He breaks up with Jane. She begins seeing a psychiatrist. He prescribes Zoloft. It helps, but not enough. On the eve of her thirtieth birthday, she decides to celebrate by washing down twenty pills with a fifth of tequila. Her body is found two weeks later, when her neighbor finally reports the smell.

. . .

"Wait!" Caine could barely breathe. His eyes flew open, and he stared at the waitress—*Ally, her name is Ally*—like he'd seen a ghost.

"You want something?" she asked.

Over her shoulder Caine could see a blond guy *(Aidan)* trying to get the waitress's attention. Caine was paralyzed, unsure of what to do. He knew he'd changed something. If he went back in, he would know what *had happened / is happening / will happen* to Ally, Tim, Marlin, Matt, Lenore, Aidan, Jane, and Tammy. And the people whose lives are touched by those eight. And their *possible / probable / impossible* offspring. And their friends. And—

"Honey, are you okay?" the waitress asked again.

"I . . . I . . . ah . . ." Caine couldn't speak. And suddenly it was all around him—the cloying stink of human waste mixed with mildew, rotten meat soaked in bile, spoiled fruit covered with maggots. As Caine's eyes rolled to the back of his head, he felt himself falling forward. He knew he would wake up with a painful headache from where his head was about to hit the table, but he didn't care; the blissful unconsciousness was rushing at him like a freight train.

He heard the worried cries of his friends. Jasper. Nava. Doc. Their voices echoed in his mind. And then, even though every neuron in his brain had begun to shriek in protest, he began to see again. His eyes were still closed, but the visions spooled before him like a horrific movie.

. . .

They live. They suffer. They die.

Over and over again, Caine is helpless to stop seeing it all.

Everything keeps happening in every which way. He is vaguely aware that in the When *he screams for nearly nine seconds, which can seem like forever when you're in the* When.

But he learns something new.

He learns how long eternity can really be.

When Caine awoke, he wasn't surprised that he had a pounding headache.

"David, are you all right?" It was Nava.

"Yeah," he said, gently rubbing his skull.

"What happened?" asked Doc.

Caine opened his mouth to answer, but he didn't have the words. He could barely get his mind around what he saw. At first the images had been clear and distinct, but as they traced over each other in the same time-space, they blurred together. It was as if he'd been watching a slide show where each new picture was presented on top of a clean white screen for a nanosecond before it was projected onto the pictures he'd already seen. By the end there was nothing except overlapping images, creating an amorphous blackness.

He knew that by the time he left the bar, he would have barely any recollection of what he'd seen; his brain couldn't possibly hold it all in. Already he could feel the knowledge leaking from his mind, out into the abyss. And he was happy to forget. If he didn't know, then he wouldn't have to choose.

He didn't know how he could live like this, so responsible, so full of choice. Even if he chose to live on a desert island, his actions would ripple through the universe. The simplest decision would cause someone to live and someone else to die. He couldn't do it. He couldn't bear it.

"I can't. I can't. I can't," Caine murmured over and over.

"You can't what?" Jasper asked.

"I can't choose. It's not right. Who am I to—"

Jasper slapped Caine hard across the face. "You're David Caine."

"But what if I mess up?" Caine asked. He could see only his brother. It was as if Nava and Doc had ceased to exist.

Jasper smiled. "Then you mess up, little bro. Even if you choose to do nothing, that's still a choice. You can't avoid a decision."

"But there are so many things that can—that *do*—go wrong."

"That's unavoidable," Jasper said. "But you have to try."

Caine nodded. He couldn't remember much of what he'd seen would happen. But even as he began to forget, he knew what he had to do. He wasn't sure that it was the right thing—in fact, he was certain there was a possibility he was wrong—but there was an even greater chance he was right. All he could do was choose the path with the least amount of errors. What happened after that was out of his control.

Caine took a deep breath and turned to Nava. "We need to get out of here," Caine said. "Is there somewhere we can go that's safe?"

"Yes," Nava answered instantly. "I know a place."

"Where is it?" Caine asked.

"You'll see when you get there."

"No," Caine said. "I need to know now."

"I don't think—"

Caine reached across the table and grabbed her hand. "Nava, you have to trust me. It's important that I know. Where are you taking us? Exactly."

Nava searched his eyes. Whatever she was looking for, she must have found, because she answered his question without any more protests. Caine closed his eyes for a second and then opened them again.

"Okay," he said. "I need to use the restroom. Then we should go."

Caine stood and limped over to the long hallway at the opposite end of the bar. When he was sure no one could see him, he picked up the pay phone directly across from the men's room. Just then a shadow fell across the floor. It was Doc. Caine put his index finger to his lips. He didn't want Doc mentioning the call in front of Nava. Doc nodded, then disappeared into the bathroom.

Caine recalled the number from three days earlier. The phone rang for a long time before the man picked up.

"Hello, Peter. This is David Caine." He closed his eyes for an instant, trying to find exactly the right words. "Please listen very closely; I don't have much time."

"Hello, James." Forsythe instantly recognized Tversky's voice on the other end of his cell phone. "I hear you've been looking for me."

"What makes you say that?" Forsythe asked.

"Let's not waste time, shall we? I know what you're after, and I can deliver it—for a price."

"There's nothing you have that I want."

"How about David Caine?"

"I'm listening," Forsythe said, trying not to sound too anxious.

"I know where he'll be at six o'clock."

Forsythe looked at his watch—that was in forty minutes. He cleared his throat.

"What's your price?"

They exited the subway in a section of Brooklyn that Caine didn't recognize. The signs of many stores they passed were in Hebrew; the men wore black jackets, black hats, and black beards. Doc smiled. Caine had to admit that he was taking everything in stride. That was something he'd always liked about Doc: Nothing surprised him.

"Law of large numbers," Doc once said to him. "It would only be surprising if something odd happened to everyone on the earth at the exact same moment. As I have but one viewpoint, I have to assume that whatever improbable event is happening to me is not happening to everyone else on the planet. Hence, as long as the chance of its happening is more than 1 in 6 billion, then the probability of its happening to *someone* is almost 100 percent, and what's surprising about an event with a 100 percent probability actually occurring?"

Nava led them through a series of dark alleys until they were in so deep that Caine could barely hear the street. When she reached the third doorway, she climbed down the stairs and knocked four times. A panel in the door slid to the side, revealing a pair of suspicious dark brown eyes. Once they lit upon Nava, however, the door flew open.

"My little Nava!" a big bear of a man exclaimed. He scooped Nava up in his hairy arms and squeezed her so hard that Caine thought her head might pop off. They spoke rapidly in Hebrew, and slowly the man's warm smile disappeared. Finally Nava turned to the others.

"This is Eitan," she said, motioning to the big man. "Eitan, this is David, Jasper, and Doc."

"Glad to meet you," Eitan said in heavily accented English. He shook Caine's hand like a jackhammer. "Nava's friends are my friends." He stepped from the doorway and motioned them inside. "Please, I am your host."

The apartment was surprisingly tidy, in contrast to the dirty side street that served as its entrance. An orange carpet covered the stone floor. A pale yellow couch with a massive sag in the middle—clearly Eitan's favorite sitting spot—sat against a wall that was covered with pictures of the big man's family. Next to the couch was a wooden rocking chair adorned with handmade cushions.

"Sit, I will get some food." Eitan stomped off. Caine maneuvered around the long wooden coffee table and sat down on the couch. The springs squealed softly, but Caine was confident they had borne much more punishment than his 175-pound frame.

Eitan returned with a plate of pita bread, a bowl of hummus, and four glasses of iced tea. Caine devoured the food while Eitan and Nava shared a cigarette. The two old allies chatted in Hebrew, and Caine tried to pretend that life was normal, even though he knew he wouldn't have much more time to spend with his friends.

"She's here."

"Excellent. Is she alone?"

"No. There are three others as well as her contact at the safe house."

"Kill the contact. Then bring her to me."

"Understood." Choi Siek-Jin clicked off his cell phone. It was dark in the alley, so he removed his mirrored sunglasses as he entered the gloom. The lock on the back door was no better than a child's plaything, and within a minute he was inside. He could hear their voices from the other end of the small apartment, but he did not make his way toward them. Instead he waited in the kitchen.

Eventually the fat man would return. And when he did, Siek-Jin would be ready.

"Are you all finished?" Eitan asked, gesturing to the near-empty bowl of hummus.

"That was more than enough-*cuff-rough-tough,*" Jasper said. "Thank you."

Eitan smiled, pretending not to notice Jasper's odd tic. "Can I get you more water? Maybe a glass of wine?"

"I could use some more iced tea," Doc said.

"Certainly," Eitan said, scooping up Doc's empty glass. "I will be right back."

When Eitan left the room, Caine felt a dull sense of dread. As he watched the big man disappear down the hallway toward the kitchen, Caine suddenly had an intense desire to stop him. But a deeper instinct held him back. Had he known earlier, maybe he could have prevented what was about to happen.

But now it was too late. He had to let the universe take its course.

Siek-Jin held his finger to his lips. Too scared to do anything else, Eitan froze, eyes wide, staring at the large gun that was aimed at his head. Siek-Jin made a quick motion for Eitan to put down the empty glass he was holding. Eitan's hands were shaking badly, but he managed to place it safely on the countertop.

His gun still aimed at Eitan, Siek-Jin pointed to the man, circled his hand in the air, and then motioned to the floor. Slowly Eitan complied. He turned around and got down on his knees as tears streamed down his face. Siek-Jin unsheathed his blade. Then, in one fluid motion, he sliced his knife across Eitan's neck. The man made a soft gurgling sound as he clutched his throat, and then Siek-Jin stabbed him in the back.

Still holding the knife in one hand and his gun in the other, Siek-Jin caught Eitan's lifeless body and lowered it to the floor. After using Eitan's shirt to wipe off his blade, Siek-Jin resheathed it. He knew that Vaner would not be nearly as easy to manage. He would definitely need a free hand.

Caine closed his eyes, trying to remember the future. This time he didn't let himself travel too far down the path before opening his eyes and returning to the *Now*.

"We need to move the couch in front of the door," Caine said, forcing himself to stand. "Along with that bookshelf."

Without commenting, Nava and Jasper picked up either end of the couch and carried it across the room. Doc took care of the shelves. When they were finished, the four of them stood back to appreciate their handiwork. The day's last bit of sunlight streamed in through the tiny window near the ceiling of the ground-floor apartment. As it lit up Nava's face, Caine felt a wave of déjà vu.

He quickly bent down and unplugged a reading lamp from the wall. It was small but heavy. He held it in his hand like a club. It would do. As Caine turned toward the doorway, he hoped that his instincts would serve him well for the next few moments. If they didn't, there was a 97.5329 percent probability that Nava would die.

"I've got a clean head shot."

"Hold," Crowe ordered. "I just want you to wing her."

"But—"

"Jim: my team, *my way.* Understood?"

"Copy," Dalton growled. Crowe had a lot of nerve, bitch-slapping him on an open channel. He'd get flak from Rainer and Esposito when this was all over.

"Leary, are you in position?"

"Back exit is covered," Leary crackled over the headset.

"Jim, you still have the shot?"

"Roger that," Dalton said, studying Nava's face in the scope. He didn't give a shit what Crowe said—he was gonna take out the traitorous bitch. Too bad, though. She was really something. He and the boys definitely could have had a good time with her. It was a shame he had to put a bullet between those soulful eyes—but not such a shame that he would hesitate when it was time to pull the trigger.

"Something's wrong," Nava said. "Eitan. He's been gone too long."

Before Nava could reach for her Glock, the Korean assassin appeared in the doorway, his gun leveled at her head. "Don't," he said, never taking his eyes off her own. "Chang-Sun wants you alive."

Nava's heart jumped into her throat. She knew by the splatter of blood on the Korean's pants that Eitan was already dead. Although the enemy was only three meters away, the distance might as well have been a mile. There was no way she could reach him before he gunned her down.

It was over.

"Winging Vaner in five," Dalton said softly into his mike. He took a deep breath and held it, counting down. He steadied his hands, positioning the crosshairs on Vaner's face.

"Four."

The horizontal line traversed her eyes, while the vertical split her nose down the middle. Her face divided nicely into four quadrants.

"Three."

He tightened his finger on the trigger.

"Two."

He prepared for the kick of the high-powered rifle.

"One."

The rifle cracked as it tried to jump from his tight embrace, recoiling from the 7.62-millimeter bullet that ripped through the air at 1,100 feet per second on its way to Nava Vaner's brain.

Just then Caine hurled the lamp at the Korean assassin. However, before the lamp could hit its mark, Siek-Jin calmly stepped aside, moving two feet to the left—exactly as Caine predicted he would.

Vaner was suddenly obscured by a dark brown shape, which instantly exploded into red. Someone had moved into the way. If that someone were David Caine, he was in deep shit. Dalton drove that thought from his mind as the shape dropped from view. Vaner was still in position, although, by the look in her eyes, she wouldn't be much longer.

Dalton unloaded the clip at her head and hoped for the best.

There was a fierce rush of air followed by a quick crunch. Suddenly the window shattered, spraying glass into the room as the Korean fell forward, smashing down onto the wooden coffee table. A hole in his forehead the size of a baseball revealed the gray meat of his brain, splashed with red. Nava acted without thinking, hurling herself across the room, and pulling Caine to the floor.

"DOWN!" she screamed, just as two holes appeared in the wall directly in back of where she'd been standing. Then she heard a crash as part of the door exploded into the room. They would have broken through but for the couch and the bookshelf, which held their attackers at bay. They had only another few seconds before it was too late.

She looked down at Caine, lying beneath her, eyes closed, breathing heavily.

Caine knew he had 15.3 seconds. At least, he thought he knew. For an instant he saw it all before him, a million branches of possibility growing from the moment. He could travel down each one and spend an infinity plotting every possible future based on any one choice. Many led to his death; all but a few to Nava's demise. In only a handful did everything work out the way Caine desired.

Each path had an infinite number of offshoots, many with horrible repercussions he couldn't fathom. With more time he could make a better decision, but he was out of time. Only 13.7 seconds left. He chose the path that seemed the most right, the least wrong, relying half on his knowledge and half on his gut.

"Sorry about this, Nava," Caine said, his eyes still shut.

Before she could respond, he grabbed both her arms

and rolled her onto her back, and smashed her head into the ground. The sound of her skull crashing into the concrete floor reminded her of the crack of a rifle.

Then everything went black.

Caine looked over at Jasper and Doc, who were trying to hold their makeshift barrier in place; there was so much he wanted to say to each of them, but there were only 9.2 seconds left.

He quickly crawled over to Siek-Jin's ruined head, dragging his own splinted leg behind him. Caine shuddered at what he was about to do but knew the clock was ticking, so he just followed the path. He reached inside Siek-Jin's skull and scooped out a handful of brains, cupping his hands to capture as much blood as he could. Its warmth surprised him—it was like dipping his hand into hot lasagna. Caine's stomach churned, but he kept going.

He crawled forward on his elbows, trying not to bend his knee. Somehow he kept his balance as he carried his gruesome package to Nava. Once he reached her, he smeared it across her face and hair. If anyone took a hard look, they'd be able to tell that the blood and gray matter weren't her own, but there was less than a 2.473 percent chance that look would occur.

Caine snatched Nava's knapsack and hobbled to the kitchen, closing the door behind him, 1.3 seconds before three soldiers burst into the room.

. . .

Their names are Martin Crowe, Juan Esposito, Ron McCoy, and Charlie Rainer. Each wears black from head to toe, body armor covering their chests. Their faces are unrecognizable behind the smoked glass of their helmets.

"On the ground, now!" Rainer barks, even though everyone is already lying on the floor.

. . .

Caine stepped over Eitan's body, which lay in a pool of blood on the kitchen floor, then grabbed a long black coat and hat off a wall peg as he opened the back door. He kept his eyes closed. It was easier to see that way.

. . .

Esposito slams Doc against the wall.

A heavy boot stomps on Jasper's back as the muzzle of Crowe's gun is thrust against his skull. When Crowe sees the faded bruise on Jasper's cheek, he knows this is not the twin he wants. A quick look around the room tells him what he needs to know.

"Leary, target is heading your way."

"I see him now."

. . .

"Freeze!"

Caine forced himself to keep walking forward, ignoring his fear. The man *(Mark Leary)* backed up slowly, keeping his gun trained on Caine's torso, just as Caine knew he would.

"Stop or I'll shoot!" the man yelled.

"No you won't," Caine said. With his eyes still closed, Caine raised Nava's Glock 9-millimeter, and

. . .

angles the gun and pulls the trigger. The bullet rips through the flesh of Leary's calf, but it doesn't stop him. He swings his pistol around and smashes the butt across Caine's skull—

(loop)

angles the gun and pulls the trigger. The bullet misses entirely, ricocheting off the pavement. Leary jumps forward, tackling Caine—

(loop)

angles the gun and pulls the trigger. The bullet slams into Leary's foot. He stumbles, madly pinwheeling his arms, bringing Caine down with him—

(loop)

angles the gun and pulls the trigger.

. . .

The bullet tore through Leary's flesh, disintegrating his femur before shredding the back of his leg on its way out.

He crumpled backward, screaming in pain. Caine continued marching forward, veering only slightly to the left to avoid the fallen commando. As he exited the alleyway, he put on the black hat.

The second Crowe saw Leary on the ground, he broke into a run, but it was too late. By the time he rounded the corner, Caine was nowhere to be seen. The street was clogged with Hasidic Jews—identical-looking men dressed in black.

"Goddamn it!" he yelled. He stared at the crowd, refusing to believe what he knew to be true—David Caine was gone.

He turned around and headed back into the house. Judging by the amount of brains that were splattered across Vaner's skull, it was obvious the woman was dead, as was the Asian man lying next to her. He didn't bother to check for a pulse. He couldn't believe that Dalton had killed them both. Crowe would deal with him later. At least the twin was alive; he and the doctor were up against the wall.

"Rainer, get those two in the van," Crowe commanded. "McCoy, go out back and help Leary. Then—" He broke off when he heard the wail of sirens. It sounded as if a fleet of police cars was descending on the apartment. There wasn't much time. The last thing Crowe wanted to do was explain two corpses to the local cops. All that mattered was to grab the others and disappear.

"You've got twenty seconds. Esposito—light it up on your way out."

His men knew what to do. Esposito planted electronic detonators on opposite walls and attached the explosives. Crowe wasn't worried that there would be any evidence left—he'd never known a demolitions man to play it safe and use too little C-4, and Juan Esposito was certainly no exception.

They were speeding away from the apartment with their two prisoners when Crowe heard a muffled *wumph,* followed by a thunderous explosion. When the authorities arrived on the scene, there would be nothing left except for two charred corpses and a lot of unanswered questions.

Forsythe was still seething at the humiliation of being escorted from the STR lab by a pair of armed guards. He tried to put it out of his mind as he paced back and forth across the floor of his new office, two stories below the streets of Manhattan. Thank God he'd secured the venture capital to fund the lab months before. All the scientific equipment was already operational, although the IT and electrical system were still malfunctioning.

Outside his glass wall, he could see Grimes rushing around the large room with his pet geeks as they installed the new servers and initialized the security system. If everything went smoothly, they'd be up and running within the hour.

Suddenly his phone began to ring. Despite the fact that Forsythe had been waiting anxiously for the call, the sound still made him jump. He reached down and grabbed the handset, abruptly cutting off its shrill ring. "Did you get him?"

"No. They were ready for us. They had the door barricaded, and the target had his escape route already planned out."

Forsythe ran a hand across his balding scalp. At least Crowe hadn't tried to sugarcoat it.

"What about the twin?" Forsythe asked.

"We got him. I gave him fifty milligrams of amobarbital. He should be under for the next three hours."

Forsythe sighed in relief. "It's absolutely imperative that he remains unconscious. If you see any sign of lucidity, administer another twenty-five milligrams."

"Understood."

There was an uncomfortable moment of silence, and then Crowe spoke again. "Sir, David Caine's bodyguard is dead, and we have his brother. Caine is defenseless and alone. He'll pop up soon enough; next time he won't get away."

"From your lips to God's ears," Forsythe said, and hung up the phone. He was disappointed that they didn't have the Beta Subject yet, but Crowe was right—it was only a matter of time. Meanwhile he could run some tests of the twin. If the Beta Subject truly had the gift, then there was every reason to believe that the brother would have it as well.

Forsythe couldn't wait for them to get back to the lab so he could start running tests. Although he wished he could skip the intermediate steps and immediately take a cross-section of the twin's temporal lobe, he knew that there would be months of chemical analyses before they would be ready. Until then it would probably be necessary to keep the twin in a near-constant catatonic state.

Only after they had learned everything they could from him would they saw open his skull.

Despite the throbbing pain in his knee, Caine kept walking. After he heard the explosion, he ducked into a Starbucks. First he went to the bathroom to wash the blood off his hands. His shirt was still stained with a fine red splatter, but there was nothing he could do about that besides keep his long black coat buttoned.

After the caffeine and sugar from his second espresso kicked in, Caine surreptitiously opened Nava's knapsack. Even though he already knew the bag's contents, it was reassuring to see them with his own eyes. There were two guns—a SIG Sauer and a Glock—twenty clips of ammo, a signal jammer, a GPS tracker, a PDA, and three complete sets of ID, each with a different name and nationality, along with backup credit cards. However, what really interested him were the three packets of twenty-dollar bills. There were 50 bills in each packet, 150 in all.

Three thousand dollars wasn't going to be enough money to pull off what he had planned, but it was a start. He closed his eyes for a moment and then walked outside. It took him only forty seconds to hail a cab.

"Where to?" the cabbie asked, his voice bored and phlegmy.

"East Village," Caine said. "Seventh and Avenue D."

In her mind's eye, Nava could see her body baking. Her flesh glowed ruby red as it began to blister and peel, sloughing off skin in long, bloody strips. The heat was like a living thing, an animal licking at her with a tongue of flames.

The smoke curled around her face, snaking its way into her lungs. It burned her lips, her gums, her throat. She resisted the urge to open her eyes, knowing that the smoke would rob her of sight. Instead she focused on breathing.

The last thing she remembered was Caine rolling on top of her, knocking her unconscious. Now her arms were pinned at her sides. She turned her wrists up and stretched out her fingertips. Old ratty fabric . . . the couch. It must have flipped on top of her, protecting her from the fire. She pushed her face into the seat cushion, using the old fabric as an air filter. She had to get out soon. She couldn't last much longer.

She had strength enough for just one push. It was now or never. She heaved her right arm against the sofa. For a moment the couch balanced at a forty-five-degree angle, the right side hovering high in the air, teetering between rolling over and crashing down on top of her. Nava stretched the fingers of her right hand to tip the balance. The fire rushed to fill the space between her and the couch, scorching the air. She gave one final heave, and the couch smashed down to her left. She was free.

Nava struggled to her feet and ran for the front of the apartment. The outer wall was almost entirely gone; all that remained was a cinder-block skeleton. She burst outside and sucked in a gulp of fresh air, stumbling away from the burning building. Then she was falling, but she didn't care; the ground was cool, and the air was clean.

Zaitsev had always said there would be time to rest when she was dead, but she decided to put her mentor's mantra aside, just this once. Right now was a good time to rest as well. The last thing she saw before she passed out was a strange man looming over her.

He was wearing a red bow tie.

Forsythe compared the twin's MRI to that of the Beta Subject. It wasn't a perfect match, but the brother did have a similar anomaly in his right temporal lobe. This was even better than Forsythe could have hoped for. If he gave the twin the experimental antiepilepsy drug, he should be able to replicate the Beta Subject's brain chemistry. Then he would have the best of both worlds—a test subject as well as a control. It was too bad they weren't triplets.

Suddenly the fluorescent lights flickered and went out.

Forsythe's heart rate immediately doubled, and he began to breathe heavily. It was remarkably quiet. He hadn't noticed the sound of the ventilation until it was no longer working. Now there was nothing except the pitch-black room and the gasping sound of his own labored breathing. He flailed out his arms, running trembling fingers over the desk. There was a loud crash as he knocked something to the floor.

Finally his fingers closed around the handset of his phone. He held it up to his ear. Mercifully, there was a dial tone. He dialed Grimes's four-digit extension. It rang eight times before he picked up.

"Yo."

"What the hell happened?" Forsythe knew he sounded frantic and scared, but he didn't care. "Where are the lights? Where are the *fucking lights??*"

"Jeez, relax, Dr. Jimmy," Grimes said. "What are you, afraid of the dark or sumpin'?"

Forsythe wanted to respond, but he couldn't. He could barely breathe. All he could think about was the closet. The enveloping darkness brought it back—his mother locking him in the closet as a child. Sometimes it was just for a few minutes, but when he'd been particularly bad, she would leave him inside for hours. He could still remember the smell of mothballs and the feeling of his father's suits rubbing against his head. And the heat. After ten minutes the closet would feel like an oven; the sweat would soak through his clothes, plastering them to his back.

But the worst was the dark. The unrelenting oppressive blackness. After a while he couldn't tell if his eyes were open or closed. He would begin to see things. And then he would scream. He knew that the screaming didn't help—his mother would never let him out when he was screaming—but he couldn't keep it in. . . .

Suddenly Forsythe heard a *whoosh* of air, and the fluorescent lights flickered back to life. Immediately his heart slowed in his chest, and he was able to take a long, ragged breath.

"See?" Grimes said. "All better."

"What the fuck happened?" Forsythe asked. He was starting to feel normal again, but he still wasn't quite himself.

"Language," Grimes said with a laugh. "Oh, Christ, I crack myself up. Anyway, nothin' to worry about. I was just checking out how the IT guys wired the mainframe into the electrical system, and I crossed a couple wires."

"Don't let it happen again," Forsythe said.

"Aye, aye, Capt—"

Forsythe slammed down the phone before Grimes had a chance to finish his idiocy. He looked at his watch—it was eleven o'clock. The Beta Subject had been missing for five hours. Without any leads Forsythe was now entirely dependent on the spyware program Grimes had released into the NSA's computer system.

It sorted through six thousand phone calls every second,

searching for the Beta Subject's voiceprint. Wherever he was, he couldn't stay off the phone forever. And when he made a call, Crowe and his team would be there. Although David Caine was smart, up until now he'd also been lucky. But eventually his luck would run out.

That was just the way probability worked.

When Caine walked into the *podvaal,* a large hand clamped down on his shoulder. He didn't have to look to know it was Sergey Kozlov.

"Where have you been, Caine? Vitaly has been worried."

"Just went on a little trip, Sergey," Caine said as he turned to face the giant Russian. "Now I'm back to pay my next installment."

Kozlov looked disappointed that there would be no need for violence today. He grumbled something in Russian under his breath and then led Caine into Nikolaev's office.

"Caine," Nikolaev said, standing up in surprise. "Sergey thought you left town, but I knew that you would never do such a thing, eh?"

"Of course not, Vitaly," Caine said as he reached into the knapsack. He extracted two packets of twenties and placed them on the desk. "For you."

Nikolaev used his letter opener to slice off the bands that held each bundle together. He fanned out the money and selected a bill from each packet. He marked each with a pen and held them up to the light. When he was satisfied that neither was counterfeit, he placed the money in his top drawer.

"This installment plan is working out even better than I expected," Nikolaev said. "I will see you at the same time next week?"

"Actually," Caine said, "I think I'll pay off the rest of my balance tonight."

Nikolaev raised his eyebrows. "Oh? You have all my money in that bag of yours?"

"Not exactly," Caine said. He pulled out his last stack of twenties. "I have a grand."

Nikolaev frowned. "You owe me another ten."

"I know. I'm going to win the rest."

Kozlov snorted, and Nikolaev's face crinkled into a smile. He said something in Russian, and Kozlov laughed again.

"Caine," Nikolaev said, still grinning, "maybe if you have an extra grand, you should give it to me instead of gambling it away. You haven't been on such a good streak lately."

"I appreciate you looking out for my well-being, but I'm going to play anyway," Caine said. "That is, if it's okay with you."

Nikolaev spread his arms wide. "Of course," he said, snatching up Caine's last stack. "I will change the money myself."

Kozlov led Caine out into the club and walked him over to his regular table in the far corner of the room. Walter was raking the pot and laughing under his breath. Sister Straight caught Caine's eye and nodded slightly. Stone merely blinked. Two other men Caine didn't recognize quickly sized him up and then returned to their drinks. Walter was the last to look up.

"Ho," he chortled, "this *is* my lucky night. Welcome back, Caine. Got any more money you want to give me?"

"Not tonight, Walter," Caine said, sitting down. He hoped that he sounded more confident than he felt. Caine put his chips on the table. He tried to remain calm as his stomach churned acid. He could do this. If he focused, he could do this. *But what if I get lost in the* everywhen *like I did before? What if I have a seizure? What if—*

Caine abruptly cut off the nervous voice in his head with his own. "Change for two hundred," he said, sliding two black chips over to the dealer.

"Changing two hundred," the dealer said as he scooped up Caine's blacks and pushed back a stack of reds and greens. Caine closed his eyes briefly and then, once he saw what he needed to see, opened them. He was ready. He pushed two reds into the betting circle in front of his seat.

"Deal."

"Straight to the jack," Caine said, reaching forward to take the pot.

"Shit!" Walter exclaimed, throwing his cards down on the table. "That's the third one you stole from me on the river."

Caine didn't respond. He was already using every ounce of concentration he had to access *everywhen.* He closed his eyes to count his chips. He had won $6,530 in the last seven hours. He was a machine. It was a nice take, but not enough to get him what he needed to save Jasper. It was time to raise the stakes.

A familiar feeling washed over him at the thought. He had been here before—high on a winning streak, confident that nothing could bring him down. Then he would find himself betting heavy on the hopes of getting a river flush and end up walking away with nothing.

But not this time. This time was different. He almost laughed at the thought, remembering all the other "this times" he'd said those very same words to himself. But *this* this time really was different. *This* this time he knew he could do it. He just had to focus—that, and keep from vomiting—and he would be fine.

"Let's say we make it interesting," Caine said, pushing his large stack forward. "I've got seventy-five hundred and some change. How about a little one-on-one action? Five-card draw, you shuffle, I cut, winner take all. What do you say, Walter?"

Walter raised his eyebrows. Caine could almost feel him debating whether or not to accept the challenge. Caine knew that Walter had won several thousand dollars the last week, so he had the cash. But even if he didn't, Walter was a compulsive gambler. There was no way he would be able to walk from the challenge. Still, Caine decided to give his nemesis a little nudge.

"If you don't want to do it, just say so—*old man.*"

Walter scowled. Caine knew that it was incredibly juvenile to mock Walter's age, but he also knew that it would work. After a second, Walter counted out a large pile of chips and then called Nikolaev over. There was a quick conversation, and then Nikolaev nodded. The dealer gave Walter three purples to add to his stack.

He pushed them forward. "Let's go."

Walter held out his hands, and the dealer gave him a new deck of cards. Walter began to shuffle. Behind closed lids Caine watched transfixed as the cards melded into one another.

. . .

The four of diamonds is on top of the jack of hearts. Shuffle. The four is between two queens. Shuffle. It is beneath the ace of clubs. Shuffle. On top of the four of spades. Shuffle.

. . .

"Wake up and cut," Walter said, slamming the cards down in front of Caine. Caine didn't open his eyes. Instead he reached forward and closed his hand on top of the deck, his consciousness still in the *everywhen.*

. . .

His fingers caress the edges of the cards as he tries to find the right spot to cut. If he does it here, he has a pair of fives, but Walter has trip eights. Here he has king-high, but Walter has a pair of deuces. Here he has—

. . .

"Stop fuckin' around and *cut,*" Walter said, pounding his fist on the table.

Startled him out of the *everywhen,* Caine involuntarily opened his eyes as his fingers jerked closed around the stack of cards. For a second he just held the cards in the air, as a terrible sinking feeling filled his stomach.

"Well, put 'em down already."

Caine lowered the cards, afraid to close his eyes. Afraid to see. As Walter began to deal, he smiled, sensing Caine's nervousness.

"Whatsa matta? All of a sudden you afraid?"

"Shut up, Walter." It was Sister Straight.

Caine was relieved she was there, but he buried the emotion. He tried to look relaxed, despite the sweat beading his brow. What the hell was he doing? Jasper was tied down to a table, and here *he* was, *gambling* to get enough money to rescue him? Caine thought it was crazy when he first saw it in the *everywhen,* but he had put his doubts aside and decided to believe. And now look at him—he was right back where he always was, risking his future on the luck of the cards.

Some demon he turned out to be.

"Well?" Walter motioned to the five cards that were facedown in front of Caine. Slowly Caine picked them up and fanned them out, one by one. Each card he saw lowered his hopes further.

Five of spades.

Seven of clubs.

Jack of spades.

Deuce of hearts.

Nine of diamonds.

Total crap.

He closed his eyes, trying to replicate what had happened when he shot Leary in the alley, to do over the cut and make things right. But when he closed his eyes, he saw—

. . .

Caine has a five, seven, jack, deuce, nine. Walter has a pair of cowboys.

Caine has a five, seven, jack, deuce, nine. Walter has a pair of cowboys.

Caine has a five, seven, jack, deuce, nine. Walter has a pair of cowboys.

. . .

It was no use. The cut, the deal—they'd already happened. He couldn't go back and change the past. He could only use the *everywhen* to inform his decision of what could be so he could choose the right future.

"How many cards you want?" Walter asked Caine. Normally the choice would have been obvious. Throw the deuce, the five, and the seven. Hold the jack and the nine. With six outs (three jacks and three nines) out of forty-seven cards, the probability that he'd pair up one of the cards he was holding was 13 percent.

But there was only about a 0.5 percent chance that he'd be able to turn either the jack or the nine into trips—which he would need to beat Walter's pair of kings—assuming, of course, that Walter didn't improve his hand. Caine closed his eyes, trying to see what the next three cards in the deck were.

. . .

Six of hearts.

Eight of hearts.

Ace of clubs.

No help.

. . .

His mind screamed in protest as the acid in his stomach sloshed back and forth. It was over. He had lost. After seven hours of masterful play, he had somehow managed to blow it. He closed his eyes to find a way, but there was nothing . . . nothing except—

. . .

The way to win.

. . .

Without hesitating, Caine reached his hand beneath the table and pinched Sister Straight's bottom.

"Oh!" she exclaimed, suddenly throwing her arms in the air. She knocked her elbow into Stone's hand, causing him to tip over his beer, which raced across the table to land in Walter's lap. The second the cold liquid touched his crotch, Walter jumped up, hit his knee on the table, and dropped the deck onto the floor.

"Shit!" Walter yelled. "Shit, shit, shit! What the hell is the matter with you, Sister?"

Sister opened her mouth to respond, but after stealing a look at Caine, she stopped. "There was a rat," she said. "It scurried across my foot." She wagged her finger at Nikolaev. "Shame on you, Vitaly."

He shrugged his shoulders. "It's the Village. The rats love it here. What can I do?"

Walter bent to the floor and began collecting the cards.

Caine put his hand facedown. "That's a misdeal."

"What the hell do you mean?" Walter asked.

"You dropped the deck," Caine said. "You saw some of the cards. That's a misdeal."

"No fuckin' way. It wouldn't have affected my decision. I've got a pair of kings, see?" Walter held up his hand. "I was gonna take three cards. I'm *still* gonna take three cards. You can cut again, but there's no fuckin' misdeal."

Caine looked up at Nikolaev. "Vitaly, I think we need a ruling here."

"Misdeal," the Russian said.

"*What?* I—"

Nikolaev held up his hand. "My club, my rules. You don't like, go somewhere else."

Caine, trying not to smile, pushed his down cards toward the center of the table. The dealer put them aside and handed Walter a new deck. Still grumbling under his breath, Walter began to shuffle. When he was through, he slammed the cards down. This time Caine was ready and knew exactly what he was looking for.

. . .

His fingers touch the cards.
Halfway down.
Three more.
He touches them.
He is sure.

. . .

Caine cut the deck neatly in half, and Walter began to deal. When Caine looked at his cards, he wasn't worried. He knew what they were—and that they would be winners. He threw the jack and the queen and kept the pair of black fours along with the eight of hearts.

Walter drew only one card. The old man tried to hide his glee when he saw what it was, but it didn't matter—Caine already knew. He had planned it that way.

"Ready to show, Walter?"

"How about we double the bet?" Walter asked, eyes gleaming.

Caine turned to look at Nikolaev, but the mobster just shook his head. "I would love to, Walter, but my credit is no good here."

"Pussy," Walter muttered under his breath.

"Hang on," Sister Straight said. "I'll back Caine," she said to Walter. She turned to look at Nikolaev. He shrugged and nodded. Then, to Caine, she said, "For half the winnings from my stake, of course."

Caine smiled. She was a player, all right. "Of course," Caine said. They waited for Nikolaev to deliver the appropriate amount of chips to the players. Then it was time.

Walter turned his cards over triumphantly. "Flush, jack-high," he said gleefully.

"Full house," Caine said, flipping over his hand. "Fours over eights." He leaned over and gave Sister a peck on the cheek. "Thank you, Sister."

She blushed like a schoolgirl. "My pleasure," she said, and squeezed his thigh beneath the table.

Caine now had almost $19,000.

Just enough.

When Nava awoke, she immediately ripped the oxygen mask off her face and struggled to sit up, trying to get her bearings. The room was spartan—white walls, gray linoleum floor, cheap furniture. It wasn't a hospital, that was for sure. It looked more like a lab; four computers lined the wall beneath an equation-filled chalkboard. Next to her gurney was a metallic cart with three shelves loaded down with syringes, scalpels, bandages, and drugs.

As she looked around the room, she heard the doorknob turn. Reflexively she went for her gun and then realized she was unarmed. Even the extra knife she kept strapped to her calf was gone. She'd have to improvise. She grabbed a scalpel off the cart and held it at her side, beneath the thin cotton sheet that covered her. The blade felt hard and cold against her skin.

Readying herself, she stared at the thin man who entered. When he saw she was awake, he nervously adjusted his bow tie.

"Hello, Ms. Vaner," he said with an awkward smile. "How are you feeling?"

"Who are you?" Nava asked, staring at the man in the bow tie. "And how do you know my name?"

"My name is Peter. I'm an acquaintance of David's. He asked me to bring you here."

"Where is 'here'?"

"My research lab."

Nava felt like rubbing her eyes. None of this made sense. "When did he contact you?"

"He called here around five-fifteen."

Nava thought back, remembering when Caine had excused himself before they left the bar. Of course—he'd gone to use the phone. But just because the time frame worked didn't mean the man was telling the truth.

"What did he say? *Exactly.*"

The man stared at the ceiling for a moment and then cleared his throat. "He said that . . . he said that my partner murdered one of his grad students."

"Julia Pearlman."

The man blinked several times. "Yes. I didn't believe him at first, but with my partner's disappearance and Julia's death, I couldn't help but wonder. In any case, David said that he knew I did tests for my partner—like the ones I did on David—and that if I didn't do what David asked, he would implicate me in this whole mess."

Nava's head was spinning. Something wasn't right. She tightened her grip on the scalpel. "*You* did the tests on David?"

The man nodded.

"*You're* Paul Tversky?"

"Oh, no," he said, shaking his head. "Paul is . . . uh, *was* . . . my partner. My name is Peter Hanneman."

Nava was suddenly confused. "Do you have a picture of your partner?"

"As a matter of fact, I do," Dr. Hanneman said, gesturing to a framed photograph on his wall. In it he had his arm around a bushy-haired man in a white lab coat. Nava knew the other man, although not as Tversky, but by his nickname—Doc.

The realization hit her like a brick wall. Tversky and Doc were one and the same. All this time he'd been right under her nose. She didn't understand. They had discussed the tests, and . . . Then suddenly it occurred to her. She'd assumed that Tversky had conducted the tests himself. So when she told David that the doctor who ran the tests was secretly plotting against him, he must have thought she meant Peter Hanneman instead of Paul Tversky.

"But Julia also referenced 'Petey,' " Nava said, more to herself than to Peter Hanneman.

"Yes, some of Dr. Tversky's students call him that," Hanneman said. "It's a nickname of sorts, from his initials. Paul Tversky. P. T. Petey."

Nava shook her head as the final piece slid into place. "Go on."

"Paul said he wanted to help David with his money problem, but he didn't want to embarrass him. That's why he asked me to offer David two thousand dollars to run some tests. I . . . I thought they were all just for show. I didn't know Paul was actually using the data for anything."

"Wait," Nava said, her mind still reeling. "What else did David say when he called you?"

"He told me the address of the apartment in Brooklyn and the time I had to be there. He said when I arrived, you would be in need of medical attention, so I brought all the supplies I had from the lab. When I got there, you were coming out of the burning building. You were suffocating. Although I'm not a medical doctor, I do know human anatomy and basic first aid, so I was able to revive you. Once I got you back to the lab, I tended to your wounds." Hanneman pointed toward Nava's bandaged hands.

"Do you know where your partner is now?"

Peter Hanneman shook his head.

"Shit." Nava swung her legs around and put her feet on the floor.

"Wait, you can't leave."

"Watch me," Nava said.

"No," Hanneman said, standing in front of her and holding out his hands as if he were trying to stop a freight train. "David wanted you to stay here and rest. He said that when he needed you, you would be contacted."

"You mean he's going to call me?"

"I . . . I'm not sure. I got the impression he was going to have someone else contact you." Hanneman lowered his arms. "Please. I'm telling the truth."

One look at his frightened face confirmed his story. She sat back down and folded her arms across her chest. She couldn't just wait here. She had to do something. Then she realized what she was missing. Her knapsack was gone. Just as she was about to stand again, Hanneman stopped her.

"Oh, David also said don't worry about . . . um, 'weapons.' He said everything will be taken care of when it's time."

Nava felt a chill run down her spine. It was as if Caine had read her mind.

He really was Laplace's Demon after all.

"How is he?" Paul Tversky asked, nervously watching Jasper's chest rise and fall.

"He's resting." Forsythe took one last look at the subject's EEG readings before turning around. "More important, how are you?"

"Better, now that I'm here," Tversky said. "Your men were quite impressive."

"Not impressive enough, I'm afraid."

Tversky nodded. "Any word on David?" he asked hesitantly.

"No," Forsythe said, slightly irritated. "But it's only a matter of time. You don't have any idea where he might be?"

"None at all," Tversky said. "But if I know David, he'll pop up soon. As long as we have his brother, David won't disappear."

"Good to know," Forsythe said, redirecting his attention to the MRI of Jasper's brain before turning back to Tversky. "If you don't mind my asking, what made you realize that the temporal lobe was the key?"

"Well," Tversky started, obviously excited to move the conversation to the theoretical, "I was reading a journal article that proposed that the mesial right temporal lobe, hippocampus, and associate limbic-lobe structures were somehow related to out-of-body experiences. A Swiss doctor studied patients with temporal-lobe pathology. Then he compared their experiences to normal patients who received direct electrical stimulation to their temporal lobe and to patients who had their neurotransmitters excited by various chemicals, like LSD and ketamine.

"Many of the 'stimulated' patients reported visual and auditory hallucinations, while others described seeing old memories, and some had visions similar to those who have near-death experiences. Others experienced déjà vu or jamais vu. I realized then that all those symptoms were consistent with an epileptic aura before a seizure, which of course reminded me of Hans Berger's experiments in the thirties. After that, it was just a matter of connecting the dots."

Forsythe nodded. "What do you think is happening on a physiological level?"

Tversky rubbed his chin. "I'm still not sure. But if I had to make a guess, I would say that the temporal lobe may allow the brain to access nonlocal realities."

"Nonlocal realities?" Forsythe asked. He'd heard the term before but only vaguely understood its meaning.

Tversky explained, "As I'm sure you know, of the twelve quarks and twelve leptons that make up all matter, only a handful exist in our universe. The rest don't exist at all or disappear after a nanosecond. But many modern physicists believe that they do exist in other universes—parallel universes, or nonlocal realities, that coexist alongside our own with different physical properties. However, instead of being composed of quarks and leptons like our universe, these parallel universes are made up of other lepton pairs."

"Fascinating," Forsythe said, although in truth he had only a tenuous grasp of what Tversky had just said. He'd always found quantum mechanics too abstract to warrant much attention. He understood that physicists had discovered subatomic building blocks that didn't exist in the known universe—he just didn't think it was very important. After all, what was the value of studying hypothetical constructs that could never be observed in reality?

"Essentially," Tversky continued, "I believe that the right temporal lobe allows for interactions between our conscious mind and nonlocal realities. I think the hallucinations and the precognitive events that David Caine experienced result from his right temporal lobe's accessing information from a timeless, spaceless nonlocal reality."

"Which is possible because, according to quantum mechanics, time and space are not constants; hence they exist outside of time itself," Forsythe said, trying to demonstrate his limited understanding of Einstein's Theory of Special Relativity.

Tversky nodded emphatically.

"And the auras and seizures?" Forsythe asked.

"The auras are conscious manifestations that occur when the brain connects to the nonlocal realities. However, that connection dramatically increases the neural activity in the brain, which in turn triggers a seizure."

"Like sticking your finger into a light socket?"

Tversky frowned at Forsythe's childish example but said, "Something like that, yes."

Slightly embarrassed, Forsythe asked another question to

get Tversky talking again. "Have you seen any other research that supports your theories?"

"A few, but they're limited. There was a controversial study a few years back in which some practitioners of Chinese Qi Gong were able to affect the nuclear magnetic resonance spectrum of certain chemicals using only their mind."

Forsythe nodded. He'd heard of Qi Gong but had always thought the people who practiced it were a cult. However, he was aware that their meditation techniques were studied throughout the world.

"In another study a German scientist showed that yoga masters could significantly alter their brain waves through intense meditation. And of course it's a well-known fact that professional psychics often have atypical readings on temporal-lobe EEGs."

"So tell me about the twin," Forsythe said. "Did he exhibit similar abilities as the Beta Subject?"

Tversky watched Jasper on the monitor for a moment before answering. "Yes and no. There were a couple instances when he seemed to know things that were impossible—such as calling me on my cell phone when I first picked up David—"

"Speaking of that," Forsythe said, turning to face him. "How was it that you happened to be driving along the train tracks in Philadelphia at the *precise moment* that the Beta Subject needed an escape?"

Tversky glared at him. "You're framing the problem incorrectly, James. My being there was random. The question you should be asking is how David *knew* that I was going to be there. *He* orchestrated the meeting, not I, although for what purpose, I do not know."

Forsythe nodded. He didn't entirely believe Tversky, as the situation still seemed a little too coincidental, but he could think of no other explanation. "So back to the twin . . ."

"Well," Tversky said, "he definitely has some abilities, although his talent is not as strong as his brother's. I suggest that when he awakes, you let me talk to him. I have an idea of how we can get him to cooperate. Also, I would like to test out a theory before you bring David here."

"What theory is that?"

"I think I know how to prevent David from using his gift," Tversky said. "Now that the proverbial door has been opened, allowing him to link his conscious mind to nonlocal realities, I expect he will be able to access them much more easily."

"Why is that a problem?" Forsythe asked. "Isn't that what we want?"

"Yes, although not if he uses his gift of foresight to escape."

Forsythe nodded. "Of course."

"But if I'm right," Tversky continued, "I think I might know a way to fix that. To turn David Caine . . . *off.*"

"Jasper . . . Jasper, can you hear me? Wake up."

Cotton. His brain was filled with cotton. Jasper struggled to lift his lids, but they were too heavy. Someone was shaking his shoulder. Again he tried to open his eyes; his lids were lighter now. The room slowly swam into focus. It was so white, almost blinding. The air was cold. He coughed. His mouth was bone dry, his tongue a thick piece of sandpaper. There was a bandage around his arm . . . a needle underneath.

"Jasper? It's me, Doc."

Jasper turned to face the voice and saw Doc leaning over him. He was smiling. Jasper started to smile back, but then he stopped. Something was wrong, though he couldn't quite remember what it was. It danced on the edge of his mind just out of reach. He wished his brother were—

"Where's . . . ?" He coughed, his voice weak.

"Drink this," Doc said, and put a thin straw to Jasper's lips. He took three small sips and swallowed. He could feel the water trickle down his throat like an icy stream. "Better?" Doc asked.

Jasper nodded and managed, "Where's David? Did he get away?"

Doc shook his head, his face full of sorrow. "They got all of us, Jasper."

Jasper closed his eyes. He didn't understand. The Voice had told him that David was going to get away. He'd done everything right . . . but it still had turned out wrong. He was supposed to protect David, protect his gift. But all he did was lead him into a trap. Now the conspirators had them. A part of him always knew this would happen. It always knew. But—

"Why . . . why are you free-*be-me-see?"* Jasper asked, voicing his confusion.

"They wanted to operate on your brother . . . to cut him open," Doc said.

"No," Jasper said. "They can't . . . Let me talk to them. . . . I need to protect him. . . ." Jasper tried to sit up, but the restraints held him in place.

"Shhhh . . . shhhh, it's okay. I convinced them to let David rest for now."

"You did?"

"Yes."

"That's good," Jasper said, leaning back on the table.

"But I had to promise that you would help them," Doc said.

"Help them do what?"

"They want to see what you see, Jasper. They want to understand."

"But . . . how-*bow-cow-now?"* Jasper asked. He was confused. And he was tired. So tired.

"With this," Doc said, holding up a shiny silver coin. "If I flip it, can you tell me if it's going to be heads or tails?"

Jasper shook his head. "I can't see the future except when the Voice shows me. But David can. . . . He can see. . . ."

Doc frowned. "Then how did you know to call my cell in the car?"

"Sometimes"—Jasper furrowed his brow, trying to remember—"I can know the *Now.*"

Doc nodded slightly. "So if I flip the coin you can tell me what it is without looking?"

"I think so . . . but I'm so tired, Doc."

"I know Jasper. But you have to do this . . . for David."

"Okay," Jasper said, aware of the slight slur in his speech. "Okay-*day-lay-may.*"

Doc looked over his shoulder at himself in the mirror and raised his eyebrows before turning back to Jasper. "Are you ready?" he asked.

"Ready."

Jasper closed his eyes. He heard the soft *flick* of a fingernail against a coin and then the quiet *ftttt* as Doc caught the coin in the air and the light *smack* as he covered his palm with his hand.

"What is it?"

"Tails," Jasper said, eyes still closed.

"Tails it is. Good job, Jasper. Let's go again."

Flick. Ftttt. Smack.

"Tails-*mails-nails-sails.*"

"Good . . . only a 25 percent chance on two correct guesses in a row," Doc said. "Again."

Flick. Ftttt. Smack.

"Heads."

"Good . . . 12.5 percent chance on three."

Flick. Ftttt. Smack.

"Tails."

"Excellent . . . 6.25 percent chance."

Flick. Ftttt. Smack.

"Heads-*beds-reds-weds.*"

"Great . . . 3.125 percent chance. Now, Jasper, I want you to do it once more, but this time with your eyes open."

Jasper was confused. "But then I won't be able to see the *Now.*"

"Just try. Come on, Jasper. For David."

Jasper opened his eyes. The white room was blinding.

Flick. Ftttt. Smack.

Jasper tried to see what it was, but it was impossible. "Heads," he guessed.

"Oh, well," Doc said, pulling back his hand to reveal the tails side of the coin. "I think that's enough. You can go back to sleep now."

"Okay-*day-lay-may*," Jasper said. He so desperately wanted to fall back asleep, but he needed to ask Doc one more question. "When . . . when can I see David?"

"Soon, Jasper," Doc said. "He'll be here very soon."

Caine slept until three in the afternoon. When he finally awoke in the dark motel room, he took a shower and headed back to his apartment. Despite his throbbing knee, he savored his walk through the cool winter air, knowing that it might be his last. Once he arrived home, he shut the door. He didn't bother to lock it. There was no point.

When they came, his dead bolt wouldn't stand in their way. The clock on the wall read 4:28:14. He had until 4:43:27 before they got there. Maybe a couple seconds more. He could know for sure if he wanted to, but it wasn't necessary. He had only two more things to set up, and then he would let the universe take its course.

His odds were decent—about 43.9 percent—that he would live through the next twenty-four hours, although there was only a 13.1 percent chance that he would live on his own terms, rather than as Doc's guinea pig. He tried not to think too much about the betrayal. If he got through this alive, he would have all the time in the world—more, in fact.

And if he didn't, well . . . it wouldn't matter anyway.

"Jesus fucking Christ!" Grimes spun around and pressed the button that connected him to Crowe. "I found him!"

"Where?"

"You'll never believe this," Grimes said as he stared at the monitor. "He's in his apartment!"

"Assemble the rest of the team. Have them suit up and meet me on the helipad in three minutes."

"Copy."

After Grimes finished with Dalton, he buzzed Dr. Jimmy. "I've located the target."

"Call Crowe."

"Already did it," Grimes said. "His team is flying out in the next minute."

"You gave him the subject's position?" Forsythe asked.

"No," Grimes said, rolling his eyes. "I told him to guess."

"Patch me through to Crowe's com unit."

Grimes flipped two switches, and Forsythe was gone. "You're welcome," Grimes said into his now dead mike. Christ. Not one "Nice job" or a simple "How did you do it?" Just "Patch me through." Like Grimes was some fucking telephone operator, for Christ's sake. Jimmy had no idea how fucking talented Grimes was. He just took it all for granted. As if it were the easiest thing in the world to hack into the NSA mainframe and steal the signal feeds of the AV equipment they had hidden in the target's apartment.

Well, fuck you, Jimmy.

Fuck you.

Having nothing else to do, Grimes settled in to watch the action live on his own "private" episode of *Candid Camera.* According to the helicopter's GPS, Crowe and his boys should be paratrooping down onto the target's roof in about ten minutes. As long as Caine stayed put, there was no way he would get away this time. And even if he tried, it was a cloudless day, which meant that the KH-12 would have no problems tracking him. Grimes had already made sure the Keyhole satellite was in position just in case.

Unfortunately, he didn't think Caine would run. Too bad. He liked it when they ran. Still, watching Crowe bust through that door should be fun. Man, he didn't envy David Caine. He didn't envy him one bit.

Caine hobbled into the kitchen for something to write on. All he found was the blank side of an envelope. It would have to do. In large block letters, he wrote the note, then scrawled his signature at the bottom. The message was only twenty-one words long, but it could very well change everything. The probability that it would be read by the appropriate person was high—87.3246 percent—but it wasn't a sure thing.

As Caine now knew, nothing ever was.

He still had nine minutes and seventeen seconds. He circled around the apartment until he found what he was looking for. He positioned his chair just right, facing his spider plant, and then began to talk. When he finished, he started over from the beginning, just in case. After the third time, he stopped. There was still an 8.7355 percent chance that his monologue had been missed, but repeating it again was too risky.

He put the envelope on his lap with the written-on side facedown and closed his eyes. He had done everything he could do. Whether or not it worked was no longer in his hands. It felt strange, giving up control like this. Despite having lived the first thirty years of his life completely subject to the Fates, now he found the whole proposition terrifying.

Part of him screamed out to run. He still had four minutes. Plenty of time to escape the apartment and disappear. He knew he could do it. If he did, there was a 93.4721 percent chance he would be able to flee the country—and Forsythe—forever. But to do so he would have to leave Jasper behind, and that was something he could not do. And so he sat, glued to the chair, his hands trembling, his knee throbbing, his heart racing, and his mind waiting.

Waiting to see whether his grand scheme would work.

Or whether he would die.

The second the phone rang, Nava was instantly awake. Dr. Hanneman hurried across the room to answer it.

"Hello? . . . Yes, hold on." He held the receiver out to Nava, and she snatched the phone from his hand.

"Nava Vaner?" asked a man with a thick Russian accent.

"Who is this?" she asked, the hairs on her neck standing straight up. Suddenly she remembered Chang-Sun's threat to tell the SVR her identity. But even if he had informed the Russian government, there was no way they could possibly know where she was—could they?

"My name is Vitaly Nikolaev. I am friend of Mr. Caine. He asked me to contact you."

"Where is he?"

"I do not know, but he said you and I should meet."

"How do I know you are who you say you are?"

There was a gravelly laugh on the other end of the phone. "Mr. Caine told me that you were a suspicious one—*Tanja.*"

Nava's heart stopped. Caine did know her Russian name, but then again, so did the RDEI.

"He also said," Nikolaev continued, " *'Trust has to start sometime.'* " Nava exhaled. Those were the words she'd said to him on the train. The message was real.

"When and where?" Nava asked.

"Sergey is coming for you now."

"He is your driver?"

"Yes," Nikolaev laughed, "he is driver. Be ready in thirty minutes." There was a click, and the line went dead. Nava hung up the phone.

"Is everything all right?" Hanneman asked, nervously wringing his hands.

"I don't know," she said. "But I'm about to find out."

"Are they there yet?"

"No," Grimes said, quickly skipping the video forward to the live feed.

"What was that?" Forsythe asked.

"What was what?"

"The video jumped. First Caine was sitting in front of the plant, and now he's halfway across the room."

"Weather patterns," Grimes lied. "Sometimes electrical interference in storm clouds causes a break in the signal. Nothing to worry about."

Forsythe nodded. "Where is Crowe?"

Grimes pointed to a flashing green dot on another screen. "He's flying over Central Park. They should be there in a couple minutes."

"Good," Forsythe said. He folded his arms across his chest and leaned in close to the screen that showed the video feed from Caine's apartment. "What's he doing?"

Grimes looked at the grainy black-and-white image. David Caine was sitting in a chair in the middle of the room, facing the door. His eyes were closed, but it was clear from the position of his body that he wasn't asleep.

"It looks like . . ." Grimes's voice trailed off. It didn't make any sense, but after what he'd just heard on his headset, nothing made sense, did it? "It looks like he's waiting."

The helicopter races high above the trees and cuts west. The five men are quiet, surrounded by the deafening sound of the rotating blades. Each is mentally preparing for battle. Juan Esposito and Charlie Rainer are looking for action. Ron McCoy is spooked; he just wants to get through this in one piece. Jim Dalton craves bloodshed. And Martin Crowe . . . he prays for his daughter.

He is different from the rest of these men. Although that difference makes him a better man, it also makes him more dangerous than the other four combined. He stops at nothing to complete the mission, although, unlike the others, his mission has nothing to do with David Caine. Caine is just a means to an end. His daughter is his only true mission.

Martin Crowe knows that the odds are extremely low he's able to save her. But he does not give up. Caine respects him. Anyone unwilling to back down in the face of impossible odds is someone to be admired—and feared. They aren't that different, he and Crowe. Each is willing to risk his life for another. It's too bad that their respective missions put them on opposite sides. Caine knows that in another world they are friends.

. . .

Caine could hear the chopper now with his ears, as opposed to his mind. It was faint but unmistakable, like the beating of an enormous set of wings. Slowly the sound grew louder, until it filled the apartment. The dishes rattled in the kitchen, and a tiny porcelain knickknack fell off his mantel and crashed to the floor, shattering into 124 pieces.

It wouldn't be long now.

"G*O! GO! GO!*"

The black-clad men slid down the ropes and landed hard on the roof. Crowe shot a quick look back at Dalton and McCoy; both were still strapped in. He knew that Dalton was pissed to be on the backup team, but Crowe didn't care. In case the target ran, he needed a couple men in the air who could follow him. However, this time it didn't look like the target was going to run; according to Grimes, he was waiting for them.

That made Crowe all the more nervous, which was why he decided to leave Dalton in the chopper. If the target did intend to make some final stand, Crowe wanted to contain the situation without having to worry about Dalton. He had always known that Dalton was dangerous, but after the man intentionally put a bullet in Vaner's brain, Crowe was forced to recharacterize him as psychopathic. He didn't want another repeat performance.

Crowe detached the rope from his belt and gave the chopper pilot the thumbs-up. The helicopter rose high into the air, trailing the rappel lines behind. Crowe saw that Esposito had already smashed open the door to the stairwell. Crowe jogged over to meet him.

Crowe nodded his approval to the man, then spoke into his mike. "Grimes, is the target still on-site?"

"Yup. He hasn't moved an inch in the last five minutes."

"Okay, give me an update if he changes position or goes for some type of weapon. Else maintain radio silence."

"Gotcha."

Crowe turned to his men. "Rainer, I want you to go down the fire escape. North side of the building, two stories down. Hold directly above the window. Enter on my signal."

"Got it."

"Go," Crowe said. Rainer trotted across the roof and

disappeared over the ledge. Crowe looked over at Esposito. "You're with me. Do not engage unless absolutely necessary."

"Understood."

Crowe stepped through the door and began racing down the stairs.

Caine opened his eyes.

He imagined that he heard them landing on the roof but knew that the sound was only in his mind. However, as they pounded down the emergency stairwell, he heard it the old-fashioned way. Five seconds later his front door crashed open. Crowe was the first one through, although there was another man at his back. Behind him Caine heard the shattering of glass as a third burst through his window.

Caine glanced at the clock with mild surprise. They were one second earlier than he'd expected. The tailwind must have picked up.

From behind, two strong hands slammed down on his shoulders, but Caine didn't flinch. Instead he just stared into Martin Crowe's eyes. He wanted the man to know that, whatever he'd been told, Caine was no monster. The last thing he saw was the barrel of Crowe's gun as the mercenary squeezed the trigger.

Before Caine slipped into unconsciousness, he did the only thing he could: He wished himself luck.

"Target secure," Crowe breathed into his mike with more than a little relief. "We'll be back on the roof in two. Request pickup."

"Roger," the pilot responded.

"That was easy," Esposito said from behind him, slapping Crowe on the shoulder. "You tranked him before I even got inside."

"Yeah," Crowe said quietly. There was something not right about this. After what had happened at the train station and the apartment in Brooklyn, it didn't make sense. The target had proved on both occasions that he was a man of considerable talents. But instead of putting up a fight, Caine had just sat there, waiting in the one place where he *knew* they would be watching.

"You want me to take him?" Esposito asked.

Crowe nodded, and the man picked up the target and threw him over his shoulder. As he did, a white envelope fell from Caine's lap and drifted to the floor. Crowe was about to leave when the first few words on the paper caught his attention.

His heart began to pound as he bent to pick it up. When he finished reading the note, he felt cold all over.

"What's that?" Rainer asked, glancing back.

"Nothing," Crowe said, crumpling the paper and dropping it to the floor. "Let's go." As they climbed the stairs to the waiting helicopter, Crowe wondered what the hell was going on—and what would happen next.

They rode in silence. When they finally arrived, the big Russian turned off the engine and climbed out of the van without a word. Nava followed him into a dark, smoky tavern. Although a few of the patrons were Americans, most were Russian. Even if they hadn't been speaking her native tongue, she would have known just by looking.

"This way," Kozlov said, gesturing toward a wooden door at the end of the bar. Once they were on the other side, it was quieter, although Nava could still hear the music through the thin walls. They went down a dank set of stairs into a private room. Kozlov navigated between several poker tables and led her into a small office.

A pale, skinny man stood to welcome her. He didn't even try to be subtle as he ran his eyes up and down her body. "Hello, Miss Vaner. I am Vitaly Nikolaev," he said with a wide smile. "Mr. Caine did not tell me you were so lovely."

"Is that why you wanted us to meet?" Nava asked.

"Okay, we will do business first, eh?" Nikolaev handed Nava an envelope. The words "Trust starts here" were scrawled across the seal. She ripped it open and took out the letter. She read it through twice before putting it down. She didn't know what she'd been expecting, but this certainly wasn't it. Caine's plan made sense, but she wasn't happy at what it entailed. Just then, exactly as Caine had predicted, the phone rang.

"That's for me," Nava said, picking up Nikolaev's phone. He raised his eyebrows, but he didn't try to stop her.

"Yeah, is this, like, Nava?"

"It is," Nava said.

"Um, I don't know if this is going to make any sense, but . . ."

"David Caine told you to call me."

"Yeah." The voice sounded relieved. "How did you know?"

"James, I think you better see this."

"What is it?"

"It's Jasper Caine," Tversky said. "A few minutes ago, he started screaming hysterically."

"I wasn't aware that was aberrant behavior for a diagnosed paranoid schizophrenic," Forsythe said without looking up.

"It isn't. However, his EEG *is.*"

That got Forsythe's attention. He pressed a few keys, and the twin's EEG appeared on his terminal. It was off the charts. Forsythe removed his reading glasses and looked up at Tversky. "What's he saying?"

"He keeps screaming the same thing over and over: *'She's coming for us.'* "

"That wasn't part of the job specification."

"I am paying you a great deal of money, Mr. Crowe. And I expect—"

"You hired me to acquire David Caine. I did that, in addition to capturing his brother. I have fulfilled my contract."

"You have fulfilled it when I say you have," Forsythe said coldly.

Crowe balled his fists. It was all he could do not to punch the man in the face. The only thing that held him back was the thought of Betsy.

"Dr. Forsythe," Crowe said, attempting to remain calm, "I do not want to argue with you. All I want is my money, and I will be on my way."

"How about this: I will double your acquisition fee if you oversee a guard detail," Forsythe said. "Just for the next week, until I am able to make other arrangements."

Crowe snapped his jaw shut. An extra $125,000. He couldn't say no. "Fine. But I won't do the interrogation."

Forsythe wrinkled his brow. "What about one of your men? Mr. Grimes has provided me with their dossiers." Forsythe pressed a few buttons on his computer, and his screen snapped to life. "It says here that Mr. Dalton has a great deal of experience in that field."

"If you care about the well-being of Mr. Caine, I would advise against using Dalton."

"But you wouldn't mind if I asked, would you?" There was nothing Crowe could say, and Forsythe knew it.

"No."

"Good, then please get him for me. In the meantime coordinate with Grimes on security." Forsythe dismissed him with a wave of his hand. As Crowe walked down the corridor, he wondered if Forsythe had any idea what he was dealing with.

After an hour Kozlov returned with the arsenal Nava had requested. As she stepped into the back of the van, she reviewed the plan in her mind. Thanks to Caine her intel was near perfect. Blueprints, personnel files, access codes, security profiles—she had it all.

There was only one problem: This was a job for at least four agents. But she was alone—and hurt, although Dr. Lukin, Nikolaev's "personal physician," had done his best to compensate for her injuries. She knew that the crash would be significant, but for now she felt she could take on the world, run a 10K, and still have enough energy to win an Olympic decathlon.

Not that she would have passed the drug test.

The water was driving Caine crazy. Another drop landed in the middle of his forehead. If they fell at regular intervals, he didn't think it would have bothered him as much, but their randomness was stripping away his sanity.

As were the earphones. The one in his left ear sounded like a radio station programmed to "seek." It played five seconds of a song, followed by a few seconds of static, followed by a snippet of another song, on and on. The bud in his right ear looped through "Chopsticks," which would have constituted its own form of torture by itself, but it was made worse by the volume's rising and falling, deafening one moment, almost silent the next.

And then there was the spinning. At first Caine thought it was just the disorientation of his surroundings, but when he pried his eyes open, he saw that his chair was indeed slowly rotating. After a little experimentation, Caine decided that his nausea and dizziness diminished slightly when he closed his eyes, so he left them shut.

Every few seconds he felt an electric shock to one of his appendages. Usually it was a finger or a nipple, but sometimes it was . . . lower. Most of the shocks were just that—shocking—although a few were quite painful. Caine's heart raced. His muscles refused to unclench, waiting for the next jolt.

He tried to get to the *everywhen* to see, but he couldn't. There was too much going on. He was helpless. He felt as if his sanity were being sucked out of his brain through a giant hose. Suddenly his chair came to a stop. His stomach, however, continued to lurch. Someone pried open his left eyelid and shone in a bright light. Then the right. Caine tried to reach up to grab the hand, but with his wrists in restraints, he was helpless. Then he felt a sharp prick as a needle slid into his skin, then a tearing sound. A sticky strip of tape was wrapped around his arm to hold the IV tube in place.

Seconds ticked by. Once again something sharp pulled back his eyelids. This time it did not let go. His eyes dried; he tried to blink, but that only made his eyelids shriek in pain. Blinking was now impossible.

A clear solution flooded his eyes. The drops continued every few seconds. Caine no longer needed to blink to keep his eyes moist, although after twenty-eight years of habit, he couldn't stop his natural reflex. He wondered how long it would take before he could retrain himself not to blink.

He felt tired, beaten, half crazed, and scared out of his wits. But beneath it all, he was determined. Then he got a shock to his scrotum, which eclipsed everything else. Between saline baths, he tried to focus his vision. A man stood before him, tall and menacing. Another shock, this one to his big toe. When the pain subsided, he tried to focus again.

The man seemed familiar; Caine tried to figure out why, but the water kept distracting him. And the music. Caine loved music, but, Jesus Christ, he'd never listen to a Walkman again if this continued. As if on command, it stopped. There was a moment of blessed silence, broken then by a cold, gravelly voice.

"Can you hear me?"

"Yes," Caine gasped.

"Do you know today's date?"

"It's, umm . . ." Caine tried to remember. His nausea intensified. "I think it's . . . *AAAAHH!*" Amazing, how painful a shock to your left pinkie could be. "It's . . . um, February . . . February . . ."

"Close enough," the voice said in a mocking tone. "All right. I'm going to stop the torture in a little while. But first listen closely, okay?"

"Okay," Caine said weakly. Anything. Caine would do anything for this man if he'd make it stop, if only for a minute. Or a second.

"We're overloading your system because we don't want

you to get away. However, this also makes it difficult to communicate. And talking to you is very important to us. But understand: If you do try to escape, your brother will suffer the consequences. You don't want that to happen, right?"

Caine thought he was going to vomit. He wanted to close his eyes and make it all go away, but he couldn't. His lids strained uselessly against the forceps, burning with pain.

"Mr. Caine." The man lightly slapped Caine's face. "I know it's hard, but stay with me. As long as you work with us, nothing bad will happen to Jasper. All right?"

Caine realized, belatedly, that it was his turn to talk. "Okay," he croaked.

"Good." The man turned away, walking out of Caine's field of vision. The chair stopped spinning, and the shocks ceased. Caine tried to relax, but his muscles wouldn't obey—every tendon was as taut as piano wire. His heart hammered in his ears, pumping blood to his muscles in anticipation of more pain.

Caine took a deep breath, held it for a second, and then exhaled through his nose. Gradually everything else fell into place. His heart slowed and he was able to unclench his jaw. He was okay. He wanted to turn his head, but it was held in place by thick metal restraints. The man must have seen Caine's head jerk slightly; he stepped back so that Caine could see him. This time Caine recognized him from the *everywhen.*

His name was Jim Dalton.

"You've had quite an interesting week, haven't you, Mr. Caine?"

Caine didn't respond.

"Do you know why you're here?" he asked.

"No," Caine answered flatly.

Suddenly Caine's body was consumed with a pain unlike anything he'd ever felt, tearing through every part in his body. The pain was alive, dancing and screaming. Caine screamed right along with it.

And then, as quickly as it had descended upon him, it was gone. Caine clamped his mouth shut, biting his tongue, tasting blood. He was so tired. All he wanted to do was close his eyes. Caine caught his breath after a minute, then slowly unclenched his teeth.

"Mr. Caine, as I'm sure you're aware, we have electrodes attached to your body. Some deliver quite painful shocks; some read your heart rate and other bioelectric signals. This tells us whether you're lying. If you lie again, we'll know. And the next shock won't be so mild.

"Most people think that if they needed to, they could withstand torture. They think, Yeah, I'm tough. I'm a man. I can take it. But in my experience, and let me assure you that I have a great deal of experience in this, most people are *wrong.*" Dalton's voice dripped with menace.

"Typically people hold out for one, maybe two minutes max, at which point they'd gladly kill their own mother to stop the pain. But by that time permanent damage has already been done, or the injury is severe enough to necessitate massive amounts of painkillers to continue the interrogation, which only extends the entire process.

"So please do us both a favor: Don't be a tough guy. When I ask you a question, answer it quickly and honestly. If you hold back, I'll know. And if I know you're holding back, you'll regret it. Are we clear?"

"Crystal," Caine rasped. His voice was ripped and torn from his earlier screams. He wondered what it would sound like after another few hours.

"Excellent. Now, let's try this again. Do you know why you're here?"

"Because you think that . . . that I'm . . . Laplace's Demon."

The man nodded. "Do *you* think you are Laplace's Demon?"

"I . . ." Caine hesitated. "I'm not a hundred percent sure," he answered, tensing his muscles in preparation for another shock. It didn't come.

"Take a guess."

"Yes," Caine blurted.

"Good. Then this wasn't all for nothing."

"What do you want from me?"

Dalton didn't answer his question. All he said was, "The doctor will be in shortly to talk with you," and walked away. When he spoke again, he was out of Caine's field of vision. It was disconcerting hearing the man without seeing his face. "By the way," he said, "don't bother trying to use your . . . talents. They don't work with your eyes open."

Caine suddenly realized that Dalton was right; with his eyes wide open, he was as helpless as a lamb. A few seconds later, Caine heard the click as the door closed. He strained his ears, trying to hear if Dalton was still there, but there was nothing. Caine was alone.

He exhaled loudly, and his mind kicked back into gear. He wanted to plan, but knew there was nothing he could do. His time for planning had passed. He'd allowed himself to be captured because he knew that the only way he could regain control was to give it up. However, he didn't know it would be so hard—and so terrifying.

Back in the apartment, when Caine was in the *everywhen,* he had seen all the possible futures. But now that he was outside his vision, Caine couldn't see which path, which possible future, he had traveled down. However, he did have a sense. It was more than intuition and less than pure knowledge, but it was there. Nava was the key. With her there were infinite possibilities.

But without her . . . Caine was lost.

Caine heard the door open and close as someone entered the room. By the sound of the footsteps, he could tell it wasn't Dalton; this stride was lighter. The person walked forward, stopped, backed up, and stopped again, as if to decide the safest route to approach him.

Then he heard the man breathing softly behind him, along with a soft, but sharp, scratching. A syringe? Maybe a scalpel. Caine's heart pounded. Finally the man resumed his walk around the room. It was Doc.

"Hello, David," Doc said.

Caine remained silent.

"I'm sorry it had to go this way, but there was no other choice."

"There's always a choice," Caine said.

"No," Doc said, shaking his head. "I had another subject like you. She told me what would happen, which path I needed to take. She told me what to do in order to fully bring forth your abilities. And she was right."

"That's why you set that explosive? Because she told you to?"

"Yes."

"But after that failed, why not kill me when you had the chance? You could have run me down in Philly."

"Don't you see?" Doc asked pleadingly. "I never wanted you to die. I only wanted you to discover what you're capable of. A life and death situation was necessary for you to take that last step. And that's what I provided."

"But why? Why are you doing this?" Caine asked.

"Science," Doc said. "Do you realize how much knowledge I—we—could gain with your gift?" Doc took a step closer to him. "David, we have an incredible opportunity, you and I, to make history." His eyes were burning bright now. Although Doc was looking at him, Caine could tell that his old mentor could see only himself. "No, not just to *make* history, to *change* history, to alter the entire future of mankind."

"I won't help you," Caine said.

"This will be much easier for the both of us if you would just—"

"No."

"Let's just run a few tests. What can a few tests hurt?" Doc was almost begging.

"That's the problem. I don't know what—or who—your tests will hurt." Caine took a deep breath, hoping he sounded braver than he felt. "I won't do it."

Doc shook his head. "This is why I couldn't have approached you in a less controlled environment. But like it or not, David, you will cooperate."

He removed a remote from his pocket and aimed it at a small television mounted high on the wall near the ceiling. The screen flickered to life. Caine strained his eyes to look up. On the monitor he saw a tired-looking man strapped down to a chair, an IV tube snaked down his arm. Jasper. He seemed to have aged ten years since Caine had last seen him.

Doc turned back around to face him. "I don't want to hurt your brother. But I will. It's really up to you."

"And what will happen if I cooperate?"

"You'll be one step closer to getting out of here." Doc's eyes gave him away. He was lying. Caine had to stall.

"I need some time to think about it."

"No," Doc said flatly. "The time is now. What is your answer?"

Caine knew there was a chance—a very good chance—that he would never leave this place. And although he was fairly certain Doc's test was harmless, he was afraid that if he said yes now, he might never be able to say no.

"I'm tired," Caine said. "Just give me some time to recuperate."

Doc shook his head. He walked to a phone mounted on the wall and dialed. "Hello, Mr. Dalton?" Caine felt his muscles tense at the mention of Jim Dalton. Doc glanced back at him. "Please attend to Jasper Caine. Level two for sixty seconds." Doc hung up, his face full of sorrow. "I'm sorry for this."

Caine watched the television screen. For the first few seconds, nothing happened. Jasper appeared to be sleeping, lying as restfully as one could with his arms, legs, and head restrained by leather straps. Then Dalton entered Jasper's room, put something into his mouth, and stepped offscreen. A shiver ran down Caine's spine, and Jasper began convulsing. His hands clenched and unclenched as the electric current ripped through his body. There was no sound connected to the images, which somehow made them all the more horrifying.

"Stop it! Stop it!" Caine screamed.

Doc glanced at his watch and then back at Caine. "Just another fifty seconds, David. It's almost over."

Caine couldn't close his lids to block out the horrible vision. He tried to avert his eyes from Jasper's twitching legs, but his pupils redirected themselves toward the screen. Finally it ended. Jasper stopped convulsing. He lay silently weeping, tears streaming down his face. Then Caine saw the final humiliation: a dark stain spread between his brother's legs.

Doc stepped back in front of Caine. It took every ounce of control for Caine not to spit in his face. Caine wondered again if he had made the right choice in coming here. But it was too late for second thoughts. This time there would be no misdeal.

"All right," Caine said, his voice filled with desperation. "I'll do your tests. But not with you in the room," Caine said, suddenly remembering how it was supposed to go. "I'll only deal with Forsythe."

Doc's face twisted into a frown. He was about to speak when a voice clicked onto the room's intercom system. "Paul," it said, "I think we should talk."

Forsythe was overjoyed that the Beta Subject had requested he be in the room instead of Tversky. If he could build a bond with the subject, perhaps he could get rid of Tversky even earlier than he had planned. Forsythe smiled and removed a small, shiny object from his pocket. As he approached the subject, the soft beeps from the EKG quickened.

"Relax, Mr. Caine. The test won't hurt, I promise," Forsythe said. "I'm going to release the lid clamps so you can . . . focus. However, if you try anything, I will know."

Forsythe glanced over at the bank of monitors on the far wall, paying close attention to the EEG readout, which showed the electrical activity in the Beta Subject's temporal lobe. If the amplitude increased above a predetermined level, the subject would receive an electric shock to break his concentration.

As an added precaution, Forsythe administered a mild sedative to make the subject more pliable. Slowly his heart rate decreased to seventy beats per minute. Only then did Forsythe release the subject's lid clamps. The subject's eyes immediately closed, and for a moment Forsythe's own heart jumped in his throat, but a quick glance at the EEG assured him that the subject was just resting—his delta waves were dominant, while the others barely registered.

After a few seconds, the subject opened his brilliant green eyes and stared at Forsythe. "Now what?" he asked.

"I want you to look at this coin." Forsythe held up the

quarter he had removed from his pocket. "I am going to flip it. When it lands, I want it to be heads."

The subject looked confused. "But what do you want *me* to do?"

Now it was Forsythe's turn to be puzzled. "I want *you* to make the coin come up heads."

"How?"

"With your mind."

Caine stared at the scientist, not sure what to say. If he lied, he would be caught. But neither did he wish to tell the truth. He hoped Nava would hurry.

Assuming she comes at all. Remember, there's a 12.7 percent chance she'll never even get here. You could be trapped forever.

Caine tried to ignore his fatalism. He looked back up at the monitor to see Jasper lying supine, a trail of drool dripping down his cheek. Then he looked at the scientist. The throbbing vein in the man's temple told Caine that Forsythe was losing patience.

There was no choice.

"It doesn't work that way," Caine finally said.

"What do you mean?" Forsythe asked.

"If you want, I can predict with a high level of certainty whether the coin will land on heads or tails. But I can't make something happen with my mind. I need to be involved somehow in order to affect its outcome." Caine opened his right hand. "Give the coin to me. Let me flip it."

Forsythe looked at Caine's palm suspiciously.

"It's the only way your experiment will work," Caine said.

After a second, Forsythe reluctantly dropped the coin into Caine's restrained hand. Caine closed his eyes. At first all he saw were a few colored spots dancing on the back of his dark lids. But then another image appeared, beckoning him forward.

. . .

It is always there. The giant tree grows out from his being. Its massive, singular trunk twists backward into eternity. Ahead, an infinite series of branches grow forth from the moment.

The image is constantly moving. Some branches grow thick and prominent, while others shrivel and die. New branches constantly spring forth; others disappear as if they never existed. The secondary branches spawn branches of their own, and those extend farther. There are so many twists and turns and combinations that all the branches seem to mesh into each other after several generations, into the shapeless abyss beyond.

The cognitive part of his brain wants to scream, to release itself from the bounds of sanity and flee the eternity before him. But another part, a primal part, calls this place home. He lets that part guide him forward.

. . .

"You said heads?" Caine asked, his eyes still closed.

"Yes," Forsythe said.

And then Caine saw how to make it happen.

. . .

There is a slight current in the air from the vents—it's almost imperceptible, but Caine can see it moving the oxygen and nitrogen molecules this way and that. The coin is a quarter, and the heads side is 0.00128 grams heavier than the tails side. The periphery of the pattern on the heads side is also larger and less aerodynamic than the tails side. But these factors are trivial when compared to the force of his fingers and the torque he applies to his cuffed wrist, which are collectively responsible for 98.756 percent of the coin's trajectory, although the trajectory is only 58.24510 percent responsible for whether the coin comes up heads or tails.

To fully understand the causes of the outcome, Caine analyzes the makeup of the coin (the core is 100 percent copper; the face is a 75 percent/25 percent copper-nickel alloy) as well as of the floor (thirty-six-square-inch linoleum tiles). These two factors account for 37.84322 percent of the coin's final outcome. Another 0.55164 percent stems from their proximity to the magnetic poles, 1.12588 percent from the speed of the earth's rotation, and 2.23415 percent from the cleanliness of the floor.

The remaining 0.00001 percent is noise—if there are 100,000 coin flips, Caine misses only once. Caine takes all the information into consideration, selects an appropriate path, and—

. . .

Caine flicked his index and middle fingers upward and launched the coin into the air. He opened his eyes and watched it tumble through space, the light playing across the two faces. Light, dark, heads, tails. When it landed on the floor, there was a light *smack* and then a *ching, ching, ching, brrrrrrrrrrrrm* as it bounced, bounced, bounced, and rattled to a stop somewhere outside his field of vision.

Forsythe hurried over to where it landed. When he picked it up, he was smiling.

"Fifty-fifty chance," Caine said, as much to Forsythe as himself. "It doesn't prove anything."

"True," Forsythe said, with excitement. "But if this coin landed on heads another forty-nine times, I think it would. Please continue."

Forsythe dropped the coin back into Caine's shackled hand. Again Caine closed his eyes, but this time he barely needed to search for the right branch. It came to him easily. Again he flicked up his fingers. Again the coin flew through the air and bounced onto the floor.

Again it was heads.

"Again."

Drop. Flip. Glint. Land. Bounce.

Another flip. Another heads. And then another. And another. And another. Heads. Heads. Heads. In between flips Caine found himself nodding off, slipping away, but each time Forsythe woke him with a quick jolt. Caine was also punished with an electric shock when he tried to look within the *everywhen* for Nava. He gave up after his second attempt; clearly Forsythe wasn't bluffing when he said he would know if Caine tried to cheat.

Finally, after what seemed like hours, they were done. Caine was dizzy and bathed in sweat, but he forced himself to look at the scientist after he flipped the fiftieth head in as many tries. Forsythe's smile slid from his face, briefly replaced by another emotion. The man quickly turned his head to mask it, but too late. Caine knew that look well.

It was fear.

"That was incredible," Forsythe breathed.

Tversky nodded. "You know what the probability is of flipping fifty consecutive heads? It's one over two to the fiftieth power. That's—" Tversky typed the calculation into the computer—"1,125,899,906,842,620 to 1. And that was while he was *drugged.* Can you imagine what he could do if he were lucid?"

Forsythe nodded emphatically. During the entire two-hour session, the subject had drifted in and out of consciousness, due to the sedative. Of course the experimental design wasn't good enough to use as proof for a paper—he would need some type of mechanical coin-flipping machine and a control group for that—but it was good enough to convince Forsythe that the subject was indeed a modern incarnation of Laplace's Demon.

Besides, neither of the men worried about publishing. With the Beta Subject at their disposal, they didn't need to worry about anything ever again. And, thanks to Tversky's work with the subject's twin, they now knew how to turn the demon off.

Although Tversky thought it had something to do with the reticular-activation system in the brain, Forsythe believed there was probably a simpler, more holistic explanation why the subject needed to close his eyes. Regardless, the reason was hardly as important as the effect—as long as the Beta Subject received constant visual stimulation, he was powerless.

"Did you measure the amount of time his eyes were closed during the various trials?" Forsythe asked.

Tversky nodded. "It's exactly as I expected—there's a linear relationship between the amount of time needed to execute an improbable event and the level of improbability of that event. Influencing higher-probability events, like the single flip of a coin, took almost no time at all, while influencing lower-probability events, like the throw of dice, required longer amounts of time in the REM-like state.

"James," Tversky said, pulling Forsythe out of his thoughts, "with the appropriate resources, I believe that David could do virtually anything he put his mind to." Tversky began to pace back and forth. "Properly channeled, he could use his infinite knowledge of the universe to help scientists achieve incredible breakthroughs in the lab. Microbiologists, astrophysicists, mathematicians, oncologists—the list would be endless! David could help us solve the universe's biggest mysteries."

But Forsythe wasn't thinking about anything as trivial as scientific breakthroughs. He had much larger ambitions. Whoever controlled the Beta Subject would control a power unlike anything ever known.

"There are other ways we could use his abilities," Forsythe mused, to see what Tversky would say.

"Like what?"

"Wall Street, for one. Politics. The military."

"Are you crazy?" Tversky asked. "We have to use him for *science.* Anything else would be too dangerous. Besides, there are so many questions that need to be answered before we even begin to discuss his uses. The possibilities are literally infinite." Tversky resumed his pacing. "We'll have to devise a way to keep him a secret. Perhaps have various scientists come work at the lab, and we'll—"

"Hold on," Forsythe said. He wanted to derail Tversky's train of thought until he had a chance to think things through on his own. For the time being, he still needed the scientist, but with any luck he wouldn't for much longer.

Perhaps he could turn Tversky over to the police for killing that grad student. That would not only keep him away from Forsythe but also serve to discredit him. Forsythe smiled to himself. Yes, that's what he would do. As soon as he understood what made the subject tick, he would get rid of Tversky for good.

"We still need to determine exactly how we can control the subject," Forsythe said, trying to get back to practical matters. "I don't think we can use the threat of harming his brother forever. Also, if we ask him to predict or perform more improbable tasks, we would risk him masterminding the perfect escape."

"Yes," Tversky said. "That's a problem. We can't continue such high doses of Thorazine. Perhaps over time, with behavior-modification therapy, we could wean David off the drugs without losing control over his psyche."

"I don't think we could ever get there," Forsythe said, shaking his head. "And even if we did, there would be no way to be sure. If our control wavered, even for a moment, we could lose everything."

Both men turned their attention back to the two-way mirror, each silently contemplating the problem at hand. On the other side, the subject lay there, involuntarily staring at the wall.

"He's far too dangerous to be allowed his freedom," Forsythe said. "I think our choice is obvious—we need to keep him in a permanent neuroleptic state."

"But that would rob him of all his free will," Tversky said, outraged.

"Isn't that the point?"

"Yes, but such a state is irreversible."

"So is death," Forsythe said coolly. "You didn't seem to have a problem with that one when dealing with your Alpha Subject."

Tversky's face turned red. "That was an accident. . . . I . . . Are you threatening me?"

"Why?" Forsythe asked. "Should I be?"

Tversky was silent for a long time. Finally he said, "I think we should test the procedure on the brother before using it on David. Just to make sure that there aren't any side effects."

Forsythe nodded. "I'm glad you see it my way."

Neither said anything for a moment. The silence was thick with tension. At last Tversky spoke. "I'm going to get some rest," he said awkwardly. "It's been a long day, and there are a lot of tests I want to conduct tomorrow."

Forsythe didn't trust Tversky, and he eyed him suspiciously. What was Tversky up to? He contemplated restraining him, but decided against it. For now, access to the Beta Subject was more than enough to keep Tversky in line.

"Good night, then," Forsythe said. "I'm going to stay a bit longer and prepare the twin."

For a moment Forsythe thought Tversky was going to protest, but then he seemed to change his mind. "Good night, James. I'll see myself out."

After the door clicked shut, Forsythe calculated the precise doses necessary to put the twin into a passive neuroleptic state. In spite of how difficult he was, Tversky was right—it was best to test the procedure on the twin, just in case something went wrong.

Forsythe hit a few keys on his terminal and clicked "OK" at the multiple prompts that asked him if he was *sure* he wanted to inject the drugs he had selected into the twin's body. On the screen he could already see the twin's eyes getting glassy, unfocused, as the drugs flowed through the IV in his arm. In less than three hours, Jasper Caine would be all but gone, replaced by someone without a will of his own, someone who would be much more subservient and respectful.

Turning his attention away from the twin, Forsythe added a narcotic to the Beta Subject's current drug cocktail. No sense risking any violent behavior. After he was through, Forsythe sighed. The experiments would have been so much cleaner without drugs. But he was confident that the twins would still be able to perform, regardless. And if they didn't, then Forsythe's team should be able to create a pharmaceutical to replicate the twins' brain chemistry, just as Tversky had done with the Alpha Subject.

Once they could do that, the twins would no longer be necessary.

The van dropped Nava off a tenth of a mile from the building. It looked identical to the other seven-story, concrete-slab structures that lined the block, but she knew that the exterior was just part of the disguise. She pulled the brim of her baseball cap down to cover her face, took one last drag from her cigarette, and then crushed it beneath her boot.

When she reached the black SUV parked on the street, she bent down and looked behind the right front tire. Her supplies were there, as promised. She stored the ID in her pocket, slipped on the wristband, and headed toward the entranceway.

Taking a deep breath, she pushed through the heavy revolving door. The lobby was wall-to-wall imitation marble. Her shoes echoed as she made her way to the security desk. The overweight guard slowly put aside his *People* magazine when he saw her approach. After glancing at her fake ID badge, he spent a whole five seconds pawing through her duffel bag.

As she expected, he only looked through the zippered compartment she opened for him. He completely ignored the larger one that contained a trank gun, two Glock 9-millimeter semiautomatic pistols, three hundred rounds of ammo, a can of Freon, and enough plastic explosives to level the building. Satisfied she wasn't a terrorist, he asked her to sign in and returned to his *People*.

With a quick smile and a thank-you, Nava walked briskly to the elevator bank. No sooner did she press the button than the doors slid open. She was about to enter when she noticed that the car contained a passenger. He was so lost in thought that he breezed by Nava without looking up. Although he didn't see her face hidden beneath the baseball cap, Nava saw his.

It was Doc.

For an instant she imagined slashing his throat with her dagger, leaving him to bleed to death in the lobby. She wanted to kill him for what he'd done to David. For what he'd done to Julia. But Nava knew that if she gave in to temptation, the guard would sound the alarm and she would be unable to save David.

And so, despite the rage screaming inside her, Nava watched him walk by without a word. Still gritting her teeth, she rode up to the sixth floor, trying to put Doc out of her mind. There would be time for vengeance later. When the doors opened, she continued her mission.

She stepped into a small foyer enclosed by glass double doors. She opened her knapsack and removed an electromagnetic device the size of a deck of cards. She held it in front of the magnetic pad on the wall and waited as it cycled through all possible frequencies until she heard a soft click as the electronic locks were released. It took less than five seconds.

She walked through the doors into a luxurious lobby. Two identical black leather couches faced each other on opposite sides of an ornate Oriental rug. On the far wall, a floor-to-ceiling window showed the twinkling lights of a city almost asleep. As she stared through the window, Nava wished that her life had turned out differently. She allowed herself a few seconds of fantasy before pulling herself back to reality. She had chosen her path, no one else. Now she had work to do.

Nava tore her eyes from the window and purposefully marched down the hall, following the route she'd memorized in the van. She picked another electromagnetic lock, and then she was at the second elevator bank. She took a deep breath and put on her game face. Once she summoned the elevator, there was no turning back. From the second she pressed the button, she would be under constant surveillance.

If her intel was correct, she should be fine. But if her intel was wrong . . . she was screwed. The elevator car could open to a team of armed guards. Or maybe some type of nerve gas. Or perhaps she'd ride safely down to the lab, only to be torn apart by German shepherds upon arrival. There was no way of knowing.

She removed her weapons and ammo from her duffel bag and stored them in a very flat knapsack. Next she removed a small package wrapped in plain brown paper. Then she withdrew a trank gun and one of her 9-millimeters, checking to make sure the safety was off. It was. It always was.

Finally she fingered the small panel on her wristband: her secret weapon. She hoped she wouldn't need it; she didn't like depending on others when her life was at risk. She reasoned that she would use it only if her death were imminent. Then, if it didn't work, she would only have herself to blame. For some reason that made her feel better.

She pressed the small elevator button on the wall and waited to see what would happen next.

For a moment Caine understood the attraction of drug addiction.

Then he felt so completely blissed out he didn't care. The cool saline solution flowing into his veins had been replaced by something else. Something amazing. He'd never known that he could feel the rush of his own blood, but then again he'd never taken a narcotic intravenously before.

The ice-cold liquid raced up his arm, making its way toward his brain. In its wake his body floated on a sea of nothingness. His arm, shoulder, neck, and then . . . *wow.* Nothing mattered. Everything was all right. His knee stopped its methodical throbbing, the ache in his back drifted away, the kink in his neck was less than a memory. His mind felt . . . doughy . . . but good. So good.

Caine's lips curved into a smile. He began to giggle. This caused his eyelids to pull at the forceps, but he didn't care. The forceps used to burn; now they tickled. Everything tickled. A wave of euphoria flowed over his body, and he sighed.

Nothing mattered, he saw that now. He wasn't sure why he'd cared so much before.

He suddenly felt very sleepy. He wanted to close his eyes and go to sleep, but he couldn't because . . . well, just . . . he couldn't remember. It didn't matter anyway; he thought he could fall asleep even though his eyes were open. That would be cool, sleeping with his eyes open.

Really . . . cool . . .

Nava tensed her grip on her gun as the elevator sped toward the sixth floor, where she waited. She stood to the side, so she wouldn't be in plain view when the doors opened. The car stopped with a soft metallic click, and the doors slowly peeled open to reveal . . .

Nothing.

Before entering, she glanced at the ceiling to make sure there were no surprises but saw only three fluorescent disks along with a tiny surveillance camera. She lowered her head and squared her shoulders as she entered the car. Given her baseball cap and nondescript gray jumpsuit, she thought she might pass for a man to whoever might be on the other end of that camera.

Once inside the service elevator, she pressed the button marked SB. The doors swished shut, and the car raced down to the subbasement. Her stomach jumped as the car slowed to a stop. She grasped the gun hidden in her oversize pants pocket, feeling the cool metal through the cloth.

The elevator opened and she took in her surroundings in a heartbeat. The room was small, no more than twelve square meters. White floors, white walls. Thick security door with a handprint scanner. A large, silvery L-shaped security desk and a bank of tiny black-and-white monitors.

Two guards sat behind the desk. Unlike the lobby guards, they were men to be taken seriously: young and well muscled, with close-cropped hair—mercenaries; one was Hispanic and the other was white. Nava put on a bored expression and walked confidently toward them. She set the package down on the desk with one hand, holding the gun in her pocket with the other.

"I have a package for Dr. Forsythe," she said by way of introduction. The white guard glanced at his Hispanic counterpart, unsure of what to do. The Hispanic guard was in charge. Good to know. She removed her gun and shot him in the neck.

He didn't have time to look surprised. He fell back in his chair, a trickle of blood oozing from the tranquilizer dart embedded in his skin. Before the white guard had a chance to react, Nava swung the gun in his direction and pressed it firmly against his right eye. He winced in pain.

"Hands behind your head," she said.

He did as he was told.

"What's your name?"

"Jeffreys."

She nodded to the handprint scanner. "Is that the only one of those?"

"Yes," he said, gulping hard.

"What are the other security measures?"

He hesitated for a nanosecond, and she pressed the cool gun barrel harder into his skull.

"There are thumbprint scanners everywhere."

"Did you hit the silent alarm?"

"No."

"How often do you check in with the other guards?"

"Every fifteen minutes."

"When was the last check-in?"

"Our last one was at ten forty-five. Next is at eleven." Her watch read 10:47. She had thirteen minutes. She would have preferred twenty, but it would have to do.

"How many guards are in the complex?"

"Ummm . . ." His left eye rolled up to the ceiling, as if he were counting in his head. "Six," he finally said. "No, no, wait . . . seven. It's seven, I'm pretty sure."

"Including you and your partner?"

"Yes."

"Will his thumbprint unlock all the doors in the installation?" Nava asked, gesturing at the unconscious man on the floor. Jeffreys swallowed hard when he realized what she was asking, but then he nodded slightly.

"Yes."

Without another word, she pulled back her tranquilizer gun and shot him in the arm. He slumped over next to his partner. She reached behind the desk and pulled the Hispanic guard's right hand toward her. Using the blade from her ankle holster, she sliced through the lateral tendons of his thumb and gently inserted the blade inside the joint; she popped off the end of the digit nearly intact, along with a fountain of blood.

Nava wiped her hands on the man's uniform. Then she cut off a strip of his sleeve to wrap around the end of the severed thumb and wrapped another strip around his wound. She couldn't believe that her source had forgotten to mention the thumb scanners. Slips like that were why she preferred to do her own recon. She wondered what else he'd gotten wrong. She'd find out soon enough.

She prowled around the desk, searching the screens until she found what she was looking for. David. His eyes stared at the ceiling, yet he appeared to be unconscious, his chest rhythmically rising and falling. White text in the lower-right-hand corner of the screen read C10. She was about to leave when another screen caught her eye.

Jasper. Like David, he was restrained in a large, metallic reclining chair, with his eyes held open. Unlike David, however, he appeared conscious. His brow was deeply furrowed, and his hands trembled. Her heart went out to him. The monitor indicated he was in D8. In D wing, far away from David. Odd that they separated the two prisoners by such distance. There would be no time for her to save both of them.

She looked at her watch: 10:48—twelve minutes left. She had to hurry.

Nava looked down the long corridor. Like the foyer, everything was white, practically glowing beneath harsh fluorescent lights. The hallway stretched forward twenty meters before splitting off to the right and to the left. When Nava reached the blind corner, she heard two deep-voiced men. She stopped and considered her options. She didn't want to come out shooting—if she missed, she would risk one of them sounding the alarm.

If she could incapacitate both quickly, without firearms, she could hide their bodies in one of the storage rooms lining the hall. But if one of the men managed to get off a shot, that would promptly end the clandestine nature of her rescue. She had to make her decision quickly.

She opted to go without guns. She put her weapons away and prepared to go straight hand-to-hand. She fought much better unencumbered, but if things got hairy, she could always use her dagger.

First she needed to separate the two. It would be easiest to debilitate one before the other knew what was going on, then attack the second. She took a few steps back and pressed herself against one of the recessed doors along the hall. Then she sneezed. Or at least she produced a noise that *sounded* like a sneeze. It was the oldest trick in the book, but in her experience only the best tricks survived to *become* old tricks.

The men immediately stopped talking. She could almost feel them listening, their ears straining for the slightest sound. She held her breath.

"Did you hear something?"

"Sounded like a sneeze."

"Yeah. Stay here, I'm gonna check it out."

Heavy footfalls thudded down the hall. She waited until he was almost on top of her before revealing herself. They eyed each other for a quarter of a second before she attacked. He was about six-two, 210 pounds, with sandy blond hair, a heavy brow, and an even heavier billy club that he immediately swung at her head. She stepped toward him and caught his forearm in her gloved hands. She continued moving forward, twisting his wrist as she did so, using all her strength to flip him over her shoulder.

But he was too fast—he brought up his other arm and punched her hard in the chest with the heel of his hand, knocking the wind out of her and breaking her hold. She had only a second before the other guard figured out that something was wrong. There was no time for elegance.

She grabbed his shoulders and slammed her knee up into his crotch with all her strength, smashing his testicles into his pelvis. The color had already drained out of his face by the time she delivered the crushing uppercut that rendered him unconscious. He crumpled to the floor like a house of cards.

"McCoy, you okay?" a voice yelled out a second after the guard's club clattered to the floor. If the other one were smart, he would sound the alarm before investigating. But since most grunts weren't known for their intelligence, she figured she had a window of opportunity. She grabbed McCoy's club and raced around the corner.

This guard was much shorter, but he had the build of a weight lifter. She tossed the club gently at the man's knees. Without thinking, he leaned down and caught it, leaving himself exposed. It was a mistake he'd never repeat.

She smashed the heel of her boot into the side of his skull with a vicious back-roundhouse kick. He didn't fall, but it was enough to disorient him for a few seconds, which was all she needed. She slammed her elbow down into his neck and then shattered his jaw with a hard knee to the chin.

He dropped to the floor, unconscious.

A minute later, after tranking both the guards and dragging them into one of the storerooms, Nava ditched her baseball hat and slipped on an oversize white lab coat. She continued down the hall toward C10.

After passing through the next security door, she entered another bright white hall that seemed to stretch on forever. The passageway was narrow, barely wide enough for two people to walk side by side. Every three meters there was a door on the right side. Two men stood on opposite sides of a door about thirty meters away. She presumed it was C10.

As she continued down the hall, she reviewed her limited options. Clearly a distraction wouldn't work, since there was nowhere to hide. There was a chance she could get close enough to trank them both, but she doubted it. Hand-to-hand was another option. On the plus side, the narrow corridor should give her a slight advantage, as she'd be better able to maneuver in the small space than the two large men would. But it also meant that if she went down, there would be nowhere to go. They would be on her in an instant.

No, hand-to-hand was too risky. Although she had taken out the other two guards easily enough, her luck wouldn't last forever. Her biggest advantage was surprise, and she had to use it. She dropped her clipboard, scattering papers across the floor outside Room C6. A guard looked over but dismissed her as one of Forsythe's protégées. As she collected her papers, she turned her back to the guards and carefully transferred her silenced 9-millimeter from her shoulder holster to one of the white lab coat's pockets.

She would have liked to use the trank gun, but there was no room for error—a bullet, even if a shot wasn't precise, would still slow the target down. Unfortunately, as the guards were next to each other, she had a clear shot at only one of them. She would need to get closer.

She resumed walking toward the guards. She kept her head down, feigning embarrassment at her clumsiness, letting her long hair fall across her face. C8. Six more meters until contact. She dropped her hand to her side, letting it fall casually into her pocket.

C9. Three meters.

She touched the cold steel, quickly running her fingers across the muzzle before grasping the handle. She stopped and glanced at the guards shyly when she reached the door. The taller of the two was toned and lean, his muscles smooth and sinewy. He clearly knew how to handle himself. The other was built like a small dump truck. She could hear a buzzing voice coming from his earpiece.

"Dalton here," he said. Nava tensed. If the other guards

had been found, she needed to attack now. But she couldn't risk letting whoever was on the other end of the mike hear any type of disturbance. She decided to wait, knowing that if the one named Dalton was alerted, she would see it in his eyes before he had a chance to react.

"Yeah, understood," Dalton said. He clicked off. His eyes were menacing, but she hadn't seen any change.

"Can I help you, miss?" the lean guard asked, his voice deep and challenging.

"I'm . . . I'm supposed to examine the patient," Nava stammered in her best nervous-little-girl voice.

He looked at her as if she were the stupidest person on the planet. "This area is restricted. You—"

He stopped talking when the bullet punched a hole through his chest.

She turned her gun toward Dalton, but he grabbed her wrist and the shot went high, smashing into the ceiling, raining down shards of plastic and glass and knocking out the overhead light. He twisted her wrist, and her gun clattered to the floor; then he grabbed her throat and rushed forward, smashing her body against the wall.

Her head bounced against the stone surface with a crack. She gasped for breath as his hand squeezed her throat like a metal vise. Her right hand was completely pinned, and his body was pressed too close for her to deliver an effective kick. She punched him in the kidneys with her free hand, but he didn't flinch. She could feel his hot breath on her skin as he continued to tighten his grip on her neck.

Recognition suddenly appeared on his face as he stared into her eyes. "Thought I already killed you, Vaner."

Black spots appeared before her eyes. She had ten more seconds before she'd lose consciousness. Her mouth opened and closed, attempting to suck in air, but it was no use. He was just too strong. Using her last ounce of strength, she raised her knee chest high, her left foot dangling in the air next to her outstretched hand.

She ran her fingers over the top of her boot until she found the hilt of her dagger. Hands slick with sweat, she pulled it loose. The force of the tug slammed her hand back into the wall so hard she almost dropped the knife, but she managed to tighten her grip along the hilt.

She pulled her arm up and stabbed down into his back. When the blade punctured his skin, Dalton tightened his grip on her throat even harder, but she kept pushing, feeling the dagger sink deeper into his shoulder. As she ripped through his tendon, Dalton let her go with a shriek. She crashed down on her hands and knees, panting. She nearly passed out but held on, grinding her bloody knuckles into the floor, focusing on the pain.

She allowed herself one more gasp before finishing the job. She had to stop Dalton from screaming. He towered over her, desperately trying to grasp the knife and pull it out, one hand limp at his side, the other clawing at his back.

She stretched out her hands, grabbed his right foot, and pulled forward. He fell back, landing hard on his side; his collarbone crunched, snapping in two. His eyes burned with pain and fury. Catching her second wind, Nava jumped atop the fallen guard, straddling his waist. She grabbed the handle of her dagger, turned it ninety degrees, and ripped it out of his shoulder. A torrent of blood shot from the wound, like water breaking through a dam.

With both hands she raised the dagger above her head and plunged it down into Dalton's chest, breaking two of his ribs before the blade cut deep into his heart. His head jerked forward, and he let out one last gasp, eyes wide, and then his head fell back. Beneath her his entire body sagged, all the life gone from its hulking form.

Still gasping for breath, she rubbed her throat and surveyed the scene. It was nowhere as neat as those of her other two encounters. The lean guard lay on his back, legs kicked out. A puddle of blood had bubbled up from his chest. He must have lived for a few seconds after being hit, because both his hands were smeared with blood; thin red lines tracked across the floor, ending at his fingertips.

Dalton had made a much larger mess. He lay in a dark red pool, blood still seeping from the wound in his shoulder. The areas of floor that weren't bloody were covered with shards of glass and black plastic from the ceiling. Anyone who came down the hall would surely see.

Her watch read 10:55. She had five more minutes before all hell broke loose. At least the light was dim, since Nava had inadvertently shattered one of the fluorescent tubes with her wayward gunshot. She looked down the rest of the well-lit corridor and then back at her little patch of darkness outside Caine's room.

She had an idea.

Crowe swore beneath his breath. The second he heard the shot outside his door, he had a preternatural sense that it was Vaner. By the time he looked at his monitor, Esposito was already dead, bleeding out on the floor. The last image the surveillance camera showed before it went to snow was Dalton grabbing Vaner's wrist. Her shot must have taken out the camera in the ceiling.

Crowe removed his .45 SIG Sauer from his shoulder holster and rushed to the door, Dalton's screams filling his ears. He was about to turn the knob when there was a loud slam—and then the yelling stopped. She must have killed him with her bare hands. Crowe released his hand from the knob. If Vaner was still alive, she might be waiting for another guard to exit the room. If that were true, she would drop him before he had a chance to squeeze off a shot.

Jeffreys, Esposito, Gonzalez, McCoy, and Rainer—he wondered if any of them were still alive. They weren't good men, but none deserved to die. He'd thought that six ex-special-forces operatives would have been enough. Clearly he had underestimated the rogue CIA agent—not only had she come back from the dead, but she'd come back fighting. The only part of his security plan that had worked was the false text on the monitors at the guard station.

All this time, instead of racing toward David Caine, Vaner

had been moving farther away, having finally arrived at Crowe's office. Suddenly the rectangular light on the wall glowed green, signaling that someone had just disengaged the electronic lock. He backed away and aimed his pistol at the door.

He put pressure on the trigger—not enough to fire, just enough so that the shot would be instantaneous when she entered. The door swung open, revealing a very battered Nava Vaner. He pulled the trigger before she had a chance to react. A half second later, the floor was covered with blood, gray matter, and a few chunks of shattered skull.

The instant Nava opened the door, she realized it had all been a trick. Just as her brain processed the information, she saw the dark man from the train station, the muzzle of his .45 bearing down on her. She wondered if it would hurt to die. She'd been shot before, twice in the leg and once in the shoulder, but none of those wounds had been serious. They'd been bloody and painful, but not life-threatening. That wouldn't be the case today.

At this range there was no way he could miss.

She felt the bullet before she heard the explosion. It entered just below Dalton's eye. She had moved the dead man into the room in order to clear the dark hallway, carrying him over her shoulder, his lifeless head resting against her chest.

Then Dalton's cranium had exploded like a watermelon, soaking her shirt with warm, sticky blood. Had she not picked up the dead man, the bullet would have ripped through her heart, instead of merely grazing her skin after exiting the guard's skull. She was beginning to wonder if maybe Caine's intuition had rubbed off on her.

But she couldn't count on it. She dropped the headless corpse and dove back into the bloody corridor. She landed on her side and slid on the wet floor, reaching wildly for her 9-millimeter—but it wasn't there. She had forgotten to put it back in her pocket. She saw it lying in the open doorway, only a few inches from her foot. It might as well have been a mile away.

The dark man would be on top of her in a second. There was no way she'd get to the gun in time. She stabbed the panel on her wristband—the emergency she had anticipated was upon her. Nava had never before trusted her life to another. She fully expected to be disappointed.

Still on her back, she removed a small throwing knife from her belt and pulled back her arm, hoping for a miracle.

Grimes was carefully selecting which Gummi Worm to eat—he liked the white ones with the green stripes—when a large flashing circle appeared on his monitor. The image was accompanied by the red-alert sound effect from *Star Trek* blaring over his headphones. He sat up, stuffing a random worm in his mouth. Cool. Game on.

He double-clicked the red sphere and sat back to watch the fireworks—or at least listen. He briefly wondered if he'd just committed a felony or something but then dismissed the thought, remembering that he no longer worked for the U.S. government. Instead he focused on all the money that had just hit his numbered offshore account. As an extra bonus, he knew that Dr. Jimmy would really flip out once the dust settled.

That in and of itself was almost better than the money. Almost. But not quite.

Crowe sidestepped the body. One look at the corpse and he understood what had happened. It was Dalton's head he'd shot, not Vaner's. But her luck had just run out—her gun was lying useless in the doorway. In the hall he could see that Esposito's pistol was still in its holster.

He stepped over Dalton and calmly walked toward the doorway to kill Vaner. As he neared the corridor, he caught a glimpse of her foot. Since she knew he was coming for her, there was no reason for him to hold his fire for the kill shot. This wasn't a James Bond movie where he waited to look her in the eye. This was real life, and he took no chances.

He squeezed the trigger without breaking stride.

The pain was electric fire. All her nerve endings screamed in unison when the bullet ripped through the sole of her shoe. She jerked back her leg and bit hard on her tongue, willing herself not to cry out. If this were her last moment, she didn't want it to be filled with screaming, especially her own. It was bad enough she was flat on her back. She had always imagined dying on her feet.

The dark man's shadow fell across the corridor as he entered the doorway. She was going to die. She steadied her knife hand, gritting her teeth against the pain, and waited for him to step through the door. Although he would kill her, she'd give him something to remember her by.

Then it happened.

The world fell into complete darkness as the fluorescent lights flickered and died.

Nava was almost surprised, even though she had triggered the blackout herself via the button on her wristband. She reacted with lightning-quick speed. Ignoring the shrieking pain in her foot, she sat up and leaned forward. If her boot had been in the line of sight of the dark man, then the reverse would also be true.

She cocked back her forearm above her boot and let the knife fly. She heard it connect with a sickening thump, followed immediately by a low grunt and the hard clank of metal against tile. He'd dropped his gun—she still had a chance. She bent forward, running her hand through the sticky blood that covered the floor, her fingers madly searching for the 9-millimeter that lay somewhere in the blackness.

Then she had it. Her hand closed over the metal grip.

She was about to raise the gun when a heavy boot stomped on her wrist. She screamed in pain as the dark man ground his heel and her wrist bones crunched and snapped.

She tried to fire, but the crushing pain paralyzed her as he reached down to pull the pistol from her hand.

She frantically grabbed for the gun with her free hand and found the trigger. In the darkness she'd lost track of where it was facing. It didn't matter; if she didn't take the shot, she'd be dead within seconds. She squeezed. She hoped it found its target, because she had no more strength left to fight.

Crowe felt the bullet slice through the flesh between his thumb and forefinger. It hurt like hell, but he didn't care; by holding on to the muzzle, he had achieved his objective—the shot went wide and wouldn't hit anything important. At least that's what he thought when he aimed Vaner's pistol at the steel doorframe.

But Crowe didn't anticipate the ricochet. Had Vaner's knife not been sticking out of his chest, it wouldn't have been a problem. But it was. Bouncing off the doorframe, the bullet whizzed an inch in front of him, striking the hilt of Vaner's knife. The force of the projectile caused the blade to pivot within Crowe's chest, ripping through the left ventricle of his heart.

Blood poured through Crowe's tattered cardiac muscle and filled his chest cavity. Although his heart kept pumping, the muscle failed to deliver blood to his body. He dropped to the ground like a stone, smashing on top of Vaner. Their faces were inches apart.

"Where is Caine?" she gasped.

He knew he had only a few more moments to live. He couldn't believe he would never see Betsy again . . . and then he remembered—the note. He closed his eyes, trying to cull its image from his brain before it was too late. He thought he would fail, when it came rushing back.

Martin Crowe's eyes only:
When Nava asks you where I am, tell her.
It's the only way I can save Betsy.
—David Caine

Suddenly realizing the note's significance, he pushed himself one more time.

"D10," he gasped. "Tell him . . . tell him I kept my end of the deal."

As the synapses of his brain sputtered, he saw a brilliant flash of color, a summer afternoon spent chasing rainbows with his little girl. If this was death, then maybe it wasn't so bad. And with that thought his synapses stopped firing, and Martin Crowe exhaled his final breath.

CHAPTER thirty-three

The darkness felt good, so much better than the light. The meds were wearing off. Now Caine could escape. He couldn't free his body, but he could free his mind. And he did, letting it sink down into the *everywhen,* where time was just an abstract concept. As he looked upon the world, the *Now,* the past, and the futures, he realized that this time something was different.

This time he was not alone.

. . .

There is a woman. She is both young and ancient. He knows She is beautiful even though he cannot see Her. Her beauty radiates from within. Like him, the knowledge She has is infinite, but unlike him, it is already inside Her, flowing through Her spirit.

Suddenly Caine is overwhelmed with knowledge.

***She**—Do you understand?*

***Caine**—Yes. The future is amorphous until it is observed. If you flip a coin, two possible futures exist: one in which the coin is heads, another in which it's tails. Neither comes into being until you observe it.*

***She**—Yes. That is why particles exist in all possible places at once, because they simultaneously represent all possible futures.*

***Caine**—But this is in conflict with the theory of Laplace's Demon. Laplace believes that if one knows everything in the* Now, *then one knows all events of the past and all events of* *the future. If Laplace's theory is correct, then the future is predetermined; it is singular—but the future is not singular; it is infinite.*

***She**—True. Laplace's theory is incomplete. It is correct in* When's *past, but not fully comprehensive in its future.*

***Caine**—Ah. Laplace's Demon knows everything in the past, because the past is always singular, as all splits are forward-branching. But Laplace's Demon does not know the precise future because there is more than one. Laplace's Demon knows everything in all possible futures.*

***She**—Yes. The* When's *future is probabilistic in nature. Because you see the multiple* Nows *perfectly, you see all possible futures; hence your observations are infinite. Because reality is a reflection of the observation, you choose your own reality stemming from each forward-branching moment because you choose which moment you wish to observe.*

***Caine**—I understand. That is why I cannot see the* everywhen *with open eyes—because as I observe the universe, it locks in the* Now, *eliminating some of the possible futures.*

***She**—Yes.*

***Caine**—But . . . why me? Why am I the Demon? Why not someone else?*

***She**—It's merely probabilistic, like the bell curve. Everyone has some "Demonic" abilities. Most have very weak abilities. Some have very strong abilities. A few have none. Hence a few must have all. Those few are the Demons.*

***Caine**—If everyone has some abilities, then why don't I know of others traveling into the* everywhen?

***She**—The* everywhen *is trapped in their unconscious minds. They may see it, but they don't understand it. Sometimes it exists as an echo.*

***Caine**—Like déjà vu?*

***She**—Yes. Déjà vu is a memory of a possible future as seen in the* When's *past. The path leading to the possible future people glimpse typically isn't followed. However, if it is followed precisely, the memory bubbles up to the conscious mind—that is déjà vu.*

***Caine**—So everyone has different levels of ability?*

***She**—Yes, some are weak, others are strong. The weak have little or no foresight. They don't intuitively foresee the consequences of their actions because they can't see the possible futures. They stumble through life blind and stupid. Their decisions are random, as are the results of their decisions.*

The strong can see much, although what they see is trapped in their unconscious mind. They attribute their good ideas to "insight," "intuition," or "a feeling." In truth their ideas come from the futures they glimpse in the everywhen. *In the* everywhen *everyone has some possible future that is idyllic and happy.*

Those who have strong abilities seek to achieve one of those idyllic lives by mimicking the decisions of their future idyllic selves, to observe the same events as their future selves. Hence their decisions are good, as their unconscious mind knows they are the "right" decisions to achieve one of the happy futures.

***Caine**—But are there any others like me? Other . . . Demons?*

***She**—Yes. Other Demons also exist in the* When. *Socrates, Alexander the Great, Julius Caesar, Joan of Arc, Molière, Napoleon Bonaparte, Hermann von Helmholtz, Vincent van Gogh, Alfred Nobel. All are Demons.*

***Caine**—They're all epileptics . . . like me. That is what the seizures are—pieces of the* everywhen *overloading the synapses?*

***She**—Yes. The sight of the* everywhen *causes Demons to suffer in the* When.

***Caine**—Back in the* When, *what am I supposed to do?*

***She**—Whatever you wish. You have the power to choose your own future and, in doing so, alter the futures of those around you.*

***Caine**—But how do I know which decisions are right? Everything is interconnected. Choosing something that is right for me could harm others.*

She—*Decisions aren't right and wrong. Decisions just are. You must choose what you think is best.*

Caine—*But how do I choose?*

She—*That's up to you.*

"G*rimes, what the hell is going on?!?"*

"Sorry, Dr. Jimmy. There seems to be a problem with one of the switches."

"I don't want the fucking details!" Forsythe screamed into the phone. He was near hysterics. "I just want you to *fix the problem.* You think you can manage that?"

"Listen, Jimmy," Grimes spit back, "I'm doing the best I can. Kirk out." Grimes clicked off.

Forsythe balled his fists. Stupid little prick. As soon as this mess was cleared up, he'd find another techie to take over. He was sick and tired of Grimes's incompetence.

He turned back to the two-way mirror and stared at nothing, listening to the hoarse sounds of his own ragged breath. The blackness was all-encompassing in the windowless space. His heart began to gallop. He kept blinking, as if to clear away the shadowy veil, but it was no use. There was no difference between opening his eyes and closing them.

Suddenly his heart stopped. Jesus . . . the Beta Subject. The lid retractors wouldn't make any difference as long as there was no light—and the computer rationed the flow of drugs. No electricity meant no sedatives. The subject could be awake in less than ten minutes. Forsythe's new fear eclipsed the old. He picked up the phone and stabbed Grimes's extension.

"You've got to get the lights back on!" Forsythe demanded.

"Ummm . . . *yeah,*" Grimes answered sarcastically. "That was my general plan, you know?"

"Grimes, I'm serious. You don't understand—it's *imperative* the electricity is restored immediately."

"Look, Dr. Jimmy, I told you I'm working as fast as I can. Talking to you on the phone makes me work *s-l-o-w-e-r.*" He stretched out the last word for effect. "Now, unless you have any other news flashes, I suggest you let me get back to work."

"Just do it!" Forsythe slammed down the phone. His heart raced. He had to do something—but what? He thrust his sweaty hands into his lab coat's pockets and began to pace, trying not to hyperventilate. He walked three steps forward and banged his knee against his file cabinet. "Fuck!" he yelled, gripping his bruised knee.

He reached around in the dark until he found his chair and sat back down, still rubbing his knee. He unclenched his pocketed fist and stretched his fingers. He felt something long and thin. He'd almost forgotten. He pulled out the object, pressed the tiny switch on the side, and was momentarily blinded by the penlight's illumination.

Forsythe sighed with relief, his heart slowly returning to a light trot. He turned the light toward the two-way mirror, but it merely reflected back at him, casting giant shadows on the back wall. He couldn't reach the subject this way, but if he went into his room and shone the light directly in his eyes, that should hold him at bay until the power came back on.

Forsythe used the light to find his way to the door and then tried to turn the handle. It was locked. That didn't make any sense. His door never locked from the inside; the electric locks were only one-way. . . . Jesus . . . the *electric locks.* He rattled the handle again, but knew it was pointless. He turned to look at his own shadowy reflection, wondering what was happening on the other side of the mirror.

He pounded the door and began to scream.

Nava wasn't sure what had kept her from passing out: the intense burning pain in her foot, the throbbing ache in her wrist, or the hot fluid dripping erratically down her neck. She wiped at her scalp. Her hand came away wet and sticky. Blood, but thankfully not her own.

She rolled the man off her shoulder and felt for a pulse. Nothing. She sighed in relief. She looked at her watch—

11:01 P.M. Now that she'd eliminated the seven soldiers, she didn't need to worry about the alarm sounding. However, she did have another deadline.

Grimes had warned her that once he killed the power, it would take the building ten minutes to send a security team to the underground lab. Under normal circumstances she wouldn't be concerned with a half dozen rent-a-cops, but she knew there was no way she could fend them off in her current state.

According to her wristband, she had eight minutes and fifteen seconds to rescue Caine.

Nava picked up the dark man's SIG Sauer in her hand, feeling its heft. She struggled to her feet. She could barely put weight on the heel of her left foot, and the floor was slippery with blood. After a minute, she managed to stand, leaning against the wall, panting. Briefly she thought she was going to pass out again. She gave her broken wrist a quick jerk, and it screamed, alive with pain.

Her eyes opened wide. Holding her knapsack between her teeth, Nava rummaged through the zippered compartment with her good hand until she found her night-vision goggles. She took off down the hall as fast as she could.

She had to get to David before it was too late.

Grimes chuckled as he unclipped his wireless headset. Dr. Jimmy was absolutely *freaking out.* Fucking classic. Classic! Grimes only wished he'd had the foresight to tape the infuriated scientist. He could have used Dr. Jimmy's curses as sound effects for his laptop. That would have been so cool. Oh, well, maybe next time. That is, if Dr. Jimmy didn't die of an embolism.

It had all been so easy. He still couldn't believe David Caine's combination of brilliance and balls. How Caine had figured out that the bug in the apartment was in his planter was clever, but when he actually sat down in front of it and slowly stated his plan . . . *wow,* that had taken guts.

If Grimes had missed it, Caine would have been leaving

himself up shit creek without a paddle. Worse, if Forsythe had seen it instead of Grimes, Caine's gal pal would have walked right into a trap. But luckily for David Caine, everything had worked perfectly.

Grimes thought back to when he'd first seen the surveillance video from Caine's apartment before Crowe's team swooped in. When he saw Caine's lips moving, he turned up the volume and got the surprise of his life.

"This is a message for Steven Grimes. I know that you're listening and that Martin Crowe is on his way to kidnap me. Once he does, I'll need your help to escape. For your services, you will be paid one million dollars. Here's what I want you to do. . . ."

After that, Caine had detailed his escape plan. His idea to have Grimes kill the lights was pure genius. Then he told Grimes to call Nava at some bar in the East Village and tell her the plan. After Nava had wired the money into Grimes's Cayman account, Grimes e-mailed her the schematics and alarm codes. Then he made the fake ID badge and a specially modified wristband transmitter, which he left outside by Forsythe's SUV. It was the easiest money he'd made in his life.

He hoped Caine would get away—Nava had promised him an extra half mil if the op was successful. Dr. Jimmy's gig was turning out to be a hell of a lot more lucrative than he'd thought.

Grimes's headset vibrated. "Grimes here."

"I'm fucking locked in!" Forsythe was practically hysterical on the other end.

"Huh?" Grimes asked, genuinely surprised.

"I said, *I'm locked in! All the doors are electronic, you asshole!*"

"Oh, right," Grimes said, choking back his laughter. "Forgot about that. Just sit tight. I should have the power back on in the next few minutes."

"I will *not* sit tight! Send someone down here to get me out!"

"Dr. Jimmy, I'm kinda busy right now, as I already explained to you. Besides, where you gonna go? There's no power throughout the entire installation."

"I need to get to the subject!" If Forsythe had been *near* hysterics before, he was all the way there now. *"Do you fucking understand me, you little dipshit?! I need to get to the subject or we're all fucked! So send someone right . . . fucking . . . NOW!"*

"Okay, okay," Grimes said, "just chill, man. I'll send someone in a second—"

"Not in a second." Forsythe's voice was suddenly deadly calm, which was somehow more disturbing. "Now. Send someone *now.*"

"Will do. Is that all?"

Forsythe grumbled something unintelligible and slammed the phone down yet again. Grimes shivered, not wanting to admit that the terror in Forsythe's voice had gotten to him. As much as he liked torturing Dr. Jimmy, maybe he should send a guard. If he lost his job, he wouldn't get these great opportunities to supplement his income.

Wait, what was he thinking? He wasn't going to risk a half a mil because Dr. Jimmy didn't have his fucking night-light. He dialed into the communications system, punched in his system administrator's code, chose the appropriate option, and hung up. If Forsythe fired him, so be it.

After today he could afford to take a long vacation.

Forsythe's heart slammed against the wall of his chest as the darkness pressed around him. The penlight's tiny illumination couldn't stave off his terror. What was taking them so fucking long? It had been at least five minutes since he'd called Grimes, hadn't it? He looked at his watch, which glowed blue in the darkness. Less than ninety seconds had passed. Still, a minute and a half should be more than enough time to dispatch a guard the hundred feet to the observation room.

He looked at the black mirror before him, seeing only a shadowy reflection of himself cast in the dull blue light from his watch. He had to get to the other side before it was too late. The subject could become conscious at any moment. He would still have some Thorazine in his system; the odds he'd wake up lucid and try to escape were incredibly low. . . .

Low probability? Had he lost his fucking mind? There was no longer any such thing as a low-probability event. Forsythe picked up the phone to call Grimes again, but there was no dial tone. He held the button down and slowly released it, willing the phone to work.

The line was still dead.

He bashed down the receiver again and again, sending splinters of plastic shooting into the darkness as another layer of his sanity stripped away.

Nava leaned against the door, panting heavily. She had to stop and rest twice during the short journey back down the hall. Her left foot felt heavy. Every step she took, she could hear the nauseating squish of blood. Fortunately, the steel toe of her boot had stopped the bullet from completely exiting her foot; at least one side of her wound was plugged.

She wondered how long she could stay conscious before passing out from blood loss. Maybe fifteen minutes tops. She would find out soon enough. She took one last breath, stood as straight as she could, and tried the handle. It didn't budge. She dug the guard's severed thumb from her pocket and pressed it down on the scanner. Nothing.

Shit. All the electronic locks were out. She took two steps back, removed the guard's .45 from her knapsack, and shot the handle three times. She pushed through the door and continued hobbling down the corridor, backtracking the way she'd come. The corridor, so innocuous when lit, now felt ominous and claustrophobic. She didn't want to die down here, ten meters underground.

She had to focus. Focus on Caine. Her mission. Her purpose.

Finally she reached a plaque in the wall that read D WING—she was getting close. It had seemed odd when she'd first viewed the facility's security system that they should imprison Jasper in D8, so far from his brother. Now it all made sense—David, in D10, was very near his twin.

She leaned hard on the nearest doorway to catch her breath. D6. She was almost there. She exhaled deeply and kept moving. Despite the stuffy air, she shivered as a chill swept through her body. She was already getting cold from blood loss.

She forced herself to take another step . . . and then another. D8. Another step. Closer now. She limped to the door at the end of the corridor, her last adrenaline reserves filling her with a sudden burst of energy. Five feet away from D10, she raised her gun.

Caine had to be on the other side, he just had to be. Because if he wasn't, neither of them would make it out alive. She aimed at the door handle and began to fire.

Caine tried to open his eyes; then he realized they were already open. He felt an incredibly bright light burning into his brain. He wanted to shield his eyes but couldn't move his arms—he couldn't even blink. Oh, God, he was paralyzed. No, wait . . . if he were paralyzed, he should still be able to blink, shouldn't he?

He heard a soft moan and realized it was coming from his own throat.

"David, can you speak?" a woman's voice asked. It was familiar. He knew her, she was . . .

"It's Nava. I'm going to get you out of here."

Nava . . . she had saved him . . . brought him to stay with her friend . . . and then something happened . . . something important. He was so confused; he felt like his head was made of putty.

More light . . . fingers touched his face, his eyelids. There was a metallic click, a pinch, and suddenly his right lid was free. Click. Then his left lid. His lids felt sore, raw and loose, as if they'd been dried up and stretched out. Despite the pain, it felt so good to close his eyes.

"Ah!" he shouted at the sudden sharp pain in his left arm.

"Sorry, just removing your IV," Nava apologized. "Almost done."

Another stabbing pain. Blood welled up from his arm after the needle slid out. He reflexively tried to bend his arm to stop the bleeding, but cold metal bit into his wrist. He tested the other arm with the same result. His legs and feet were similarly restrained. Now it started to come back . . . being captured . . . waking up in this room, bolted into the chair.

He looked around. Nava hovered over him, a pair of goggles on top of her head. A light stick she had placed on the table cast the room in long shadows. She bent down out of his field of vision. Then he heard tearing. Nava was sliding a strip of cloth between one of the cuffs and his flesh.

"David, I'm going to spray the restraint with Freon. It'll feel cold for a sec."

Caine heard the unmistakable hiss of an aerosol, and his wrist felt icy beneath the thin layer of fabric.

"Don't move."

Before he had a chance to process what she said, Caine heard a sharp crack like breaking glass. His arm was free.

"You okay?"

"Yeah, I think so," Caine said, flexing his arm experimentally. It crawled with pins and needles. He still felt tired and slow. Nava set to work on freeing his other arm and then his legs. She had just sprayed his last restraint when Caine heard a heavy thump.

They both turned toward the sound; at first he saw only a dark reflection in the mirror, but then, as he looked closer, he thought he saw a pinprick of light from the other side. There was another thump . . . and another as a thick crack spiraled out from the center of the mirror.

Suddenly Caine's and Nava's reflections shattered as the mirrored wall exploded out at them with an incredible crash. He raised his arms to shield his face from the flying debris as it rained down glass around them. A thousand miniature mirrors spun toward him; a few ripped into his skin. Blood oozed from seven tiny lacerations, pulling him out of his fugue.

However, it was the hysterical screaming that brought him fully back to lucidity.

CHAPTER thirty-four

Nava jumped on top of Caine to shield him, as a metal chair smashed through the mirror and crashed to the floor, momentarily eclipsing the sound of tinkling glass. Then a short man with thinning hair climbed through the other side. He was screaming.

"YOU CANNOT TAKE THE SUBJECT!"

She turned to face their attacker. His face was flushed such a deep red that it was almost purple. A long gash stretched across the length of his forehead, dripping blood. He wiped at the wound distractedly to keep the blood from obscuring his vision.

She aimed her gun at his forehead and pulled the trigger, but instead of a thunderous explosion, all she heard was a dry click. Her clip was empty. Before she could react, the man launched himself across the few feet that separated them and landed on top of her, knocking Nava to the ground. She smacked her head hard against the floor as he wrapped his hands around her neck.

Unlike Dalton, this wasn't a trained killer, but Nava was in less than prime fighting condition. Her left arm was useless, and she was weak from blood loss. The only thing the man had on her was a fountain of energy fueled by pure rage. Unfortunately, Nava thought, that might be enough.

Still, she wouldn't give up without a fight. She reached out, grabbed the man's testicles in her good hand, and squeezed. Instantly his hands flew from her neck to his crotch, and he shrieked. She didn't let go. Unable to pry off her fingers, he pulled his fist back and punched Nava in the face. She couldn't see the blow coming, and she caught it full in the mouth.

Her head ricocheted off the floor. She let go, and he rolled off her, clutching his crotch and moaning in agony. Nava spit a mouthful of blood and struggled to her feet. She had to get Caine out of there.

Ignoring his whimpering, Nava returned to work on Caine's last intact restraint. She smashed it with the butt of her gun and helped him from the chair. His legs were weak, and he put all his weight on her, nearly knocking them both over.

"Easy, David. I'm in rough shape myself."

"Sorry," he said. "I think I'm okay now, really."

"Can you walk?" Nava asked.

Caine took a couple of steps forward, holding Nava's arm for balance. "Yes," he said, a little unsure, "I'm a little wobbly, but I can walk."

Nava nodded and loaded a fresh clip into her Glock. "All right, then, let's go."

"NOOO!" Forsythe yelled. Something crushed Nava's wounded foot, dropping her to her knees. The doctor had stabbed a glass shard into her boot. Now it was Nava's turn to scream. She whipped her foot away, falling forward, dropping her gun.

Forsythe seemed to gag as he crawled forward, leaving a trail of blood. Nava delivered a kick to his head with her good foot, but it didn't have enough power to knock him out. He kept coming. Desperately, she swept her hand through the broken glass, searching for her gun.

Finally her hand closed around the grip. She aimed it at Forsythe and pulled the trigger. At that moment Caine grabbed her wrist, pulling her arm up. The bullet went wide, missing Forsythe and embedding itself into the wall behind him. Forsythe stopped screaming. The room went dead, the only sound the ringing in her ears from the gunshot.

Nava looked at Caine in confusion.

"No more killing," he said simply.

Nava hesitated for a moment and then spun the gun around in her hand and smashed it down on Forsythe's head. He slumped to the floor, unconscious.

"I didn't kill him," she panted.

Caine blinked and said, "We have to save Jasper."

"Follow me."

Caine grabbed the light stick as Nava hobbled out of the room, almost falling twice. Her foot was a mass of screaming nerve endings. The third time she stumbled, Caine grabbed her arm to steady her.

"Looks like I'm not the only person who needs help walking," he said.

Nava pushed ahead. "Stop here," she said as they halted in front of D8. "Cover your ears." She shot the door handle until it was nothing more than a piece of twisted metal. Caine pushed the door open, shining the light stick in front of him.

"Oh, God, Jasper . . ." he whispered.

Jasper lay on a table, arms and legs held in place by thick leather straps. "David," he croaked, "is that really you?"

"It's me, big brother," Caine responded, choking up, "and Nava." As Caine went to work unbuckling Jasper, Nava leaned against the doorframe to catch her breath. *Almost there,* she said to herself. *Almost there. Almost* . . .

And then she felt herself start to fall as she lost consciousness.

"Nava. Nava, wake up." Caine gently slapped her face. "Come on, we're almost there."

Her eyelids fluttered.

"She's coming around," he said to Jasper, who was nervously peering over Caine's shoulder. "Help me get her to her feet." Jasper took one hand, and Caine took the other.

Nava groaned as Caine pulled her hand. "Wrist . . . broken," she panted.

"Oh, Christ," Caine said, releasing her hand as if he'd touched something hot. "Nava, I'm sorry."

"It's okay." She shook her head. "Just help me up with my right arm."

Jasper pulled her right arm gently as Caine supported her left side. Nava was standing, although rocking slightly from side to side.

"Let's go," she said. "There's not much time."

With Jasper and Caine on either side of her, Nava directed them down the dark corridor and through a security door, which she blew open with her pistol.

"Watch the bodies," she advised as they entered a tiny elevator bank. A man lay on the ground.

"Is he . . . ? " Caine started to ask.

"They're not dead," Nava said matter-of-factly.

Caine sighed in relief as she reached forward and stabbed the elevator button. Nothing happened: There was no sound of an elevator whirring to life. The numbers above the car didn't light to show the speed of descent. The lights . . .

"Doesn't the blackout affect the elevators?" Caine asked.

Nava slapped her head in frustration. "Damn it," she said. "We've only got two minutes."

"Then what?" Jasper asked.

"Then this place fills with the building's backup security and we're screwed," Nava responded. "Come on." They went back down the corridor to where they had come from. She had them count off twenty paces and stopped. She removed some gray putty from her backpack and attached it to the bottom of the wall by the floor, then attached a small device with a tiny black keypad.

"Get ready to help me," she instructed. "When I say 'go,' we run down the hall to the elevator bank. Got it?"

"Got it," the two brothers said in unison.

Nava punched in "0:45" on the keypad. Her finger hovered over a green button and—

"Wait!" Caine said.

"Caine, there's no time—"

"If you detonate the bomb here, it will set off a chain reaction that will kill innocents. We need to move it. Get cover—I'll set the timer. Jasper, take her!"

Before she could fight him, Jasper grabbed Nava around the waist and pulled her to safety. Caine removed the bomb and limped farther down the hall to find the right spot. Once the explosive was in place, he reset the timer. He had only twenty seconds. He knew there was still a 37.458 percent chance he was too late, but he had chosen his fate. He didn't look back.

Nava felt the explosion before she heard it. She flew into Caine, who took the brunt of the fall. The hot wind was followed by an enormous roar. The second she heard the last stone crumble to the floor, she rolled off him.

"Come on, let's go!"

Caine and Jasper helped her stand, and they all moved toward the rubble. There was a gaping hole where the wall used to be, and a good chunk of the floor had caved in. Nava looked into the hole, hoping her memory of the blueprints was correct.

"Is that what I think it is?" Jasper asked.

That was when the smell from the raw sewage hit Nava's nose. She nodded.

"Jasper," Nava said, "set this last charge right there." She pointed to a spot in the ceiling above a pile of rubble. Jasper shot a look toward Caine, who nodded. After Jasper was finished, the twins helped Nava into the hole. Once inside, Jasper picked her up, threw her over his shoulder, and began jogging down the tunnel. Ten seconds later they heard another explosion, followed by a small avalanche as part of the ceiling collapsed, filling in their escape route.

No one followed.

Jasper groaned as he pushed up the manhole cover and climbed onto the sidewalk, then turned around and carefully pulled Nava to the street with her good arm. Caine was right behind her. Within seconds a large white van pulled up beside them. Sergey Kozlov was at the wheel. Its side door slid open, and a bearded man jumped out.

Caine blinked his eyes. "Dr. Lukin, she's badly hurt," Caine said.

"How did you know my name—" The man cut himself off when he saw Nava.

"My God," he said, pulling one of her arms around his shoulders. "Get her into the van. We must hurry."

As they raced across the Brooklyn Bridge, Lukin sedated Nava while Caine and Jasper struggled to control her bleeding. Outside the back window, Caine watched the Manhattan skyline until it disappeared behind a line of buildings as they sped through Brooklyn. The neighborhoods became more and more run-down the farther they drove along Flatbush Avenue.

Caine's stomach, which was sinking by the minute as he watched her slip away, suddenly dropped entirely when the van went airborne and smashed down on its front tires before screeching to a halt.

Dr. Lukin popped open the door, grabbed the end of Nava's stretcher, and jumped out; Jasper followed suit, grabbing the other end. Caine hobbled after them into the cramped elevator.

Lukin pressed a button, and Kozlov squeezed in just as the doors thumped closed. As the elevator ascended, no one spoke. The only sound was the hum of the gears. Jasper was squeezing Nava's ankle, acting as a human tourniquet. Finally the elevator came to a stop, and the doors slid open.

The five of them raced down a dank hallway, and Lukin fumbled a key into the lock. His apartment was half bachelor pad, half emergency room. There was a brown, coffee-stained couch in front of a thirteen-inch television on one side and a stainless-steel operating table on the other, complete with medical equipment and a stocky middle-aged woman, who seemed to have been waiting for them.

Without breaking stride, Lukin and Kozlov transferred

Nava's limp body to the operating table. Caine and Jasper immediately backed away to let Lukin do his work. In Russian, Lukin shouted out Nava's condition to the woman, who immediately began attaching sensors to Nava's chest.

Nava's blood pressure was low and dropping fast. Her heart monitor beeped at an alarming rate. There was a brief discussion as the doctor and the woman who Caine now realized was his nurse talked excitedly while tending to Nava's wounds. Finally a cloud descended over Lukin. His nurse looked at him solemnly, then went back to Nava's wound. But the urgency in their voices was gone; they had stopped moving as if a life hung in the balance.

"What's wrong?" Caine demanded.

Lukin ignored him, but the nurse shot Caine a sad look and then returned to her duties.

"What?" Caine nearly screamed.

At length Lukin muttered something in Russian under his breath and then walked toward Caine, blood-soaked hands held up.

"She's lost too much blood. I don't think we can save her."

"Can't you give her a transfusion?"

He looked guiltily down at the floor for a heartbeat, then back up at Caine. "Her blood type is O-negative."

"And?"

"And . . . She can only accept O-negative blood . . . and we do not have enough. It's a very rare type. I am sorry."

Caine backed away, clenching his fist. There had to be a way. There had to. Wait . . . what the fuck was he thinking? He could figure out a way. Caine closed his eyes, willing himself to see the way, the path. But there was nothing. Nothing except bright spots of color dancing on the backs of his eyelids.

"Are you all ri—"

"Shut up and let me concentrate!" Caine shouted.

He let himself go, remembering how it had felt before, calling up the image of the tree as he dipped into the *everywhen* . . . and then, as if it had always been there, it was again. Huge and majestic, with infinite complexities stretching out to eternity. He looked down the branches, following path after path, abandoning one after another until he found it.

It was so obvious. He'd been trying to find some obscure, improbable solution, when the answer was so simple. Caine opened his eyes. He spun around and saw Kozlov watching the scene from the back of the room, his thick, bulky arms crossed over his chest.

Caine turned back to Lukin. "He's O-negative," he said, pointing at Kozlov. "Use him."

"Ahhh . . . it could be dangerous, she's lost so much. . . ." The doctor seemed very unsure of himself.

Caine shot a glance at Kozlov.

"What do I get for my blood?" Kozlov asked calmly.

Caine blinked. If they didn't start the transfusion in the next minute, there was an 89.532 percent chance that Nava would die. He didn't have time to argue with the hulking bodyguard. He grabbed Nava's gun from the table and fired off a shot. The bullet whizzed by Kozlov's ear and buried itself into the wall behind him. Then Caine aimed the pistol at Kozlov's head.

"You get to live," Caine said.

Kozlov didn't argue. He walked over to Lukin and rolled up his sleeve. The nurse began to prep him. As she scrubbed his arm, the unmistakable scent of alcohol filled the room. Kozlov winced slightly as she slid the needle home. Caine closed his eyes and sighed in relief. There was a 98.241 percent chance she was going to make it. A warm hand gripped his shoulder, and he opened his eyes to see Jasper smiling deeply.

"I'm proud of you, little bro. I knew you could do it."

Caine smiled back at his twin, giving his hand a quick squeeze before closing his eyes again. A wave of exhaustion washed over him. Suddenly Caine wasn't worried about the future. He didn't need to be . . . now that he was in control.

The next few days passed peacefully as Dr. Lukin repaired their wounds and fed them painkillers. Although Caine, Jasper, and Nava stayed together in the small apartment, they didn't talk much; they didn't have to. The three were comfortable in the silence that typically comes after people have known each other for years.

Caine did his best to stay out of the *everywhen.* He only dipped inside once, to see how Bill Donnelly Jr. was doing—seven pounds, six ounces, a head full of blond hair just like his dad's. Besides that one glimpse, Caine kept his mind firmly planted in the *Now.* He didn't even allow himself to visit the past, despite his intense desire to witness—to understand—Doc's betrayal. He knew that nothing could be gained by such knowledge. And so he refused to immerse himself within the *everywhen.*

By avoiding it, terrible things happened that he could have prevented, although joyous events occurred in their wake. But he had no guilt. He knew that one could not exist without the other. And so he let the universe alone, allowing its inhabitants to determine their own futures without his interference.

For now all he cared about was Nava, Jasper, and his promise to Martin Crowe. He was still unsure how he was going to keep it, but he knew that soon it would come to him. In the meantime he focused on his brother. In the *everywhen* he learned what was wrong with Jasper and why no amount of psychiatric medication had ever been able to calm his demons without dulling his mind.

Yes, Jasper was schizophrenic, but that was not his true disease—it was only a symptom of what ailed him. Jasper's problem was one of perception. His doctors had been only partially right when they'd said his brother had trouble discerning reality. In truth Jasper's perception of reality was far greater than that of most of the so-called sane people who surrounded him. His problem was that instead of perceiving only one reality, Jasper often perceived several at once.

When a coin was tossed in the air and came up heads, Jasper would also see tails as he observed multiple futures. Hence every moment Jasper saw his own reality alongside infinite parallel potential realities, echoing in his mind like visions in a house of mirrors. Caine knew that the cure for his brother lay not with biochemistry but with knowledge, meditation, and, oddly enough, chess.

As soon as Caine spied the dusty old board beneath the coffee table, he knew. So he set out the pieces, and the two began to play. It was the perfect game for Jasper to learn how to stay focused on the present, in that the object was to predict, overcome, and control the opponent's future moves, but to do so it was necessary to have a supreme knowledge of the here and now.

The twins played all day, one game after another. The constant matches reminded Caine of when he used to play with his father as a child. But instead of making him feel sad for his lost parent, the games filled Caine with a happy sense of nostalgia, as he realized that as long as he remembered his father, his dad would always be with him.

But more important, the games taught his brother control. Slowly, as Jasper learned to focus his energy on the present—the reality that existed only before his eyes, between the thirty-two pieces on the sixty-four squares—he learned to cordon off the visions from the infinite mirrors in his mind.

Each day Jasper showed more and more improvement. David Caine knew that his brother would never be normal in the classic sense of the word, but he also knew that over time

Jasper could find a level of comfort that previously had been denied him. Although Caine had already glimpsed a saner future for his brother in the *everywhen,* all he really needed to do was look in Jasper's eyes to know that his twin was going to be okay.

It wasn't until the fifth day that Nava began to get antsy. That morning she woke up at dawn, alert and aware. Jasper and David were both still asleep. Neither of them had left the apartment since they'd arrived. Although neither brother said so, she knew it was because each man felt that he needed to watch over Nava in her time of weakness—just as she had tried to watch over them in theirs.

She had so many questions she wanted to ask David, but whenever she was about to form the words, he would only shake his head.

"We have all the time in the world for answers, Nava. For now, rest. Nothing will happen to us for the next few days, that I promise."

Had anyone else spoken those words, Nava wouldn't have believed them. But she had learned to trust David, and so she did as he asked. Now, as she stared at him, he lifted his head and smiled.

"Hey," Caine said, rubbing his eyes. "How long have you been awake?"

"Just a few minutes," she said.

He stood up, stretched, and walked over to her makeshift bed on the couch. He sat down on the coffee table beside her and ran a hand through her hair.

"Will you tell me now?" she asked.

"Sure," Caine said, as if he'd been waiting for her to ask.

"When I found Julia . . ." Nava let her voice trail off for a moment, remembering the naked, broken girl lying in the Dumpster. It seemed like a million years ago. Shrugging off the image, Nava pulled herself back to the present. "She told me that after I saved you, you would be able to tell me why I lived and why my mother died. But now I think I know.

The dreams . . . the nightmares I had when I was little . . . the ones that made me afraid to fly . . . the ones that saved my life . . . they came from you, didn't they?"

Caine smiled and shook his head. "No."

"Then where?"

Caine pointed his finger at her chest. "You took them from the collective unconscious. You must have glimpsed one of your possible futures, and you avoided it."

"How?" Nava asked.

"You really want me to repeat Jasper's physics lecture?"

"I suppose not," Nava laughed, but then her face clouded over again. "But why? Why did I see and my mother didn't?"

"Oftentimes children see things adults can't. When we're young, our minds are so much closer to the collective. But, more important, children *believe* what they see there. That's why kids can picture themselves as firemen, astronauts, and heroes. Only when we're older are we taught to ignore our 'irrational' images of the future.

"Maybe your mother did catch a glimpse of her death. Maybe she didn't. I can't answer that question for you, Nava. All I can tell you is at that moment when you refused to get on that plane, the little girl you once were saw your possible future and made a choice.

"And your choice was a good one. You have done more good in your life than you can possibly realize. I know, it hurts that the one person you most wanted to save was the one you lost, but you can never go back and change that.

"Mourn your mother and sister, Nava. But don't mourn your life."

Caine took Nava's hand. "You have an incredible gift to choose the right path—even more than you realize. Trust yourself, Nava, and you will be able to control your destiny."

"But I can't choose like you can," Nava said. "I can't be *sure*."

Caine shook his head. "Neither can I. Yes, I have a talent, but it's not infallible. My gift allows me to see far enough ahead, be it a second or a millennium, to choose the path with the highest probability of success, but I'm never a hundred percent certain. Even I don't know everything that will happen. Like you, my future is dependent on everyone else's choices, because their decisions form the collective *reality* that we all share.

Nava's head was spinning, but she thought she understood. Sort of. Finally she broke the silence. "Now what? You know the future—you can do anything."

Caine shook his head. "I don't know *the* future, Nava. I know them all—which, because they are infinite, is tantamount to knowing nothing."

"But everything you did to set things in motion . . . it all happened just as you predicted."

"I just predicted the most probable outcome in every scenario. I didn't know for certain everything would work out. Had you not *chosen* to save me, had you not created your own success, I would still be trapped in that lab."

Nava shivered. "But you still didn't answer the question: What are you going to do now? And what about Tversky and Forsythe? Where are they? Will they come after you again?"

Caine shrugged. "I don't know for sure. But I'm sure I'll find out."

Suddenly Nava felt an icy hand grip her heart. "The RDEI. They'll be coming for me. I have to—"

"Don't worry," Caine said, cutting her off. "I gave them some information that will save more than a few lives—and in return they agreed to eliminate the price on your head."

Nava sighed in relief. She wanted to probe more deeply as to what would happen next, but before she could, Caine announced that he was going to take a shower. Although he didn't say it, she knew that he wouldn't answer any more of her questions. At least not today. After he padded off to the bathroom, Nava walked over to the table to retrieve her pack of Parliaments. Talking about her mother made her want to smoke.

She put a cigarette between her lips and struck a match,

already anticipating the nicotine rush. But just as Nava was about to light it, she did a strange thing: She closed her eyes. For a brief moment, she thought she glimpsed something behind her lids that was at once both foreign and familiar. She opened her eyes, and a wave of déjà vu washed over her as she stared into the flame.

Without thinking, she blew out the match, her cigarette still unlit. Slowly she returned the perfect stick back to its case and threw the whole pack away. As she closed the lid of the garbage pail, she realized that she'd quit smoking for good.

Nava had made her decision.

That night Caine knew it was time to go back in. He'd put it off as long as he could. Even though the *everywhen* was timeless, in the *When,* time—artificial construct or no—was ticking, and he had work to do. When he opened his eyes a few seconds later, a sad smile crept across his face.

"What did you see?" Jasper asked

"How did you know I was looking?"

"I have my ways," Jasper said. "So answer the question."

"I saw how it all works out. And I wasn't alone."

"What do you mean? There was someone there with you?"

"I'm not sure," Caine said, rubbing his chin.

"You couldn't see who it was?"

"I suppose I could have," Caine said, "although I know the answer will come to me soon. So I decided to wait."

"How come?" Jasper asked.

Caine grinned. "Even Demons like surprises."

Caine didn't have any dreams that night, but when he awoke, he knew it was time to make the call. After he dialed the number, Caine listened for two full minutes without saying a word, then hung up. His second call was much quicker than the first. When he was through, he put on his coat and headed for the door.

"Where are you going?" Jasper asked.

"To meet with my lawyer," Caine said and walked out.

It took him over an hour on the D train to get into midtown Manhattan from Lukin's Coney Island apartment. It felt weird, being back in the world after existing in a closed environment for nearly a week. As Caine limped up the subway platform, he tried to stay in the *Now,* knowing that if he dipped into the *everywhen* and saw the effects his every step had on the throngs of people surrounding him, he might lose it.

When he reached the thirtieth floor of the Chrysler Building, a thin man with a conservative dark red tie approached him.

"Mr. Caine?"

"Yes," Caine said.

"Hello, I'm Marcus Gavin," the lawyer said, extending his hand. "Thank you so much for coming in today. If you would follow me, I have some very exciting news for you."

Once Gavin closed his office door, he opened a manila folder on his desk and extracted a thin sheet of paper, which he held gently, as if it might suddenly turn to dust. At first it appeared that he was going to offer it to Caine, but then he seemed to change his mind, and he carefully laid the paper back down.

"Can I get you some water or a cup of coffee?" the lawyer asked, stalling for time.

"No thank you. I'm fine."

"Ah, well," Gavin said, clearing his throat. "I'm sure you're wondering what this is about."

"Yes," Caine lied. He already knew but decided it was simpler to feign ignorance.

"Well . . . um, gosh, this is all very surreal." Gavin nervously clicked a pencil against his desk. "Mr. Caine, I presume you were good friends with Thomas DaSouza?"

"Yes," Caine said, "although we hadn't seen each other much during the last few years."

"Really? Well, then this is even odder than I thought."

Gavin picked up his coffee mug and took a sip. When he began speaking again, his voice was softer. "I'm not sure if you know this, but about a week ago there was an accident and Mr. DaSouza was critically injured. He is currently at Albert Einstein Medical Center. Although the doctors did everything they could, his prognosis is not good. I'm afraid Mr. DaSouza is brain dead with no chance of recovery. I'm sorry."

Caine closed his eyes for a moment. The fact that he'd already known about Tommy didn't make it any easier to hear.

"Well . . . er, you're probably wondering why I called you here to tell you that," Gavin said. The nervous tone in his voice had been replaced with a tenor of excitement. Evidently, now that the bad news was out of the way, it was time for celebration. "What I have here"—Gavin delicately picked up the sacred piece of paper—"is Mr. DaSouza's last will and testament. It was found on his refrigerator."

He handed it over to Caine. Caine let his eyes linger over the document for a moment before handing it back.

"It gives you power of attorney and also names you as the executor of Mr. DaSouza's estate," Gavin continued, staring at Caine, "including Mr. DaSouza's lottery winnings of over $240 million. Of course, his money will remain in a trust until you decide to . . . um"—Gavin lowered his voice to a near whisper—"pull the plug."

He paused for a moment to let this fact sink in before he continued. "As Mr. DaSouza has no living relatives, it is your right to make that decision."

"And if I choose not to?" Caine asked.

"Not to what? Decide?"

"No. If I choose not to terminate life support—then what?"

"Well . . . ahh, if you don't . . . um, then the interest from his trust will more than pay for his medical expenses for . . . well, eternity I suppose. Oh, and you will be given a salary of $100,000 per annum for overseeing his trust."

"Oversee how?" Caine asked.

"Well, his will stipulated that if he were ever to become incapacitated, his money should be put into a charitable trust to . . . ah, and I quote, 'make people's lives better.' As executor you will decide how to distribute the annual proceeds from that trust. Obviously, though, since there is no hope of recovery, after Mr. DaSouza . . . ah, passes, you can dissolve the trust and do whatever you wish." Gavin gave him a broad smile. "You're a millionaire, Mr. Caine."

Caine shook his head. "No I'm not." He paused. "And I never will be."

"But . . ." Gavin looked confused. "You do understand that Mr. DaSouza is brain dead. . . ."

"Yes."

"And the doctors say it's impossible for him to recover," Gavin said, obviously flustered.

"Nothing's impossible, Mr. Gavin. Some things are just very improbable." Caine stood up. "I assume I'll need to sign something before I go to the hospital?"

"Yes, of course," Gavin said, pulling out a small stack of papers.

After Caine was through, he shook Gavin's hand and headed for the door.

"Um," Gavin said, "do you mind if I ask a question?"

"Of course not," Caine said, turning around.

"If you aren't going to . . . er"—again he dropped his voice down to a whisper—"unplug Mr. DaSouza . . ." He paused. "Then why are you going to the hospital?"

"To run a few tests," Caine said.

As Caine walked out the door, he could sense Gavin's confusion, although he had no desire to extinguish it.

Once Caine obtained a vial of Tommy's blood, he paid a private lab to run the tests. Twenty-four hours later, the tech called him with the good news. Although the woman on the other end of the phone was surprised at the results, Caine was not. When she asked him how he knew, he just wished her a pleasant day.

After Caine hung up, he picked up the file, bought a small rainbow-colored teddy bear, and headed back to the hospital. This time, when he walked onto the fifteenth floor, he knew what he was doing there.

"Caine!" Elizabeth exclaimed when he walked into her room. "You came back!"

"Of course I did," he said. "And I brought a friend." He removed the stuffed animal from behind his back. A smile lit up her face.

"Excuse me," a worried voice asked, "who are you?"

Caine turned around to face the woman. Her eyes were red and puffy, as if she'd spent the last week crying. Even though Caine had never seen her before, she was familiar to him, as if he'd seen her in a dream.

"Hello," Caine said, holding out his hand. "I'm David Caine. I was a friend of your husband's."

"Oh," she said with a slight sniff, "I'm Sandy." She gently shook his hand. "It's nice of you to come by. We don't get many visitors."

"I know," Caine said. "Um, could I have a word with you outside?"

"Sure," Sandy said. "Honey, we're going to be right back, okay?"

"Okay, Mommy," Elizabeth said.

Once they were in the hall, Caine began. "I know this will sound odd, but I have some good news for you."

"What is it?"

"I found a bone-marrow donor for your daughter. He's a 99 percent match, and he's ready to do the transplant as soon as Elizabeth is well enough."

A mixture of emotions crossed her face—shock, joy, and then sadness. Before she had a chance to speak, Caine continued.

"Don't worry about the money. I represent a large trust that was founded to help people like your daughter. All medical expenses will be covered."

"Is this some kind of a joke?" Sandy asked, her face suddenly stern. "If it is, I don't think it's very funny, Mr. Caine."

Caine pulled out Tommy's medical file, showing that he was a match.

"This is for real?" Sandy asked after looking through the file. "Are you serious?"

"I've never been more serious in my life," Caine said.

"Oh, my God! Oh, my God!" Sandy grabbed Caine in a monstrous hug as tears streamed down her face. "I don't know what to say. I mean . . . oh, God . . . How can I ever thank you?"

"No thanks are necessary," Caine said. "Let's just say we're even."

Sandy looked confused but only nodded. Then Caine reached into his pocket and brought out Gavin's business card.

"This is my attorney. Once you talk to Elizabeth's doctors, give him a call. He will make all the necessary arrangements."

"Thank you, Mr. Caine," she said, squeezing his hand.

"If you call me Mr. Caine, then I'll have to call you Mrs. Crowe. 'David' will be fine."

"Okay. Thank you . . . David." Sandy Crowe wiped her nose. "I'm going to tell Betsy the good news." Just as she was about to go back into her daughter's room, she turned. "You never told me how you knew Marty."

"Oh," Caine said, scratching his head. "I guess you could say I knew him from work."

Caine walked out of the hospital feeling better than he had in weeks. He knew that there was still a chance Elizabeth's transplant might not be successful, but there was a 93.726 percent probability she was going to be just fine.

He had decided to walk a few blocks to clear his mind when suddenly the stench filled his brain. Before his physical body crashed down onto the sidewalk, his mind had already slipped into the *everywhen*.

. . .

The woman, the She, is with him. But She is different. Smaller, somehow, and more familiar. He can see that She is both happy and sad. Caine feels sorry for Her.

She—*Thank you, Caine.*
Caine—*What for?*

As Caine asks the question, he suddenly sees.
He understands.
She is in When's *past, helping Tanja see her future so she does not get on a plane.*
She is in the dreams of Tommy, helping him see numbers.
She is the Voice inside Jasper, telling him how to help his brother.
She is trying to show Caine the everywhen, *triggering his seizures.*
All of Her actions coalesce to form a cascade of events that lead to Tommy's impromptu Will and his improbable accident, Nava's rescue and Caine's awakening. All to save one little girl, dying of leukemia. A girl named Elizabeth "Betsy" Crowe.
Caine sees why She is familiar. She resembles her sister, Sandy, and her niece—Betsy.
Caine—*It is You, making all of this happen.*
She—*No. We only help people to see. We are powerless beyond that. You make this happen, as do Nava and Tommy, Jasper and Julia, Forsythe and Tversky, along with millions of others, each on their own path, each making their own choices.*
Caine—*All this . . . because of Betsy?*
She—*No, Betsy is only a piece of the final objective. You don't understand. But later in the* When, *you do.*
Caine—*In the* When *. . . you are Julia.*
She—*No. In the* When, *We are not singular. We are many. We are the Will of the collective unconscious. However, you perceive Us as Julia, as she serves as Our Conduit, Our*

Voice. In her final moments, she sees in your mind a common desire, and so We enlist her to help accomplish Our goal. However, it is you who unconsciously seeks her voice, for she can speak only to those who wish to hear.

***Caine**—But Julia is dead.*

***She**—The* everywhen *is outside the* When. *Here Julia is alive. She is a little girl. She is growing up. She is falling in love with Petey. She is Betsy's Aunt Julia. She is dying in a garbage Dumpster.*

***Caine**—That is the smell. Julia's consciousness carries the smell into my mind.*

***She**—Olfactory memories are the strongest. Since she is Our Conduit, her memory of the stench where she is left to die accompanies Us.*

***Caine**—In the* When, *why tell Dr. Tversky to try to kill me?*

***She**—It is the only way to cause Tommy's accident.*

***Caine**—You choose Betsy's life over Tommy's.*

***She**—No. In your* When, *Tommy kills himself. By helping him know his dreams, We extend his life. Nothing is lost.*

***Caine**—Are You eternal?*

***She**—It is . . . uncertain.*

***Caine**—How is that?*

***She**—In some futures We are eternal. In others We are extinguished. Our fate is linked with yours and your brethren, for you are Us and We are you.*

***Caine**—Why am I here?*

***She**—You need to understand your place. You must use the* everywhen *to help Us all.*

***Caine**—How do I help? With Tommy's money?*

***She**—The money will help a few but will ultimately change little.*

***Caine**—What then? How do I help?*

***She**—It is not for here. It is for later in* When.

***Caine**—Why not here?*

***She**—You need some . . . time.*

. . .

“Hey, I think he’s coming back around,” a voice said above him. “Are you all right, buddy?”

Caine rubbed the back of his head, which had already begun to throb. He gently sniffed the air. The smell was gone.

“Yeah,” he said. “I think I’m okay . . . for now.”

Tversky clicked *"Si,"* and the sign-in screen was replaced by a purple desktop littered with icons. He double-clicked the blue lowercase *e* and waited impatiently for the browser to open. Before the home page could load, he typed in a new URL. It took him only a minute to find the story that he was looking for.

EX-NSA DIRECTOR ON TRIAL FOR TREASON

By Patrick O'Beirne

Washington, D.C. (AP)—Dr. James P. Forsythe was arraigned today on 131 counts of conspiracy and treason against the United States. Dr. Forsythe, formerly the director of the National Security Agency's Science and Technology Research division, was formally charged today in a packed Washington courtroom.

Authorities first learned of Dr. Forsythe's alleged wrongdoings when firemen were called to the scene after a bomb exploded in a New York office building (see related article) on February 7. In addition to finding Dr. Forsythe and his staff trapped beneath the rubble, rescue personnel also recovered three dead bodies, along with hundreds of computer files. Dr. Forsythe allegedly stole the files from the NSA after being terminated for coordinating an "illegal FBI operation" linked to the Philadelphia Amtrak shooting (see related article), said one Washington insider.

> Despite what the prosecution described as "overwhelming evidence," Dr. Forsythe pleaded not guilty on all counts. Federal prosecutors, however, are optimistic about securing a conviction.
>
> "We have literally a mountain of evidence as well as a witness. . . . It is extremely probable that he [Dr. Forsythe] will be convicted." The prosecution's star witness is Mr. Steven R. Grimes, a current employee of the NSA.
>
> "Quite frankly, I was shocked that all this was going on right under my nose," Mr. Grimes said in a statement today. "I never thought that Jimmy [Forsythe] would steal secrets from the government. . . . I'm going to do everything I can to assist the U.S. Attorney's office in their case. I'm an American—and I don't take kindly to traitors."

Tversky scanned the rest of the article, but there was no mention of his name. He breathed a sigh of relief. Although the police still wanted to talk to him regarding Julia's death, he knew they had officially ruled the case a suicide. Tversky smiled. He couldn't believe his luck. If he hadn't left the lab that night, he would have been caught, too. Hell, he might have even been killed in the explosion.

Considering all that had happened, he couldn't be in better shape. With Forsythe up on conspiracy charges, Tversky was nearly in the clear. Even if Forsythe told anyone Tversky had murdered Julia—not that there was any reason for him to do so—who would believe him? It was almost too perfect.

It was a shame that he'd lost most of his data, but he was certain he could re-create the chemical compound that had triggered David Caine's initial emergence. All he needed was time, and now that he was safe in Mexico, he had it. Each morning Tversky would roll a pair of dice to determine where to go next. He hoped that if he kept moving around the country at random, David would be unable to find him.

Logging off the computer, he paid the man behind the counter twenty pesos and headed outside. Within seconds he was bathed in sweat. The Mexican sun was blistering, and Tversky shielded his eyes. Christ, it was hot. And the smell of garbage was suddenly everywhere, a disgusting stench that seemed to eclipse all his other senses.

He'd begun walking quickly back to his cabana to get away from the stink when he spotted an ice cream stand across the street. It was perfect timing, really, since the second the stench had infected his nose, he found himself overcome with a powerful craving for chocolate ice cream. Without looking, he dashed across the street toward the vendor.

He didn't see the bus until it was too late. The impact sent Tversky flying through the air. He landed on the ground just in time to get crushed beneath the bus's front tire, his ribs cracking into hundreds of pieces, simultaneously puncturing his heart and lungs.

He heard several people screaming for help in Spanish, but he knew it was too late. As the darkness closed in around him, he was grateful that at least the smell seemed to have dissipated. He wondered why he'd felt so compelled to run across the street. Had he lived a few seconds longer, he might have understood the smell's significance, but he was out of time.

As his consciousness winked out, one last thought sped through his mind: *I don't even like ice cream.*

A month earlier in a garbage Dumpster, Julia gave Nava's hand one final squeeze and died, a smile on her lips, and ice cream on her mind.

ACKNOWLEDGMENTS

I started writing this book in part because I wanted to create something truly unique, all by myself with no one's help. The funny thing is, along the way I discovered that in many ways, writing a novel is the most collaborative endeavor I've ever undertaken. At every step, someone helped me move forward, and without each and every one of the people listed below, this book never would have been published.

As I have no desire to rank people in their level of helpfulness, I decided to go in chronological order. Here goes:

Stephanie Williams. You were with me in Starbucks when I wrote my very first page and were the first person to read my book when I had written my last page. Without you, my dream of writing a novel would still be just that. I owe you more than I can say. I miss you.

Daniela Drake. You read through each draft and were the only person I could trust to give me the gut-wrenching criticism I so badly needed to eliminate all the "RNW." (Plus you are the only WCN who can intelligently discuss the complexities of reality television.)

Erin Hennicke. The first person "in the industry" to read my book. More important, you were always there with advice once I finished the "easy part" (writing).

Suzanne Gibbons-Neff. Not only did you serve as both conscience and cheerleader during my entire writing process, but you also made a fairly critical introduction to . . .

Barrie Trimingham. I barely know you, and yet, you

helped make publishing this book a reality when you answered Suzanne's call and put me in touch with . . .

Ann Rittenberg. Quite possibly the best agent in the world. You believed in me when my book was still in its infancy and were the first person to tell me that I really *could* write for a living.

Ted Gideonse. International man of mystery. Without you I'd have to find my own way through Japanese contracts and German tax code, which would not be pretty.

Mauro DiPreta. You got HarperCollins to buy my book. Then you edited it. Then you convinced me to fix the parts that I didn't think needed fixing (even though they did). Then you edited it again. I couldn't have asked for more.

Joelle Yudin. My lifeline to everything HC, you answered all my stupid questions without ever making me feel stupid.

Maureen Sugden and **Andrea Molitor.** Without you guys, there would be a lot of commas in the wrong place and a bunch of en dashes where there should be em dashes. You make me look smart, for which I am truly grateful.

Julia Bannon, Jamie Beckman, George Bick, Lisa Gallagher, Karen Resnick, Pam Spengler-Jaffee and everyone else at HarperCollins who do all the things that I don't even know about.

And lastly, all my foreign agents. You guys rock.

I also must thank all the people who've added to my life in so many ways:

The 4000 Pine Brotherhood, especially **Andrew "Andefiance" Burrows** (a great friend but a really lousy *Halo* player), **Cyrus Yang** (who knows more than he should about guns and ammo), **Donald Johnson** (the only guy I could ask to meet me at the end of the earth who'd say, "Okay, what time?"), **Brady O'Beirne** (you're in the book now, happy?), **Kei Sato** ("ACH!"), and **Rick Sibery** (the one true pony). OK, and **Tad,** too.

All my friends from Dartmouth, specifically **Leon Hsu**

(you still know everything), **Jeff "El Jefe" Geller** (if you were any more laid back, you'd be dead), and of course **"S.K. & the evil van groupies."**

The Stanford GSB Tuesday Night Poker group ("Is there a straight in there?").

My own personal IT department, including **Ron McCoy** (the man, the myth, the legend), **Marshall Simmonds** (search engine optimizer extraordinaire), and **Spur & Mav-daddy** (keepers of my data).

Miscellaneous New Yorkers, especially **Margo "Abo-rakyiraba" Wright** (Go Bodanna!), **Ori Uziel** (hedge boy), **Kimberly Krouse** (Pagoo, Pagoo), **Dave Otten** ("Survivors ready . . . *Go!*").

All my phone friends, especially **Mina Song** and **Iris Yen,** who were kind enough to be unemployed while I was writing my book, and **Emily He,** who called me back even though she had one of those job thingies. Plus the irrepressible **Jason Meil** (the only one who knows the truth about the free-willed monkey).

My doctors, without whom my tired eye would have given up long ago, with special thanks to **Dr. Janice Cotter** and the Boston Foundation for Sight, **Dr. C. Stephen Foster,** and of course **Dr. Alan "DG" Geller.**

Joanie and **Billy Felder,** for giving me the biggest gift anyone can bestow in New York City—a 700-square-foot, pre-war, rent-stabilized apartment.

My mother **Lois** and my "dah-ling" sister **Cheryl,** who've always supported me in my endeavors, even though I don't call as often as I should.

Marge and **Steve Hoppe,** who make the best damn ribs in the world.

George Davis, for calling me three times daily, and **Toni Davis,** for not.

And finally, **Meredith.** What can I say besides that you make everything better? I love you.

AuthorTracker